PENGUIN BOOKS
LAMENT OF MOHINI

Shreekumar Varma was born in Trivandrum. After an M.Phil in English Literature from Madras Christian College, he took a diploma in Journalism. He worked in the *Indian Express*, Bombay, and has also been editor, publisher, printer, and lecturer in English and Journalism. He has published articles, interviews, short stories and poetry in several newspapers and magazines, and has written a children's book, *The Royal Rebel*. He has designed and broadcast radio programmes. He has also written two award-winning plays.

Shreekumar Varma is the grandson of Sethu Lakshmi Bayi, last ruling maharani of Travancore, and great-great-grandson of the artist Raja Ravi Varma. He is married to Geeta and has two sons, Vinayak and Karthik. He lives and writes compulsively in Chennai. (Email: varmashreekumar@visto.com; home page: itsshree.homestead.com/itsshree.html)

Shreekumar Varma

■

LAMENT OF MOHINI

PENGUIN BOOKS

Penguin Books India (P) Ltd., 11 Community Centre, Panchsheel Park, New Delhi 110 017, India
Penguin Books Ltd., 27 Wrights Lane, London W8 5TZ, UK
Penguin Putnam Inc., 375 Hudson Street, New York, NY 10014, USA
Penguin Books Australia Ltd., Ringwood, Victoria, Australia
Penguin Books Canada Ltd., 10 Alcorn Avenue, Suite 300, Toronto, Ontario, M4V 3B2, Canada
Penguin Books (NZ) Ltd., Cnr Rosedale and Airborne Roads, Albany, Auckland, New Zealand

First published by Penguin Books India 2000

10 9 8 7 6 5 4 3 2 1

Typeset in *Sabon Roman* by SÜRYA, New Delhi
Printed at Rekha Printers Pvt. Ltd., New Delhi

This is a work of fiction. Names, characters, places and incidents are either the product of the author's imagination or are used fictitiously and any resemblance to any actual person, living or dead, events or locales is entirely coincidental.

This book is for my mother

ACKNOWLEDGEMENTS

—————————◼—————————

A   for Amrita Chak, Jacaranda's editor, for that first unforgettable ray of optimism from outside my family.

B   for Balan and Vidya, for all their help in Bangalore.

C   for Chetan Shah, for showing me the door to opportunity each time.

D   for David Davidar of Penguin, for the half-hour that helped restructure the book.

J   for Jayapriya Vasudevan of Jacaranda Press, for everything she did to set me off on my journey.

K   for Karthika of Penguin, for resurfacing each time with hope.

K   is for Kerala, mentor, muse and music.

L   for Lakshmi, whose book was an important source for the description of the wedding in Chapter 21.

M   is for Madras, home.

S   for Sayoni Basu of Penguin, my invisible friend and editor, who remarkably and rapidly saw through this book.

S   for Sriram and a lifetime's friendship.

S   for Sukumar Nambiar, for his perennial interest.

U   for Uma, cousin, critic and well-wisher.

And, beyond alphabets and words, Geeta.

ACKNOWLEDGEMENTS

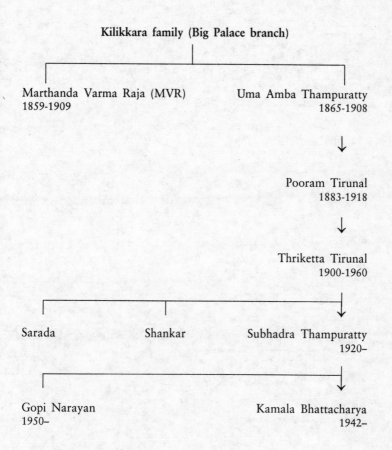

Kilikkara family (Big Palace branch)

Marthanda Varma Raja (MVR)
1859-1909

Uma Amba Thampuratty
1865-1908

Pooram Tirunal
1883-1918

Thriketta Tirunal
1900-1960

Sarada

Shankar

Subhadra Thampuratty
1920–

Gopi Narayan
1950–

Kamala Bhattacharya
1942–

(Arrow points from mother to eldest daughter)

POINT ZERO

———————————————— ■ ————————————————

Ganapathy was the beginning.

I'm back now, like a bad coin minted from morsels of memory.

An old monk, oozing hair and claws, standing at this very same spot, once grabbed my hand and predicted big things for me. This is the Beginning, he had announced. Iyer, tufted-warted-deaf priest of the temple, had scratched his belly and nodded approval. Of course, he couldn't hear a thing. Ganapathy sat inside, noncommittal, knowing all things will come to pass. Ganapathy is still my only witness.

Nothing will stop you, the ash-stained ascetic had continued, you'll become big, and break every rule and then you'll repent because you have to return to the Beginning. A couple of months, before that, a goatee-sporting professor had warned me, 'History flows, don't think it's deadwood behind you. It f-l-o-w-s!'

Prophetic pronouncements. Here I am today before this tiny temple, more than a decade later, drawn by chapters of an unfinished manuscript. A breeze staggers in from the ocean bed, laden with the cold roar of waves and shaking an orchestra of leaves. Perhaps this is the beginning of a new life, that hushed instant before curtain rise.

The temple in Doctors Colony is dwarfed by a monstrously maternal banyan. Decades ago, Ganapathy had sprung from gnarled flesh and become a popular boon-giver—Ver Ganapathy, Ganapathy of the roots, attracting devotees from all over the city. Fireflies rush at me in a wild starry procession between the hanging roots. I blink and they vanish.

Shadows shift. It is nearly five now and the priest continues to snore, his rumbling lullaby competing with the sea. He lies curled up and shrouded whitely, a badly-packed parcel in a log shed that has risen beside the temple, a new convenience for today's hi-priests. Ganapathy, his prisoner for the night, waits patiently. The temple has a nose-blocking smell of incense, oil, camphor and damp old flowers, indeterminate plight of yesterday's prayers.

My taxi had stopped outside the gates with a final sputter. The old driver looked back and his face lit up with a toothless grin when he saw I was still in the car. I added a generous tip and walked on to my tryst with the past.

The buildings of Doctors Colony are typical Housing Board constructions built with little imagination.

I mark crucial spots on the map before me. The wood apple tree under which I spent languorous dusks with Lekha. Sometimes we walked out and down the main road till the Circle, returning and going down to the beach and sitting on the sands till it was time to make dinner. The temple steps where I'd sit with Iyer and discuss God and politics, his tuft swinging madly as passion grew. And right there, where I ran to get ice for Uncle Shankar on that fateful night. And the distant glimpse of the Kali temple on the beach, with the large black idol; her glaring eyes and the trident raised to strike had stopped me as I ran calling in desperation. Each memory is a mirage, wrapped cloud-like around a core of nostalgia or pain.

And there is the balcony of our 'C' building. I have stood on that balcony, watching life being played out in the slum across the glass-spiked boundary wall, wondering whether life at its rawest is the most rewarding.

On the balcony, a child's illustrated table has been pushed against a corner, overflowing with brown-bound notebooks. Clothes hang on a line, a sari, two gaudy lungis, towel, a brown-stained brassiere. The door leading to the bedroom is shut. A sudden resentment wells up: what right has this newcomer—whose wife proudly exhibits her underwear to the world—to impinge upon my years in this house?

Without warning, an image crops up. One morning, I've only just risen from bed, sipped my coffee. I stand in my dhoti and vest, feeling the cool breeze, watching the spread of colour in the sky and listening to the birds. There is a blankness within me, blanket of languor that will lift only after the first mugful of a cold bath shocks me out of it.

Lekha emerges from the bedroom, smiles and stands beside me. Her loose hair dances gently. 'You look so impressive standing here, like a general.' Pleased, I square my shoulders. 'Thanks!' Rare compliment indeed from a retired colonel's daughter, it's not to be taken lightly. She adds: 'Like a general supervising his men.' She points to the field below where the men from the slum are armed with water and squatting in three neat rows. I join her burst of merriment and chase her right back into the bedroom.

A crow startles me, calling crankily from the higher branches. I'm an intruder in this land of snorers. Walking back to the temple, I stand and watch parallel battalions of red ants and a couple of gold-tinged black centipedes, metre-gauge and broad-gauge crawlers, filing inquiringly towards the sanctum. The banyan begins to tremble, a multi-stringed instrument in a mummified world of its own.

A drop falls on my head, another on my nose, and on my arm. Magically, the sky begins to darken. Point zero, and I'm back . . .

THE BEGINNING

---◼---

4 March 1998

My day begins early, hours before the sun starts his.

I am jolted awake by a grey breeze; it sweeps up and encircles me in welcome. I rediscover myself slumped in a cane chair in the hotel balcony. I'd been leafing through the night, squinting down occasionally at the yellow garlands swelling and changing shape. More than ten years separate me from this electrified toy city that's grown beyond reach or redemption—Madras, city of doom and desire, now renamed Chennai, a large electronic idli laced with red chilli powder.

I can hear a tap leaking to a slow countdown in my three-star bathroom. I shake myself and take a white shower, braving the cold water. My spirit soars.

The lift slithers down. The Hotel Maharani Madras International lounge stretches before me like a pleasantly decorated mausoleum. The doorman is six feet tall and costumed like a Rajput warrior. He salutes smartly as he opens the door, stiff purple beneath a fierce moustache.

The air outside is crisp. A sharp liquid, mercury-like, pops and fizzes through my veins. All is quiet. Night kneels, savouring its last moments. Small boys lie sleeping in front of shutters, sharing their jute sacks with white, black, brown and spotted dogs. The shutters are pasted with a series of political posters in Tamil that continue on the adjoining wall.

A line of yellow and black taxis wait just outside the hotel gates, hugging the pavement. I walk up to the first. The driver lies in the back seat, drooling deliriously into the cracked rexine. He starts violently. 'Airport?' His voice is thick. 'No,' I say. 'Stationaa?' I shake my head. He introduces a forefinger into his ear and pumps accusingly. 'Enna saar, where at this time you're wanting to go? Everybuddies are sleeping. You come after five.' I walk to the next cab. But they are all pledged to discourage early risers.

Turning back to the hotel for a tourist cab, I run into a rebel, an old one-eyed Muslim with a finely cultured white moustache. His car is inscribed with flowery messages in English and Urdu, and haunted by a trace of old incense. 'Doctors Colony,' I tell him. 'Past Besant Nagar.' When the car lurches forward with heavy rumbles of protest, I feel as if I'm crouched inside an electric mixie.

I sit shakily in the sagging back seat and think of Mehra's monologue. 'The spirit of the times is distinctly commercial. One unguarded moment, sala, they'll cut out your balls! Pull the other bastard down so you'll have room to stand.'

Dilip Mehra is plump, shining, smiling, reeking of Kouros. I'm vice-president of his publishing company based in Bangalore, moving smoothly with the system. Mehra's gel-jowled face swam against a rectangular canvas hanging in his gleaming M.G. Road office. It showed an amused camel plodding through a grey desert, a better reflection of his work ethic than his pronouncements. There was a painful crick in my neck as I faced him across his largely empty table, after he had read my three-word report on Rangachari's new manuscript. 'For heaven's sake,' Mehra told me, 'let's get this book, yaar!'

No one knew quite how to take Rangachari. His story

was already legend in publishing circles. It began with his retirement as a professor of history at the Madras University. Retired life insulted Rangachari. He kept haunting the university campus, and pursuing old acquaintances and new methods of reinsinuating himself into academics.

Three years ago, he wrote his first book—the one that still doesn't count among his works—where he took a fresh look at the history of the city under British rule. 'Maternal, myopic, madly milling Madras—but the thoughtful welfare measures of the British are evident even today,' he wrote, nearly half a century after their departure. He waxed eloquent on the white man and his civic sense, on the heavenly conditions when the British were in charge. Finding no publisher adventurous enough, he scraped together his own finances and printed the book. It was bound expensively and had two-colour maps and five pages of moth-tasted photographs showing sprawling colonial buildings, tree-lined avenues and unspoilt stretches of cow-graced greenery.

White City was a flop. Of the thousand copies printed, less than two hundred were sold by the end of the year. Colleges refused to touch the book unless it was prescribed, bureaucrats were unwilling to recommend such a patently unpatriotic treatise. The lone review in a city tabloid wondered what 'this author is so anti about. Does he, we fail to understand, want a brown or white city?'

Rangachari was shocked and demoralized. Later, after his second book, he declared in an interview to the *Sunday Express* which I had hunted out for information about him, 'Booksellers and reviewers are like that. When a man is unknown, they play tricks. And when he becomes big, they wag their tails and run after him.' The accompanying photograph showed a faded thin man in a kurta.

But that was later. The fate of *White City* subdued him. Faced with penury and a scoffing set of relatives, he withdrew into a shell, surrounded by hundreds of hardbound scatterings of his dream—white city turned white elephant. He'd used up most of his gratuity and savings. To confound matters, his wife found the time ripe for pneumonia. Closeted with this headstrong ponderous visionary, she embraced the first alternative affliction that sought her out. Rangachari was shattered. He still believed his life had failed only because the world was too petty to recognize true talent. And he would most likely have ended up as one more extinguished writer or eccentric widower.

Were it not for Veda Vyasa. He read a children's version of the life of Vyasa, which led him to the Mahabharatha. The gorgeous descriptions and an exciting range of characters danced before Rangachari's eyes. Krishna, cowherd, lover, master schemer, king, philosopher, compassionate miracle-man; Arjuna, epitome of brave manhood; Draupadi, wife of five heroes, wonderful woman; Karna—was there a better man in mythology? Son of the sun, brought up by a horse-keeper and befriended by princes, fighting his own brothers because he held loyalty was thicker than blood!

Tatachari Rangachari became convinced he was the torch-bearer of a cultural renaissance, a mythappropriator. Perhaps the next-in-literary-line—even a reincarnation—of the writer of the Mahabharatha. So he sat down and wrote an opus modelled after the great epic, recreating the ornate palaces of British South India, nawabs and maharajas with frustratingly familiar names. He conjured up smug club-hopping Englishmen and their alarmingly frail wives. Lord Krishna was reflected in Dr Teddy, a quixotic dark-haired Londoner with a pipe hanging from his lips instead of a flute. The doctor performed miracle cures on the natives and was satisfied when three out of ten survived. To complete the analogy, he succumbed to a small septic wound on his toe. The book struck the imagination of a confused readership, who couldn't tell where fact ended and fiction crept in.

Sage of Reason was published by a former student of his named George, a Kottayam Malayali settled in Madras. He ran a corner-shop publishing unit in Kodambakkam, V. George's Guides and Sons, that brought out exam guides. The first limited edition caught the eye of K.C. Shetty, the respected Mumbai reviewer and columnist, who was floored by the sheer audacity of Rangachari's imagination. Though he probably received hundreds of books from similar small-time publishers, Shetty granted this one a quarter-page review. It wasn't all praise. 'The author betrays emotions that verge on the dangerous,' he wrote. George reissued the book with a quote from Shetty in blood-red letters on its cover. 'Amazing! Definitely worth a read.' He dropped the rest of the sentence: 'if only to witness the high eccentricity of amateur authorship.' George was an astute man. He kept the copyright and all profit. He handed out small rewards now and then to his author, and continuously grumbled about the high cost of printing and distribution, and the expensive marketing gimmicks he had to dream up.

To drown his despair, Rangachari started on his next book. This dealt with the life and times of a nationalistic Nadar from Thanjavur district who gets caught up in the Independence movement, vacillating in an equal number of pages between terrorism and non-violence. The book was appropriately titled *Groping in the Dark*.

Rangachari went into raptures about everything his protagonist did. The Nadar made voracious love to Radha, a fiery co-revolutionary who taught him the ABC of pain and pleasure, then to a half-sister who'd already seduced him in childhood during a temple festival and then went on to become a renowned classical singer, and still later in his 'twilight years' came the mature relationship with Jagadamma, an older woman he loved deeply and sacrificed ('because the country's Cause comes before all else, including woman's love'). Simultaneously, he was blowing up trains and buildings by the dozen, or lecturing a tribe of nomadic snake-catchers on the significance of sacrifice, or investigating—somehow again in the national interest—the intricacies of black magic in secret caves behind the thundering Courtallam falls under the blind and benign tutelage of a dying saint.

But the old man was wiser now. He made it clear that he was going to have no more dealings with V. George. The book was gobbled up by a Mumbai publishing house, Winsome Publications, famous for fathering six clone-faced fortnightlies that differed only marginally in their degree of luridity. They came charging to add *Groping* to their showcase of painful passion and kinky killings. A sexy woman on the cover beckoned readers to come grope in the dark.

Perhaps he acquiesced on the rebound. Perhaps the Mumbai house was the highest bidder and Rangachari's new priority was cash. But now he was well and truly branded, and bigger publishers turned away.

Which is why, a year later, Dilip Mehra did a double take when, after reading the first two chapters of Rangachari's latest, I made my three-word report: 'Take it, Dilip.'

I had got the manuscript from Krishnamurthy, a self-appointed literary agent from Coimbatore. He was a distant nephew's nephew of Rangachari, a forty-year-old 'boy' who'd gravitated to Uncle Rangu in a sudden rush of family feeling. What I read was pulp. But pulp that left me shocked. I sat stunned. Like a cartman woken to find his trusty bullock vanished, and himself caught in the fumes of a strange-known country, diabolinquished . . .

There I was reading, and I was halfway into my own ancestry, helpless, taken by surprise, led there by some pruriently-inclined word vendor, a complete stranger! It was all there in black and white. Normally I would have dumped such a manuscript without another thought, sent it straight back to nephew's nephew in Coimbatore and forgotten all about it. But this was no coincidence, this was another one of Rangachari's historical forays, and the background he'd so carefully recreated was my own.

Consider the falling father in the opening chapter, the monsoon tragedy where he loses his footing and plummets three floors down. Take the explicit little geographical essay in the second chapter—the distance from the capital, the ring road and the fields all along it, the warm summer smell of the river, the temples and the elephants. The family partitions and quarrels, celebrations and aberrations, the relationship with those formidable priestly neighbours, only too familiar. It was turning out to be a ghost story, and the ghosts were all mine.

Granted, it isn't so difficult to hunt down Kilikkara history. There must be memory-ridden uncles and legacy-laden garrulocals willing to shake out branches of the old family tree, share folklore with a prying professor-turned-hack. It's also easy to find school textbooks in Malayalam tracing the origins of Kilikkara and talking about our family's role in Kerala history. But the eccentric personal bits, where does he get them from? What else will he get?

Who is this Rangachari, and how does he know what he knows?

My first concern was to stop the man before nephew's-nephew got lucky and someone bit the bait. Imagine having the story of your clan immortalized by Winsome Books—sultry sirens beckoning from the cover, promising that your family saga was 'definitely worth a read!'

So I went to Dilip Mehra and said, 'Take it, Dilip.' I couldn't think of anything else. Honestly. The best thing was to jump straight down into the arena and take all this bull by the horns.

And then it was Mehra all the way. I described how a cell makes a man, and a thought makes a philosophy, and how two good chapters could make a best-seller. I recycled commercial concepts he himself endlessly spouted, and added gravely: 'Times are changing, we need an acceleration.' That was it. 'You go, Gopi,' Mehra said. I remained silent, watching him steadily as if considering this new burden. 'To Madras!' He winked. 'Go man, get the old bugger to our side. No more Georges and Winsomes!' I should go to Rangachari and convince him about Enterprise Publishers and Associates instead.

Nostalgia whipped at me the moment I got off the night Mail. Everything from the archaic red building of the Central Station to the way people behaved on the traffic-crazy roads was achingly familiar. Even as I visited the EPA office and discussed Rangachari with the local manager, Nagarajan, a bald self-effacing man whose vocabulary centered around a wondering 'appadiya?'—is that so?—an inner voice kept telling me that this wasn't what I was really here for. Things beyond my control were working—synmeshing, soul-vaulting, supragalactic things! I was a reluctant pilgrim being hassled by primeval gods, forced to return to the fold. Thirteen years in Bangalore, straining and kneading and pushed into positions of compromise. And now this mission to Madras—shoved back to the edge of historia.

I pulled myself together and got Rangachari on the line.

'This is Gopi Narayan from EPA, it's about your manuscript,' I began. He grilled me for ten minutes about the history of EPA and cross-examined me to find out if I'd really read his two chapters.

The rasping voice finally said, 'Come to my house at eleven tomorrow. We'll talk.'

MORNING FALLS

When his father, Narayanan Namboodiri, fell from the roof of the three-storied ancestral house in Kilikkara and lay peacefully as if embracing the vast earth that had raised him, Gopi didn't immediately see it as the first of a series of notches Fate had claimed for itself.

It was the monsoon of '65. He stood beside his mother and stared in fascination at the lifeless body on the drenched grass. He was aware of a feeling of profound relief, and then guilt that seared through him like physical pain. The guilt was to last, eternal, unreasonable. Forever after that he could do nothing on his own without a disturbing sense of being assessed by some unknown They who kept a tally of his shortcomings and watched over him like a disapproving bench of judges.

The rains had been heavy that year. During a lull that fateful morning, Narayanan decided he would venture up onto the tiled roof to repair a faulty ventilator cover which was banging away, disturbing everyone's sleep and depositing rainwater into the hall on the third floor. His wife Subhadra tried to dissuade him.

'Shankaran or Bhaskaran will do it,' she said rather gently, as if the prospect of his clambering up in the fine drizzle that made everything wet and slippery had subdued her.

'It's not a big thing. I can easily do it.' When an idea got into Narayanan's head, no one could get it out. Especially not his wife. The upshot of it was that he conveyed himself laboriously up to the roof, Bhaskaran the rubber estate supervisor steadying the ladder on the sit-out. Narayanan was a maniac with his hands, he could never keep them idle.

RV uncle, married to Subhadra's sister, called out, 'Be careful, you'll slip. Better to come down and send up one of the servants.' Narayanan's short laugh dropped to where they stood like an invisible bundle. His stepbrother, who had arrived only the previous day from their family home Kunnupuram illam, emerged from the outhouse at this point. A corner of his dhoti was secured within his armpit and his mouth churned endless betel through which he shouted out a muffled thick-throated warning, 'Narayana, you're not so young any more. This isn't the age for acrobatics!'

Narayanan looked down. 'Don't worry unnecessarily. Your younger brother is built like an ox.'

Subhadra said in wild desperation, 'Why does he do such things? Kilikkara Appa, please look after him!'

'There, that should do it,' he said, arching like a brown rainbow to pick up the hammer and box of nails from the ledge. 'I'll be down in a minute.'

It was the shortest minute of his life. His foot slipped, extending the arc in a daring ballet. Gopi heard his mother cry out. For a brief unnatural moment, a large outstretched bird struggled in the air while the nails hailed down, sending them trotting back. RV uncle, who was a nervous and emotional man, raised a hand to his bare chest and produced a long-drawn sickening wail, 'Ayyooooo!'

The stepbrother said, 'Now see what he's gone and done.'

Gopi stared. He was fascinated, scared and repulsed. The hammer was still clutched in his father's hand as if he'd held on to it for support. The nails were strewn on the grass like

artificial dewdrops. 'That's the end!' he thought briefly. Then
he heard his mother sob and saw the thick wet hair that
bordered his father's baldness and lay plastered to his neck,
and he felt the first movement of guilt within him.

The body was taken inside, bathed and laid out grandly
as if it were a display at an exhibition. It was dressed in fresh
clothes and surrounded by an outline of grain, and a brass
lamp was lit above the head. His mother sat grimly in a
corner, her eyes puffy with tears. All of Kilikkara Palace, with
the exception of a few immobile old uncles and aunts, were
there. Gopi's mother decided, autocratically they said then,
that the body would be cremated in Kilikkara itself and not
in Kunnupuram illam. She sent for his brothers and cousins,
saying the body could wait.

Later the men carried him off in the rusty blue ambulance
from Dr Sahadevan's hospital to the family cremation ground,
a kilometre away from the Palace on the western side. The
women and children stayed behind to mourn and to examine
past deaths. Gopi hung around and realized that when a man
dies, it isn't his departure but the phenomenon of death that
claws at people. He was fifteen then.

His father had alienated himself from their family because
of his callous plainspokenness. He was intolerant of other
people's opinions even as he realized his own didn't cut much
ice with them. This led to a permanent grumpiness which
acted as a buffer between him and his wife's people.

The trouble was Narayanan had come into the family on
a confused footing. Being a namboodiri Brahmin, his priestly
caste made him superior to his wife's family. Stature-wise, he
was rungs lower. Being of royal lineage, that too in a
matriarchal milieu, she had an edge over him which she
unthinkingly cultivated despite her basically gentle nature, and
he was reduced to playing second fiddle with poor grace. Each
was thus forced to assume a role that went against the grain,
and kept manoeuvering and side-stepping and sparring forever
afterwards.

Gopi was witness to several of their disagreements, which
would have been amusing if they didn't generate so much
tension. In the end, Narayanan resorted to staying away as

much as he could. He attended court cases in the district courts and in Trivandrum, and personally supervised operations on the lands that were scattered like grain about the district rather than trust the Big Palace manager, the wizened Pappu Iyer. Narayanan's frequent long disappearances from Kilikkara made him the subject of rumours that solicitous uncles kept regaling his wife with.

But Gopi noticed that most people had only praise for his father now. Death had obliterated all the wrinkles of his life. The relatives who stayed on to console his mother were offered lunch in the common hall of the Palace, away from the polluted house. They lingered and left only after dinner that night. 'We didn't even boil water in our kitchen today,' an aunt said briskly, 'poor Subhadra!'

One aquiline uncle bounded up to his sister Kamala, who was twenty-one that year, and said, 'You know, we have to examine the financial aspect now.' He kept standing there, slightly bent, perversely scanning her face. Kamala, who didn't know what he was talking about, nodded miserably. A long string of cotton trembled in her dishevelled hair, and Gopi felt like pushing aside the uncle and pulling it out.

Another uncle, not much older than him, kept disappearing and emerging moments later with a glassy scowl pasted on his face. Curious about this surprise mourner, Gopi followed him as he ran to the veranda of a house outside the Palace precincts. A melancholy group of youngsters sat around a radio that crackled out details of a cricket test in which India was taking a steady drubbing. The uncle shook his head and participated in the collective groan before rushing back.

Inside, the conversation became morbidly melodramatic. 'When you think of that Tamilian with the shop on Cloth Road, this is nothing. Goldsmith, yes. He fell off his roof two months ago.'

'Two months? I saw him in his shop yesterday.'

'Some people are born lucky. He bounced off a parapet and landed on a heap of bricks. Broke his hands and legs and cracked his skull.'

'And continues to sit in the shop?'

'It's like that in his family. His aunt had leprosy. No one

would go near her. She came to massage my feet one day. I told her to be off. Imagine, leprosy! And then she went to Chottanikkara to pray to the goddess, and now she's perfectly all right.'

'You're joking!'

'I tell you, her fingers had started becoming stiff and all that. I said, you get well and come, otherwise I'm not trusting you with my feet—I have only arthritis now, I don't want leprosy as well. She went away, and now . . .'

'It's the will of the goddess.'

'True, that family is blessed . . .'

'With leprosy and cracked skulls!'

'They survive everything, that's the great thing.'

'Coming back to this one,' a Northern Palace aunt added, signalling discreetly with her heavily lined eyes, 'first time such a thing has happened in the Palace.'

'Well, Narayanan Namboo'ri wasn't one of us.'

'Still, married into the family.'

'Poor Subhadra, she must be suffering.'

'That's nothing new, if you ask me.'

'Shh, she's sitting there.'

'There should be some sort of justice, shouldn't there? Going through life like that, and then having him jump off the roof!' The aunt began to quiver. 'And why couldn't they take him to his own illam instead of cremating him here? You noticed? There were hardly five people from Kunnupuram . . .'

'He didn't jump, he fell. And it was Subhadra herself who wanted him cremated here.'

Gopi's grandmother's cousin, their Matriarch, was a brittle, toothless lady past ninety who lived in Eastern Palace. She conducted herself with a natural imperiousness that would have been frightening had she been taken seriously. She insisted on being escorted to his mother. Clutching her arm in claw-like fingers, she said in a low hoarse voice, 'Don't worry, Subhadrey. Now you can relax at last.' Those within hearing looked shocked but preferred not to comment. The Matriarch was famous for her sharp stinging retorts.

'After all,' she continued, acknowledging the silence in triumph, 'outsiders will be outsiders. And we women should stick together . . .'

Another thing Gopi realized later was that his mother, too, fell that day. She lost her bearing and composure, her unwritten status as the calm and unassailable centre of the joint family, more dependable than the Matriarch herself. Who but the most dedicated persecutor, the Northern Palace aunt asked pointedly, would add his own death to his list of torments?

There were certain clear-cut, neatly-etched events that guided Gopi Narayan's life just like banks and boulders direct the path of a stream.

That day was a boulder. It was Saturday, the second day of March 1985.

He opened his eyes early to the day, hours before he usually did. The freshness of the morning promised much. It's going to be great, he thought. Not because he expected spectacular things to happen. It was a gut feeling. The light struggled in and granted slow shape to the furniture like a transition from one dream to another.

Thirty-five! It crept upon him, shocking him, stepping stone to maturity . . .

Only a month ago Uncle Shankar, his mother's brother, had silenced him, triumphant at the winning end of a see-saw debate on junk food, 'We oldies can't afford those luxuries.' He was reduced to defending his age. Very much like dozens of grand-uncles and aunts strewn all over Kilikkara Palace, shuffling and thrusting up their existence in one way or the other.

Lekha and Shobha lay on his right, their breathing conjoined and gentle except when Shobha missed a breath and gulped in air. He couldn't remember lying in bed like this and proprietorially watching them sleep. Not so early anyway.

His birthday was an AGM where he reviewed life's assets and speculated on what was ahead. He lay back with his hands folded comfortably beneath his head and tried to empty his mind of all thought. Yogi-like, he contemplated a gentle shaft of bronze light spilling from the window.

Faded grey faces watch him squarely from the wall.

His father, Narayanan Namboodiri, in a white jubba, his long hair collected in a bunch drooping like a limp beehive to one side of his head, looks starkly into the camera. He is young and thin-lipped, photographed in the bemused wake of his marriage. Gopi has been on the verge of replacing the cracked glass of this picture for some seven years now.

His mother, Subhadra Thampuratty, stands straight and proud and big-bosomed, an aristocrat in every respect.

His grandmother, Thriketta Thirunal, a thin-faced old woman, her forehead covered in holy ash, rudraksha beads around her neck, photographed during the last days of her life.

A small photograph of Colonel S.K. Raja and his wife Sumangali, Lekha's parents. He in uniform, looking more armyish than he ever did in real life, she comfortable and homely and looking completely vague as she always did.

A huge brown spider patiently harnessed thread-like arms to spin a fine web to bridge the distance between his parents. Atta boy, that's it, you're doing fine, go to it! And it became his own clarion call, for the duration of the birthday at least, like so many earlier efforts at self-motivation. An old marching song, picked up during college days, welled up at this point and he began to hum. Lekha moaned, stretched and opened her eyes at the sudden melody. She stared at the ceiling, swept her face in an arc to take in the room, and finally settled on Gopi. She smiled and clutched him like a drowning person. Gopi continued bravely with the song. She planted a sleepy kiss on his cheek. 'Happy-happy-happy birthday, Gopi.'

Abandoning the song and all thoughts of spiders, he fell upon her.

'Gopi!' She giggled weakly. He felt his spirit soar. He stroked her hair lovingly, wading his hand in as if he were leaning from a boat and testing the waters. He caressed her face with single-minded devotion, paying obeisance with fingertips and lips to eyes, nose, cheeks, lips and ears. Her breath was warm and unsullied. An investigative hand wandered to the slightly damp rise of her hip between blouse and sari, and travelled in deceptive languor down to the back of her thighs. Hands still on his back, she held on tight.

He was content to lie thus for the moment, breathing the trace of shampoo on flowing hair, feeling the breath of her body on his. He pulled back; time is precious and she's not going to remain unwary for long. He allowed his fingers to sail gently over her belly, played like a child in the dip of her navel. Her blouse was soon a bigger tent over his incursions, passion began to rise.

Lekha exhaled sharply and wriggled away, shooting a pained glance at Shobha who was curled up at the foot of the bed, having reached there in her frequent security manoeuvres. Lekha put both arms around her, gathered her like a peevish pillow and hugged her tightly. Shobha's protest was loud and clear. From a safe distance, Lekha whistled in wonder, 'Gopi, how time flies!'

He didn't relish her attempt at distraction. Shobha's presence hadn't cooled his passion, early-morning passion is hard to cool. He clenched his teeth and lay back, hands behind his head, staring furiously at the spider. His irritation mounted. 'What's wrong with thirty-five?'

'Don't. You shouldn't mention your age on your birthday. Not done.' She shook her head gravely. She stretched out on the bed and curled her toes, then made a bundle of herself, bringing her knees sharply up to her chin. 'Don't tell me what time it is,' she drew out in a half-purr, 'I'm so slee—eepy.'

He had half a mind to say, what a lousy birthday present first thing in the morning. He closed his eyes and forced his mind to go blank. When he turned to look at her again, she'd already gone back to sleep. She looked like a small girl, her face round and fair and carrying a perpetually thoughtful expression. The thick black hair cuddled on the white pillow, the pale yellow sari flowing out. He watched her gentle breathing.

Two days ago on a tired evening, he'd got back from the press and settled behind his paper. She brought him his coffee and slipped behind, ferreting out those unruly grey hairs. He pretended not to notice. Her fingers tickled the base of his neck. 'Soon,' he began mournfully through the newspaper, 'people will think you're my daughter.'

She must have blushed. 'What nonsense! You look young

for your age.'

A note of sadness in his voice. 'Even with all the grey?'

'Just because you have a few grey ones here and there doesn't mean you're old. I found only two today.'

He lowered the newspaper. 'Where?'

'I pulled them out.'

The sadness grew. 'And let's say you pull out three tomorrow, four the day after. So on and on, multiples of two every other day. Quite soon I'll be bald.'

Lekha stifled a laugh. 'Then they'll think I'm your granddaughter!'

Now, lying next to his wife, who was seven years younger than him, he considered his advancing years and chuckled loudly.

He got up hastily to avoid waking Lekha again. The clock showed a quarter past five. He went to the Godrej cupboard and opened the door cautiously, trying to mask its metallic protest. Finally, draining out his laughter into the blue-grey metal cage, he took out clean clothes. Everything was neatly arranged, his shirts and trousers and dhotis in one section, Lekha's saris in the other, Shobha's dresses and school uniforms below. The interior had a close smell of starch, mothballs, metal paint and soap, an oily trace of sandalwood. He leaned forward and shut his eyes. The combined smell stirred out a vision of childhood in Kilikkara. He thought of his mother. He locked the cupboard and went into the bathroom.

There he launched into a robust classical bhajan, his favourite nerve-nudging Shree Ragam sobering him and misting his eyes. He propitiated his new thirty-five-year-old body with mugfuls of water from the bucket. By the time his concert was over, Lekha was awake. She slid guiltily past him into the bathroom. He stood before the cracked mirror that hung on the bedroom wall, struggling fussily with his damp hair. He tested its creativity moving this way and that, elongating his nose, squashing his lips, widening his eyes. Then he stood back and studied himself critically, seeking a stance that made the mirror least abusive.

Medium height, trimmed moustache, ordinary looks. His nose was sharp. 'It's the Kilikkara stamp,' his mother said, 'not something you can duplicate easily.' Gopi concentrated on the nose, blurring everything else. Sharp sloping descent, the sudden attempt at freedom, a disturbance of the perfect line, and then the return describing an equally sharp angle. The nostrils, shiny at the edges, flared in equine impatience. He went down from the nose to the sparse frame within the vest.

It had been a different story in the early days, a pot belly that spoke of glorious inactivity. Lekha used to badger him. 'Play a game,' she'd say as if to a moody child. She hastened to add, 'We're husband and wife, so it's not about looks, just health. This,' caressing his excess with forbidding prescience, 'is not a good sign. Allow it to go on, and things will get out of hand—definitely problems later on.'

'What problems?'

'You know, heart and things.'

He had no alternative but to give in. He tried several fitness programmes. Brisk morning walks, jogging, even yoga. After five weeks of yoga, during each of which he absorbed a new set of exercises, he found he was becoming energetic and smoking less. But the enthusiasm was hard to maintain. Being woken at five by a terribly duty-conscious Lekha and spending two hours in positions of acute discomfort was a heavy price to pay for good health. The sixth week fortune smiled. His instructor called to say he wouldn't be available next morning. 'I've a wedding to attend, but please do it at home.' Gopi was shocked. 'Do it at home! What am I paying him for?' With great relief, he cursed the man's irresponsibility and went back to sleeping till eight.

But Lekha wouldn't leave him alone; and he took up jogging. One day, followed by a vicious and single-minded street dog that pursued him clamorously down the street, he sought breathless sanctuary behind Aunt Sarada's gates. Badly frightened, he refused to jog. Aunt Sarada backed him, saying she'd rather have a fat nephew than a rabid one. He secretly blessed the dog. He'd grown to hate those huffing public forays, pretending to ignore the amused looks of spectators who rose early to witness his discomfiture. He went back to nursing his paunch.

It struck him later that his reluctance was part of a larger cycle of inactivity and despair.

Those were the days when he pottered around Greenacres, Aunt Sarada's large colonial house, thinking up things to do. Or read. Or tried conscientiously to write something. Finally, ultimately, in the end, what he wanted to do was Write. His ambition to be a writer had once amused his friends in college. 'Writer? Like in a police station?' 'Okay, and I'm all set to be a Lefter!' 'What are you going to write, letters, cookbooks, porn?' 'Tell me when you finish, ya, I'll buy hundred copies and distribute to my friends and employees.'

Perhaps it was the strength of their scepticism. He'd never gone beyond a single chapter, though he commenced many books. He kept telling himself, his mother, Aunt Sarada and later Lekha, 'I've several stories in me. One day . . .'

He spent hours soaking in RV uncle's ruminations. He religiously attended functions organized by Aunt Sarada's Lotus Ladies' Club ('Like the lotus that blooms in the mud, we create beautiful things from the lowest of the low'). He accompanied Lekha everywhere, even when she shopped for provisions, or visited a friend. At first it didn't matter that the friend's husband wasn't around, that he was off at work like everybody else. The women joked and made small talk. They exchanged culinary notes and bits of film and neighbourhood gossip. Gopi enjoyed these sessions, their sheer lack of consequence. Besides, he was far more comfortable with the escapades of housewives than with their husbands who spoke decisively about abstract things like politics and finance and discussed their work with easy authority. He felt guilty when these men flaunted their jobs. He led them to believe, without actual dishonesty but through a devious process of wishful logic, that he was in a state of flux, between jobs.

His guilt loomed larger during confrontations with Lekha. A housewife comes to expect an employed husband. She expects to have the house to herself while the husband does his bit in an office or factory. That's what the children come to know when they reach the age of understanding. He dreaded his children growing up believing home was a cosy little place where Mother did domestic chores while Father slept or read.

The major problem with unemployment, Gopi discovered, was that you had to appear to be active all the time. It's different for someone with a proper job, his leisure hours aren't suspect. But the onus of explaining his movements fell heavily upon Gopi. He was constantly having to dodge the omnipresence of an invisible unknown They.

If he wanted desperately to find a job, any job—he wouldn't mind becoming an estate hand or an office clerk— it was because he'd had enough of trying to justify himself. He bit his teeth and attended interviews on Purusuwalkam High Road and Linghi Chetty Street, in Chintadripet and Korukkupet for insignificant ill-paid jobs, displaying his sincerity like a flag for the benefit of pompous shabby managers. Maybe I'm overqualified, he thought. Maybe I'll never get a job. Maybe I'll go back to Kilikkara and spend the rest of my days in slow and regal splendour like some of my great-uncles who think of nothing beyond food, culture and oil baths.

The die was cast the day Lekha declared briefly, 'It's not your fault, Gopi, it's mine. I'll get a job, you sit and write.' He was jolted by the absence of bitterness or irony in her voice; the deathly cool of the plain decisive statement cut to the bone.

One evening, not long after that they were all on the terrace of Greenacres. Those were the carefree days before they moved to Doctors' Colony. RV uncle paced up and down like a nervous wild animal. Aunt Sarada regaled Lekha with funny stories about Lotus Ladies' Club members. There was a strong breeze and RV uncle's dhoti kept spreading out like a skirt. Boys on a nearby balcony were flying kites. Suddenly Aunt Sarada swooped down and slapped Gopi's knee painfully. 'Why not Panikkar?' she shrieked. They looked blank. 'Panikkar, of course, he's got his press, why didn't anyone think of him?'

RV uncle said moodily, 'Why are you shouting?'

He was an intense man who did everything by the book. Reminiscing was his hobby, and his friends and relatives were resigned to sharing it with him. A man of delicate constitution and manners, he was repulsed by anything crude. Of course, he did trot out his standard set of naughty jokes—though he rarely got beyond 'busts' and 'bottoms'—after that third peg, but he blushed so much that his audience felt sorry for him. His long meandering stories—meticulous in detail and historical accuracy—ran on, and he paused to scratch his head and think deeply and to call Aunt Sarada over a dozen times to clear his doubts. By the time he was quite finished, his listeners, though impressed by his storytelling ability, were weary and dislocated. They also knew of his bowel movements, insomnia and the plethora of tablets that scores of doctors had prescribed right from the time he was dragged into manhood.

Aunt Sarada was fiercely loyal. She projected him as an ideal human being, his role of husband-father-socially committed citizen being eminently fit to be emulated. Sadly though, RV uncle was frequently brusque with her. And yet they couldn't do without each other, so completely dependent were they. When she brought up his friend Panikkar with such passion, he enquired coldly, 'What are you talking about?'

Unfazed, she said, 'Gopi can see K.P. Panikkar. I'm sure he'll fix something. Why don't you talk to him?'

His lips twisted in disdain. But whatever was poised to emerge from them would forever remain a mystery. At that precise moment the wind pushed forward and caught hold of RV uncle's dhoti and lifted it playfully over his face. Three startled pairs of eyes beheld a wispy strip of bulging loincloth above sagging bony knees. He let out a cry and scrambled to bring down the dhoti. His bespectacled face struggled into view, reddening like a beetroot. Aunt Sarada couldn't help the guffaw that burst out of her. Lekha jerked a hand to her lips, but too late. Gopi, pretending nothing had happened, said in a normal voice, 'So what are we to do about this K.P. Panikkar?'

Before a fortnight was out, he was accompanying his uncle to Panikkar's office at Vimala Art Printers. Panikkar bantered loudly, discussing everything under the sun except Gopi's employment. Finally when they rose to leave, he said casually, 'So he can come tomorrow morning. That should be okay—what?'

Gopi stood and marvelled at the unexpected turns life has

in store for all of us. He continued to study himself critically in the mirror. Years of erratic work schedules at VAP had melted all that fat. Now the only suggestion of roundness was on his face. 'Lekha was quite right,' he told his reflection. 'A paunch is a definite insult to the Kilikkara nose!'

He had the spooky feeling of being watched and turned around. Shobha lay on her stomach, chin propped up on her knuckles, studying him sleepily. 'You're talking to your nose?' she asked, knowing him.

TEN ELEPHANTS AND A MONKEY

■

They had ten elephants.

That, of course, was long before Gopi Narayan's time.

The three main branches of the Kilikkara family—Big Palace, Northern Palace and Eastern Palace—had yielded a fourth in the 1870s when Northern Palace, grown too big and quarrelsome to contain itself, split like an overripe pumpkin to give birth to Southern Palace. Being a split and not a formal partition, the development had no immediate legal ramifications, but a foul smell hovered in the air for some time. The new branch occupied a pole as far away from Northern Palace as possible; members forgot their descent from the same grandmothers and met like strangers during feasts at the agrashala, their common dining hall.

Big Palace was the smallest branch. Its members were easily housed in a single building named Raga Sudha, a large three-storied affair with twenty-four sides and six red-tiled gables, that had risen magnificently from the earth, its lower half still modestly skirted with an ancient muddy hue—it was reputed to be the oldest building in all of Kilikkara. Gopi Narayan belonged to this branch.

The two family partitions and the break-up of the joint family into several disparate units changed everything. For a decade after the second partition in 1952, the divisions were more or less continuous. Kilikkara royalty exploded, radiating nuclear families to every corner of the country, and outside the country as well. It was happening all over Kerala. Large old families were beginning to split up. Kovilakams—big, small and self-styled palaces—with their 'royal families' were submitting rather reluctantly to the new social order. Property was being partitioned off. The micha bhoomi reform, which plucked excess land from big landowners to redistribute to landless labourers, made sure that land, too, would soon become a perishable commodity. Some of the thampurans or noblemen realized the blissful palace life wasn't going to last forever, and sought out jobs and opportunities outside, going as far as Africa, America, England and 'Persia'.

Elephants were a part of the sacrifice Kilikkara had to make.

In those days, temple festivals were elaborate affairs that went on for several days. The entire town participated. The kovilakam, literally 'inside the temple', shouldered the financial brunt and hosted sumptuous feasts for the duration of the festival. Palace life revolved around the temple, and the number of gaily caparisoned elephants proclaimed the importance of each Palace. Ten elephants was no mean achievement. Until the family realized that these enormous, taken-for-granted creatures were depleting stores at an alarming rate. It was finally Grand-uncle Rama Varma Raja, author of Kilikkara's first partition, who came down to brass tacks. 'We've reached a stage when we must take a decision. It's up to all of us, *oru kudumba prashnam*. Tell me, who is more qualified to remain in the Palace, we or the elephants?'

It created a furore. 'Get rid of the elephants! What's the use of saying we're from Kilikkara?'

And the Patriarch replied calmly, 'Sheri, very good, we'll leave, elephants can stay!'

When they were shown cold figures, they couldn't help

agreeing with him. Besides the cost of feeding and maintenance, they had to retain several mahouts and an elephant doctor, all essential elements of a pachydermal retinue. A large fenced-in field far away on the western border of the Palace grounds housed the elephants. Members who lived in that direction were often driven to complain about smells and sounds floating in the languid palace air, and even occasional damage to trees and property as the animals lumbered about their duties. But this was dismissed as a geographical inevitability, no one questioned the elephants' right of residence.

The accident at the Kilikkara river proved more sobering. It happened during the monsoon towards the close of the last century. There was much more water in Kilikkara river those days. Some of the elephants were taken periodically to the forest to fell timber and guide the logs down the river. One massive tusker, a favourite called Suryan, lost his footing and was swept downriver. The river was in spate. The body was found four days later, two miles down, mauled by crocodiles.

This was a big blow, and the family went into mourning. A commemorative wooden plaque was planted in the elephants' compound. It was inscribed with two verses from the Rig Veda and the sketch of an elephant solemnly saluting. Members of the family went about as if a relative had passed away. For days after that, conversation centred around elephants, living, legendary and mythical; elephants who'd died in accidents 'but not like this, my God!'; and elephants who'd departed in a spirit of sacrifice.

Worse, they only had nine elephants left.

The second casualty occurred during the temple festival. The five-metal festival idol of Kilikkara Appan was brought out with fanfare to be taken in procession. Sankaran, who'd been lately acting cranky, rebelled against the indignity of having to stand humbly by as drums rolled and pipes blew and the god he carried on his back extracted ceaseless hours of obeisance. And while the women were roused to religious fervour and the men thrust out their chests in proprietorial pride, Sankaran swayed his trunk in ominous rhythm. Finally the old one decided enough was enough. He let loose a deafening scream and ploughed into the startled crowd.

Dislodging his mahout and the image of the god, the bright-coloured umbrella and caparison.

Three people from the village lost their lives, including an eighty-five-year-old woman and a child. An uncle who escaped a massive foot by a small inch went into shock. He remained delirious for a week. At the end of the week, his hair had turned milk-white. He became known as Aanathala ammavan—Elephant-head uncle—in memory of this incident.

Sankaran scampered down the slope as if he were a goat. He paused at the Kilikkara Appan temple, hesitating since it was one of his halts during the procession. Then he carried on resolutely till he reached the stone steps leading down to the river. Giving a final yell he stopped, waving his trunk madly.

There was nothing else to be done. Old Sankaran was sold to the first comer with scant regard for his worth. Though he was still alive, another plaque went up in the compound. Simultaneously, three plaques were raised in the Kilikkara village square to honour the memory of the three victims, organized bitterly by a group of young rebels who were stung by the Palace's tribute to a murderer.

There was a deadly aftermath. The mahout who, by coincidence, had been responsible for both the ill-fated elephants, fell into a deep depression. He took to drinking heavily. He would travel all the way to Kilikkara from the estate of the elephant's new owner and offer an outpouring of guilt to the family members. Twice he had to be forcibly removed. Later they heard that he had, in a rare moment of sobriety, bid farewell to Sankaran and his master, and strung himself up on a tree, dedicating his life to his oversized ward.

And then there were eight.

After the 1920 family partition and the Patriarch's ultimatum, the family agreed to make do with two elephants. But that was hardly felt to be a shadow on their prosperity. After all, how many families are there that keep elephants?

The last one was a fine tusker named Arjunan. Early every morning he lumbered from the compound to the temple. Chained to a post, he'd flap his majestic ears and devour a green carpet of fronds. He carried the idol in procession to the tune of pipes and drums. The Palace children made daring

attempts to touch his wrinkled grey skin, and loved him with
all their hearts. When adults condescended to ask what they
wanted to be when they grew up—lawyer-doctor-engineer-
diplomat?—invariably the smaller children looked solemn and
said, 'I will become Arjunan's keeper.'

Arjunan was a mischievous elephant who selected unlikely
members of the family for his frolics. It was RV uncle's
pirannaal, day of the star under which he was born. He was
walking around the main sanctum with his upper cloth tied
around his waist and his hands folded in prayer. As he came
to the elephant, he didn't pause but proceeded stiffly along.
Arjunan, trying to get his attention, stuck out his trunk and
gave him a playful nudge on the buttocks. RV uncle staggered
forward. And then to help him regain his balance, Arjunan
gave another quick nudge on his stomach, sending him flying
back. The next thing they knew, he was flat on his back on
the stone floor, waving arms and legs like a giant baby.
Arjunan shook his head and returned guiltily to his fronds.

RV uncle, unlike the watching children, was not amused
by the incident. The beast had lost his reason like old
Sankaran. He said, his mouth set in a grim line, 'Get rid of it
before we lose any lives.'

Even Aunt Sarada said, 'He was just being playful . . .'

'We can't let him play with our lives!'

Then Gopi's father stepped in. Narayanan Namboodiri
was more fond of elephants than people. When he was in
Kilikkara, he spent hours with Arjunan. His constant
companion was Thanu, Arjunan's mahout, a thin man with
lumpy muscles and quick toothy smiles. Thanu knew no life
outside the elephant compound and gratefully shared many a
secret about elephant maintenance with the namboodiri. He
was flattered by the attentions of 'Namboo'ri thampuran'.
The address, begun as a sarcastic reference by old uncles in the
family—actual thampurans—who poked bitter fun at the
namboodiri's appropriation of their duties and rights, had in
time become a respectful term used by unenlightened menials.

When RV uncle insisted that Arjunan should go, Narayanan
put his foot down. Whatever they said behind his back,
Kilikkara had a healthy respect for Gopi's father. He had a

sharp legal brain and an amazing head for figures. Almost all
of the Palace administration had been entrusted to him. In
addition, there was his famous temper. It was like a heavily
drugged maneater, no one knew when the drug would wear
off. 'Arjunan will stay,' he said. There wasn't much RV uncle
could do after that. He was essentially a weak man whose
weakness bubbled up in the presence of his 'co-brother'.

Three years after Narayanan's death, a council of elders
met. It included family members as well as those married into
the family. Citing reasons of economy and conjuring up the
ghost of Great-uncle Rama Varma Raja, the council decided
Arjunan should go. 'Remember what he said? It's Us or
Them!'

Gopi was eighteen. Even today he can see that scene. The
youngsters watched as Arjunan's chain was draped over him
like an enormous iron caterpillar. He walked heavily from the
compound to the temple and paid his last respects to Kilikkara
Appan. The bundle containing the silk and umbrellas was
handed over ceremoniously to the new owner's representative.
Thanu wept openly. Watched by a small silent crowd of
admirers, Arjunan ambled down the main path, outlined
against the setting sun. His bell rang in cold rhythm. He was
made to pause at each house on the way, raise his trunk in
salute and bid farewell. They accompanied him for a while,
through the main arch, and then watched his massive wrinkled
back retreating down the slope that led to Kilikkara village.
Even after they lost sight of the elephant, the bell rang and
Thanu kept wailing in their ears.

Arjunan didn't get a plaque.

Not long afterwards, the compound which was temple
property was sold for a moderate consideration to the brother-
in-law of a Southern Palace aunt. The gentlemen had made his
fortune in the Gulf. Undaunted by the funereal presence of
commemorative plaques, he erected a large modern house.
The bright mass of white-brown-browner squares and its
stucco facade stood in awkward isolation from the quiet
traditional grandeur of the Palace buildings. Despite its plush
interiors and the man's generous hospitality—including cool
drinks made from imported powders, assorted biscuits and

exotic tours through his travel albums—visitors were rare. The Palace elders expected him to visit them and those who did turn up complained snootily of elephants in the air—not just the overpowering smell, there was a general aura of elephants. Stories circulated about people tripping over phantom balls of dung, of groaning whispers and sweeping trunks. Invisible chains rattled enormously in the night. The aunt's brother-in-law bravely persevered, having sunk money in the house. He was the first outsider to be allowed to build a house within the palace grounds. In deference to his predecessors, he named his two-acre property Aana Muttam. Elephant Estate stood as an awkward monument to the dying grandeur of Kilikkara.

There were other such attempts to bridge the gap with nostalgic devices, reflecting the crude sobering reality of the times.

The Palace office where Rama Varma Raja and then Gopi's father had sat and pondered over the intricacies of a family partition, some five hundred yards from the temple, was now largely shut up. The front room became a library-cum-meeting place, 'a den for idle young fellows', according to one prim uncle. The air here was thick with bidi smoke and laughter as youngsters discussed politics, cinema, women and sports.

The uneven surface of the large open maidan, where ten elephants had waved their ears like royal flags during the temple festival, was now planted with goalposts.

The Palace school was situated on the road to the village, cutting through paddy fields and a stream. The rarefied wisdom of specially imported tutors had once nourished rows of struggling blue-blooded brains. It was now a government school. The only reservation for admission was for the socially deprived classes of society, as certified by the government. Strikes and 'gross incorrigible indiscipline' (another avuncular opinion) became a way of life.

The school was still known as MVR Higher Secondary School after Kilikkara's greatest man of letters, Gopi's grandmother's grand-uncle. The swirling library was nostalgically—and optimistically—named Kilikkara Palace Cultural Club. Times had changed, but they were still remembered.

Several other traditions continued uninterrupted though. The lure of the temples, Kilikkara Appan within the Palace grounds and Manjoor Devi across the river in the middle of the forest. The gong suspended from the entrance arch that still boomed out its noon and midnight toll. The common lunch or dinner at the agrashala on important days. The common fund for temple maintenance. And, of course, the annual temple festivals. Despite their diminished grandeur, they still drew crowds from Kilikkara and neighbouring villages. The Kilikkara Appan festival brought all the family members together every year from whichever corner of the world they'd migrated to.

Today, when these emigrants return to Kilikkara, they find the transformation complete. Every branch, every family unit for itself. Common traditions hang by slender threads, radiating mostly from the two temples. Outsiders have come to stay within the Palace, someone's brother-in-law, someone else's husband's uncle, a namboodiri rolling in Gulf money. Villagers come daily to worship inside the temple, a sacrilege in earlier times. Even the stretch of river adjoining the palace is no more an exclusive domain. At certain times, like during the festivals, no one can tell who is family and who is from outside. There are just bare wet bodies everywhere.

Gopi studied in the MVRHS School till the tenth standard.

In keeping with the prevalent custom, he joined school only at seven. He preluded this by gathering worldly wisdom at the feet of Monkey Krishna Iyer, an irritable old taskmaster from Nagercoil. Krishna Iyer's father was Mankambu Srinivasa Iyer, a Sanskrit scholar of repute. The family name was soon distorted by the previous generation of students which included Subhadra, Gopi's mother.

'Monkey's coming, Monkey's coming!' his students whispered as the stout balding gentleman with his soda-bottle spectacles came lumbering up to the Northern Palace office room where classes were held. God help the youngster who was overheard! The fat cane sang down brutally, a couple of thick fingers descended upon flushing ears.

'What did you say?' the grating voice demanded.

'Nothing.'

'Repeat that!'

'I didn't say anything,' the unfortunate one would whine.

Amazingly, these were the offspring of a hallowed family whose history was closely allied to that of the Travancore rulers. The children grew up to become top-ranking bureaucrats, judges and diplomats. But Monkey Krishna Iyer was licensed to pinch. Such was the importance given by the Kilikkara family to education and good breeding that Monkey Iyer could flay till they squealed and still keep his position. It was all for a good cause.

The students composed a poem in Malayalam, an ode to the Monkey, and it remained their pre-school anthem. A rough translation:

Alas! we have a monkey
Whose tail is stiff and long;
He wags it on our bottom
And tells us we are wrong.
There's nothing we can really do
To chase away this pest,
Our uncles think him very cute
And keep him as their guest.
We'd rather stay as dunces
Than study with a monkey;
And when he dies we're pretty sure
They'll send out for a donkey!

The children even dreamed up a Monkey Estate full of plaques, the biggest with the ode inscribed on it and carrying an illustration of Monkey Iyer saluting with his cane.

Towards the end of his career, which dragged on and on, he grew deaf. He shouted out his lessons and grew even more strict. Sometimes, as senility took a firm grip, he would digress and talk about politics and the decadent times and even about his own life, which his students considered his most amusing subject. Some of Gopi's cousins dared to call him Monkey to his face, taking care to keep a straight face since they suspected he could read lips.

To relieve the deadening monotony of his classes—this monotony amidst the warm air and chirping birds and the cool river and, ah God, thousands of fleshy mangoes waiting for their greedy little hands—to save them from the constant drone of Monkey Iyer's voice, nature took pity on them and issued her call. Monkey Iyer treated these calls with the utmost respect. He struggled to his feet, asked a student to take charge and hastened to the outside toilet way behind the office room. A collective sigh of relief filled the room at this sudden freedom. One or two pruriently-inclined pupils, prone to profane forms of entertainment, dared to follow him, grinning and dancing and gesticulating. They unfolded shocking details of the master's enormous scrotum and 'elephant's trunk' that seemed to take on a life of its own when he uncovered it for his relief. They soon ran back to issue their report, of how wearisome it was to get the elaborate dhoti untied, of how long the stream lasted, of the belly that danced and gurgled like an enchanted mountain. For Monkey Iyer never bothered to lock the door, fearing a toilet mishap that would render him inaccessible to outside aid.

One day he caught them at it. The two boys rushed in, their faces pale. 'He's seen us!' they hissed. But apparently Monkey Iyer's sight was almost as bad as his hearing for he believed that Gopi was one of them. He stood darkening the doorway, fuming.

'Balan thampuran! Gopi thampuran! Get up!' He used the respectful form of address, but his tone was anything but respectful. Every word burned. 'I wasn't there,' Gopi mumbled, trembling with anger, sorrow and fear.

'How dare you talk back to me!'

'I wasn't there.'

'Hold out your hand!' He got three 'cuts', one more than his cousin, because of the additional crime of rebellion. 'Have you any idea about the family you have the good fortune to belong to?' he shouted in Gopi's ear, looming over the boy like a short-sighted ogre. 'Do you know your grand-uncle had written a literary masterpiece by the time he was twenty-five?

Do you know your uncle from Southern Palace is a most respected judge in the Madras High Court? And you, thampuran, desecrate your family name by peeping on elders when they pass water! You dedicate your childhood to voyeuristic pursuits!'

Though unsure of what a voyeuristic pursuit was, Gopi guessed it wasn't a desirable quality. 'I didn't do it!'

Innocence is a cruel joke when no one else recognizes it. Gopi burned with the injustice of it. He was furious at the real culprit. But no one in his right senses would confess to Monkey Iyer. The guilty cousin made mute appeals to Gopi to shoulder the blame without fuss, crinkled his eyes pitifully to demonstrate how sorry he was. Gopi was in no mood to forgive anyone. Neither was he strong enough to let the righteous indignation that washed over him pass without expression. He was soon facing his father. His accuser stood beside him, red face twitching like an epileptic. 'Thirumeni, I find this hard to take!'

Narayanan looked stern, but somehow his attitude betrayed something less than anger. It was as if he was only acting a part. He dismissed Monkey Iyer with a promise of appropriate redressal and turned to Gopi. 'So that's what you do?'

'I didn't do it.'

'Are you telling me that your master is lying?'

'It wasn't me, there were others.'

'What others? Come on, tell me, what others?' Gopi continued to stare. 'Let's see what your mother has to say about this.'

'He punished me though I didn't do it!'

His father took a firm grip of his shoulder and steered him to the courtyard where his mother was supervising a couple of maids laying out lime cuts to be dried in the sun. He beckoned to her and the three of them went into the privacy of the storeroom, which was cool and dark and smelt of pickles, fresh coconut oil and grains. They negotiated their way through the glass and earthen containers and sacks of raw rice from the Palace granary, and stood under the small netted window which threw a swirling yellow light on the floor.

She stood impatiently with her hands on her hips, looking

fixedly at her husband. By now Gopi felt everything hinged on her verdict. If she believed Monkey Iyer's story, he was lost, sullied for the rest of his life. His father related both versions.

She turned to Gopi with anger in her eyes. 'Aren't you ashamed of yourself?' she asked coldly. He flinched. Already he burned with shame. He cursed his cousins and Monkey Iyer for his exhibitionism and poor vision. 'That punishment is not enough. Everyone in the Palace will know.' She advanced towards him in a fresh burst of anger.

'Wait!' Narayanan put up his hand. She stopped, turning irritably. 'I don't think Gopi did it.'

'Do you mean Krishna Iyer is telling a lie?'

His father placed a hand on Gopi's head and rumpled his hair. The boy's eyes filled and at that moment he felt closer to his father than ever before. 'Krishna Iyer is old. He's deaf and half-blind. Anyway, I don't think Gopi would do such a thing.'

Gopi pressed against his father, his shoulder feeling the sweat on his bare midriff. His fingers found the sacred thread his father wore over his shoulder. It was drenched.

His mother sighed. 'Don't lie to me now. Is your father right?'

'Yes,' Gopi said in relief, hating this inquisition.

'Then I will explain to Krishna Iyer. You can go.'

Gopi lifted his head. His father's eyes twinkled.

This incident occurred when Gopi was six. The special relationship with his father continued for about four years. Narayanan rarely sought him out. In a place like Kilikkara, it wasn't common for a father to be openly affectionate. Nor did Narayanan forsake his brusque manner. But his feelings surfaced at times like the sudden sparkle of sunlight through trees.

There was another moment Gopi stored. There were events he thought of as red asterisks dotting his life's horizon, egging him on. Sometimes they faded at his approach, sometimes they justified his faith. Among the luminous landmarks he still remembered was his ninth birthday. His father was in Trichur in connection with a squatters' case and he had promised to be back for the birthday lunch. That promise stuck in Gopi's mind. It was something to look forward to, to round off the day.

Hope coursed through the climbing day like gossamer tendrils. He shut his eyes and prayed to Kilikkara Appan. His mother gave him a silk dhoti with a gold border that glowed beneath his restless fingers. He wore it proudly, showing off impartially to his cousins and anyone who cared to stop. Tomorrow the dhoti would be washed and stored away until another occasion. He walked up and down the temple path a hundred times. It was customary for boys of his age to wear nothing more than a pair of shorts—in earlier days it was a leaf-wrap or a towel around the waist. A silk dhoti was a luxury, how they stared!

He didn't have to go to school. His mother took him instead to visit relatives and get their blessings, making him feel like Arjunan the elephant carrying the festival idol to each house in the Palace. By the time they returned home, they were tired and streaming despite periodic rewards of cool glasses of buttermilk, coconut water and lime juice.

'What, boy, getting bigger, is it?' an elderly uncle asked with a bloated attempt at good cheer.

Gopi knew he probably hated him just then. The uncle's clock was six hours behind everyone else's and he'd made special efforts to receive them. The Big Palace people, especially Subhadra, had that privilege—they were VIPs in a manner of speaking. His rousing himself to honour a mere boy's birthday was a measure of their importance.

'In our days we celebrated birthdays with elephants and pipes,' he continued. 'Pe-pe-pe-pe-pe!' He mimed a nadaswaram player with angled arms and puffed-up cheeks.

Kochu Kelu ammavan—literally Small Kelu uncle—was a huge man with pregnant breasts and a comfortably settled stomach. His enormous brown nipples demanded attention. He was smooth and shining, a giant bald baby having succumbed early in life to the addictive pleasure of the *sarvanga kshouram*, whole-body tonsure. The barber shaved his vast domains with devout concentration as Kochu Kelu held court, discussing, debating and joking with friends from Kilikkara village seated behind a large white sheet strung up as a screen. These sessions were referred to as KK's roma durbar, his hair court sessions.

'And then, little boy, you'll grow bigger and study in school and college and get a big government job and go to the city to make your living. Who'll be left to safeguard our traditions? We people won't live forever. Take care, don't forsake Kilikkara!' He leaned forward and hooked Gopi with fish-shaped eyes. Wads of flesh sagged beneath them like storage bags. Gopi was fascinated, torn between eyelashes that represented his only hair and staring nipples. He sat with a small grin, unsure whether old KK was joking or scolding.

'How old do you think I am?' he asked suddenly. Gopi continued to sit and grin, confronting such a question for the first time. He didn't know what to make of it. KK carried on his person none of the usual indicators of age; no grey hair since he had no hair at all, no thin and stooping frame since he was fat and jolly, and no vacant gums, being blessed with large white teeth. 'Sixty?' he asked cautiously because he had heard that no one lived beyond sixty.

'Sixty!' Kochu Kelu laughed, producing a deep swirling sound like sambar being stirred in a cauldron. 'When was that, thirty years ago? What do you say, Subhadrey? Your boy has gifted me exactly thirty-three years of life!' He continued to laugh and his belly undulated monstrously. It fascinated Gopi and his grin began to fade. 'Have you heard of MVR?'

'I don't think he has,' Subhadra said.

'Well, you should! He was one of the greatest poets our language has produced. He was your great-great-grand-uncle. Same MVR who wrote the epic. And he was from here, from our own Kilikkara. Did you know that?' Gopi shook his head silently. 'And do you know, I was only seven years younger than him? I am from that time, that blessed era when Kilikkara was Kilikkara. You see?' Gopi nodded silently. 'When Kilikkara was Kilikkara! Now see what is happening. People are going away and forgetting our traditions and forsaking our Mother!' Gopi hung his head, not knowing what sort of expression was now called for.

His mother laughed. 'He's too young to be upholding traditions. There's plenty of time to think of his future.'

'I'm only making a prediction. At the rate everyone's leaving, soon we'll have to shut up the Palace. Deivamey! Did we ever think of a time Kilikkara Appan would be left to fend for Himself?'

'I should think He's the one who looks after us.'

By the time they got through several such conversations, it was half-past twelve. People had gathered at the agrashala for the feast.

'Where's he? He hasn't come.' Gopi's voice was squeaky with emotion.

'He'll come, don't worry,' his mother said. 'He promised, didn't he?'

But he didn't. They finished lunch and everyone was cheerful and chatty. Nobody noticed his father's absence. Gopi didn't eat much, everything tasted salty. He had to sleep in the afternoon though he wanted to wait up. In the evening, they had banana fry and a coconut and jaggery sweet wrapped in banana leaf. He was permitted a glass of coffee as a special favour. 'Don't keep thinking of your father. Something has delayed him. Go and play.' So the boys played cricket. Gopi was out three times and graciously given the benefit of the doubt. They allowed him to keep wickets and, in his excitement, he forgot his father for a couple of hours. When the light began to fade, Subhadra sent word that it was time for the temple. They bathed in the river and got to the temple in time for the evening puja. Gopi stared accusingly at Kilikkara Appan. He glowed bright and fresh and seemed happy in His own world.

After that, a resigned depression set in. He allowed himself to be bundled off to dinner and bed. Before he dropped off, he thought, I'll never speak to him again.

It must have been near midnight when he woke up. Lights shone in the outer room. Gopi strained his ears to catch the whispers.

'That's silly, he's gone to sleep. You can tell him tomorrow.'

'I can't wait.'

'Well, it's too late now. He was miserable throughout the day.'

'I must see him.'

'He's sleeping.'

'It doesn't matter if he loses some sleep.'

The door opened, sending the light tumbling in. He felt a gentle touch on his forehead. 'Gopi.'

He was up instantly. He didn't even make a pretence of waking up. Narayanan sat down on the bed and peered gravely at him. 'Father promised to be with you. Something came up and he couldn't.' The orange light played against his head like a halo, darkening his face and sharpening his eyes. 'Don't feel bad about it. See, I've brought this.' He thrust a paper packet at him. He didn't apologize in so many words because he never did. Gopi opened the packet with wraith-like fingers. Everything in the room glimmered with a light of its own, the room itself was getting darker. The paper tore. He pulled out the white silk shirt. For a long time he couldn't speak as his fingers rubbed the soft sheen of the fabric. He gazed at the shirt, then at his father.

'Do you like it?' Gopi nodded. 'I'm glad.'

'I-I knew you'd come,' he stammered.

His father held his shoulder and said, 'That's why I woke you up.'

It made up for everything else. He was one of the first boys to own a shirt! He screwed his eyes shut and thanked Kilikkara Appan. It was a brief joy. A year later, and their relationship would turn topsy-turvy. It probably had nothing to do with Gopi and his father—it probably had to do with something that had happened centuries ago.

When I return to the hotel from Doctors Colony, I'm drenched. Hair and clothes stick to the skin.

I reach my room, strip off my wet clothes and take a hot shower. I pick up the phone and order food. The 'Indo-Continental' breakfast—toast and marmalade, cornflakes, crisp dosa and chutney, rich brown South Indian coffee—is wheeled in by an old friendly waiter who makes a big thing of arranging the cutlery meticulously on the table and then refuses to leave me in peace to enjoy my food. He hovers and smiles and fusses over me like a fond mother. I sit down and eat before he actually starts feeding me.

Long before eleven, I'm in Rangachari's neighbourhood. It is a vile street. The traffic is heavy, slow and very noisy. A large lorry stands squarely in the middle of the narrow road, causing confusion. Curses, angry honks, desperate raising of engines. A dog yelps excitedly. A youngster in torn shorts runs around with precise cheeky instructions on how to back up the vehicle.

I cross an open drain gurgling with a greenish brown sap, thanking God the rain has stopped. A small child of indeterminate sex is defecating profusely into the drain, straddling it adroitly, its back to me. I ache for the customers who will stop by the vendor displaying his tray of sliced-open jackfruit. Flies play hide-and-seek between slimy yellow fruit and the drain. (All flies and no lid, I want to caution him, makes your jack a sick fruit indeed.)

There are hundreds of small shops and offices on this street. Motor spares, electricals, sweetmeats, paper, travel agents, cargo booking, advocates.

Above the shops are residences. This is advertised by the clothes flapping on lines, the idle women and bored young men deep-frozen in balconies, watching life without interest. Finding Rangachari's number is not so easy. There are at least three numbers on each door—old, new and very old number. 'Where's 17/2?' I ask a passer-by. He shrugs eloquently and moves on. Another listens carefully, makes me repeat everything and then says, 'Sorry, I'm new here.' I'm shown the number twice, but it's the old and the very old number.

An old gentleman with a cellphone growing out of his ear responds kindly, 'No use looking. No number like that. Yes, I'm sure. You can go back home.'

I've half a mind to. But I persist, and then have the brainwave of asking at a cold-drink stall. This is a pettikadai—a wooden box perched on four thin beams—stacked with bottles of soda and different kinds of 'colour' drinks, a large coil of rope, medicines for cold and headache and fever, cigarettes and plantains. Two or three Tamil film magazines sporting acrobustic starlets on their covers are clipped to a nylon string. An electric switch, displayed prominently, will heat up a coil of wire to light cigarettes. All this is presided over by a cheerful vendor with a huge moustache.

As I approach, I slip on a banana peel and totter dangerously. I steady myself by grabbing the counter. Heart beating fast, I grumble in Tamil, 'They have to throw it on the pavement!'

The man is amused. 'You have to be careful where you walk.'

I buy a single cigarette from him though I already have a packet. 'I'm looking for an address.'

He laughs. 'Unless you're born in this place, you won't find it.'

'I'm looking for 17/2. It's a residence.'

'17/2. Now where is that? Residence? There's a shop there, that one selling spare parts.'

'Yes, I know. I want the new number.'

He moves a few empty bottles like an absent-minded chess player. 'Whose residence?'

'Rangachari. He's a writer.'

'Ranga—oh, Prof'sar Saar.'

'Right! I have an appointment with him.'

He points. 'You see that water pump? Shop next to it? Prof'sar Saar stays just above that shop.'

Stroke of luck, I tell myself. I have the name and the number. Now I need flesh and blood. And this is exactly the fellow who'll give it to me.

'What sort of a man is he?'

'Good man. Straightforward.' The vendor looks curiously at me.

'I'm a publisher. I'm here to see him about his new book.'

Someone comes up and asks for a goli soda. He picks up a bean-shaped thick-skinned bottle and smacks the top briskly with his palm, freeing its mouth of its blue marble. Some of the liquid fizzes out. He hands it over to the customer who drinks up greedily. While counting out the money, the customer discovers gauze-covered breasts making purple eyes at him. Shooting a swift glance at me, he yanks the magazine from its string and adds a couple of extra notes. After he's left, the pattern is rearranged to accommodate the new bottle.

'Saar is always writing,' the vendor says, returning to me.

'There was an interview in a Tamil magazine some time ago—colour pictures and all. I used to tell people, read the interview, it's good. Some free publicity, you know! Let me do my bit for Saar.'

'You know him well then.'

'Mari is here every day. He does the cleaning and cooking, everything, in fact. After Amma went, Mari's all-in-all. He comes here every day for a bidi, sometimes a soda.'

'How long has he been living in this house?'

'Oh, many years, long before my shop. He was in the university. But they lived a quiet life. A student may have come, another prof'sar, that's all.'

'She died, didn't she?'

The man nods. 'Amma was a quiet lady. Not a word out of her. Sometimes she went out to the temple. Once a week for provisions. There's no need to go out actually, everything comes here, vegetables, milk, kerosene. After retirement he's even more busy. Always sitting up there and writing. But nowadays he doesn't like to go out. Sometimes people come over to see him. Like you. He may meet them, he may not. He's a real recluse. You wouldn't think he's a big author.'

'Do you see him often?'

'No one sees him! For days, sometimes weeks. Mari comes up for fresh air once in a while, how long can you stay locked up like that? Sometimes he dashes out for a Small.' He winks. 'Don't mention that.'

'I won't. What sort of a man is he? A bit short-tempered?'

He sniggers. 'A bit!' I've grossly underestimated Saar. 'He'll bite your nose off. They're all scared of him. He was like that even then, but now he says whatever he likes, straightforward, exactly what he feels.'

'He's written only two books. Why do you think he's so famous?'

'Wrote three, actually.' He scans my face for surprise. 'No one has read the first one. That's what they asked him in the interview. You've written only two books, how come you're so famous? And Saar said, if you commit only one murder, you're still hanged, aren't you?' The man chuckles, shakes his head, clearly a fan of Saar's humour. 'He said, if you're a

writer from the south, you can never become famous. Someone
from the north has to say you're good. Saar wrote a book
first, the one no one read. Then he wrote another one and
someone in Bombay wrote in a newspaper that it's a good
book. Now see where he is!' He frowns, probably considering
the north-south divide. He suddenly switches from Tamil to
English. 'What is in our hands, gentleman? All God-above's
drama, no? God-above pulling, we playing, that's all.'

'What's he pulling?' I ask, taken aback.

The vendor shakes his head. 'God-above pulling string,
like fuffet we playing. All fuffet!' He turns away, moved by
his own homily.

'About his temper . . .'

'He simply kicks them out!' He shakes his head admiringly.
'Mari was telling me the other day, some journalist came for
an interview. His magazine had written a gossip column, Saar
is a drunkard and lost his memory, and wrote his book when
he was drunk. You should have seen him. Have you ever seen
me drunk, he asked, are you the guardian of my memory—
like that. The journalist was only a reporter, some other
writer-biter had written that column. Saar said, then why
work for such a stupid magazine? He told Mari to pick up a
stick and drive him out. The journalist ran.'

I smile nervously. 'You're scaring me!'

He lovingly twirls his gigantic moustache. 'I haven't
finished. Then, within ten minutes, he changed his mind. Go
and bring him back, he told Mari. Now where is Mari to go
and look? He thought he'd go out and smoke a bidi, come
back and tell him the man had gone. But there that journalist
was, waiting for an auto. So he was brought back and left
with his interview.'

I shake my head, impressed by Saar's chameleon-like
qualities. 'What made him change his mind?'

'Who can say? Saar's like that.' He looks thoughtful.
'Those days Saar made history, now he makes money!'

'Mari says that?'

'What does Mari know? Saar must have told him.'

That will have to do for the time being. It is eleven.
Armed with this Saar-crossed saga, I walk past the shop

to the dark doorway. The staircase is crumbling and dirty. There is a warm smell of rancid hair oil, diesel, cooking and urine. I climb. The sounds of the street fade out and silence takes over. It is cool. A narrow white plastic board nailed to a green door says TATACHARI RANGACHARI.

I ring the bell and wait.

LOVE STORIES

—————————◆—————————

Excerpt from the diary of Kochu Kelu, 1885:

Perhaps it is foolish to think that I can accomplish what many others—more proficient, knowledgeable and enthusiastic—have attempted and failed to do. We have never been known for detailed and accurate cataloguing. I believe there are many instances that have been deliberately discarded from the collective memory!

I have had to meet some of the old uncles and aunts variously to piece together our history. Even so, I find there are significant gaps and intriguing mysteries. For instance, there is the matter of the Chakram, that scarcely ever finds satisfactory corroboration. There is the relationship between Kilikkara and Kunnupuram illam, the house of namboodiri priests twelve miles from here. The Chakram seems to be a wedge that is eternally stuck between the two houses.

As far as I can tell, this particular Chakram is made of copper, and is a thin sheet that has been inscribed with a powerful set of incantations, guaranteeing peace, power and prosperity to the family it is intended for. (That is very important—it is not the family that owns it or takes possession of it that reaps the benefit, but the house that employs the priest to inscribe the incantation in the first place.) From the various interpretations, it is fairly evident that Kunnupuram had the Chakram in the first place and we took possession of it in some adventurous manner. I have no doubt that a great deal of all this is an elaborate fabrication of great romantic minds.

The priests in turn cursed us, and that curse confines us all to the brink of a precipice in each succeeding generation. No one is clear about what will happen. Each generation will see terrible death and misfortune, that much is certain. Sometimes I don't know whether to laugh or cry. Every family has its own misfortunes. And all this when there is no physical sign of the Chakram any more! I have spoken to some of the younger namboodiris from Kunnupuram who agree that there may be much more myth than history in these stories.

Narayanan Namboodiri's alienation from his wife's family was perhaps a product of prevailing customs and attitudes. Narayanan was the fourth of five brothers—the last two were born of a different mother.

The eldest brother married a woman of his own caste. He was a grim-looking ritualist wedded to the rule book, both in life and vocation. He slaved impassively through life, bent upon straightening the straitened status of the illam. His wife existed like a shadow of his entombed desires. No one knew what she felt about anything, least of all he. But she was eminently qualified to be his wife. The Bhagavad Gita says do your duty and don't bother your head too much about the fruits thereof. Their marriage bore no fruit. Nevertheless both husband and wife continued to do their duty.

Besides the brief bequeathed to successive family heads of Kunnupuram—to raise the family's financial and social position—Narayanan's eldest brother had also to contend with another duty: replenishing the assets of the family regularly sloughed off by the two irresponsible brothers immediately younger to him. Numbers Two and Three were travellers; and if there ever was a land version of the sailor with goodies in every port, then it was the travelling namboodiri.

The travelling namboodiri had sammandhams—relationships—in several noble houses. He was a dabbler who flitted from flower to flower. But life wasn't just a bed of flowers. He could be summoned to a rich Kshatriya or Nair family where the women gave him the once-over—in terms of looks, colour, family background, qualities of body and mind—and then if they selected him, asked him to stay on. These were the eating-sleeping-making-love namboodiris who had to necessarily leave their self-respect at home and pretend to a dignity they didn't feel they deserved. If they felt they could do without the comforts they found in these households, they left. And perhaps returned at later times. Thus 'their' women too were free to dabble if they were so inclined. In a matriarchal system where women were supreme—and brothers and uncles took precedence over husbands—it was perhaps easier to have a husband who wasn't always getting in the way.

(Even today some old gentleman might tell you: 'Ah yes, my mother was from such-and-such family, daughter of so-and-so, granddaughter of so-and-so, etc.' Ask him about his father's family and you'll get: 'Er, I'm not too sure, he was a namboodiri—he was from this-particular illam, that much I can tell you.')

The second and third brothers were happy-go-lucky—happy to go around getting lucky. The sort who lusted after the prospect of a grand meal. The sort who surveyed a woman from head to toe and breast to breast on first sight, and gauged their bodies and their desires simultaneously. They believed in laughter and easy living, and were grateful to life for not imposing too much on them. They gambled and watched kathakali performances and attended weddings and engaged in idle debates that could lead anywhere as long they were kept occupied.

They were connoisseurs who believed in chasing the last frontiers of satiation. They were, naturally, different from their elder brother. Quite the opposite, in fact. They loved fruits; duties were dismal. They were dilettantes; nothing enduring or focussed about their relationships. They loved their elder brother—especially his willingness to let them live as they pleased. At last count, Number Two had five women and Number Three seven. No such count was undertaken for the number of children they sired—who can count the stars in a fertile sky?

But not everyone was lucky to be happy. A namboodiri who married within his caste could prove to be extremely insensitive—like a gardener crushing underfoot the blooms of his own garden. Namboodiri women were called athaenmar or antharjanam, the ones inside, they are not seen or heard. Once they arrived at their husband's home—since namboodiris are patriarchal—they left only as a corpse. They were rarely educated as much as the male. Sometimes they had to endure competition, one, two or even three companion-wives. The husband could do no wrong. But if a woman herself 'strayed', she was subjected to an internal court of inquiry comprising learned Brahmins, led by one trained in the art of such interrogations, and she could be slighted and banished. Widows were shorn of ornaments and virtually declared a nonentity.

It was, as in most cases, one set of rules for the male, and another for the female.

These circumstances were, in fact, the very provocation that triggered the defiance of younger namboodiris earlier in the century who formed themselves into reformative groups. Or embraced communism. It led to an awareness which eventually led the namboodiri women out of the inner rooms of the illam, into arenas where they competed with men and shone, and guided others too timid to break away on their own.

After the birth of his third son, the old man became tired of seeing the same face on his bed. He took another wife. The first wife moved aside, stepping into an advisory post. Narayanan was the fourth brother, new son from the new wife. And he took one wife. The fifth son, also born of the later alliance, was a scholar and a bachelor. He ferreted out ancient palm-leaf manuscripts and dedicated his life to their study. If he had any other interests, no one knew of them. He excelled in learned debates and discourses. He was even more responsible than his eldest brother for getting Kunnupuram up a notch or two on the social scale.

It is possible that the last two brothers took after their mother. There was in both an unbending streak, a defiant edge that equipped them with a strong sense of independence along with a formidable moral fibre. It is possible that their mother was like that. Who knows—those inner rooms of a namboodiri illam!

There were, during that time, wealthy namboodiri families who commanded immense respect. If that wealth was inherited, and none of the members had to actually earn a living, the respect grew. Other families were weighed by their scholarship and expertise. Kunnupuram, unfortunately, had enough of neither. They had fallen upon evil days long, long ago. Son One with his ritualism, Son Four with his unexpectedly lucky 'royal' match and Son Five with his learning did their bit to push the family name up the social register. Against heavy odds. Like past prejudice, for one. Like the merry escapades of Brothers Two and Three, for a second. And who can tell, the weight of sordid history for a third.

Narayanan was married to Subhadra of Kilikkara Palace. Both were young enough to be attracted to each other without the system getting in their way.

Kilikkara was one royal house where the sammandham system did not have much impact except for an instance or two in each generation—even that had stopped by the twenties. Marriage was for keeps, and to one partner. And if that partner passed on, the family was large enough to accept widow remarriage long before it was touted as revolutionary in other parts of the country. Also, matriarchy in Kilikkara was not simply a trick of nominal protocol as it was in many families. Where woman held the title, and man the bridle. It was common in such families for brothers and uncles to take over administration and thus the key to the treasury. They indulged their whims and high-spirited fantasies at the expense of the joint family, leaving the women satisfied with an impression of superiority. The brothers and uncles often succumbed to an expected proclivity towards protecting their own families—wife and children, rather than sisters and nieces—perhaps a prescient propulsion towards the nuclear family that would burst upon them decades later.

Funds of the joint family being siphoned off by brothers and uncles to their wives' families was a rather common occurrence. Most perpetrators felt no guilt. Women who did realize what was happening brought up the subject but preferred not to make too much of it, since they were yet to perfect a mechanism where a woman could really rule without avuncular-fraternal help.

Siphoning was a natural emanation from a bit of night-magic—thalayana manthram or the pillow-spell. Where wily-wife-whispers before, during or after nocturnal satisfactions—depending on whether the husband had to be caught during urge, surge or purge—deflected loyalties and wealth to such an extent that entire families have been known to sink into easy decay. Which proved to be a raw deal for the joint family's women since they were provided for neither by their husbands nor by their own family.

When Narayanan married Subhadra of Big Palace, it was the first such alliance between the two families. From providing temple priests to providing husbands is a definite promotion. Kunnupuram was justly proud of itself. At last, after several decades, they had regained for themselves something of that eminence among namboodiris they'd been used to. Narayanan did everything to justify Kilikkara's faith in him. He handled legal matters. He loved to liaise with British officers in Trivandrum. He travelled once in a while on family errands. He helped with temple and family administration. He helped in the family partition. He was something of a hit with children. Above all, he was deeply in love with his wife, and she with him. Yes, he got along.

Then he became a father. It was after the birth of their daughter Kamala that the discomforts really began. Narayanan had a volatile temper. His wife's relatives were slyly snobbish and sarcastic. It was her calm that kept conflict at bay. But after her first delivery, Subhadra changed in a way that took even her by surprise. She was quick to take offence. Patience turned to tears, then irritability, often anger. She was often too tired to retort when her uncles scoffed at her husband.

Subhadra wasn't prone to making allusions to grandeur, unlike her haughtier married cousins. Nevertheless, she became a victim of her husband's paranoia. Showered by the thunderous sparks of their constant confrontations, he blamed his outcast status for their tension. Rather than his temper. And her hormones. Uncles now came forward to feed fuel to their fire. Her weakness, they imagined, had toughened her against her husband. This man had come from an unworthy illam to usurp their privileges. He deserved to go. Narayanan thus fell from favour years before he landed, three floors down, on that bright wet grass.

He sought out preoccupations outside Kilikkara. She, insecure in this province of soured intimacy, created a hard shell about her and withdrew into it. The uncles and well-wishers 'took the side' of Subhadra and told her not to worry—'we'll be a buffer between the two of you.' It became a tripartite tug of tension.

And then that sordid piece of history cracked open like a volcano and the first cinder flew up and fell on him. And all because of an old Chakram, which didn't seem to exist— perhaps never did. One day, Narayanan went up to Uncle Kochu Kelu who was Kilikkara's Patriarch and asked him one question. Where is the Chakram? He'd kept that question wrapped up in a trembling corner of his head, till there came a time when he felt he had to spit it out like some purple pulp of poison or die with its stain. The Chakram belonged to my family, he said reasonably, and now that we've come together in this relationship, isn't it just and isn't it time that we took it back?

And that did it. It brought to life an ancient enmity, it rekindled old and cantankerous memories, it swept him in one swell sweep out of the pale of the family.

Past the flush of youth and the crush of middle age, having but briefly tasted the gratification of senility, Kochu Kelu stood at the pinnacle of his life at seventy-eight. He surveyed the undulating expanse of time all about him with startling clarity. Future, past and present were equally sharp. Within his soft pampered body he now found a strong will, a clear vision and rare understanding of people and events. He took a long and grave look at Narayanan and said, 'That story is over and done with. Never mention it as long as I'm alive and the Patriarch of Kilikkara Palace.'

The large smooth timeless thampuran had left everyone else behind in his journey to graceful greydom. Age hadn't dimmed his insight nor custom paled his infinite patience. He took the world on his own terms, and that included the sun and the moon and the tyranny of time. When he spoke to Narayanan, no one realized he was putting his final seal on history, on events more than half a century old, events that owed their finely-sculpted completeness to none other than KK himself. For he was a man who straddled generations, who lit a fuse at one end of time and saw it explode at the other.

His day was typical of his life. He was independent and isolated, autocratic and understanding. Kochu Kelu opened his eyes to the world at half-past nine. He had a half-hour's silent communion with the gods and his inner self, still in bed. His bedroom was large, airy and high-ceilinged. One could spend most of one's life in such a bedroom. And KK did. His faithful manservant Paramu turned up with a basin, warm water, a neem stick, toothbrush, paste, tongue cleaner, soap, face cream, talcum powder, large fluffy towel, mirror and a transistor radio. The transistor was switched on, pre-tuned to a station providing Carnatic music. The mirror was propped up to let him see himself.

Sitting in bed, KK indulged his teeth and mouth first. Both neem stick and toothbrush were needed to maintain his healthy white (and still original) teeth. His face was washed with soap between every operation. His whaley pink tongue flopped out, and the tongue cleaner was employed mercilessly. After a last scrubbing of his face, he rubbed cream on it, taking his time, using fingertips and little swabs of cotton, dab-dab-dabbing in time to timeless music. Paramu removed his sleep-crumpled white shirt and dhoti, leaving him in a loincloth that turned invisible within all that flesh. Paramu helped him to sprinkle powder all over himself, under arms, within joints, on the vast smooth back. KK crinkled his eyes as he watched the procedure in the mirror.

This lasted an hour. As a finale, he pulled off his loincloth like a tired cabaret artiste and threw it at Paramu. He was then dressed in fresh starched clothes.

That over, it was time for his morning coffee. 'Coffee' was a drop of decoction in a large glass of very sweet milk. He sat for about thirty minutes, clutching the glass between his hands, turning it gently, sipping and contemplating. Paramu then brought him his newspaper. He transferred himself wearily to a nearby couch with green satin upholstery. The newspaper was always two days old. Somewhere in the past he had missed a couple of issues on different days. Instead of skipping them and going on to the current paper, he took them one at a time, never catching up, always two days late. He was very thorough in his reading, going from first to last line, cover to cover. During the latter half of his reading, he sipped from a glass of orange juice. Every now and then, he popped a couple of freshly boiled peanuts into his mouth.

By the time he finished the paper it was time for breakfast. One p.m.

He ate ten idlis. In his younger days it used to be twenty. He spent several minutes pinching out the middle of each idli, which he ate, and he discarded the rest. The idli was dipped in bland white chutney and chewed relentlessly. He drank a glass of Horlicks along with it. KK was loyal to his brands. His soap was Lux and toothpaste Colgate, his talcum powder was Cuticura, the cream on his face was Pond's, he read only the *Hindu*, and drank only Horlicks. His storeroom was well-stocked so that he never missed his brand. All this activity was too much for him. He had to take a half-hour nap.

When he woke up, he readied himself for the Audience. The time between three and five was reserved for people who wanted to meet him. For people he wanted to meet. For the dharmakkaar,people who came to your doorstep so you could perform your dharmam by helping them, brutally dismissed as 'beggars' by the rest of the world. He had a standard clientele for dispensing his dharmam, and a standard range of dispensation: twenty-five paise, fifty paise and one rupee. They had to be blind or severely lame to merit the rupee.

Once in three days, KK had a bath. He used two kinds of oil, three kinds of scented water, scrubbed himself with a fibre called eenja, used soap, and had warm and then lukewarm water poured over him, was dried thoroughly with a large towel, and finally his scalp was rubbed briskly with *rasnadi podi*, an ayurvedic powder that helped to ward off the evil effects of a bath like cold, cough and pneumonia.

Also once in three days, a barber came and shaved his face. Once every month, he had his *sarvanga kshouram*, full-body shave. Both these sessions were vicariously enjoyed by his audience which was allowed to stay on, conversing behind a white-sheet partition. But they were dismissed at five when it was time for his lunch.

Lunch was full-blooded and vast. He moved to the dining room. He sat at the head of a long, fully-laid table and rolled careful balls of rice, dipped them in each side dish and chewed meditatively. He loved the sound of crushing pappadams and crushed more pappadams than he ate. After he finished, he went back to the drawing room to catch up on his sleep. He lay on a large couch, snoring worriedly for half an hour. He woke up fresh and ready for some entertainment. Since their mealtimes never coincided, this was the time to exchange notes with other family members. He laughed and joked and had little children come over. He gave them sweets and biscuits which they were allowed to eat only the next day since it was so late in the evening and already time to rush through the evening bath and hurry to the temple.

Or Kochu Kelu listened to music. He had an old funnelled crankable His Master's Voice record player on which Paramu played 78 r.p.m. records from vintage plays and movies and concerts. This was one of his favourite times of the day. He lay back, swaying his head to the music, smiling and humming along.

In a delicious daze of musical aftertaste, he set out for his walk. He stepped out from the drawing room into the open veranda. The soft breeze or the sheeny heat, depending on what the weather had in store for him, coupled with the rush of blood in response to his body's sudden mobility agitated his vast frame like a sexual tremor. He walked the length of the veranda—up-down—three times, five at the most. That was enough, he was refreshed and glowing like a successful runner.

By then it was half-past eight, teatime. The exercise made him hungry. He went back to his bedroom and had pale tea along with biscuits/buns/crisp vadas, sitting on the satin-covered couch. Still sitting there, he waited for Paramu to clear the cutlery and switch on the bright light behind him. This was when he read. His reading was eclectic, embracing history, science and theology. He read fiction too. His vast library brought together Dickens and Proust, Hardy and Goethe, Kalidasa and Checkov. Much later in life, he appended a secret cache of thrillers that he consumed unknown to the outside world. In a rush of adolescence after his ninetieth birthday, he sampled Harold Robbins but abandoned him with blushing haste.

On most days, with the book on his lap, he would lapse into a winding tour of reflection. Sometimes he considered the book he was reading. Or he drifted off into realms of reverie where vaporous visions shrouded his brain and he slipped into a brief deep doze from which he jolted awake, leaden, scared and moody.

His dinner was at eleven. It wasn't much, a couple of idlis, a couple of vadas, the inevitable hot Horlicks. After that, he gave himself to the first of his nocturnal passions, writing. He wrote letters and updated his diary. And sometimes he took up his 'notes'—these were emotional responses to events that didn't fit into the formal format of his diary. He also did his bit to fill in the blanks in his family history. As he wrote, he listened to the tinkling notes of a small carved music box, lined with red satin, kept open by his couch.

The second passion wasn't regular at all. Sometimes the intervals were far too long—and it died, as if at retirement, once his sixtieth birthday was celebrated grandly in the Palace. It generally happened like this. When Paramu came to clear the dishes, he'd tell him, 'Ask Janu to bring my Horlicks

today.' Janu. Or Karthyayini. Or Chellamma. They were the
maids in the household.

Even that was only the first exploratory stage. The assigned
maid would come in with the drink. After he finished the
glass, taking his time, he would call her close and run his eyes
over her body. Janu, Karthyayini, Chellamma. Thirty, thirty-
five, forty. Or thereabouts. After his eyes, came his hands.
With slow purpose, they travelled over her breasts, hips and
buttocks while she stood still like a cow in the market. Even
that wasn't final. Sometimes he would nod abruptly and say,
'I'm going to sleep.' But if he felt up to it, he said, 'You can
come back.'

The woman took the glass from him and left. If all was
well, she prepared herself, sent word to her husband and
returned. If that wasn't possible—if the husband was reluctant
or she had her period or there was a sick child to be looked
after—she sent a substitute. Spending the night with Kochu
Kelu thampuran was remunerative. On certain days, it was
enough that the maid stayed, and what didn't happen gave
him a far more serene pleasure. KK was happy to remain a
bachelor. He didn't miss marriage, and with his crowded
hours, he had absolutely no time for it.

In his youth, which stretched longer than the lifetimes of
some of his companions, he'd clung to his bed and habits with
practised ardour. Bolstered by bolsters, pillowed by pillows,
blanketed by blankets and bedded by whoever heeded his
summons. His whole life was a steep breathless ascent in
reverse, like a river regaining its source or a child wanting the
womb.

But when Narayanan of Kunnupuram came out with his
rude request, asking for the Chakram, he frowned and sent
him on his way. There were some areas of the past he wasn't
too comfortable with.

Aunt Sarada's house, Greenacres, stood in a well-to-do
neighbourhood. Massive private and company houses with
long driveways and neat lawns. Uniformed gatemen killing

time on the roadside, reading, flirting, gossiping, an ironing man with his cart of customers' clothes, and only the occasional sound of traffic. It had the hush of a road that realizes its own importance. Every now and then, a sweating jogger in expensive regulation attire panted by, red-faced and vulnerable. Their neighbours on Mehtaji Road (abbreviated from Diwan Bahadur R.N. Mehta Road) were mostly Raj retirees who'd bequeathed a legacy of civil service postings. The houses held more servants than masters, and were invariably guarded by grim growly dogs superceding the time-killing watchmen.

Greenacres sat impressively on twelve grounds of prime land, valued anywhere between five to six lakhs a ground even in '85. Built in the last part of the last century by a wealthy English couple named Watts, it was sold to RV uncle by Junior Watts when he bundled up his furniture, memories and parents, and departed the country shortly after Independence. It combined an old-world elegance and solidity attempted but rarely achieved in modern constructions.

Gopi stood on the porch and smoked a cigarette. The drive, flanked by grizzled prolific trees and obese bushes, circumambulated a dried-up stone fountain and a lawn studded with chairs and a round table, all carved out of stone. It led up to the large portico where RV uncle's shining green Buick used to preen before the times and crowded streets forced him to opt for a Fiat, small and guilty in its grand surroundings.

As a young boy visiting from Kilikkara, he had found delight in lazy lawn gatherings, the conversation fuelled by tall glasses of lime juice, and the air rich with scented night and leisurely droning mosquitoes. The cold damp stone beneath his thighs, feet tickled by silken heads of grass were sensations of memory that had never left him. Laughter and family chatter, sudden silences as the night closed in about them, punctuated by ringing slaps as mosquitoes claimed their share of blood relations.

White steps led up to a veranda that hugged the curving face of the house. The steps were the venue of several childhood combats and chases and games, of self-conscious assemblies before the family photographer—ah, okay, okay, now smile, pleeeesss, not so much! Yee—ess, that's it, one, two—yesss! Four doors opened into the drawing room—a booming carpeted hall full of carved overstuffed furniture, antiques and knick-knacks from all over the world, several life-sized paintings, including two by Ravi Varma. And a sepia-tinted air of nostalgia.

Gopi walked through this hall, pausing to examine delicately carved daggers, Chinese vases that sprouted red scenic veins on concave bellies, Russian and Japanese dolls, a clock of gold and glass that offered an immodest view of its complex innards, a hollowed-out elephant's foot lined with solid silver that invariably served as a waste-paper basket for under-cultured visitors. And locked up in glass cases were innumerable wine goblets, crystal caskets, gently moulded glass decanters—mementos of frequent trips abroad when RV uncle's health was still in the mood for it.

He stood looking at all these rare expensive objects of art and he grew sick to the heart. They aroused the same bitter wrench every time, symbols of a lifestyle he didn't share. It came unbidden, originating less from envy than a sense of injustice. He lived in a rented single-bedroom flat with his family, and went about on a scooter, he had to slog out a living at Vimala Art Printers, unsheltered from the shocks that life dealt out, with the unstomachable status of a poor cousin.

While Aunt Sarada threw parties and RV uncle indulged his hypochondria to a fine art. While a cousin was a consultant in the U.S., and another probably saw even more money in Delhi with her psychiatrist husband.

He couldn't escape it, he himself was responsible to an extent—years ago, the magazine had drained a chunk of his family share. He'd plunged into business with the suave and practised ease of a born entrepreneur, little realizing the truth. That a crow's child is, after all, a crow's child.

'We're not businessmen,' his Grand-uncle Cherunni warned. 'We are good masters. We can order our servants about and relax, that we can do! That's how we'll live till the end of our days. A businessman cannot rely on other people, he needs to have Initiative and Drive. He has to be in the office every day. And if his employees take off, well, he jolly well must fold up his sleeves and do it himself. Do you see any of us cut out for that?'

It was true, every word of it! But Gopi went back to Big Palace muttering, 'What a snob! There's nothing you can't do if you're determined. All he knows is theory. You have to wade in to know reality.'

He turned away from the familiar dryness gnawing at his throat. On the opposite wall, as though wooing him away from his gloom, hung a small reproduction within a carved gilded frame. Another lost vision.

The original oil painting hung in the front hall in Raga Sudha in Kilikkara. Krishnan Thampi (1867-1917), the artist, used to copy European masters and exotic landscapes. He was related by marriage to the Travancore royal family. Thampi had held an administrative post in the Sri Padmanabhaswami temple in Trivandrum, but devoted all his spare time to churning out recollections of images that now adorn the walls of almost a hundred venerable family mansions in Kerala. Endowed with a melancholy brilliance, he lived during the time of Gopi's great-great-grandmother, Uma Amba.

Lament Of Mohini. Against the trembling background of an angry sky, bleeding with a single slash of lightning, stands Mohini, her long black hair loose and struggling in the wind. Her sari has tumbled to her waist and barely hides one rounded breast, the other stands revealed, proud and firm. One hand is raised against the sky, against its rampant cruelty; the other clutches her falling sari.

Gopi stood like an intruder in a forbidden museum, staring at the painting. Lament of the temptress! Thampi's visual rendering of a scene from a Malayalam epic. The poem had been written by Kilikkara's most famous literary personage, Marthanda Varma Raja, Uma Amba's brother. It was a long and exquisitely crafted masterpiece of love and loss, and considered his most important work, surviving on the Kerala University syllabus for more than three decades.

Gopi knew the story it told. Excerpts were even now

offered up at akshara slokam competitions, literary merry-go-rounds where combatant connoisseurs were required to recite, taking off from the last phrase of the preceding poem.

MVR's first version of the poem retold the classical myth of Mohini in pure pedantic painstaking Sanskrit. Lord Vishnu takes the form of a beautiful damsel named Mohini to defeat the demonic Bhasmasura—the Ash Demon—who has been terrorizing the kingdom of the gods. Having received a virtual boon of terror from Lord Shiva, the devious demon chases Shiva himself to test its efficacy. Shiva hides. Mohini appears before the demon in all her enchanting beauty. She dances, challenging him to recreate her every pose. Smitten, he complies. At one point she points to her head. He mimics her, pointing to his own head, and is quickly reduced to ashes. Because he's been granted two boons—one, of indestructibility; the other that the person whose head he points to would be reduced to ashes. And, pointing to himself, he has eaten into his first boon. The story goes that after the demon is destroyed, Shiva, seeing the beautiful woman who is really Vishnu, falls madly in love with her. Their love results in a son, the Kerala cult figure Lord Ayyappan who is enshrined in the Sabari Mala temple atop a high and arduous hill.

In the classical versions of the poem, it's Shiva who pines, needing to see the divine Mohini once again. In MVR's rendition, Mohini is loathe to return to her male form. She pines for Shiva who leaves her soon enough and returns to Mount Kailash. This pining is the lament of the temptress. It is a new and interesting idea, of Mohini's reluctance to give up her femininity, her continued attachment to Shiva. Full of teeth-crunching phrases and oblique classical references, *Lament of Mohini* would have been a 'learned tome'.

But the second and final version has nothing to do with the legendary Mohini. Here instead there is a prince who loves a priest's daughter—a girl whom even the sun thirsted to see, so rare was a sight of her.

Mohini is the motherless daughter of a Brahmin priest. The king's son Narendran sees her while she's bathing in the river and falls hopelessly in love with her. She is of a higher caste, so their union is impossible. Narendran's agony is terrible, he knows he may never see her again. He uses the slightest pretext to visit the priest's house without raising suspicion.

The descriptions of these visits and of the gardens that surround the priest's house are exquisite, and the imagery is dazzling. A peacock reflects the mind of the girl, preening its gorgeous feathers or turning away in sudden blushing shyness. The sky and the trees and the wind mirror the emotions of the hero-lover, bristling with rage or swaying gently or roaring with agony. Mohini—thus named by her lover because he's too timorous to ask anyone her real name!—has a parrot which is either psychic or divine. It tells her of the mystery lover she's never seen, and describes accurately each emotion he goes through. It is through the parrot that she comes to know her admirer. Finally, one day, he's rewarded by the sight of his beloved, unhampered by others. The father isn't at home, and her aunts are preparing for the evening puja.

They gaze at each other, communicate silently. They pledge themselves to each other till and beyond death, even without uttering a single word. The parrot chatters excitedly, but it has lost the feel of human speech in the face of such powerful passion! There's no parental opposition because the parents don't know of their love. It is the lovers who realize they will never be able to live together. So they decide to die. Again, without a word being spoken.

Mohini runs into the forest where the elements let loose a reign of terror, joining in her lament and raging against the cruel world which won't let them be together. Her parrot struggles pathetically on her shoulder, imploring her in its new-found gibberish not to leave it behind. When the king's son reaches the forest, he does not find Mohini, only the mists of her memory. The fury of the forest and the mourning parrot remain to remind him of his love. He does not die, because the king's men find him and take him back. He goes home, carrying the parrot with him.

The poem tells a simple story in radiant verse. The descriptions of nature, the beauty of Mohini. The mute expression of their love for each other. The strength of character as they decide they cannot live together. Each word has been interpreted differently. Several theses have been written on the meanings embedded in the poem. Mohini is the seductress, the sensuous female who attracts the male. But once she's got him, she becomes the victim and yearns for his return. She cannot live without him. The plight of Mohini becomes the tragedy of all women. She is shy and proud, alluring and haughty, reserved and romantic; but once he comes under her spell, he's everything in her life. The enchantress becomes the enslaved. The man is also the weaker of the two. He escapes the final promise of death.

The face in the painting is not conventionally beautiful, but it captivates Gopi each time he sees it. It is rounded with the suggestion of a dimple on the chin, sleepy haunting eyes and thick eyebrows. Right from his childhood, it had a strange attraction that has never died. Mohini, the eternal temptress, had claimed another victim.

He told RV uncle one evening, 'I sometimes keep looking at that painting.'

'Lament of Mohini.' Three thick words in a sombre monotone. 'The poem was in our syllabus.' As though that summed up everything! 'It is not the story, it's the poetry,' he added. 'When I was young they even had it for a year in high school. It was withdrawn to protect our young minds. Once they started fiddling, you could be sure they'd come out with the strangest things.'

'Who started fiddling?'

'Bureaucracy. They found descriptions that bordered on the obscene.'

'But isn't it sheer poetry?'

'Well, there are descriptions . . .'

'Like what?'

'Certain descriptions.'

'For instance?' he persisted.

'Of Mohini.' RV uncle cleared his throat. The famous third-peg glint flickered in his eyes. 'The scene where Prince Narendran sees her for the first time. She's having a bath in the river and several young girls, her companions, have formed a shield around her. He is on the other side and, through them, he—mmm—sees parts of her body. Leg! Thigh! Bust! Her back!' Each loaded word fluttered breathlessly. 'Very exciting descriptions!' A rainbow dawned on RV uncle's face. 'A schoolboy might think of nothing else. And then they move away, allowing her to climb up from the water. She is completely revealed in her wet lower garments.' He paused, as if beholding a vision. 'I will tell you it's very . . . erotic.'

Gopi smiled. 'I didn't know it's that sort of poem.'

'That sort!' RV uncle shook his head irritably. 'No, no, no! That sort? Do you know that some of our Sanskrit verses have graphic descriptions?' His lips curled. 'The human body became obscene only after Victorian prudery. I'll tell you this, it was rigid fundamental Christianity that first put a cloak on beauty.'

Gopi was surprised. Had he underestimated him? Here was an advocate of appetite, vindicator of the voluptuous! 'Must have been very popular in its time,' he said cautiously.

'Actually, it was buried under all his other work. The short poems were thought to have more appeal. It was only in the '30s or even later, I should think, the '40s, that it was rediscovered and given a special place. Now it's seen as his best work.'

'But MVR has never been major, has he?'

His lips twitched. 'Never been considered major. How's it possible? No one to promote him! You think it's pure merit that gets you to the top?' He fixed Gopi with an accusing stare. 'If your community pushes you up, you stand a chance. Otherwise, you're lost in the crowd. All the famous poets of Kerala have had that push. Not our people!' RV uncle shook his head. 'We're too busy pampering our own children or fighting. Look at Bengalis, learn from them. They made Tagore a world figure, even as a painter. And our own Ravi Varma? Any Tom-Dick-Harry will come along and criticize his art, find a hundred faults, who's going to protest?' There came a grim bass chuckle. 'But our Kshatriya community will not go out of its way! Mark my words, promotion matters.

Ask your Uncle Shankar, ask him what they do in his advertising agency. You should be nicely packaged and labelled and sold to the consumer. Otherwise . . .' He made a suggestive thumb-down gesture. 'This one single poem should have been enough. *Lament of Mohini*. But MVR was sidelined. And the highest honour they gave him was a place on the university syllabus!'

They sat silently in the drawing room as if suddenly engulfed by a silence from the quenchless past.

BOWELS OF DISCOMFORT

He'd waded in too deep. The magazine had always been a pet idea, an offshoot of the writing dream. It was nurtured through adolescence, guarded jealously in college and finally ignited the year he passed his Masters. He discovered a kindred spirit in Chacko, his classmate, a tall thin youth sprouted from an over-enlightened Thiruvalla family. He sported an absurd Van Dyke and hair so flossy that a friend swore, 'Before we pass out of college, I'll use him once to mop my ceiling!' Besides being a prolific man of letters, Chacko was also a storehouse of preposterous and unlimited ideas. And he had the gumption to put them to work. Dismissing granduncular and other warnings, Chacko simply said, 'Nothing ventured, nothing gained.'

'What we need first and foremost,' he proclaimed during the first general body meeting of their company, 'is an accounts man.' The general body consisted of Gopi and Chacko.

Gopi agreed.'We won't go the way of so many rags. Mere idealism can kill it at birth. We need creativity backed by sound business sense.'

'That's why you need an accountant. A good man. I've got just the person for you.'

'Who?'

'Me.'

The general body was being conducted in the ditch outside the college cafeteria. It was their last day in college. 'You! You're Literature. What the hell do you know about accounts?' Gopi couldn't remember exactly how Chacko sold him the idea.

The magazine was named *Symbol* and registered with the registrar of newspapers. Gopi swore himself in as publisher and editor at the metropolitan magistrate's court in Egmore along with his printer. The company that owned the magazine was Gocha Communications, an unregistered partnership company that celebrated both their names. Gopi was publisher, editor, proof-reader, financier and office manager. Chacko was reporter, assistant editor, business manager, advertising executive, accountant and special correspondent. They agreed to draw a salary only after they saw profit. The first issue carried interviews with Mr Hande, the state health minister, and I.S. Johar, the late Hindi film comedian, specially requested poems from Kamala Das, and a modest and memorable editorial from Gopi's own pen.

'You may wonder about the role of yet another magazine,' Gopi wrote. 'Enthusiasm rouses life. And it will be our humble endeavour to provide that enthusiasm.'

They finalized arrangements with Welldone Press, a highly antiquated letterpress which endeared itself by agreeing to give them a fortnight's credit. The inaugural issue had a run of three thousand copies. With great difficulty they managed to sell 350 to friends, relatives and tired local train commuters. The rest of the copies were bundled up and thrown out of sight so that no one could claim the first issue wasn't a success.

But failure became incentive. The more sales fell, the more inspired they grew. They had general bodies every day. Chacko was the ideas man and he had no dearth of them. 'Enthusiasm!' he'd remind Gopi during his brief moments of gloom. They would review previous issues and Chacko drew up new and daring ideas for the next. It soon got to a point when the format of each issue was different.

'We need a "Dear Uncle" column,' Chacko said one day. 'You know, readers write in their problems and a professional replies. Real money-spinner nowadays. Our circulation will simply shoot up.'

'We're really not in a position to pay professionals.' This was during the latter part of that fateful year. Gopi was finally becoming careful about expenses.

Chacko produced an impatient sound. 'You don't have to have a psychiatrist! In fact, that spoils the whole thing. "Uncle" must be someone who's educated just enough. What he needs is experience in these matters.'

'Where do we get such a person?'

'We already have him.'

'Who?' Gopi asked, slow to learn.

By the year end Chacko was writing ninety per cent of the magazine. As Uncle, he invented letters and answered them. The first three were classics:

Dear Uncle, I'm a girl of sixteen with a sheltered upbringing. There's a boy in my class who sits next to me and shows me bad pictures. The other day I took courage and threatened to report him to the teacher, but he lifted up his shorts and showed me his underwear. Please tell me what to do. I don't know what else he will show me. Yours sincerely, Sheltered Girl.

Dear Uncle, I'm a married businessman. My old father stays with us. The problem is whenever my wife and I start making love, he gets up in his sleep and wanders into our room. The doctor has warned us not to lock our room in case he has a stroke at night and cannot reach us. I'm going mad with worry, torn between my old father and the children we'll never have at this rate. Yours worriedly, Out-of-business Man.

Dearest Uncle, I have no one else to ask my question.

I'm working as a secretary in a big firm. The other
day a dear colleague opened his pants and showed me
his kidney. When I told my mother she became very
upset and told me never to talk to him again. I don't
know what all this fuss is about. Tell me, is it wrong
to show a friend your kidney? Yours sincerely, Puzzled
Girl.

'I can't print these!' Gopi protested. 'No one writes letters like
this.'

'How do you know?'

'They're repetitive and . . . you're obsessed with
exhibitionism and voyeurism!'

Chacko asked patiently, 'What experience do you have of
these things? I know for a fact there are people like this. In the
little schools, in the far-flung corners of life.' He shut his eyes
as he did during such moods.

'But this is ridiculous. Kidney, for God's sake!'

'To you it may seem unreal. But not everyone's educated.
Real people are out there with real problems. A word of
comfort from Uncle would help.'

Uncle's replies were equally colourful:

Dear Sheltered Girl, All this is part of school and
growing up, so please don't waste your time worrying.
I don't know what exactly you mean by bad pictures.
Anyway, you did right in discouraging him. Showing
one's underwear is well within legal rights. But if he
tries to show anything further, please tell me what it
is. I'll be happy to advise you.

Dear Out-of-business Man, Yours is a strange but
misunderstood plight. It is significant that your father
walks into that room at that time. Your doctor is
perfectly right. At this rate your father runs the risk
of a stroke—so please lock his door from the outside.
The rest is up to you! Don't forget to give Uncle the
Good News.

Dear Puzzled Girl, I'm moved by your innocence.
Your mother is justifiably upset. The kidney is certainly

not for public consumption. I suggest you go through
a book called *Gray's Anatomy*. There are kidneys and
kidneys.

It didn't matter what Gopi thought. Chacko had shouldered
this burden along with all the rest. Before long, he was
Starman predicting the future, Runner Up, an expert on
sports, Captain Glamour churning out film gossip and
interviewing stars, and Legal Eye providing free legal advice.
He wrote an occasional poem or short story, speaking in
different styles and moods. Gopi had started the magazine as
an outlet for his own creativity, but was rendered barren, like
a lavish host nursing his hunger and gazing wistfully at his
gorging guests. He found himself worrying about money
instead. Everyone wanted money, and they wanted it
immediately.

The stringer, printer, office boy, the delivery boys who
bounced around ineffectually covering agentless areas, the
typist who became the first cursing casualty of depleting
resources, the middleman who procured cheap newsprint from
the surplus stock of a financial daily. Worst of all, their dour
landlord who invaded the musty second-floor Gocha office on
the fifth of every month. Gopi heard their demands in his
dreams.

He realized how right his grand-uncle had been. But it
wasn't a question of snobbery, it wasn't that he didn't work
hard. It was a question of attitude. Biblical sayings came to
mind: ask and ye shall receive, knock and the door shall open.
But it depended on how stridently you asked, how loudly you
knocked. His creditors always managed to make him cough
up. But when he asked for the money he was owed, the
agencies and the distributors and the small shops pleaded and
shielded and dazed him with excuses. And that was the
difference. They could, he couldn't. They were in it for
survival, he was only a dabbler. They could press on and push
it in and twist it till it hurt; he operated within a veneer of
restraint and politeness. And They were always with him,
looking over his shoulder, judging and mocking . . .

The venture benefited only those who regularly extracted
their pound of flesh. Some of the stringers collected certificates

from Gocha and went on to join *India Today*, *Femina* and other periodicals. *Symbol* continued its hand-to-mouth existence. Gopi gave up all hope of turning into an acclaimed author or even a moderately appreciated editor. He counted uneasy days to breakeven, jumping when the telephone rang, hiding from a gallery of predatory creditors.

The stray articles he wrote, masterpieces in their own right, remained largely unread. The only encouragement came from uncles and aunts in Kilikkara who were regular subscribers. 'Very good. Forceful!'

'I read your piece on education, Gopi. I'm impressed. You should stop all this *Symbol* business and start writing for the papers . . .'

'I knew you had it in you. Remember those stories you used to scribble when you were ten? Don't worry, I'm always your fan.'

The other subscribers were so silent Gopi wondered whether they read the magazine at all. Chacko had to invent their letters as well.

From the beginning, it was Chacko who'd thrown the gauntlet and picked it up. 'See if I don't get us enough ads.' He ran to all the agencies in town. 'Increase circulation,' they said. So he ran to all the distributors and book shops. 'Improve your get-up and give articles like . . .' Each of them had their own idea of what the reader liked. So Chacko ran back to Gopi. Finally, they realized they wouldn't get more than a couple of discounted ads each month. For the rest, they had to sprinkle the magazine with 'goodwill' ads in the hope of a future pay-off.

The December '71 issue was the last. *Symbol* folded grandly, leaving Gopi poorer by 1.25 lakh rupees. He had broken into a 1.5 lakh fixed deposit, and Chacko was urging him to make further investments. But the ominous phone calls and his landlord's grouchy face proved too much for Gopi. He had never handled so much money in his life. He had never seen so much money disappear so fast. *Symbol*'s epitaph came from Chacko: 'We sank under the weight of talent. How can there be two suns in the same sky?'

Even as he surfaced from those murky depths, the post-

mortem began. As if all of Kilikkara had nothing else to
discuss. 'I heard you stopped that paper of yours.' 'Tighten up
circulation, Gopi. I haven't received November as yet. I paid
for full-year, you know. Ha, ha, ha!' An old aunt, who spent
her widowed life recycling prayer beads in a dark corner of
Eastern Palace, roused herself briefly to whisper, 'Gopi, ende
kunjey, you lost all your money, didn't you? May God save
you.'

And that was the reason for their outrage. The money, the
family inheritance, lost indulging a whim, playing with a toy.
It whipped up silent displeasure in a few, including RV uncle
whom he accompanied to Kilikkara that bleak vacation.
Others grumbled and gossiped from the river to the temple.
Though Kilikkara's joint family had split beyond redemption,
Subhadra's children, they felt, still needed higher guidance.
Subhadra had rapidly traversed the Kerala female's inevitable
journey from dominance to dependence. And it was all the
more evident because of how she'd been before.

One cool December evening, when stars burst juicily from
the sky and temple bells and drums had drawn their wild
mosaic in the air, seated on platforms, parapets, chairs and
benches, on the porch of Raga Sudha, they began a family
discussion. Gopi did not sit in the centre of their circle, but
that was how it felt.

RV uncle: You must realize that inheritance passes on to
the female members. In a way, you've let your mother down.

Grand-uncle Cherunni from Northern Palace, old beyond
his years: The money is not an individual's asset. It must be
preserved for the next generation.

Aunt Sarada: It was a mistake. Don't be harsh on him.

RV uncle: It's not a question of being harsh. It's for his
own good.

Uncle Rajan of Eastern Palace, a retired colonel with a
two-chhotas-daily routine: You talk as if he's the first Kilikkara
thampuran who went into business. Shall I remind you of the
hatchery, the lorry service, the furniture showroom, the cinema,
the hotel and the industrial fan factory? And several others if
you start counting! Can you tell me of one single unit that
didn't lose money?

Grand-uncle: All the more reason he should have been careful. You learn from mistakes, not follow them! We should preserve the family wealth. The partition doesn't mean we've stopped being a united family.

RV uncle: I suggest we look after Gopi's share till he can handle it wisely. We'll give him, say ten years. He will be old enough to do as he pleases.

Gopi's mother couldn't stop herself: How will he live?

RV uncle: He will continue to stay with us in Madras. I'll get him a job. The money will go to him automatically.

There was nothing Gopi could say. When his Uncle Shankar returned from Bombay after a fortnight, he said, 'Are you a child? How dare they behave this way with you! And how dare you take it all!'

Ten years progressed to twelve, and there was still no sign of his money. He wasn't about to ask RV uncle, and he knew his mother wouldn't. But why was Aunt Sarada silent? He often quarrelled with his mother about her unshakeable contentment. 'I live in my house, Sarada has hers.' Her bland response was typical. She now took life at face value, it was stupid to argue about the given.

Two months before Gopi's thirty-fifth birthday, Uncle Shankar disappeared.

Even Aunt Sarada, who mothered him rendering his bachelorhood easier to bear with whopping culinary detours, had no idea where he was. Her brother led an unorthodox life at the best of times. He said he was going to Kilikkara, a sudden urge to worship at the temple. He should have been back in Madras by now. She didn't start worrying till much later. In any case, she'd plenty of other worrying to do.

Her husband's errant bowels churned and turned, yet refused to deliver, causing him great mental and physical agony. 'Am I going to die?' he kept asking. He would get up in the middle of a conversation and rush to the bathroom, only to return a few minutes later with a hangdog expression. He would jump up in the middle of the night and embrace the comfort of the commode. He left the door open and chatted interminably till something did or didn't happen. Aunt Sarada lay in bed, mumbling weary acquiescence at appropriate intervals.

His doctor, used to advising him on tenuous ills, now took up the challenge of a real and substantial enemy. His diagnosis changed according to the varying intensity of his patient's complaints. His evening pastime soon became the vigorous kneading of RV uncle's writhing abdomen, much to the pleasure of his patient and Aunt Sarada's alarm. 'Stop it,' she cried. 'You'll break him open!'

The elderly doctor, grown silvery in the service of loyalists like RV uncle, waved her away. 'Don't you worry, my dear. There's more to this gentleman than meets the eye.'

'I was afraid of that!' RV uncle gasped, writhing in half-pleasure, half-distress.

'Please don't do that, doctor. He'll go!'

'Go?'

'On the bed.'

'There's nothing inside to go,' whined RV uncle.

'That slice of watermelon you had in the morning . . .'

'Watermelon!' yelled Dr Bhat in delight. 'After all that cautioning yesterday. You're asking for it, Kunju!' The playfully abbreviated name made its owner flinch. RV uncle was 'Kunjappan' to his peers and elders back in Kerala. The doctor insisted on being even more intimate.

Evenings were thus full of drama at the Kunjappan household. Aunt Sarada, who wore good health like a mantle about her, was generally dismissive of hypochondriacs. But she humoured her husband, though with the sharp eye of the practical housewife.

Gopi, Lekha and Shobha went to enquire about his health one warm afternoon. Throughout the ride, Shobha acted like a hijacker bent on diverting the scooter to the beach. Finally, Gopi said in exasperation, 'If I hear one more complaint, no ice cream for the rest of your life!' Miraculously, there was not a sound from her after that.

RV uncle lay with an air of theatrical fragility. Aunt Sarada sat in a chair by his bedside, looking anxious.

'What does the doctor say?'

'He's not too worried. He says it's only bad digestion.

Compounded by his usual constipation. Mixture of opposites—
you know how Bhat talks! But he's prescribed a lot of tablets,
that's what's worrying me.'

'Why should Bhat be worried? It's my system that is
failing.' RV uncle told the ceiling darkly, 'I don't think I've
ever suffered so much.'

'I'm sorry we didn't come earlier,' Gopi said.

'Some days I feel I won't last. People will realize it wasn't
an idle complaint.'

'It's Gopi's birthday two months from now,' Aunt Sarada
said. 'I'll make a magnificent feast and see that you enjoy it.'
She sounded as if she was consoling herself.

'If God keeps me till then.'

'Don't make it worse than it already is!' She turned to
them. 'You know, I was worried to death last night when he
suddenly began moaning. I brought him some water and he
was all right.'

'I get bad dreams.' RV uncle shut his eyes and shuddered.
'Last night it was a fairy story.'

'I want to hear, Kunjappappoo-oooppa,' Shobha said,
showing interest for the first time.

'Shobha,' said Lekha in a warning tone.

'I was in a high tower. They kept threatening to throw me
down because I had some information they wanted. And I
couldn't remember what it was. So they kept torturing and
threatening and pouring cold water all over me.'

'Did they throw you down?' Shobha's interest was turning
into a perverse excitement. Lekha directed a large-eyed look at
Gopi. 'Did they tie you to the bed and stretch you till you
screamed?'

'How do you know all this?' Aunt Sarada asked mildly.

'It's there in my Russian storybook. And then they pull
out your hair one by one till you die.'

'Your uncle has very little hair to pull out.'

'Shobha, that's enough!'

But RV uncle was now in the mood. 'They did throw me
down. That's when I screamed. Your grandmother thought I
was having a fit and held me tightly. That only scared me
more and I shouted louder. She threw water on my face and

I thought it was part of the torture.'

Lekha laughed. 'Good God!'

'Anyway, he's much better now. A couple of times I was really worried. There were loud noises in his belly and he'd be pressing it and moaning. I don't know how to handle all this. The problem with Bhat is he's so old he needs regular naps. If you ring up, they say he can't be woken up.'

'Even if you're dying,' said RV uncle, 'you shouldn't wake up Dr Bhat.'

'What noises did he make with his stomach?'

'Shobha . . .'

Aunt Sarada brought her close and spoke gravely. 'When your stomach isn't feeling too well, you get strange rumbling sounds.'

'Does he have gas?'

'Shobha!'

RV uncle laughed. 'You know everything, don't you? Come.' He began to stroke her hair. Gopi let out his breath in relief. There was no saying how RV uncle would react. Once he'd stopped talking to his ten-year-old granddaughter when she held out a rose for him to smell and scratched his nose in the process.

Later, as they were leaving, Shobha shouted, 'I didn't complain, no? Where's my ice cream?'

'Oh, so this is blackmail,' said Aunt Sarada. 'You'll come to Greenacres only if you get an ice cream.'

A high-pitched voice sailed across the hall. 'Did Kolappappooppan hear someone talking about ice cream?'

Shobha laughed. 'Yes!'

Kolappan had a tall broad head and a short broad body separated by an invisible neck; he looked like a mud pot balanced on a mud jar. His voice echoed like a mud-jar whistle. He was about the same age as RV uncle. 'How's he?'

'Better,' Aunt Sarada replied. 'Bhat's coming later to see him.'

Despite staying in the same house, Kolappan inhabited a world of his own. Occasionally, they politely exchanged information if it was important enough. Kolappan was the house guest who'd stayed on. Next month, February '85, would be the eighteenth anniversary of his arrival.

Eighteen years ago, when Kolappan developed a malignant tumour in some recess behind the undulating stretch between his nonexistent neck and ample left breast, it was cousin Kunjappan—their mothers were sisters—who came to his rescue. Good old Kunjappan, who'd married well and wisely into the famous Kilikkara family, had taken the trouble of bringing him down from their ancestral home in Poonjar in order to sponsor the entire treatment—medication, surgery, comfort and rehabilitation.

Kolappan was so nicknamed because he had allegedly resembled a stick when he was ten years old. He'd rapidly outgrown the name, but nicknames die hard.

Kolappan brought his wife along to Madras for some extra comfort. The couple stayed at Greenacres. The doctor advised Kolappan to continue his medication and wait a bit before surgery. 'Hold on, let's see how it goes, Mr Appan,' said the Edinburgh-returned specialist who was probably under the impression that Kolappan's first name was Kol. But after two months of medication, it was formally proclaimed that miraculously the tumour had disappeared, 'medically melted away, malignancy and all.'

Aunt Sarada told Kolappan and his wife to stay on for a bit more, 'just in case.' Since they were childless and Greenacres had extra rooms, Kolappan and his wife were comfortable enough in their downstairs room. The wife, being a serious diabetic, couldn't eat whatever was made in the kitchen so she began a separate kitchen for herself and her husband. Thus Ambi, the cook, was saved the trouble of cooking for them as well. After two years, Kolappan severed all connections with Poonjar during a vacation there and made Madras his permanent home. He transferred all his worldly belongings to Greenacres. Even then he was still referred to as 'the guest' or 'patient'. He was always being asked polite questions like, 'So now how're you, how's your you-know?' and Kolappan would nod bravely and say, 'It's quite all right.'

Some years after that the wife died, and Kolappan began his lonely existence. Aunt Sarada sent his meals to his room during the period of mourning. But one day Ambi was overheard complaining about 'this daily room service for that other thampuran'. Kolappan decided touchily to revive the second kitchen which had died with his wife. He began to cook all his meals himself.

Kolappan soon developed a strain of paranoid nervousness that made him suspicious of everyone in the house. At one stage he even passed on desperate SOS messages to dinner guests. Then he started suspecting the guests themselves of trying to attack him when no one was looking. This was embarrassing since Aunt Sarada was a gregarious soul and loved to have plenty of people home every week. They arranged to have Kolappan see a psychiatrist. After three months of weekly sessions, he felt that the psychiatrist was a naattukaaran, his countryman, come to smuggle him back to Poonjar with the active support of cousin Kunjappan.

But the sessions did help. Kolappan improved, though he always considered himself a martyr, a brave and lonely recluse in Greenacres. When others enjoyed themselves, he peeped out of his room and smiled tolerantly. When Aunt Sarada's children and grandchildren came down, Kolappan looked abandoned and let down, the suffering childless widower harshly reminded of what he was missing in life. But Kolappan stayed on; in spite of his 'T'-word being a formidable rival to RV uncle's less dramatic ailments; in spite of his uncanny ability to embarrass at least one dinner guest at a time; and in spite of RV uncle's strong but unvoiced resentment, born of his inability to simply ask him to leave.

Today Kolappan was in a mood for martyrdom. 'Come to see Brother, is it?' He smiled courageously. He circled his towel like a turban around his big bald head. 'Good! I hope we'll meet next time. There's a pain on the left side—just below Left Nipple. Carrying on, what to do. If all goes well, we'll meet next time.' He took elaborate leave of them.

Before they left, Aunt Sarada told Gopi, 'You simply must contact Shankar and tell him about your uncle's illness.' She looked even more worried than before. 'I've been trying to get through for days. Where on earth can he be?' She managed a self-consoling smile. 'Maybe there's something wrong with his phone.'

But as Gopi edged his scooter on to the road, he looked at his watch and cursed. 'Four thirty. Traffic will be hell.'

'We must see Uncle Shankar,' Lekha said. 'You promised her.'

'All the way now?'

'You promised. And Shobha'll get a ride.'

They wended their way through atrocious traffic, cursing and getting cursed. Cars honked madly, buses crossed lanes and came careening into them, pedestrians jaywalked bravely, policemen yelled and sweated and swatted the air trying to bring about a modicum of order. At one point, the signals weren't working and they had to wait for more than a quarter of an hour. Shobha kept muttering irritably, 'Let's go, let's go!' till Gopi snapped. 'Go where? Why don't you get down and walk if you want?'

In a lateral world where personal growth is seen as a spreading out, a comfortable sticking on to familiar terrain, where people explored horizontally and swam sideways, Uncle Shankar shot up like a passenger in a bubble lift. Watched and watching, knowing exactly where to go once he'd made up his mind, he punched the right buttons, zooming up to dizzy heights. He knew his floors and he knew his buttons. But his freedom wasn't all that promiscuous, aware as he was of being enclosed in his capsule of tradition and Kilikkara expectation. Now it appeared that Shankar had stepped out unexpectedly at a middle floor . . .

The landmarks of Shankar's life were fairly uncomplicated. Born in Big Palace. Armed with an MA in History which was unfocussed and yet flexible enough to support any venture he might undertake later in life. Involved himself in the Arts, an exciting twilight world of rehearsals, greasepaint and frustration no one in Kilikkara had any clue about. He also dabbled in amateur dramatics and lent his voice for documentaries and the radio. He had a sensitive voice that touched the listener in a special place.

Shankar had worked for a multinational. Their consumer goods division had at least nine soaps and toothpastes in the market, each competing with the other like a family quarrelling before outsiders. No other soap or toothpaste in the country stood a chance unless they claimed herbal miracles, rock-bottom prices or rooted traditions. Yet he had sparkled so brightly they offered him regular advertising commissions on a platter through their sister concern even after he quit them over 'principles of freedom'. Even as he worked to bring about fragrance and fresh breath, he had a dim growing realization of misplaced allegiance till he could bear it no longer.

He gave up his suit and tie for a khadi kurta, his five-figure salary for creative freedom and heaved a sigh of relief. His advertising commissions kept him comfortable. His inheritance left him fret-free. He took to the stage in right earnest, directing, acting and odd-jobbing without a care. The famous voice touched people in all sorts of places.

He was known as the Kilikkara thampuran who'd slipped, a bachelor at fifty. He had forsaken the security of a hefty income and was known to be experimenting with unorthodox areas of life. But there was an undeniable dignity in whatever he did, in how he lived. There was an old-world charm, a tinge of tragedy like the grave nobility of a fallen hero. His tall kurta-clad frame, grey beard and fair fragile skin, his faraway frown and sudden transported smile were an integral and familiar part of the city's creative environment.

His 'second life', as Lekha put it, was closed to all else and derived from the prerogatives of grey bachelorhood. It probably had to do with an early failed relationship that had wounded him forever. Beautiful young things were seen hanging on his every word. Actresses 'simply loved' his direction. His ultimate unavailability enhanced his appeal.

Shankar lived in a rented house in the cantonment area of St Thomas Mount, an hour from his sister's house. Today it took them two hours. By the time they left the traffic behind them and coasted down, they were sweating and dirty and angry. Only Lekha remained in good spirits. 'Quite some time since we came here,' she said. They entered the shaded road where Shankar lived. A group of very young boys had appropriated an entire stretch for a cricket pitch. They stopped their thunderous game to let them pass, then resumed with shouts and swaggers.

Beyond the gates were twin houses. Shankar lived in one, his landlord in the other. They went up the tree-lined path and Gopi parked the scooter. The houses were old, quaint and colonial with tiled roofs, green-painted pillars, and creepers stumbling up the walls. In the other house, three chickens and a hen strutted around like invigilators in an exam hall. A dog barked half-heartedly. Otherwise all was silent. Shankar's house looked uninhabited. Gopi rang the bell. They could hear a faint echo. Shobha remained silent, obviously tired, rubbing her knee and scratching her elbow. 'Try again,' Lekha said. He did, and they stood uncertainly for a while, watching the chicks in the distance and hearing the occasional yells of the cricketers. 'Come. Let's go ask him.'

They walked to the next house, more lived-in and homely. A rich smell of dosas being fried in ghee made Shobha look up pitifully at Gopi, but she remained silent, knowing his mood. They disturbed the chicks who clucked impatiently and Shobha clung in alarm to her mother's sari. Gopi rang the bell. For a while there was no response, then the door opened and the landlord, attired in a vest and dhoti, stuck his head out. His eyes popped up enormously through extra-thick spectacles.

'I don't know if you remember, I'm Mr Shankar's nephew. We rang the bell, there's no response. Do you know where he is?'

The man studied them sharply as though to store every detail. 'He comes, he goes.'

'He doesn't seem to be here. Did he tell you anything?'

Something like a grin moved his lips. 'Does he tell me?' He looked down at Shobha who promptly took refuge behind her mother. 'One morning I saw him. Last week, week before . . . He was trying to start his car, having some problem. He had to bring in a mechanic. I haven't seen him after that.'

'The car,' Lekha said. 'Let's go to the back and see if it's there.'

'I can tell you that. It hasn't been taken out at all.'

'Do you have any idea where he could have gone?' The man raised an expressive eyebrow. Lekha pulled at Gopi's sleeve. 'Get his phone number. We'll call later to check.'

As they walked back to the scooter, Lekha said, 'Strange.'

He knew what she meant. Uncle Shankar simply wasn't a disappearing sort.

MARTYRS

Excerpt from a note by Shankar, 1984:

I feel like a participant in a game of hide-and-seek.

When I promised to help you out with material for your thesis, I didn't expect this—hardly! Like a child running into corners searching for his hidden comrades and discovering trapdoors and cubbyholes and niches, secret passages that run away into the dark—I've embarked on an innocent journey and run into goblins of the past.

I am entrusting you with whatever I have gathered. Your purpose is less personal than the nature of most of this material. I don't feel guilty about loading you with all this, since I am positive that you will be selective as befits a professional and make use of only the relevant parts. There is so much to sift through and I hardly have the time to wade in. Anyway, best of luck for the project. Definitely let me know . . .

5 March 1998

I recognize Mari the 'all-in-all' at once.

He is thin and rat-faced and frowns. Pokey hair that defies liberal swabs of oil. He reminds me of a gangster's Filipino chamcha in an old American film, Hollyhood in torn vest and shorts. 'Mari?' That surprises him and his features soften briefly in deference. Then his eyes narrow into slits and he falls back into condescension. 'Gopi Narayan from Bangalore. Appointment.' He nods, but makes no move. We wait past the moment of ease. 'May I come inside?' I ask politely in Tamil.

He retreats reluctantly. The room is cool and dark. The sounds from below, the heat have no way of reaching this padded cell. But the hair oil, diesel, cooking and urine from outside have congealed into a composite stale breath. I don't know if it's in the room or stranded in my nose. Mari waves a magician's hand. A dim light settles in the room.

'He's in?' I prompt, to get things going.

'No.'

'He told me eleven!'

He shrugs indifferently. 'You can wait. He'll come.' Another shrug which says, maybe. And he leaves the room. His scratchy nasal voice hangs around like a ghost. I curse him soundly under my breath. There's little I can do except take him at his word and wait.

The room is long and narrow, a veranda furnished as an afterthought. Plain steel folding chairs. A table covered by a blue cloth embroidered with a rider in a feathered hat. At the far end, struggling to manifest itself in the dimness, a low-slung writing desk. A thin mattress has been laid out before it. A shelf is packed with books, writing paper and plastic tumblers sprouting ballpens and pencils. This is where the great man works, all those Mahabharatha sahibs and the Nadar's dedicated lovers were conceived right here. This is where he sits and fashions, lovingly, libelously, those juicy bones he'll fill our Kilikkara closets with, his dog-eat-doggerels.

I sit in one of the chairs. My eyes dwell idly on other things. A covered earthen water pot balanced on a three-

legged stool. A framed picture of a woman with a pale
pinched face. The picture is garlanded with plastic flowers.
There are several more pictures, all gods. Green chillies and
lime, large pieces of browning sugar crystal strung over
doorways to baffle the evil eye.

Chasing ghosts, I'm now here. There are worlds within
worlds. Worlds of time, space, ether, action and inaction.
Worlds of maya and worlds of substance—and swimming
with practised ease through them all now I'm here. Is this free
will?

Have I done the right thing? By poor trusting Mehra, by
me? What do I hope to achieve playing gladiator? What if
Rangachari takes one look and sympathizes: you've come all
the way for this? He probably filched pieces of family history
for the earlier books too. To make everything that much more
authentic, of course. And no one's bothered to protest. So why
should I make a big thing of it and draw attention to
similarities that people may not even notice? Still I'm now
here.

The room is intimate and functional, the visitor is an
intruder. I sit absolutely still, but my legs are getting cramped.
There is another framed picture on the wall opposite and I go
over. Plastic beads of different colours depict a girl with long
hair standing stiffly in front of what I presume is a fountain.
The girl's face is gentle and green.

'Come, come . . . Namaskaram!' I turn with a start. A
silver-headed man has materialized by my side. He smiles
pleasantly, hands folded in welcome. His white cotton jubba
and dhoti are crumpled. A touch of sandalwood has entered
the room with him, mingled with Dettol.

'Eh—namaskaram. I'm Gopi Narayan.' I edge away from
the green-faced girl.

'Sit down. Let us talk.' His voice is full-throated. He
catches my elbow and guides me to a chair. Flips up the back
of his jubba and sits down. He leans forward. Two deep
points light up his eyes. Have I seen him before? Some chord,
ancient or near-forgotten, has tickled a vibration somewhere
in the room that teases me as I study Rangachari. His face is
vertical and wrinkled, embedded with eyes that never leave

me. The silver hair is long and untidy, giving him the air of a musician or mad poet. A tight crop of white needlepoints carpets the lower half of his face. I sense an air of intense nervousness. As if his whole frame is trembling, numerous tiny folds charged with a deep-seated electric current.

'You're the publisher.' Perspiration dots his forehead, his head goes up-down, up-down.

I fumble out my business card. He scrutinizes it as if he's a connoisseur of business cards. 'We're well-established in the south,' I inform him.

The card travels up to his nose and he breathes in. His eyes close; there is a delirious look on his face. 'So you're a publisher.'

'Yes, sir.'

He looks up eagerly. 'You will publish my book?'

I try to hold my smile. 'That's what I'm here for.'

'I'm glad that is settled.' He studies me intently, looking for second thoughts.

This is the writer hounded by publishers? He holds my card between his fingertips as if it is precious. Is he playing with me? 'Society, you know, has a debilitating influence.' Rangachari leans back comfortably in his chair. 'Writer—it is from him that ideas are generated for the rejuvenation of society.' He rolls his r's like a Tamil-accented Scot. 'So you'd say he is the central point?'

I mumble warily.

'It is not what they think.' He pulls back the sleeve of his jubba and I'm shown the play of rebellious veins. 'The prophet is always a martyr. Don't you think so?' I open my mouth to mumble assent and close it, defeated. 'Rejuvenation—re-joo-vi-nay-shun.' He munches the word, savouring and pulling it apart. He shakes his head in admiration. 'What it implies, actually, is one kind of upheaval. It will come only when the common man recognizes martyrdom. The prophet has to be persecuted first.' He produces a sad chuckle. 'I should know . . .'

'Very true,' I agree solemnly.

He is obviously thinking of the flopped *White City*. We could go on and on, time someone pulled the chain, belled the cat, killed the crap. Let's get down to brass tacks and stop this trasharade! 'Doesn't history give us examples all the time?' I contribute to his facile philosophy. The professional in me gloats: Dilip Mehra, you lucky bastard. There's no need of a sales pitch at all. He's fallen hook-line-sinker. 'We find your books so refreshing, a change from the new barren journalistic styles. We'll take it up immediately—if that's your wish, of course.' Frustraitor! Are you here to stop him or encourage him?

'That's my wish, of course. Yes, certainly—my-wish-of-course. Reality is the form of persecution they're using. You should know that.' I nod, wondering how to turn him back. 'You're a perceptive young man, I can see that. We dwell within mostly. That is how we're able to remain isolated from society and face it at the same time. The trick they use is to make us confront reality.' He looks steadily at me, having no doubt that we're on the same wavelength. 'After all, what is reality? It's only our way of looking at the outside. Is reality one and the same for all of us?' He waits, a magician who's just completed a neat trick and wants his audience to react.

I have a strong sense of the absurdity of this moment. Instead of a no-nonsense fellow with a temper, here's a gentle eccentric! Dazed, I make a compulsive effort. 'You have a strong sense of history. Very significant. The way you look back and interpret events and characters.'

'Have you read the books?' I nod heartily. 'I have not been well,' he says softly. 'That's why they're all gathering dust. But I am recuperating. There are several books here now.' He taps the side of his head.

'I'm glad to hear that.' He does look tired, older than in the picture I've seen.

'Have you read my poems?' he asks suddenly.

'No, I didn't know you wrote poetry!'

'Yes, yes. I'm always writing. There are rhymes and concepts in the head. The first writer is the poet, others are only followers.'

I swallow, unable to stop being carried away. 'Are you thinking of publishing?'

'Yes, they should be published, shouldn't they? To tell

people what to expect in these degenerate times. Prepare them to face what is to come.'

Professional is all excited. Pulpfiction and pulppoetry! Two birds with one stone. In the Ramayana, the monkey god Hanuman sails the skies to Lanka taking Lord Rama's message to Sita. After handing over the message, he goes one better and burns Lanka as well. Dilip Mehra's going to get a two-in-one.

'I use different languages,' Rangachari continues. 'I write shairi in Urdu, ghazals in Hindi, paamalai in Tamil and couplets in English.' He smiles benignly.

And haiku in Telugu? Surprise refuses to leave my face. 'You're a linguist!'

'Language doesn't matter.' He frowns. 'It's nothing but a cloak to dress your thoughts. You need a dress for every mood. The emotion must become the language.' Should I pinch myself? Or should I pinch him? Rangachari shifts to a businesslike tone. 'If you're planning to publish, I might as well bring them out.'

'Your—your novel?'

'Maybe next time.'

I gulp back my frustration. 'What about your latest? I told you over the phone, your nephew gave me two chapters. About the Kerala family.'

'You're never quite finished with a novel.' His voice trembles. He traces a thick vein from his wrist, a slow journey to his elbow. 'There are always . . . changes to be made.'

I feel propelled and impotent. 'Obviously you look for influences in real events. This one, where is it from?' It's a line totally out of place, unscripted, malacropupism! He stares blankly at me. I clench my teeth. 'Are you in touch with people from this particular family?' Unbidden, jittery.

'Wait here. I'm going to bring them.' He stares at a point behind me, making no move to get up.

He's drunk! That's it, he's forgotten why he's called me and blabbers on. I should come back later. But before I can say a word Rangachari winces as though he's in pain. Then he begins to weep. I make sharp awkward gestures of protest. He shakes his head and wails, growing louder and louder.

Mari comes running, wiping his hands on his shorts. He takes in the situation and clicks his tongue irritably. He swoops down and pulls the old man roughly up by the shoulder. I make a half-hearted attempt to stop him but he glares at me almost threateningly. I stand up and make a move forward. Mari ignores me and steers the unresisting old man, still wailing, out of the room. Just before he disappears, Mari turns to tell me coldly, 'You can go.'

Now there is only the deep silence. And the Dettol in the air.

The remainder of the day and the next day, I sit in the EPA office and listen to sloppy Nagarajan grumbling about sloppy authors.

The office is country cousin to our Bangalore HQ, getting step-Mehra treatment. It is a clutch of three rooms and veranda, held tightly together by a string of smells: exhaust and petrol, vadas frying in the ground floor teashop, and talcum powder and cigarette smoke bestowed by the old barber who calls himself Balu's Delux Saloon.

'Technical books are the worst, sir,' Nagarajan explains. The 'sir' is an occasional reminder to himself that I'm half-boss. 'We have to keep running back to them.' His baldness reflects a soothing shaft of sunshine.

I sit silently. He's been trying to distract my attention, waving routine office affairs in my face. I feel swamped by the roar of traffic, the soft clatter of computer keyboard and the louder protests of a large Godrej typewriter pounded in the next room by a muscular woman who keeps turning her face this way and that like the MGM lion.

I look pointedly at my watch. He sighs. 'Still no call, eh?'

'It's more than a day.'

He looks surprised. 'Appadiya? Okay, it's our need, we'll have to run after them, isn't it?'

He picks up the phone and proceeds to dial. Once he gets the number, he talks rapidly in Tamil, then grins. 'Success!' He nods at me as if I'm a lucky boy who can expect a treat. 'Sir? Ah, just one minute.' He thrusts the reciever at me.

I clear my throat. For some reason I am nervous. 'Mr Rangachari? This is Gopi Narayan. I came there yesterday . . .'

'Yes, Mr Narayan, I heard.' His voice is brisk, quite unlike yesterday's jumpy monotone. The r's are still rolling though. 'I'm sorry I missed you. I was called away unexpectedly. Mari must have told you.'

'We spoke about . . .' I stop, not knowing how to proceed.

'You met my brother. I regret you had to go through that.'

'Brother?' I repeat the word stupidly. Nagarajan, infected by my wonder, adds an extra dash of surprise to his face. A hundred appadiyas swirl within his head.

'I will explain everything when we meet,' Rangachari says. 'This evening? We will have dinner together in my house.' He waits briefly for my response, then laughs shortly. 'I must make amends!'

Nagarajan and I stare at each other like mirror images. 'He has a brother?'

'Who, Rangachari? Appadiya?'

'I don't know! I'm asking you.'

'No, I haven't heard of that. No, no,' He shakes his head, looking distressed.

'He was just like Rangachari's pictures, naturally I thought . . . The funny thing is he spoke about his writing and all that—this is ridiculous! Of course, he looked older.'

'Appadiya?'

'We'll wait till tonight, I think . . .'

In a train moving north-east, Shankar stood at the open doorway and watched the rolling landscape. Fields and trees and monstrous caterpillar-bushes. Everything was green. He saw stray houses and people looking up briefly. If he moved back further, the scenery slid away from its own sharp reflection on the red polished door, creating a circling picture.

He edged forward, hanging out as far as he dared, straining his arms. The tracks thundered below him. The air blasted his face. His knees began to buckle and he forced himself to move away from the door. He ran a hand over his face and hair. Tomorrow morning, the train would reach Madras and life would pick him up once again. The same lonely house and the determined faces and the slow predictable grind of creativity.

All that would be behind him, perhaps forever.

Shankar walked back slowly till he hit the opposite locked door. To his right was the door to the air-conditioned sleeper. To his left were the toilets and the precarious walkway above the coupling.

The last month had been a whirl. I must keep travelling, he had told himself, if I stop I'm done for. The work at the agency had grown so predictable, pressure was mounting on him and he realized he was becoming an instrument in the hands of others. He no longer felt deeply about his work. One day at work, he sighed and pushed back his creatives and said, 'I need to get away from everything.'

One of the girls had laughed. 'Go to Benares. That's the place for people like you!' He hadn't laughed. It stuck in his mind and grew bigger and bigger. To escape it, he took a train to Kilikkara. It would help him recuperate, he told himself, a brief return to the womb. But it was there he had met her . . .

At the station, he heaved his large suitcase into a taxi and gave directions to his St Thomas Mount house. When the driver swerved into the main road, he changed his mind and said, 'Go past the beach.' As the car sped past the university buildings on the right, the morning walkers on the left, the statues and the sand beyond, he closed his eyes and took a deep breath. The car was hurtling away to some destination that hinged upon his decision. If he remained silent, the taxi driver would take over, just as something else was taking over his life.

The lighthouse on his left. It had been closed to the public since more than a few people had walked casually up the steps and then jumped down. How had it been with them? He tried to figure out their logic. Had their lives been too crowded or too empty? Had it been easy or difficult?

'We keep on going?' the driver asked conversationally, as if hoping they would.

They were caught up in the school traffic snarl in San Thome. Horns and revving engines and impatient motorists, running children and a grim policeman. He felt equally hedged in within himself. 'No,' he said sharply. 'Stop!'

So here he was in this room in the Sea View Lodge, barely big enough to contain him and his suitcase. You probably had to get up on the terrace with a periscope for the sea view. And the lodging, he was sure, was typically confined to a couple of hours of steamy heaving on the iron bed. If you got hungry you had to pay the 'boy' to get food from across the road. He had five idlis and coffee, and still felt so empty that he ordered another round. The 'boy' looked at him with new respect.

Now he sat tense and waiting in his chair. The room was getting darker. Street sounds peaked shrilly and dipped. In the corridor outside his room, two voices argued desultorily. Someone somewhere dragged something heavy, an iron bed perhaps, across the floor. What would people think? It was crazy. He stared, trying with his eyes to push the light away from the bars. He needed a couple of days more to himself. A whole month of travelling hadn't done anything for him. Let them wait, let them think he was taking his own time returning. They probably hadn't even missed him.

He tried to predict their reactions to his Kilikkara trip and to her. Why was it so wrong? These were new times. People had no trouble doing what they felt deeply about. And yet he had remained silent. He'd probably come across as a mildly interesting old uncle, kind in a distant sort of way, a rather surprising visitor from the other camp. He'd been three times to Kunnupuram in the course of his two trips to Kilikkara. He had discussed the Chakram and the relationship between their two houses down the ages—he dwelt on nothing for long. He skimmed and swerved and touched nothing. And he left as he came, like a messenger who'd lost his message.

Shankar sat and listened, hearing nothing, as the bars ate up the remaining light.

MAKING WAVES

Excerpt from the diary of Shankar, 1985:

However much I reason this, try to extricate myself, I'm done for. Perhaps they're right, those who swear by history as if it's some living thing, some beast that must have its pound of flesh. Maybe I'm the chosen one of this generation, the sacrificial lamb.

But I can't leave, can't forget—this is a curse that's compounded by old age! I think of MVR, but he was only twenty-five, half my age. I'll keep silent and simply hope it doesn't burst within me—

One thing is certain. If I think, at any point of time, that she or the family will suffer because of this, I will not hesitate to sacrifice, truly become the victim of this generation.

With the threads finally tied up, Aunt Sarada announced a dinner. Her parties were famous. She could celebrate just about anything, very much like the politician who leaves no occasion unsqueezed.

For Gopi, childhood in Greenacres had been a series of gastronomical adventures. Dinners graphed out of the pages of exotic, patiently assembled cookbooks that formed rows and rows in the downstairs library. These pages provided the substructure; the chief ingredients, vision and daring, were her own. She turned the printed instructions this way and that, pumping out exquisite modifications that stimulated eye and palate in equal measure. Ambi the cook surrendered the kitchen to her and kept a safe distance.

She sailed through her drawing room with its colonies of carved furniture, making anxious enquiries, as her guests drooled and chomped. They lay back gasping, clutching postprandial coffees and fulfilled bellies. 'Aaah! Never knew veg could taste like this!' 'That was no trifle!' 'Sarada, I'll treat a mushroom with more respect after tonight!' 'My poor sugar, I'll never live it down!'

At times she surprised her guests with a completely naadan sadhya, the traditional Kerala feast, assembling with near-accuracy thirty- and fifty- 'item' lunches from old Kilikkara menus, an array of mouth-watering preparations laid out on enormous plantain leaves and eaten seated on a mat on the floor. Her friends and rivals demanded recipes. She gladly obliged, knowing well there exists many a hurdle between word and method.

Her husband's digestive system had rebelled early in life. It dictated tiresome terms, condemning him to bland diets that ruined his spirit and killed his tongue. RV uncle's loss became a stomachful for family and friends. And Aunt Sarada flowered from domestic dabbler to grand hostess.

Remember the year the Emergency was repealed? The country, left dazed by a strange new discipline, was waking up to sunshine and business as usual. A nationally overrated Delhi swami cheerfully predicted the end of the world. 'That's It, Says Swami,' screamed one headline. Another interviewed the 'Divine Doomsayer'. A conservative Madras paper relegated the story inside: 'Delhi Godman Claims That World Will End.'

Aunt Sarada, a shaken supporter of Mrs Gandhi, threw a

grand dinner meant as a signal of solidarity in the new world. Being a firm believer in life, she had no doubt the world would last forever, but the occasion was tempting.

She pored over her epicurean bibles like a besotted bookworm. She called only seven couples, but it became the talk of her circle for ever after. It was sadass-mehfil-soiree-virunnu, call it what you will. Besides serving fare to challenge a five-star food festival, the guests were treated to a virtual seminar on life and death. Given her culinary command and RV uncle's penchant for the morbid, the evening wove itself into a strange blend of death and appetite, a Last Supper, deliciously trembling hiatus between Now and After.

Gopi remembered the deliberately dim-lit room. The gorgeous central chandelier with only one lighted bulb dripping eerie shadows. The nervousness and bravado, the giggles and guffaws.

'The sun's core is running out of hydrogen,' their friend Chakrapani warned. He was a scientist at the Murugappa Research Centre. 'The sun will become a big fat red star. And its neighbour the earth, unable to bear all this, will be roasted alive.'

'When will all this happen?' someone breathed.

'Soon. A few thousand million years from today . . .'

Dr Bhat laughed. He said: 'Death is an illusion, sickness is an illusion, ignorance is an illusion. There's only Love.' He was a devotee of the Mother at the Pondicherry ashram. 'Love, love and nothing but.'

'You didn't say sickness is an illusion when you got my hernia last year!'

'What's a little hernia in a universe of illusion?'

'Why wasn't your fee an illusion?'

'Wrong note,' Aunt Sarada said. 'Here Death is no illusion.' She smiled quickly. 'At least for today.' A delicious tremor passed around the dining table. They discarded desserts and held hands, solemnly repeating after her as she swore allegiance• to the next world.

There was only one sour note. Cousin Kolappan, recuperating from the scourge of fresh widowerhood, lay in his room listening to the whispers and the gasps. He had been reflecting upon the devious handiwork of a whimsical God, who'd served him notice and evicted his wife instead, cursing him to eternal loneliness.

He was distracted by the dinner guests. He heard the discourses on death. He ventured out his mud pot of a head and witnessed the shadowy charade. He realized they were challenging and laughing at Death, belittling it while he was still smarting with the pain of loss. What did they know of death?

'What do you know of Death?'

They froze.

RV uncle shook off the tight hand of his frightened partner. He rose and began, 'Kolappa, that's enough. We were only . . .'

'Mocking at death!' The bald death's head grinned humourlessly. 'Weren't you?'

Silence. Then clearing of throats, breathing, an elbow upsetting a glass which threw a slowly widening wine stain on the white tablecloth.

Dark silhouettes leaped as he raised his voice. 'Death laughs at your games. Don't sit and wait for Death. Death will come unbidden.' And then his dark room swallowed him up once again.

The reactions varied. One woman, deeply affected by the entire spooky evening and shattered by its climax, sobbed hysterically. Aunt Sarada said, 'He didn't have to turn up like that!' Nambiar, a retired high court judge, summoned a determined laugh. 'The last was the best!' RV uncle sat back in his seat, looking pale. Gopi, who'd already traversed the distance from post-graduation to entrepreneurship to full-time leisure, felt his heart thumping. There was no end to the wonders at Greenacres!

'So what are we celebrating this time?' Lekha asked.

'Come to the party, you'll know.'

Lekha made a sound of protest. 'Come on!'

'His recovery. Bhat's given a clean chit,' Aunt Sarada said.

'Now that's a reason.'

'And Shankar's return.'

'He's back?'

'Yes, he is!'

'Where on earth did he disappear?'

'He called this morning and refused to say.' There was a pause.

'What is it? Cheriyammey, is he all right?'

'I hope so, Lekha.' She heard her take a deep breath. 'It's probably nothing, something in his voice. Must be tired, of course. When you've known a person for so long . . .' She laughed. Then, delighting further in stretching the suspense, she said, 'As for the guests! You'll never guess!'

Shankar turned up at Doctors Colony that evening like a wandering spectre.

Wild-blown hair, dressed in his trademark khadi kurta and pyjamas, darker and thinner, and carrying a new depth in his eyes. He sat down and removed his gold-rimmed spectacles and wiped them with the edge of his kurta. 'Lekha, some water.' Shobha was outside playing with her friends. Faint screams and laughter kept perforating the air. Shankar told Gopi, 'There's so much I have to tell.' He sounded exhausted, like someone looking to unburden himself.

When Lekha brought the water, he drained it and asked for more. Tiny crystal drops clung to the salt-and-pepper of his untrimmed beard. 'We were all worried,' she said. 'Your landlord said you'd disappeared without a trace.'

'I'm not a baby.' He shook his head. 'It's chechi, isn't it? She must have panicked and sent you. Chettan being ill—on top of it, I'm missing! Next time I'll put an ad in the paper before I leave, so everyone's properly informed.' The irritability and exhaustion in his eyes were chinks in a personality they thought they'd understood. 'I was in Kashi—Benares.'

'Kashi!' they cried out and looked at each other, surprised at their own surprise.

'Wait, let's get out of here and get some fresh air.' Shankar rose, full of tired determination like a traveller refusing to be tied down. 'We'll go down to the beach. I'm suffocating in here.'

'Okay, let's go.'

'Come, Lekha.'

'No, I've a whole lot of things. You go ahead.'

'Then we'll all stay,' he said.

'No really, I'm fine. You two go on.'

So they did. Moist soft evening sand. The flighty breeze, dead one moment and sailing high the next. The sky spread silver-grey, a blanket that sagged dangerously close. A stereophonic roar of the sea filled the earth, muffled by the sky's cotton, waxing and waning like a child opening and shutting its ears, playing with sound.

They sat and stared at the drama before them. A giant moving coliseum where waves played with each other. A couple of boats bobbed up and down, fatigued fishermen intent on survival. A few groups of people sat around, some youngsters throwing a frisbee, shrieking children chasing and being chased by the waves. Beyond their world, countless life forms lived, multiplied, died, within hidden kingdoms. Where crabs dived and pounced and streaked through mysterious whirlpools in the capricious sand.

'So we'll all be in Kilikkara soon. Some peace and quiet—temple and pure food!'

'And a lot of pure gossip,' Gopi added.

'You'll be celebrating your birthday in two months, won't you?' Shankar asked. 'Thirty-five years, right?' Gopi nodded. 'Right! We aren't getting any younger.' Before Gopi could respond tongue-in-cheek, Shankar turned to him abruptly. 'You must look after Lekha.' Gopi looked at him in surprise. 'She shouldn't feel she's alone.' Shankar gave him a quick look. 'Don't think I'm interfering.'

'No, of course not.' Gopi felt strange, like a disembodied speck among sea, sky, sand and strangers. He shivered, not his limbs but inside—a knotted twine grating through bones.

'We men are like children,' he continued, 'we carry on as if life's a game. When it's too late, we are helpless and don't know what to do!' He was looking at the sea but Gopi wasn't sure whether he saw it. There were new crow's feet trailing Shankar's eyes.

'Why?' Gopi asked, confused.

'We marry our women and bring them into the family. They may be educated, girls with minds of their own.' He shook his head. 'They all become extensions of ourselves. You may deny it, but that's how it is. Finally, they're all the same.'

'Not everyone . . .'

'We've indulged ourselves far too long. We can't change now.' He chuckled breathlessly. 'We make them think it's a privilege to be married to us. Then they'll bury their own lives and live for us . . .'

'What do you think is wrong with her?'

'She looks spent. It shouldn't be like that at her age. She should be happy, welcoming life.'

'You think Lekha's not?'

'She should have no reason not to be. And it's up to you to see that.' Shankar turned and placed a hand on his shoulder. His eyes looked doleful, his fingers clutched making Gopi wince. 'There should be no regrets for you.'

A demon wave rumbled up, baring silver fangs before crashing down on the sacrificial sand. Gopi couldn't speak after that, feeling choked.

'I'm on the edge,' Shankar said, sounding as if he were drunk or talking to himself. 'Time only will tell. You're better placed . . .'

They sat straight and watchful, two sad sentinels—thirty-five-year-old nephew and uncle fifteen years older. What did he mean? But it didn't matter, the effect was already upon him like a pall of regret. The sky was sinking, the sea rose. A strong breeze ran up and down. Sun and moon shared the sky in a dense moment of camaraderie.

'What happened?' Gopi asked.

'I went to Kilikkara last month. A strange thing happened.' He smiled at Gopi, and his eyes looked even more exhausted.

'What?'

'That's what drove me away—to Kashi and then back again to Kilikkara.'

'You went to Kilikkara a second time?'

'Yes, I did.' He turned and grinned again at Gopi. 'To make sure.'

'You don't look the same, you look tired . . .'

'Of course, when the time comes, I'll tell you. Before anyone else. I'm tired, Gopi, really tired of everything. It's as if everything's turning to ashes!'

Gopi stared at him. 'Why?'

'Why? Why? I don't know why! It's too . . .' His voice was thick as he said, 'Everything's too heavy, everyone's play-acting . . .'

'What on earth were you doing in Kashi?' Gopi's fingers found a whorl-shaped shell treasured by the sand. A crab moved away quickly.

'I simply needed a little peace and quiet, to get away . . .'

'How was it?'

'Dirty, especially after Kilikkara. And crowded and crude and commercial. Otherwise, it's heaven!'

'I've always wanted to go,' Gopi said. His father, who had travelled to Benares a couple of times, had conveyed the impression that it was an ancient abode of the gods.

'In spite of all the beggars, and the priests who literally pounce on you waving this and that puja in your face, and the violent politics that's come up . . .' Shankar swept a charitable hand. 'In spite of it, there's still something undying, ancient.' He paused as the sky darkened rapidly, the moon shone like a secret window. 'You see life and death juxtaposed. I stayed in a choultry along with fifty people all sleeping in the same hall, each speaking a different language, eating whatever came my way, bathing under a tap in the open. I was up with the sun. I sat on one of the ghats, watching people drown the ashes of their dead, sanyasis sitting still with their eyes closed adored by flies, absolutely immune to all that went on around them, people bathing and shitting on the banks.' He shook his head. 'I saw two people come on a motorbike and grab a boy—a college student. They beat him up with sticks and chains. The blood spattered on the mud along with the red paan spit and the filth, and he lay writhing like an epileptic before he collapsed. No one came to help, not even a policeman, who turned his face and continued to smoke his bidi. I thought of getting up and doing something—something heroic to stop them. But I couldn't move.'

'What happened to him?'

'Some tourist family from Bombay came and looked shocked and took him to a clinic in a rickshaw.'

'He survived?'

'Who knows? Must have. People do there. Two or three girls came up then and propositioned me. Their faces were all painted up—like tragic clowns. They were barely fifteen or sixteen. Some Americans were walking around with cameras, tape recorders and notebooks as if they were peeling off strips of raw India to take home and paste in scrapbooks like colourful dead butterflies. And still I sat there as if there was something else, as if I was waiting for something else to happen. Flowers and blood and shit and kumkum, rose water, refuse and paan, incense and song and wailing—so much wailing!' He laughed, a short humourless sob of a laugh. 'But they're much stronger. The very air gets you tough and resigned at the same time. You could go to sleep and wake up years later, and nothing would've changed.' He grabbed wet sand in his hand and watched it dribble heavily down through his fingers. 'They've set up camp in Kashi, the gods . . .'

They were silent for a while. 'You were gone for a month.'

'After Kashi, I went to Goa.'

'Goa!'

Shankar smiled. 'Wonderful experience. It's transformed from last time, more hotels and tourists, but Goa remains Goa. And you won't believe how closely it resembles Kerala. You'd think you were home if it weren't for the number of churches. And booze parlours instead of our toddy and arrack joints!'

'Nice place?'

'You haven't been there, Gopi?'

'Where have I been?' Gopi asked dryly.

People were beginning to desert the beach. Only some stray dogs remained.

'You should get around, Gopi. Travel broadens your outlook.' Gopi turned away, stung. Shankar continued without noticing. 'There is a temple near Ponda, temple of Mahalsa. I was in a bit of a hurry but the priest insisted I wait for the puja. There was this large group of people around me.' He held up a hand, fingers spread out. 'All silent! I closed my eyes, and it was as if there was no one else in that hall. The bell would ring now and then, breaking the silence. The air was cold. The floor was cool marble. And then the priest opened the door. She came into view—I can't describe that moment. All the lamps and the goddess in her grandeur.'

'I never thought of temples in Goa,' Gopi said. 'Only churches and beaches!'

'She's also called Vishnu Maya. Mohini.'

'Mohini!' Gopi turned sharply to look at him.

His face looked unreal in the moonlight, the beard painted on, eyes glowing. 'Yes, Lord Vishnu's female form.'

'The temptress,' Gopi said.

'Right, temptress.' Shankar turned to him. 'Also Maya—illusion.'

Clouds of dark transparent glass sailed the sky, disappearing the next moment they looked. Shapes changed, messages merged, a glass miragery. Without warning the sky rumbled. They looked at each other in surprise. 'Strange!'

Shankar nodded. 'Strange indeed.' He added, as if telling himself, 'After going back to Kilikkara, I'm more sure of myself—even though I know what doom can follow!' Gopi nodded as if he understood everything, resigned to all this suspense.

Shankar seemed lost in thought. Then suddenly he began to chant: *'Thasmin kaley jaladh yadhi sa labdhanidra sukha syadhanvasyainam sthanithavimukhaam yaamamaathram sahasva, maabhoodhasyaha pranayini mayi swapnalabdhey kathaanchith sadhya kashthachyutha bhujalathaagranthi gaadhopagoodham . . .'* His voice shuddered, giving meaning to unknown words.

Gopi sat listening till the end, then he said, 'What?'

'If she's asleep—fortunately!—when you arrive, then, oh Cloud, arrest your peal of thunder and wait while my love has embraced me close in her dreams—do not loosen her arms from my neck!'

'What?'

'From Kalidasa's *Meghadhootham*, the yaksha's words to his cloud messenger as he sends him off to his beloved.'

The sky rumbled again and Shankar turned with a smile. 'Something like that!'

'It may rain,' Gopi said. 'Freak . . .'

'Shall we wait and see?' Gopi smiled. They waited. 'Wonder what messages they're taking,' Shankar said, looking up. 'And to whom?'

They were now all alone with the night and the ocean. They could hear the voices of the Meenavar Kuppam fishermen and their families from the huts. Shankar said, 'But it's something else I wanted to tell you. It's an old story, no one knows exactly, something to do with an old Chakram.' He shook his head. 'Each time you go back you get a new story. This was from Northern Palace. I was there and we were sitting and chatting over tea and biscuits, and this one came up.'

'What sort of Chakram?'

'A Chakram that was installed in Kilikkara a long time ago. They say it originally belonged to Kunnupuram. It was removed from there a couple of centuries ago and consecrated in our temple. The Kunnupuram head, of course, took it badly and cursed us to high heavens. And then it disappeared from Kilikkara too, stolen most probably. Under somewhat mysterious circumstances.'

'And no one knew all this till now?'

'It's always been there, I believe, like a sting in the air. That's the major reason for the discord between us and Kunnupuram. Your father got into trouble because of it. Some of his people felt the Chakram never left Kilikkara, that it wasn't stolen at all.'

'Meaning?'

'Meaning someone in our family has kept it hidden all along!'

'That's ridiculous. Why should we?'

'Why did we take it from them in the first place?' Gopi pursed his lips and remained silent. 'So your father was asked to find out if it really was there.'

'And he did?'

'Your father was young, and those days he was popular in the palace. He didn't realize how sensitive the whole issue was. He asked the Patriarch whether the Chakram had really disappeared or we were holding on to it secretly.'

'And all hell broke loose.'

'Right. As if he was a Trojan horse.'

A sleeping dog raised its head with a long mournful howl. They waited patiently till nature regained her breath. 'What is this Chakram?'

'It's a small copper sheet engraved with a consecrated design, made strong by reciting mantras several times over. And the more pujas are done to it the more powerful it gets. It gets difficult to control after a stage. That's why it was buried in the inner room in our temple where the Devi's idol is located. Someone broke into our temple a hundred years ago and dug out the Chakram, a namboodiri from Kunnupuram.'

'So they've taken it back . . .'

'No, he was found dead inside the temple. The Chakram was missing.'

'And they think we kept it?'

'That's one idea. It was hidden somewhere in the Palace, and no one's found it even after a hundred years.'

'It could be buried somewhere,' Gopi said.

'Sure. But there's no benefit in keeping it buried—unless it's inside a temple. You bury it to contain the power, and it has to be inside the temple so the regular worship can keep it charged. But it's not in the temple any more, according to all the oracles who've been called.'

'So where is it?'

Shankar shook his head. 'Who knows? I took a little trip to Kunnupuram to see what they have to say.' He grinned. 'They've more important things to think of, this is just one of those things from the past.'

'They're not interested?'

'Not as much as our fellows in Kilikkara were.' He sat up and looked around as if he'd suddenly realized where he was.

'Are we planning to spend the night here or what?' He pointed. 'Look! Look at those waves. They are like ghosts from the past, crashing down again and again on the sands of life.'

THE PARTY

The first of the guests came in at eight.

An hour, and the party was well under way. The room expanded miraculously to accommodate the steady influx. Minutely carved sofas stretched, corners and angles and islands of space shifted and welcomed. The glow from variously designed lampshades—bright ethnic, dull chic, sharp grill, elegant glass and snooty silhouettes—and the three chandeliers so amplified the room that it seemed now capable of continually opening up to contain all who came.

Gopi's alarm grew. How many people were expected? Aunt Sarada's list was a Pandora's box, there was no saying what might emerge. Cars crunched up, announcing themselves with hurled-out headlights that briefly ricocheted on a glass showcase, sending RV uncle hurrying to the porch again and again.

A familiar guffaw rang out. Gopi froze. He stood up stiffly, a sickly smile torturing his lips. RV uncle walked into the room followed by Gopi's boss K.P. Panikkar, his wife Leela and daughter Sulochana Panikkar (briefly Menon during

a disastrous alliance). Panikkar halted in his tracks and
frowned as though he was trying to place Gopi. 'Gopi
Narayan!' He was wearing a red-and-white striped T-shirt,
Panikkar-on-vacation. 'Enjoying yourself!' he bellowed. His
guffaw rang out grimly. He dumped his tall frame heavily into
a carved sofa. RV uncle winced.

His wife was a tall slim woman made of delicately veined
bone china, her severe lips and thin nose offset by kindness in
her eyes. Aunt Sarada came up with welcoming arms. Without
further ado they switched to the Lotus Ladies' Club, a subject
that sinuously stretched through successive parties and meetings.
Watching them, he realized Lekha had been left to look after
final table-laying details. *She should be happy. And it's up to
you to see that!*

Sulu Panikkar sank into the couch beside his chair,
clouding him in shrill perfume, and smiled—this was a different
proposition altogether! Full crimson lips and heavy-kohled
eyes. Did she have the slightest hint of a squint, Gopi
wondered. The smile made his legs begin to tremble.

'Gopi, long time, isn't it?' She pronounced his name 'Gou-
pee'. Her voice was husky, her eyes opened wide to show
flowery irises, as though she were referring to some previous
occasion they'd been secretly together. Gopi clenched his
teeth: this is the effect she has on all males!

Sulu, who'd reverted to her maiden name with a vengeance,
wasn't like her mother, more ripe poppy to her mother's lotus.
She wore a flowing turquoise blue silk kaftan and a sleeveless
sequinned jacket over it, looking like Alladin or Ali Baba or
someone like that from a costume film. His eyes stayed
stubbornly on the round white column of her upper arm.

'Your wife has come?' she asked sharply. Gopi started to
answer. 'Where do you stay?' she asked. He prepared to
answer that. She turned abruptly to her neighbour on the
couch, an old thickset ex-planter from Coonoor nursing his
drink, leaving Gopi in mid-air. She said brightly, 'So, Jacob
uncle, missing the open air?' Gopi's smile froze and he sat
staring at her long unbroken sheet of jet black hair that fell
uselessly to her hips.

Shankar, sporting a grey raw silk kurta and his freshly

trimmed salt-and-pepper beard, commandeered an animated
group: sweating businessman bundled up in a shiny blue suit,
imperiously underlining his words with a gold ballpoint pen
pasted between his fingers; his wife who attempted desperately
to edge in a word; a tall thin nervous man in a goatee; and
a straight-backed woman in a relentless red sari. Aunt Sarada,
in her welcoming expedition across the room, shouldered her
way into this group. Gopi heard her say, 'Guess where
Shankar ran off this last month.' Others gathered.

'He went to Kill-karrah,' came a slightly bored drawl.

'Right,' said Shankar.

'That was first. Too easy. I'm talking of after . . .'

'He flew to Singapore. I was there last month. What a
hectic trip, plane just wouldn't . . .'

'No!'

'To Bangalore. To be with your niece Kamala.' Aunt
Sarada shook her head, laughing. Gopi watched Lekha enter
and stand in the doorway.

'US, of course,' the shiny blue businessman said. 'Simply
rotten cold in Washington this year. Or January I'd've been
there. I had unavoidably urgent business.'

'And yet you avoided!'

Shankar looked at Gopi and winked. 'Did he go to
Kashi?' Gopi asked self-consciously. He paused. 'To Benares?'

'No, he was in Delhi. These secret trips are always to
Delhi! I hear Rajiv's seeing businessmen from all over
nowadays.'

'Shankar's not a businessman.'

'And then, perhaps—Goa,' Gopi murmured, smiling at no
one in particular.

Aunt Sarada squealed. 'Gopi's right!'

'What? What did he say?'

Gopi backed away as they converged on her.

'Why on earth Benares, Shankar?' came Sulu's husky
voice. 'You're not growing old on us?'

'Only old people go to Kashi?'

'You either pray for dead souls or make peace with your
maker. What did you do?'

RV uncle wandered up to investigate this revelry. He

looked pale. He said in his steady story-voice, 'In the old days you had the four stages of life. Brahmacharya or bachelorhood, grahasthashrama or family life, followed by vanaprastha, going away to the forest to be at peace with yourself, and then sanyasa, total communion with God. Shankar probably wants to skip all the interim stages!'

They all laughed.

'Arrey, you sure it's not some commercial op-haurch-unity?' the businessman asked suddenly. 'Benares and Goa. Could be, I bet.'

'Hardly,' Aunt Sarada said drily. 'Just Shankar's whims!'

'Not even married. Why bloody rush off to Kashi?' Jacob the ex-planter swirled whisky in his glass, cornering Shankar almost belligerently. He was one of RV uncle's oldest friends.

'Just a pilgrimage. What's wrong with that?' He added pleasantly, 'I didn't even want anyone to know.'

'Bet you didn't. Come on, Shankar, spill the beans!'

The group melted, leaving Shankar at the old man's mercy.

Like vagrant drops of mercury, they melded, parted and regrouped in slackly faithless combinations.

A sunset group was dominated by Aunt Sarada. Beside her sat Dr Bhat and his pastily made-up wife who sprouted a browning hairpiece profuse with white and orange flowers. She was fat and kindly, an uncomplicated woman with none of her husband's dry humour.

Aunt Sarada was already into her next monologue. 'It was the art show of the season. But the Academy just spends all its time bringing out booklets and monographs on retired old art professors. Typical government office—hundreds of dusty copies piled all over the place. Who's going to buy all that?'

'It is just like that in the Doordarshan also,' said Chandrachudan, an earnest-looking man, from a small wooden stool. He seemed to prefer the stool to sharing the sofa with J. Kunjumani, a retired Southern Railway general manager and long-time drinking partner of RV uncle. 'Like some tahsildar's office. How can you make TV programmes from a government office? Will art come out of bureaucrats' files?'

Chandrachudan was the timeless, rather shabby secretary

of MMA—the Madras Malayali Association. This was a
parochial outfit thriving obsessively on nostalgia, 'news-sharing'
and card games. Having worked for an insurance company all
his life and being unable to shake off its coils, he now
freelanced, leasing out larger variegated doses of life. He also
claimed an artistic temperament, having done several walk-on
roles in Malayalam films where he was alternately typecast as
loyal family retainer and vituperative policeman. This left him
with a snarled personality, a rigid bearing married to a servile
manner. His popularity rested upon the fact that he knew
precisely what to do during the panic of Marriage and Death.

'Exactly,'Aunt Sarada growled in response to his
interruption. 'So they wake up and find they've done nothing
to promote art or keep in touch with the public, and they try
to compensate by holding a series of exhibitions. This girl I
know, Shruthi, was trying to show her paintings. It's too
expensive organizing an exhibition, you just can't do it by
yourself.'

'Why not let our MMA handle?' Chandrachudan asked,
jumping up. 'She's Malayali?'

'I'm talking of ten years ago,' she said briskly. 'Today, if
she sells three paintings, she can buy up your MMA!'

J. Kunjumani held up his hand. 'Wait. This Swathi, is she
Rangarajan doctor's daughter, by any chance?' His thin face
split briefly, showing wolf-like fangs. 'Rangu was railway
doctor those days. All chums, we were. Our RV knew him
very well. Too bad about that dog, but.'

'What dog?' Mrs Bhat asked, her eyes opening wide.

'Got bitten to death by his own dog. Dripping with rabies.
I always told him, get rid of that dog but they kept it in the
drawing room, waiting to lick visitors.'

Chandrachudan nodded. 'Our city is full of that.
Corporation isn't doing anything at all. In our Association
itself, the watchman has been bitten twice.'

'Nonsense!' said Dr Bhat. 'Dr Rangarajan had a stroke.
Nothing to do with dogs.'

'We're not talking about Swathi,' Aunt Sarada cut in with
terrible patience. 'This is Shruthi, my friend's niece. She was
crying to me, what's the use of studying in art school if you

can't even be seen? You remember?' RV uncle nodded with a tight smile, knowing the shape of things to come. She carried on blissfully. 'He told her he'd fix it up at the Academy with his friend, a government official. Girl was so happy she kissed him—have you seen him blushing? The exhibition came—you know what happened?'

Dr Bhat said, 'Continue. Are you afraid our Kunju will object?'

Mrs Bhat said placidly, 'Why you're hurrying her? It will all be coming out in good time.'

Chandrachudan added admiringly, 'Amma will have her drama after all.'

Aunt Sarada laughed. 'So we went for the opening day, there were speeches-beeches and all. The chief guest started talking—and here we also have this beautiful set of paintings by a new artist called Shruthi. We felt really happy, and Shruthi looked so proud. He said, now you must be expecting a beautiful young girl to be the artist, in which case you're going to be surprised. He paused dramatically, and, of course, we really were surprised! Because our Shruthi is a beautiful young girl.'

J. Kunjumani intoned, 'Beauty lies in the beholder's eyes.'

'Maybe,' Dr Bhat said acidly, 'but you don't tell an audience things like that about a young girl.'

Chandrachudan quickly added, 'The beauty is not important actually. Especially for the artist. No need of good face if you have one good brush.' Everyone paused to figure out what that meant.

Aunt Sarada ploughed ahead. 'The Academy man said, actually Shruthi is the pseudonym of a mature well-respected man in this city, Mr Rama Varma. Ladies and gentlemen, let me present to you our surprise artist, Shruthi alias Rama Varma!' She clapped her hands. 'We didn't know what to do! And poor Shruthi almost in tears.'

Dr Bhat let out a roar. 'Shruthi!' He poked a finger in the air. 'Our Kunju!'

'Shruthi,' echoed Chandrachudan, 'iii—iiii—iii!' He fisted his palm in embarassment as his voice slipped out of control.

'It was a total mess,' Aunt Sarada went on. 'I kept

prodding him—I said, get up and tell them you're not the artist. And he justs sat there. Shruthi was looking accusingly at him as if he'd deliberately arranged the whole thing. Finally I got up. I said, excuse me, sir, sorry to interrupt, but there's some mistake, Mr Rama Varma's not the artist at all, it is this girl and there's no alias-valias—her name really is Shruthi.'

Chandrachudan whispered, 'Ammey! You only can do such things.'

'And Kunju sat there thinking, what a spoilsport!' Dr Bhat shook his head. 'You should have let him have his moment of glory.'

'Shhu! How can he say he's Shruthi when he's not at all Shruthi?' Mrs Bhat chided. 'But why is that Academy man saying that in the first place?'

'The government official who recommended her sent a note to the joint director. He wrote a reference on the note: Shruthi/Rama Varma. So, all the correspondence after that said Shruthi/Rama Varma. How was the chief guest to know?'

'What a mixture,' said Chandrachudan. 'It will never happen in our MMA.'

'These government people,' Mrs Bhat swore. 'Look at him, anyone will think one nice old man will be called Shruthi?'

RV uncle sat desperately in his chair. His eyes had become convulsive balls behind his spectacles.

Gopi turned to hide his laughter. The conversation drifted to pseudonyms and aliases. He saw Panikkar coming purposefully towards him. Backing away, he bumped into Shankar and hid neatly behind his tall frame.

'Dislodged Jacob?' Shankar nodded, scowling to indicate the effort.

They gravitated to the carved ebony table on which bottles, decanters and glasses, an ice pail and bowls of snacks were lined up artistically. Shankar poured himself a drink.

'What are you hanging around for?' he asked. 'There's so much exciting conversation going on!' Gopi smiled and remained silent. 'You know what your problem is? You should learn to mix with people.'

Gopi tried a laugh. 'Oh, I try. They should learn to mix with me.'

'Have a drink,' Shankar said. 'It'll loosen you up.' It seemed a casual remark. He let it go. 'Come on, have a drink.'

Gopi stared. 'Not for me!'

'Nonsense, I'm taking charge of you tonight.'

He laughed. 'I don't drink!'

'You look like you could use a drink.'

'Why's that?'

'Things you'd like to forget, perhaps? It's in your face.'

'That I need a drink?'

'You need to relax,' Shankar said firmly. 'The more you keep gritting your teeth, the more it stays with you.' He quickly prepared a cocktail of Thums Up and rum.

'I'm not gritting my teeth . . .'

'You could use a drink,' he repeated, handing him the glass. Gopi stood holding it at arm's length. 'Come on, nothing will happen!'

Gopi made feeble noises of protest. During a hall day in college long, long ago, under the pressure of classmates, he had dipped a reluctant forefinger in a glass of neat Hercules XXX and touched it to his tongue, the first and last time. His tongue shrivelled and burned, his resolve to remain a teetotaller strengthened for all time.

'This won't hurt,' Shankar said gently like a doctor. 'The cola takes away the sting.'

Gopi raised the glass to his lips. Not bad, he thought, then the acid, progressively metallic, slightly rancid aftertaste caused him to screw up his face. Shankar watched him, grinning. Gopi tried another sip. He smiled as he took a third.

'Yes, that's how. And the bitterness is slowly replaced by the cola. I don't care much for water, too raw. Hey, it's not tomato soup! Take your time, you need decent intervals between sips.'

Gopi thought, what an uncle! Liquor wasn't taboo at Aunt Sarada's place, it was smoking before the elders that offended. Unfortunately, he was a smoker. He had to slink away or hide his cigarette behind him. It was an unwritten rule, even though they all knew he smoked. With Shankar there were no such hang-ups.

'Did you forget?' he asked.

'What?'

'See, I told you you would!'

Shankar took his glass, he made two drinks for them. Gopi's hand was unsteady, but he accepted the glass and took a large sip. His stomach turned, he felt the bile rise in protest. He fiercely retained his smile. 'Mohini!' He took a long draught and pointed the glass sloshily at the small reproduction hanging on the opposite wall.

'MVR's, not my Goa goddess!'

'I know that.'

'This is the enchantress.' Shankar smiled. 'The timeless lament of woman—hunter and victim, mother and beloved.' He waved his glass. 'Let's drink to that. Sad story.'

'There's despair among our young men?' rose a husky voice.

'Hello, Sulu. Refill?' Shankar took her glass.

'Why do you both look so sad?' Her perfume seemed even stronger now. The kaftan floated about her like blue liquid.

'We were talking of women,' Gopi said. He could talk endlessly to her, his brain felt free and uncluttered.

'No wonder!' She tested her drink delicately. 'Where's your wife?' Why was she so interested in wives? Gopi looked up to find Lekha standing with Aunt Sarada, Mrs Bhat and some other women. She was staring at him. He shifted back to Sulu Panikkar. He raised his glass and said, 'Cheers!' She grinned and did likewise.

'Excuse me,' Shankar said, edging away.

'Oh come on, Shankaa-ar, don't leave!' She threw out a delicate crimson-clawed hand. But Shankar backed away swiftly. Sulu pouted accusingly.

'He's a busy man,' Gopi explained in a jovial voice. Now that Shankar had left them together, he felt her closeness heavily. The round white shoulder pulled him like a magnet, like a lighthouse drawing a floundering ship. She asked, 'Have you been to Paris?'

'Why's everyone asking about my travels?' he laughed.

'I was there two months ago.'

'Oh!' His reaction had nothing to do with Paris. Her soft damp hand had floated upon his arm. A hot flush covered his cheeks. A nervous glance showed Lekha preoccupied with old ladies. He turned back to smile at her. The smile felt like a leer even to him.

'You must go to Paris!' she said, as though she wanted to extract a promise right there.

Fat chance, on the measly salary your father gives me!

She backed to an armchair against the wall and dripped herself into it. The Ali Baba jacket gaped open. His eyes digressed perfidiously to the magnificent surge of her (not-perhaps-too-big-only-too-tightly-contained, Gopi conjectured trying to remain clinical) breasts, the sharp valley that slashed down, smothering a tiny diamond drop on a silver chain surrounded by friendly pinheads of perspiration.

'It's so different from any other place,' she said softly, picking up and fingering the diamond drop. 'Art and love and freedom. That's what they say . . .' Her tongue writhed out, moistening scarlet bee-stung lips. He stood staring stupidly. The sight of her glistening lips was getting too much for him. O my God, he thought. His head was already in a shambles with sweet-tasting insidious rum.

'I'll never drink again,' he breathed.

'What?'

'No, nothing. But I never will!'

She squinted narrowly at him. 'Excuse me.'

He watched dismally as she rose, eyes pinned on him all the while, and moved rapidly away, leaving him in her sharp perfume. He heard Aunt Sarada call out for the second or third time, 'Dinner, anyone?' No one seemed to take her seriously. This is a deadly draught, this cocktail of conversation and alcohol, he thought as he watched people swirling merrily about the room. He drained his glass with determination, burped, looked around guiltily and then bumpily gravitated to another group. They occupied the space abandoned by the sunset group, and only RV uncle remained, still folded across the sofa, still looking red.

He identified two of them. Shanthi Rajan, the thin dark woman in the impossibly red sari, with her halo of frizzy hair and thick spectacles. She was part-time social worker and full-time spinster. She was blessed with strong views and an easy ability to outshout. She sat up straight as usual (the only time she leans, it's to the Left, Gopi chuckled), carefully assessing the man who was speaking. The other person he recognized was Rohit Sharma, an ad film-maker and amateur playwright, a shy and contemplative young man, one of Shankar's proteges.

The thin man with the goatee was standing and speaking earnestly. Gopi studied him through a fog. His spectacles were as thick as Shanthi Rajan's and he had the same intense air. Gopi grinned. Definitely twins separated at birth!

'In fact, you get to know more, feel more when you're outside. When I was in England two years ago, attending a world history forum, I could think of nothing else. I kept harassing people—India, India, always India, yearning to get back.'

RV uncle attempted to sit up straight. 'Absence makes the heart fonder.'

The thin man continued, 'Something in this country holds you like an umbilical cord.' A finger dipped behind his spectacles to wipe an eye. 'Roots are so strong.'

RV uncle cleared his throat elaborately. 'Our culture has stood the test of time. While others wilted and died, we survived.' He nodded at them like a college professor. 'Because we go much deeper. Our scripture is not myths and fairy stories. Our religion is a way of life.' He held up a fragile finger. 'Our traditions are of the noblest. We didn't condemn the sinner or kill the non-believer. We looked inside to bring out the finest . . .'

Goatee waved his hand. 'Here you have a son of the soil!'

Shanthi Rajan made an impatient movement of her torso, squared her shoulders and lodged a fist beneath her left breast like a conquering hero. 'Is that how you see India?'

Her twin turned to smile at her. RV uncle said stiffly, 'That's how we all see our country.'

'Politician's rhetoric,' she said dismissively. RV uncle jumped. 'We had our golden ages, not now.' Her voice rose. 'We're as greedy as the rest, believe me. Fiercely jealous of territory, language and religion. This culture you talk about remains on paper—a few concerts and stone temples, crumbling stone temples! And we're competing to become as faceless and standard as any other modern monstrosity of a nation.'

Goatee stared. Her sudden open defiance, rather than the content of what she said, had taken him by surprise. He swallowed noisily. 'Madam!'

Shanthi Rajan savoured his condition. 'Look around you.' Her thin arm swept an entirely rotten world. 'Bhopal slaughtered by fumes of imperialism—Bihar starving while Gandhi-topis feast—Punjab, our greenest state, reddened by blood—what more? What more do you want?' Her face coloured to match her sari.

'Shanthi is a communist,' RV uncle explained.

She shook her head. 'I'm a realist. You cannot even talk of progress until the nation is proud of its present and not simply its past!'

'Do you know whom you're talking to?' RV uncle struggled up from his own discomfort to accuse her. 'This is Dr Chari, history professor at the university.'

They nodded politely at each other. 'I'm Shanthi. I'm with EPV.'

'What is EPV?'

'People's Education On Values.'

'People's Education On Values,' Gopi rolled the words softly on his tongue. There was something wrong somewhere. He also felt a sudden tight build-up in his bladder.

'We press . . .'

'You press!' Gopi echoed softly.

'Yes?'

'We press for value-based education, not stick to stale school and college texts. Today every student is running a race to get into one of the IITs. Or medicine.'

'What options do you offer?' Dr Chari asked gravely.

'In the first place, we expose them to what happens in the lowest reaches of society.' Her fist went home beneath her left breast. 'We show them how to use education as a weapon against white-collar exploitation and unethical politics.'

'That's a very noble aim,' Dr Chari said in surprise.

'We let them see life at different levels. On the streets, in the pavements. In the night markets, where young girls are sold. Tribal areas, where innocent people are victimized.'

RV uncle looked shocked. 'You take young children to see brothels?'

'College students, mostly,' Shanthi said impatiently. 'Please, uncle, trust us to be sensible!'

But Dr Chari was impressed. 'I'm glad,' he said. 'I'm so glad.'

'So there's no place for empty patriotism!' she barked. The brief honeymoon was over. 'We have to push out the stale air.'

Gopi looked jerkily at each face and chuckled. 'Yes, I'm going to get some fresh air myself . . .' As he backed away, he saw Shanthi Rajan's spectacles flash coldly at him.

He took in cool night air and acrid tobacco smoke with the same ardour. He sat down on the white steps and waved his cigarette in the air, watching the flaming button dance and stretch. Large pots with green hairstyles hung on either side of him. He remembered running feet and screams and hiding places and bitter gangs, ice cream and films and beaches and drives—when he would have preferred a home on these steps rather than go back to Kilikkara after the vacation.

He got up and walked out to the garden. The grass felt ticklish, stimulating beneath his bare feet. He turned back and looked up at the house. His head swirled. The house, blind with a lighted smile, echoed with ghost sounds. A dog whined from the road, frightening him. He felt his bladder struggle.

He looked around. What the hell! He threw away the cigarette with a stylish flick of his fingers. He unzipped. He was digging desperately within when he froze, seeing the grim shadow at the gate. The watchman! Was he looking? Or facing away? There was no way he could tell, the wretched man was just an unmoving dark silhouette, an accusing gurkha silhouette.

He hastily zipped up, his eyes fixed on the gurkha. The gurkha stood like a statue. Perhaps he was a voyeur! Well, he certainly wasn't going to oblige him. For a brief moment he thought of going up and challenging him, but gurkhas carry lathis. And daggers. Gopi scowled into the darkness and turned back, heaving an unbearable bladder.

He stumbled back into the bright crowd, now but a

shadow of the guests he'd left behind. Nowhere but the toilet, he cried out within his head, but found himself helplessly embroiled in matters of state. RV uncle stopped him short. He looked so drained, yet so red that Gopi halted in his tracks.

'The state,' Shanthi Rajan said, 'will always remain an instrument of exploitation and force . . .' This was a different voice, a sharper mood. 'Uncle may call me a commie, but I recognize reality. Exploitation stops when there's no state left.' RV uncle sighed deeply, there seemed little hope of stemming the flow. 'When class is abolished, when we become a society of cooperation not exploitation, the state will wither away . . .'

'And who will administer?' Dr Chari asked earnestly.

Gopi stood clutching the carved headrest of Shanthi Rajan's sofa. His hips jerked involuntarily as he made a discovery. 'It's not EPV!' he cried. 'It's PEOV.' Something within his head was unfolding with cloying slowness.

At the same time, Rohit Sharma said mildly, 'There's nothing wrong in being positive. You must have hope.'

'Hope!' Shanthi Rajan snorted. 'Hope is the opium of the oppressed. A carrot!'

'Carrot, that's good.' Gopi laughed. 'Hope is the sop of dopes! Or the dope of sops!' They all turned to look at him.

RV uncle said in a small voice, 'This is Sarada's nephew Gopi.'

A cloud lifted. Dr Chari gazed at Gopi as if he were a rare bird he had sighted. 'Pleasure! I'm honoured!' He walked quickly around the sofa and placing a hand on Gopi's shoulder, drew him away from the others. 'The past is a gift.'

Gopi said, 'What?'

Dr Chari shook a finger. 'Don't let anyone tell you otherwise.' Gopi must have looked surprised because he added, 'I was telling your uncle, don't forget the family background, it's too precious. You're the blessed people. The custodians of history! Promise me you'll never forget that.' Gopi grinned. 'Promise me!' The historian's head came swooping down to his. Gopi nodded, retreating uneasily. 'Thank you,' Dr Chari breathed. His goatee looked as if he'd perhaps used an eyebrow pencil on it, it seemed so perfect.

'History flows. Don't think it's deadwood behind you. It f-l-o-w-s! The past will come home to roost.'

Gopi said sharply, 'Sir?'

'Yes,' Dr Chari said. 'History is a lighted fuse. It can cause explosions at the other end. Your ancestry is charged with history. It won't be long before you too begin to feel the current.' Gopi shivered as if a cold hand had clutched him by the neck. Dr Chari continued to speak, about Kilikkara and historical processes and electric wires. The words skimmed by. Gopi couldn't concentrate. He saw RV uncle struggling to sit up in his chair.

His bladder was close to bursting. He made a tortured movement. 'One minute!' It came out louder than he had intended, almost a scream. Several heads turned. Dr Chari stopped talking and looked alarmed. Gopi blushed and lowered his eyes. 'No, nothing,' he said weakly. 'I'll just go to the bathroom and come . . .'

He heard RV uncle call out in a slow, disapproving voice: 'Go-pee!'

'Okay, I will!' Without looking back he charged away.

He almost didn't make it upstairs in time, but when he did, it was such ecstasy he wouldn't have traded the experience for anything else. He listened to the gushing as if it were the surge of a mountain stream. He heard the cries of birds and the laughter of happy people. He caught sight of himself in the full-length mirror and was so amused he began to laugh.

It took a long time before he could sober up. He washed his face again and again. He looked in on Shobha, side-stepping the stentorian snoring of the old maid on the floor. He sat beside her and stroked her hair. Her innocence moved him so much it brought a lump to his throat. He finally wiped his eyes and got to his feet.

He could hear a dog begin to howl, which made him uneasy. He hurried to the staircase. As he reached the foot of the stairs, it seemed that the commotion of the party had metamorphosed subtly into something else.

Bobbing heads created a new pattern in the lush drawing room. They were all crowding around RV uncle's sofa. Aunt Sarada's voice came distinctly, rising from breathless panic into a moan. Dr Bhat's round face surfaced. 'Call an ambulance,' he said.

Gopi caught a glimpse of RV uncle's face embedded on a cushion, eyes screwed shut, overflowing with red shadow. 'Ayyoo-oo-yyooo!' Chandrachudan's voice broke sharply, scaring him even more. It echoed RV uncle's own cry, a hopeless wail that had shivered through a faraway monsoon twenty years ago.

Gopi stumbled into the shattered pattern of the drawing room. As he did so, he couldn't help noticing the bald head shaped like a mud pot sticking out from the barely open doorway of a dark room. And eyes bulging with fright.

AFTERSHOCKS

Like a cathedral abandoned after its most impressive service, Greenacres echoed cavernously in the throes of silence. Among the many shadows that crowded the house, the most active presence was that of its master Rama Varma—RV uncle.

Aunt Sarada, Kolappan and Shankar, who'd packed his bags and moved in, Ambi the cook and the other servants— they were all sterile half-dead beings sweeping sluggishly through its rooms. RV uncle was a strong grim presence, more alive than anyone else.

It gave the lie to the grimy white waves of acrid smoke that had billowed skyward that strange sweaty afternoon. The white smoke carried away colourful particles of RV's life: his childhood and schooling in Poonjar, his marriage at age seventeen to the younger daughter of the redoubtable Thriketta Thirunal, his early aborted attempts at pursuing an ICS career, his nervous existence among giants in Kilikkara's Big Palace, the journey to Madras and the purchase of Greenacres, his slow emergence as a man of stature in the city's high society, his bundles of stories, the bowels of his discomfort.

The smoke crackled hysterically, carrying RV-Sarada quarrels, Kunjappan-Kolappan cold wars, his undoubtable pride in the success of his children. And as the liberated particles grew in number, tingeing the sky like a stained glass canopy, the burning embers below depleted, retaining the balance of life. For the sky has to accept the ghosts of the earth.

It had been Chandrachudan's suggestion that they finish the cremation the same day. Dr Bhat agreed. 'I don't believe in keeping the body till everyone comes, it's just not decent.' Shankar conveyed the decision to his sister. 'The children?' was all she asked. Then she clutched at Mrs Bhat and went back to her frightening silence.

The cremation was done at the Nungambakkam ground. Gopi was shocked by the attitude of the vettiyans, the men who did the final job. They kept haggling till Shankar pulled out his wallet and hissed, 'Now do it!' As Gopi stood by the burning remains, seeing a hundred images of RV uncle down the years, he heard two vettiyans quarrelling drunkenly near the entrance.

Surprisingly, the strongest feeling that ran through the house was guilt. Aunt Sarada broke her silence and said, 'Why didn't I leave him alone? He was going and I was telling those stories.'

Dr Bhat growled, 'My fault, professional failure!' No one had seen him like this.

Shanthi Rajan said, 'I shouldn't have argued. He got excited.'

'We saw he wasn't well,' J. Kunjumani said. 'He should have been resting inside.'

Shobha had slept through it all: the first realization that something was wrong, the wailing of Sarada, the paleness of Bhat, the horror of Chandrachudan, the shocked murmur that ran through the guests, Shanthi Rajan's wide-open mouth, Chari's trembling goatee, the discovery that crept in on Gopi like a hangover of pain. And then Chandrachudan rallied. After all, death was his area of expertise. It was he who phoned the ambulance, literally pushed Dr Bhat and Shankar into the antiseptic rustiness of the vehicle to watch over RV, and instructed Gopi to stay on in the house and help. Chandrachudan scrambled into his old Standard 10 and followed the silent ambulance—no sirens, no bells, as if caught unprepared at this late hour.

When the ambulance finally returned, jolting those left behind from their hours of strenuous vigil, Aunt Sarada was too tired to weep. The furniture was moved to the fringes of the drawing room and RV uncle's body laid out on the floor. His thin brown face looked grimly satisfied. During the course of that morning as well-wishers filed past to pay their respects, Aunt Sarada told Lekha, 'Look at his face, it reminds me of that time he dyed his hair. It was so awful, I told him don't do it again, like an old actor painted young!' She began to laugh softly. When Lekha turned in surprise, her face looked crumpled as if laughter was running out forever.

Shobha slept through it all. Lekha looked in on her a couple of times. Early that morning the little girl woke up to an empty room. The maid wasn't there. She could hear several voices endlessly murmuring below, probably in the garden. She went to the window but she couldn't see anything. She came carefully down the stairs, a small uncertain figure. She stuck her head through the curtains and peered out. She saw RV appooppan lying on the floor, covered with a white blanket. She was about to laugh and run up when she saw other people seated on the floor further ahead. They all looked angry, with their heads down.

Shobha felt scared. She was backing away when she felt a hand upon her shoulder and screamed.

She was whisked away into a dusky room. A sad-faced Kolappan sat her on a chair, and gave her fruits and Marie biscuits despite her protest that she hadn't even brushed her teeth. He then warmed some coffee for her. This being a forbidden beverage, Shobha accepted it and entered heartily into the conspiracy. 'Don't worry, don't you worry,' he kept telling her. While Lekha and Gopi scoured the house looking for her, the child and the old man sat in that shy room gravely exchanging stories. While others were recovering from sadness and shock, these two felt nothing but fear, comforting each other as long as they could.

After the initial shock, Aunt Sarada seemed to dry up. All her friends had come and gone. The only time she showed some emotion was late in the evening when Mrs Bhat went home. She clutched her arm and held on. But Mrs Bhat had to leave, the flowers had staled in her hairpiece, her eyes bulged with exhaustion. Aunt Sarada shut back her tears and gulped, 'Everyone is going.'

By that time, some relatives of RV uncle had arrived from Poonjar. They were accommodated in one of the downstairs guest rooms. After bathing and eating and taking a quick look around the house, they soon established some order in the proceedings. They conversed with Kolappan with the excitement of siblings separated in childhood. Their voices rose high, sounding normal, like any other day. Endless cups of coffee and tumblers of lime juice were circulated in the drawing room.

Gopi's sister Kamala flew in from Bangalore. He thought, if there's anything positive come out of this death, it's Kamala. She and her Bengali husband were successful architects in Bangalore. It was more than a year since he'd seen her. She had put on weight and her face glowed with good health. After marriage, she'd developed a trace of a puzzling British accent. Her husband had done his schooling in London and that was the only possible explanation. Another occasion, and he would be teasing her about it.

She was pleasant as always, a breath of fresh air in the staleness of this house. She sought out Shankar that evening and took him to a corner along with Gopi. 'I thought I might as well bring this since I was coming,' she said, and drew out a gold necklace from a violet satin pouch.

'This is . . . the necklace.' Shankar took it from her and held it up against the light. Three large diamonds twinkled with a life of their own. 'What a beauty!'

It was the Kilikkara Matriarch's legendary prize, a reward at the beginning of the century for the birth of a female child, at a time when all the births in Kilikkara were mysteriously and monotonously male. Their grandmother Thriketta Thirunal had obliged by being born just in time to bag the prize. The necklace stayed in Big Palace, going to the eldest girl born in each generation. They stood with Kamala, staring like feverish diggers come upon a pharoah's femur. She pointed to a gold link that had detached itself and was hanging loose. 'I remembered you told me once not to give it to unknown people. You have a friend here who does a good job.'

'I'll get it fixed, though maybe not before you leave.' Shankar handed the necklace to Gopi. 'You keep it. You know Naresh, don't you? We'll go meet him when things have settled down here.'

She said, 'Sorry to bring this out in the midst of everything, I didn't want to forget.' She was still the same, quickly finishing off chores, quite different from Gopi.

That night, Gopi saw her come up and whisper to Lekha. She looked puzzled and embarrassed. In the middle of their conversation, they both seemed to freeze. Kamala pointed at something, looking shocked. Lekha bent her head, her hand rushing to her mouth. Later he asked her, a little coldly, 'What was so funny back there?'

Lekha shook her head and said mildly, 'Just a small mix-up.' His sister had bathed in the downstairs bathroom that afternoon. She had dumped her clothes in the laundry basket but washed her panties herself, hanging them out to dry on a peg. Later she'd gone in to retrieve them. 'They were missing,' Lekha said.

'Who'll take panties?' Gopi asked reasonably. 'Must be the maid.'

'That's what I told her. Chechi said no, she already asked her.'

'So?'

'Suddenly, as we were talking she saw it.' Lekha took a deep breath and carried on, 'That old namboodiri who accompanied the Poonjar relatives.'

'The bent one with the white moustache?'

'Yes. He was wearing them.'

'What—Kamala's panties?'

Lekha tried to keep a straight face. 'It was clearly visible through his thin dhoti. Blue in colour.'

'Those people wear loincloths!'

'He probably ran out of stock, I don't know.'

'They have a refined sense of purity, they don't touch other people's underwear!'

'He must have thought we'd put in guest underwear.'

'It must have been tough,' Gopi gasped, 'you know, pulling them on . . .'

The laughter came like a waterfall, keeping him shaking in the dark for a long time. Kamala! It was like seeing his mother, a closeness he realized he'd been missing. It washed away everything else—the exhaustion and sleeplessness, the misery on Aunt Sarada's face, on top of everything, the letter.

Going home that afternoon to pack an overnighter, he'd found a nasty note from the Sindhi who'd lent him money last September. The money had been given for two months, interest deducted at source. January, and Gopi was still looking for funds to pay back the amount, principal plus two months' interest plus penal interest. He pleaded for more time, he asked for an advance from Panikkar, nothing had worked. One day, the Sindhi rang up the press and shouted at him. 'Arrey baba, I gave money because you're from royal fam'ly and all. Must be one kadka royal fam'ly, I say!'

Today's note said the next communication would be a lawyer's notice. But supervisor Sebastian had once told him prosecution was 'peanuts actually'; default on the market and you could expect to find two well-built fellows outside your front door any time. 'And if you have a family, boy—just watch it!'

Gopi sat clutching the paper. He tried to think, to come up with solutions. His mind stayed blank. The months of wretchedness, the false calm from the loan and the frustration as he realized he'd brought upon himself an even greater burden. Last night, his first ever drink had actually melted away his phobia, leaving him free and light. The effect had died with RV uncle.

Aunt Sarada broke down as her daughter Uma, son-in-law and grandchildren flew in from Delhi just before nightfall. Her son and his family were expected from the US in a couple of days.

As they were waiting for Uma to arrive from the airport, Shankar took Gopi aside. 'There's something I want to tell

you.' Struck by his expression, Gopi followed him outside and
along the veranda, away from the visitors. 'Perhaps this isn't
the time . . .' Gopi pulled out and lit a cigarette. 'There was
a brief moment in the hospital when chettan regained
consciousness.'

'I didn't know that.'

'Very briefly. We haven't told chechi.' Gopi drew in a
long puff. 'They were trying all sorts of things—thumping his
chest, oxygen, injection. At one moment the duty doctor
stopped to take a breath. He looked so tired himself, young
guy. And suddenly he opened his eyes.'

'RV uncle?'

'It was eerie, just opened his eyes and looked straight up
at the ceiling. There was a flurry of activity, doctor, nurses,
attendants, all congratulating themselves.' Shankar wiped sweat
off his forehead. 'And he spoke to me—' Gopi stared, holding
the cigarette dangling between his fingers. 'He was clear and
very sharp. Even the doctor was surprised.'

'What did he say?'

'He wanted us to go to Kilikkara. I told you about that
Chakram, didn't I? He said, go clear up that matter and things
will be better.'

'How?'

'He felt the family's facing problems because of that
Chakram. He wanted us to bring in an oracle to see what can
be done—and also speak to the Kunnupuram chief. Apologize
on behalf of the family for what was done in the past.'

'For taking some Chakram two centuries ago?'

'What's the harm, if it will ease things?'

'I don't see—'

'Then he spoke about you.'

'About me!'

'He's holding your money in trust. He wanted me to have
it cleared and returned to you.'

'Let's not talk about that now.'

'It was his last wish.' Shankar placed a hand on his
shoulder. 'I believe he's invested in land somewhere. His
lawyer knows the details. He's been negotiating to sell the
land so he could return the money to you. And then he gave

a long sigh and that was it.'

They stood watching groups of people on the lawn for a few minutes. Then Shankar gave Gopi's shoulder a squeeze. 'I'm going in.'

Gopi stood staring after him. He thought of the Sindhi's letter. Smoke wisped out and rose up from between his fingers. Sometimes the earth has to accept the sky's ghosts too! His eyes filled. This was suddenly another burden in his life.

Gopi took to taking walks. He had four days' leave from the press and little to do. If Greenacres was gloomy, Doctors Colony was perhaps worse. There you had four depressing faces bearing down upon you, comparing notes and sharing your silence, taking the edge off your shadows, but here you were alone, you and your spirits. So he remained in Greenacres all of two days, and shared and compared and stared till he began to feel guilty about harbouring a personal burden that was different from theirs. He rushed back home. When Lekha chided him for making too much of his predicament, he said, 'What more can there be?'

'Money isn't everything,' she said.

'Okay, what is?'

'Everything else.'

'What use is everything else if he's going to, you know . . .'
He couldn't bear the thought of those two goondas standing outside their door. He'd told Lekha about the note after promising himself a hundred times he wouldn't; but she seemed to take it much more calmly. To please her, he stopped gazing vacantly at walls and went on long purposeless walks instead. He walked across and around Doctors Colony, he went down the main road till he reached the Circle. The traffic caused him to cringe and retreat. He stood in a safe corner and contemplated those lost landmarks.

The colony and the circle were spiritually joined. They were named after two brothers, Ponnappan and Chinnappan Chettiar. The first had followed the second to Madras from Ammanur town (in the present Chidambaram district) early this century. Other chettiars, they found, were doing worthy things and being recognized for it. So they folded up their dhotis and got down to building an empire for themselves, sure that they too could match the pace of the city's life.

Ponnappan opted for education and sports. He built several colleges and schools. He championed sports meets, financed foreign trips for Indian sportsmen and established a football coaching centre in a city college. He did so much for education that towards the end of his career he began to miss a degree of his own. Finally, in the twilight of his life, the Madras University was pleased to confer an honorary degree of letters on him and he became Dr Ponnappan Chettiar. Among the memorials to his illustrious career was Doctor Chettiar's Colony, situated past Besant Nagar, on land that had belonged to him.

His brother got a Circle, an oval fountain-and-statue park in the middle of a crossroad. The fountain had degenerated into a dry trough filled with interesting kinds of rubbish. It saw water only during the monsoon when dogs, cows and crows queued up for a drink or bath. The statue had disappeared, a victim of excessive love.

The statue had caused a rift in his community. Chinnappan had been a champion of cinema and industry. Two factions from his hometown Ammanur, belonging to different political parties, appropriated his memory for their exclusive use. Each insisted the statue would be unveiled by their leader. It was pointed out that neither political leader was a chettiar. It would be a lot wiser to get a neutral chettiar to do the honours—for example, one of Chinnappan's many grandsons who were all eminent and willing. But politics, which easily fuels communal and community feelings, is stronger than both.

'Either our thalaivar or no one else!' said the first faction.

'Either our thalaivar or no one else!' said the second faction.

Finally someone solved the problem. He came in the night and vandalized the statue with a hammer and a can of tar. Chinnappan Chettiar was left looking like a bitter surrealist's depiction of a handicapped dwarf. He remained on his pedestal for a month after that, accusing passers-by with his good arm. He was then towed away for repairs, never to be seen again.

The DMK Government in its rationalistic enthusiasm, chopped off caste and community names from all signboards, thus lending an informal air to the state with roads carrying only first names of VIPs. Doctor Chettiar's Colony became Doctors Colony. Chinnappan Chettiar Circle became Chinnappan Circle. An official in the government's name-pruning department smelt casteism even in that first name and the circle was renamed Circle. All that remained of its fleeting glory was the pedestal vacated by the Chettiar, inscribed with his biographical sketch.

Gopi shook his head in wonder. A colony with a degree. A degree without a name. A fountain without water. A pedestal without a statue. A circle without a name. It was indeed a locality of lost landmarks. Briefly consoled by the fact that his problems were a lot less complicated, he backed away.

Harassed by the unruly traffic around the Circle, he went down to the beach. Frothy waves churned on the yellow sand. He bent down to examine crabs which ran for shelter from his interest. It was after a whole day of this that a deep sense of peace descended.

For a man who in life had seemed evanescent compared to the substantial presence of his wife, RV uncle in death proved larger than life. He spread across the old house like a sore damp memory hung out to dry.

Greenacres had turned into a mournful mansion of dwindling energies. Aunt Sarada succumbed to the accumulated exhaustion of years. That endless third week following the twelfth-day rituals, life grunted to a standstill. And leaving her in the care of Shankar, her busy son-in-law flew back to Delhi, whisking away Uma and the children. No one blamed him. Dr Ranjit was a sought-after psychiatrist who consulted at the AIIMS as well as in his private clinic. A single hour's absence could result in severe setback to a host of precarious psyches. His wife Uma was indispensible to his routine, so she couldn't send him off alone. As for the children, their school held that discipline and attendance were the two pillars that supported education. So they came as a family and left as a family. No one blamed them, openly that is.

'How can they leave her like that?' Lekha fumed, serving dinner at Doctors Colony. 'Other people have jobs and families too!'

'Could have been worse,' Gopi said mildly.

'How?'

'They could have stayed!'

It was true. Everyone felt every minute Dr Ranjit was away from his practice. It wasn't only his patients who suffered. The house bloated like a pregnant woman on the brink, red from holding her breath before the final push. Finally, Aunt Sarada tearfully accompanied them downstairs, kissed her grandchildren soundly, held her son-in-law's hand, hugged her daughter and said in clear tones of relief, 'I don't know why you have to leave so early.'

Her son, stuck in the US, was unable to get away immediately. He waited and waited for clearance long after the funeral, long after the rituals. 'We'll be there,' was all he could mutter each time he called his mother. Aunt Sarada's disappointment was obvious, it stretched like a grey weary mask over her face, unnerving all condolers.

Back home in the flat, Gopi tried to dismiss that mask from his thoughts and pulled out Kamala's necklace from its satin pouch. He held it up for Lekha and Shobha to see. The light from the overhead bulb fell fawning over it and their two-hundred-square-feet front hall took on a charmed look. 'Show, show, let's see.'

'No, show me!' Gopi grinned as they huddled before him, gazing devoutly at the legendary legacy. 'Is it ours?' Shobha asked reverently.

'No,' Lekha said. 'It's valiyamma's.'

'Maybe one day . . .' Gopi said and fell silent.

Lekha frowned. 'What do you mean?'

'It's for the eldest daughter, isn't it? They've stopped with Sandeep!'

'So?' Lekha asked almost belligerently.

Gopi grinned. 'Little miss may wear it for her wedding after all.'

'Don't even joke about it.' Lekha grabbed the necklace from him and returned it to its pouch. 'We're here and they're there!'

'Meaning?'

She didn't bother to explain. 'For your kind information, this is not a joint family any more, the necklace has reached its final destination. She can give it to her daughter-in-law or granddaughter or sell it or pawn it or donate it or do whatever she wants with it. It's nothing to do with us.'

Shobha looked cheated. 'You said you'll give it for my wedding.'

Lekha glared at Gopi. 'See?'

He gathered Shobha into his lap. 'Who wants this? I'll get a brand new one for my little chuchi-puchi.' With the necklace safely back in the pouch, that brought little smiles all around.

Gopi's mother was also scheduled to arrive in the first week. Aunt Sarada waited impatiently, but time grew lazy and stretched and so did Subhadra's resolve. It was more than twenty years since she'd left the portals of the Palace. Now a fear of the unfamiliar rooted her to a centuries-old system, entrenching her within the fortress of home-temple-relatives-ritual.

When the sisters next spoke on the phone, the equation had subtly altered. Aunt Sarada would dispose of the house and go and stay with her sister in Kilikkara. They agreed it would be tough to remain in this old house, enduring the ghost of her husband's companionship. 'It will take time, of course,' Aunt Sarada said. 'Can't say when. I'm hopeless at this sort of thing. If he'd been here . . .' She was finally left with Shankar. Gopi visited her almost daily. Every morning Shankar left for urgent pending work at the agency and returned only at night.

That left the melancholy triangle of Aunt Sarada-Ambi-Kolappan to supervise the disintegrating fibre of Greenacres. Kolappan sat and stared at the wall in his room, sometimes he sobbed out aloud. Aunt Sarada lay in the upstairs bedroom she'd shared with RV uncle. Day and night, dawn and dusk, light and shadow moved like travellers on a platform, past her silent waiting room.

Ambi retrospected continuously, plucking old events off the dying air. He'd had his moments with the master, corrosive moments where a piece of biting criticism was enough to send him sulking, skulking about the kitchen hauling ages of royal family members through the coals. Now that RV uncle was gone, he silently and dolefully paid homage to the many facets of their relationship that could have been.

Greenacres collected a thin film of dust, coating its lungs and breath. It wheezed out sounds from time to time, startling its robotic residents. No one paid much attention to the disarray and dust, they were too immersed in themselves and their depressing reflections. Grass grew, bushes bulged, trees shed, a mildewed wind blew across the garden shaking down its defences.

The drawing room, with its muted colours and lush reminders, took on the aspect of a neglected musuem. The maid's movements grew desultory as she heaved her mountainous frame from room to room, passing her broom over carpet, upholstery and carved wood alike. Rats peeped in and discovered that no one was interested in hampering their movements. Soon the silver-lined elephant foot had a hole the size of a man's fist. The inner curtain had a vertical rent, sitting on which a squirrel swung to and fro in languid play. The carpet was littered with rat leavings. A Thampi oil began to change colour near its edges, accumulating a pale cloudy pattern the artist had never intended. The room that had glowed against the paleness of RV uncle alive now faded beneath the sharpness of his memory.

One afternoon, there was a small crisis. Ambi scampered up the stairs and knocked on Aunt Sarada's door. 'Come, come,' he breathed.

'What is it, Ambi?'

'Come, come!' She went down with him. He stopped outside Kolappan's room and pointed meaningfully. With a puzzled expression, she knocked. 'No, no, go in!'

It was the first time in years that she was entering this room. It was dark and packed thickly with memories and grief. A musty crushing smell of complex origins hit her as she walked in. 'Kolappa.' There was a flurry of movement as though of a hundred hushed wings. She switched on the light and stood for a moment, adjusting her eyes to the sudden dawning of the present. There he was, lying in bed. At first she couldn't locate any movement. Then she saw it, the slow fluttering of his right arm and leg, swishing, twitching, wrenching the mattress off the cot. She came up closer. His head was shaking from side to side. She saw the flecks of white lining his mouth.

Sarada swung into action. She grabbed a heavy bunch of keys and ran back to him, wrenched open his fist and pushed the keys into his hand. She shoved a thin leather-bound notebook, the only thing she could find, between his teeth. She instructed Ambi to run upstairs and fetch a bottle from the first shelf of the medicine cabinet in her bedroom. After that, she rang Dr Bhat.

When Kolappan had come out of his convulsions, Aunt Sarada looked sharply at Ambi. 'Ambi!' (The silence rang out: you stupid idiot!) Ambi flinched.

'Ambi!' she said again. (How could you play around with a man's life?) 'I will have to look after him,' she decided.

When Dr Bhat arrived from his afternoon siesta, all was peaceful. Kolappan, a half-dressed barrel with a towel across its shoulders, was lodged in a sofa in the drawing room, holding a hot cup of milk. Aunt Sarada sat opposite him. Ambi stood by with a look of uncharacteristic humility.

Later Dr Bhat reported to his wife, 'I feel Sarada's somehow come back.'

Twice every week Shankar took Gopi to see RV uncle's advocate. They sat in his stuffy office and discussed the property held in Gopi's name. There was a problem—'not really a problem, a small delay,' the old man said. The buyer, who'd staked his claim with a small advance, wanted time to gather his finances, and Gopi now found himself in a precarious water-water-everywhere situation.

The asking price was a crore. Gopi spent sleepless nights. He'd notched up a neat debt of over thirty thousand rupees— only Lekha knew his situation. His salary was a pittance compared to his needs. He and Lekha had periodic fights over their pathetic condition. They blamed Panikkar, themselves and each other's family before creaking to a compromise, since pointing fingers rarely touch a solution.

A crore. A hundred lakhs. Ten million rupees. His fifteen

lakhs in fifteen years had grown more than six times. He was a millionaire with not a paisa to his name! Gopi laughed bitterly. Lekha suggested they ask her parents for money. He said, 'Don't even think of it.' She suggested writing to his mother. He said, 'We've waited so long, let's wait a bit longer.' He promised to threaten dissolution of the contract. But when he was with the buyer, he just couldn't speak out. The advocate advocated patience. 'He's a good party, it's better to wait.' So what if he's a good party, he thought, I only want money from him, I'm not marrying him! He wanted Shankar to put in a word, but he was equally unreasonable and said, 'Wait, don't hurry.'

They went to temples and astrologers. Their horoscopes were studied minutely by grave old men with sighing eyes who said they could expect relief by the beginning of the next Malayalam month. One numerologist said the fault lay in his name. Change the spelling to Goppi and fortune would smile instantly, money would flow like a river. He asked Gopi to write the new name a hundred times each day so that it became a part of him. 'You don't have to change it officially if it's too difficult, but you have to internalize it.' So every day he rose early and wrote 'Goppi' a hundred times, more painstaking than even his yoga days. Finally, when nothing seemed to work, they tried another numerologist. He listened to the change suggested by his predecessor and sniggered. 'Some people will say anything. Some people are simply commercial, what to do?' He suggested the spelling be changed to Goopy. 'Write thousand times, not hundred.' Gopi glared at him, flung the man's fees on the rush mat between them and walked out.

'Imagine—Goopy!' he said bitterly as they came down the stairs.

Lekha studied him gravely and said, 'Let's be glad he didn't say Goofy.'

In Greenacres, there was a change of mood. The maid worked more briskly. Aunt Sarada was back on her feet. She evolved a new and strict timetable. Every hour of the day was accounted for. She went back to supervising the kitchen. Kolappan's meals, medicines and moods were dictated by her.

She made sure he watched TV and went out for a walk every evening. She suggested books from her library. She scoffed at his hobby of watching walls. She made sure he was around when people came to visit her.

It was a double-edged miracle. The waning of grief and the building of a new relationship. It was the grief that made it happen. Like glue that runs in treacly trickles and then binds fast. RV uncle remained the missing world that filled in their blanks. At first, Ambi and the other servants were at a loss to explain the nature of their relationship. Kolappan belonged to a world that had breathed its last ages ago, he was being returned after years of hibernation.

A week after RV uncle's death, the Poonjar relatives had offered to take him away with them. He looked scared and locked himself in his room. After Kolappan's convulsions, things changed. Aunt Sarada seemed to find a new reason to live. Kolappan rediscovered life. Shankar realized his sister had given up her idea of selling Greenacres. 'For the moment at least,' he said hopefully. 'She feels some sort of responsibility towards him!'

His formal blossoming to life and business-as-usual took place shortly thereafter. Kolappan drained his mid-morning beverage and said loudly, 'He was fated to die.' There was a strained silence. 'Don't you see? Brother took it upon himself!' They looked away in different directions, always uncomfortable when Kolappan spoke beyond his limit. 'Your family has a curse upon it.'

'What has that got to do with it?' Shankar asked him.

Kolappan nodded with an air of wisdom. 'Brother took it upon himself for the sake of your family.' What irritated Gopi was Aunt Sarada's silence. She seemed to accept everything the old man said, humouring him.

There was a current failure one night, leaving them hot and sticky and at the mercy of mosquitos. Kolappan went silent in mid-sentence. He sat still, wrapped in darkness and fear, not contributing a word. When the lights came on, they saw Aunt Sarada sitting close to him, holding his hand.

It was Ambi who put things in perspective. 'Not even brother and sister. From her behaviour, you'd think he was her son!'

One night, Gopi lay awake after Lekha had turned over and gone to sleep. He rose and opened the door to the balcony, his limbs frozen and sweating.

What have I done to merit all this, he thought. The strangeness of the night did justice to his state of mind. The sky was pale metal, a breeze pushed and rustled. The clouds continued to make grey gargantuan shapes. The moon raced across the sky. He saw himself as a speck in a grand design whose proportions couldn't even be imagined.

In the maidan below, labourers and their families slept outside makeshift huts. One man lay straight and stiff, wearing only a lungi, his head protected by a cloth tied like a turban. Beside him was his woman, her sari riding up her thighs, a hand on his stomach as if to make sure. Another woman, looking vacant and sleepy, sat leaning against her hut with a child on her lap, one large brown breast out of her blouse. As far as he could make out, the child was asleep.

They work themselves to the bone for this. Their food salted with the day's sweat; no place for petty emotions or mighty egos in their daily drudgery. They live, work and love on the raw edges of life, precarious, tenacious. They have the will to live, ignoring anything beyond the bare business of existence.

What am I? Why do I place myself at the centre of the universe? Why can't I look around, take in the ebb and flow? Why am I embroiled in petty longings and emotions? God help me, tell me who I am and where I belong—Gopi Narayan, on the balcony between stretching sky and ocean roaring below.

WAYBRIDGES

■

6 March 1998

Rangachari. Again.

Or so it seems. He's clean-shaven, neatly dressed in a fresh kurta and pyjamas. He isn't nervous, he's brisk, brusque, clear. And no Dettol, only sandalwood.

Mari opens the door and lets me in. He wears a lungi today. A surly bubble rises from between his eyes but bursts instantly. I wait for Rangachari in the same room with its pictures, green girl, horseman, shield against the evil eye. Virgin pages waiting for his impregnating ink. This time it doesn't take long. He strides in and looks at his watch. The room is brighter, more lights switched on. Twins, if indeed they're brothers!

The shave, controlled hair and clothes do make a difference. Though how can you rub away veins and wrinkles? Truth is, he can't. A film actor 'double-acts' his way into your credibility, multiplying himself and making you think each image is a different person. The lights in your world have been switched off, you're given the parameters of the bright adorned world before you—adorned so it's larger than life and you believe anything you're told depending on the skill of the teller. Realchemy. Sensorcery.

In real life, you know. The lights are still on. Especially if you've spent time with the man, spoken to him and watched him closely, which I have. More than physical details, there is a sense or spirit of a person you carry away with you. Like scent on a handkerchief. It can become as familiar as a name or label. The way a person moves, laughs, gestures, talks. The way he reacts to you. Relationship is a waybridge opening you to the ways of a person.

In this case, I'd sat and warily watched Brother One for half an hour as he raved. I sat close to him, studied him and his mannerisms. Every inflexion of his voice, caught breath, eye-clench, cleared throat, is familiar to me. Like a picture I've played back and forth in an internal VCR. And here's Brother Two before me. We sit down. I touch him as we shake hands. I smell the sandalwood, store the gestures, catch his briskness, impatience, smile.

Well, are the scents different, are there two of them? Rangachari and Brother?

Honestly, I can't say, can't decide. My vacillatent mind's been beaten. He looks different, speaks different, but . . . The face is the same, the mannerisms are almost the same, but . . .

'Mari!' he shouts and orders coffee. Even their relationship is different. Today Mari's on the lower pedestal.

Rangachari crosses his legs and smoothens the kurta over his knees. He clears his throat. He peers, frowning at the labour section of his room. He consults his watch. He leans back comfortably. And then looks at me. That's how long it takes to wipe off yesterday's embarrassment and come to the present. 'So you know Kittu,' he says. Who's that? 'You got the work from Coimbatore, didn't you?'

The forty-year-old boy—nephew's nephew. 'Through a contact. I haven't met him.'

'So what do you think of it?' Even before the question is

complete, he abandons it. 'You know I already have a publisher in Mumbai.' He pronounces it like any other non-Mumbaite, stretching out the second syllable in a Yankee drawl, Mum-baai.

I smile. Not scoffingly, gently. 'Yes, I know. I'm here to see if you can get a better deal.' He laughs, a strong laugh, halfway towards scoffing. Having dealt my first card, I make a motion of retraction. 'I didn't put that very well. EPA sees a better deal for the book. In EPA, we don't consider the author and the publisher—you and us—separately.' (Already bringing him into our fold.) 'I've been following your career. I read the two chapters you've finished and I told our chief it shows great promise.'

The coffee arrives. Mari is now a deafmute, an efficiently controlled robot. He places the tray on a side table bending low, hands out the coffee. It is typical South-Indian-filter-coffee served in the typical South Indian way, an upside-down stainless steel tumbler of piping hot coffee locked in by a small base vessel. I keep smiling at Rangachari. He sips loudly, enjoying himself. I blow into it, waiting, inhaling the delicious aroma. And deal my next card.

'I had a very interesting conversation with your brother.'

He looks up. 'Yes, yes.' He skims over the information, carrying on. 'Where is this EPA? Bangalore, you said?'

'That's right. We're one of the largest private publishers based in the south.' I take a sip of the coffee. It is delicious and scalds my tongue. I keep smiling. 'Your brother is not well,' I add, my tone gentle, interested. The smile creates a waybridge.

He is forced to pause. 'My brother has become a liability,' he says flatly. 'He's harmless but he cannot face people. You saw him, didn't you?'

Before he can proceed to other things, I add, 'He's also a writer?'

Rangachari peers into his tumbler and finds there's nothing else he can vacuum into his mouth. He reaches forward and places the vessel and tumbler on the tray. He sighs deeply. 'My brother was a scientist. Professor at IIT.'

'In Chennai?'

'No—Mumbai.'

'What happened?'

He frowns, looking as though he might fly into one of his legendary tantrums. 'You know how scientists are.' (Yes, of course, quite different from safe predictable historians.) 'It's a good thing he didn't do anything drastic. There's a history of that nowadays in the IITs.'

I nod gravely. 'Why does he have this . . . thing for publishers?'

'I'm to blame! After my books succeeded, he felt at a loose end. There he was, nothing achieved, you see. And the brother is a big author.' He smiles, matter-of-fact and mocking.

'Mari didn't tell me about him.'

'Why should he?' he barks. 'Is he a violent animal that we should keep a sign "Beware of Brother"?' I hang my head. It is at this point—something about the way he rushes out his words—that I suddenly realize I've seen him before. No, not that mad meeting day before yesterday, much before that, something from the past. It just crops up, shaking me up.

'His name is Seshan,' he says defiantly, challenging me to dispute that as well.

'Can I see him?'

This pesky publisher. I see it in his eyes. 'He's not here. He's been admitted for a day or two.' Rangachari says it reproachfully, staring at me, two golden pinpoints.

'Okay.' As if accepting defeat, sealing the matter now and forever.

'Now let's get back to my book. How much have you read?'

'Your nephew gave me two chapters.'

'He's got two more.'

'How many chapters have you written?'

'Many more.'

'It would be good if I could see them. To have an idea.'

'You know what I've been through,' Rangachari says. He pushes back the sleeve of his kurta, very much like his brother did yesterday, and studies his arm. 'I'm very careful about publishers.'

'The beginning was striking,' I tell him earnestly. 'I'd

certainly like to read more of it. At least those two chapters.'

'Ask Kittu. He'll courier them to you.'

'I've been trying to contact Mr Krishnamurthy all afternoon.'

'Yes, he's quite busy. Some shop of his own, something like that.' He is silent for a while. 'Coimbatore is a small place, but big in terms of business. Now that he's come into money, he's making good use of it.' There's a dry note in his voice, reaching towards bitterness. Kittu's not going to be in Uncle Rangu's good books for long.

'All thanks to your books.' I smile warmly to lighten his mood.

He shakes his head so that his hair swirls up and settles untidily over his forehead. 'What is your offer anyway? We must talk business.'

'I have a letter typed out for your benefit,' I say, business like. 'You can go through it at your leisure. Everything is given in detail. Percentage, publicity, advance—one thing we believe in is to give you a say in everything. Design, cover, pricing, even typeface. That's an EPA speciality. You can read it, take your time, think about it, maybe even discuss it with your friends.' I give him time to weigh EPA against the crass commercialism of V. George's Guides and Sons and Winsome Publications, and add solemnly, 'It's usually when you're hurried that you tend to make mistakes.' He looks at me and now a new dawn is rising within his eyes. I continue in my gentle professional manner, 'How many pages do you think there'll be?'

He closes his eyes as if he's begun to count. 'I don't know, it's difficult to say. But this one could become very big. Twenty, twenty-seven chapters? 350 pages?' He waves his hand spiritedly. 'It's a very exciting story. Personally for me.' For me too! I fill that pale vacant moment by handing over the pink manila cover which says 'Dr T. Rangachari'. Printed below is EPA's logo in green and the address in black. He accepts it with a cursory glance and shoves it into his kurta pocket.

'In both your books and this one, there's a strong thread of reality running through. So much detail, very familiar events and characters . . . You do take from history, don't you?'

He shifts in his chair. 'Worried about libel, eh? I've never faced that problem.'

I laugh as if that's a joke. 'I meant the literary aspect. How do you manage historical and fictional elements so smoothly?'

'Don't forget, I'm a historian first, that's my background.' He adds acidly, 'I'm the poor historian-turned-rich-novelist.'

Rich? Unless it's all stashed away, windfalls of swindled heritages.

'*Sage of Reason*, for instance. You've said the Mahabharatha inspired you, the epic kind of writing and the flow of characters. What used to happen in the south—that's what you used, isn't it?—during the British times.' I shake my head at his ingenuity. 'I saw perfection there.'

He looks at me through half-closed eyes. 'I don't aim for perfection.'

'Oh, why not?'

'No work is perfect till it's reached the reader.' He's smiling. 'If I want to write the perfect book it, will never leave my hands! You leave it with me long enough and I'll keep perfecting it—and even if a perfect book reaches the reader, it will be of no use to him.'

'Why is that?'

'There should be silences which only he can fill.'

'That's true,' I say mildly.

'He's the final frontier. And then the book is complete, the connection has been made. You see?'

I sit and think of a suitable reply, then give up and decide to get back to my attack. 'You realized you could present history on a fictional platter, combine your expertise with this new interest, using actual settings and characters . . .'

'How do you know they're actual characters?'

'Aren't they?'

'Every writer uses material picked up from experience— whether consciously or whether it just comes in. That's why you people carry your disclaimer at the beginning. No resemblance to anyone living, dead, yet unborn, et cetera, et cetera.'

'How has it been with you?' I edge in casually.

'Both,' he replies, equally casual.

But I'm determined to make something of this visit. 'In *Groping in the Dark*, your Nadar hero. There must be some seed. You couldn't have picked him off the air.'

He smiles, laid back and slightly teasing. 'Why, do you doubt my creative powers?'

'No, no! Just that I can breathe easier if I know—all of us at EPA.'

'What do you want to know?' He folds his arms across his chest, a martyr like Brother yesterday, another victim of siblingering torments.

'We won't go into the others. This work.' I'm on another waybridge now, a delicate balancing act. 'You've described this place, a palace somewhere in central Kerala. I took out a map, I couldn't find the name. Is there really such a place?'

He smiles. Who's conning whom? 'Yes, there is. Take it that there is such a place, and I've changed its name.' He folds one leg over the other, drums on his knees.

I take a deep breath. 'Is there such a family? You say they're close to the Travancore ruling family.'

'What if there is?'

'Well!' My little laugh curls in the air like a cynical lip. 'Here we finally do come into the area of . . . Some pretty interesting scenes you've drawn up in that palace, right in the beginning which means there must be more. How will they react? And if indeed they're so big . . .'

'Yes, yes, they're big all right.'

'So won't they react?'

'I have the greatest respect for that family.'

'On a personal level, but who's to know that? Anyone reading your book will . . .'

'It's not a true story.'

'But if there is such a family . . .'

Rangachari cuts in. 'Listen, there are two ways one does this. You talk of the particular and your story is universalized when the reader gets hold of it. Or you go right ahead and paint the bigger picture in the first place. Either way you don't remain with the particular.'

'I think,' I tell him dryly, 'you may be particularizing a little too much here.'

He's not offended. He simply smiles. 'Who'll know whom I'm talking about?'

'All of Kerala! Everyone will know. Your descriptions are very convincing. Even to me,' I add bitterly.

He removes his spectacles and looks through them, moves them left-right, up-down. 'My admiration for the EPA increases by the minute. Look before you leap. It's a good policy.'

Look, I've already leaped, you petty boozewashy! Now I've no doubt. This is both Rangu *and* Brother. Rangu *is* Brother. With a split personality due to drink, drugs or brain damage. Mr Ink on the brink, fatally plunging into defamatory depths in the fond hope that his victims will remain perpetually silent. How wrong you are, how very wrong!

During my silent deliberations, Tatachari Rangachari carries on. 'There's a definite market for this now, that's what they tell me. Take a slice of history and twist it to suit a mood, use your imagination and retell the story. They feel I could be a pioneer there.' His eyes drill into me, seeking tribute.

'Yes, that's something new.' There's your epitaph, villain—killed pioneering. 'So there's a lot of research involved,' I say, meeting his drilling stonily. 'Going to places and doing all that digging.'

'Yes, very hard work.' He accepts everything as a compliment! 'But definitely worth the trouble. This one will make some noise, I can tell you that. There's this family, and I'm examining how much the past can affect the present.'

'Interesting!'

He frowns, wondering whether I'm good enough to be drawn into his charmed circle. 'Imagine a string stretched till it can no longer be stretched. That's how we trace the path to the past.' He demonstrates with his fingertips. 'String—stretched—taut. The present can bear the weight of the past thus far and no further. When the string snaps, the present is left to evolve its own conditions, it can no longer depend on the past. You follow?' He cocks his head earnestly, sparking off some pale old vision, and I can kick myself for not remembering even now—it's sitting on the edge of my brain, that misty-past-morsel, waiting to jump down triumphantly. 'It happens everywhere, to everyone. Civilizations change and break down when they can no longer bear the weight of the past. Once the string snaps, you sweep away the broken pieces and start afresh. In families, it's the same thing. They carry the burden of the past till they can't cope. Then they break.'

'Like joint and nuclear families?'

'It's a symptom,' he agrees. 'When that happens, when the family splits up into manageable constituents, the smaller units are free to make use of the past as they see fit—in this case, tradition, religion and other rules. To suit their new lifestyle, you follow?'

'This book. You're using it as a sort of . . .'

'You've got it.' He chuckles. 'That's why this will be a major work. I'm taking a family who've tasted the magnitude of history. I'm tracing their journey down to the present. What happened, how have they coped, how close is the string to snapping. It would take longer for such a string to snap because it would be a strong thick twine, maybe even a rope! Such a family has a definite role to play in the making of history, their descendants cannot escape the broad brush of destiny.'

'And what have you found—have they coped?' I keep treading this treacherous path he's fashioned for me.

But he refuses to follow. 'My book is a textbook on history, clothed in fiction for the people.' His voice lowers as if he's hatching a conspiracy. 'Past, present, future—what is the difference? It's just like fencing in your piece of property for identification, nothing more, to put your stamp.'

'In your book, does this family succeed? Does the string snap?'

'The book is nearing completion. You'll know.'

'But you know, don't you?' My voice sounds tense even to my own ears. (I know this man. Unmistakably—from somewhere!) 'What happens to that family? How does it end?'

He eyes me strangely. 'You're very, very interested . . .'

I manage a short laugh. 'You lead us to that so soon, two chapters flat.'

I must slow down, make him reveal more before I'm ready

for the kill. But he waves away all that we've said and jumps up. 'We'll have dinner now.' He looks at his watch, goes to the doorway and shouts for Mari. I can hear Mari's reply: ten minutes. We stand around idly, forced to kill those minutes.

I point to the venue of his creative labours. 'This is where you write.'

'That is where I used to write. Now there's no particular place.'

'Isn't that unusual?'

'I've got myself a laptop.' He smiles, showing his teeth. 'A sign of the times! It makes things much easier. So I keep going from room to room. It's IBM, they say it can do some wonderful things. But if I keep playing with computers, who'll do my writing? Mari?'

Later, as we walk into the dining room, he is talking of how writing leads to publishing, publishing leads to celebrity, celebrity leads to irritable interruptions, interruptions that interfere with writing.

I bend over the washbasin. I wash my face and arms. When I straighten up, I see a framed photograph on the wall, a spidery man with a French beard posing with his wife, both young in an old photograph. I stand frozen, the water dripping from my fingers. 'Who is that in the picture?' I ask. 'Is it you?'

'Yes, yes. You can't recognize, eh? My wife and I. A very long time ago—late '70s?'

But of course! String stretched taut, wire lit on one side causing explosions. History isn't deadwood, it flows! Chari— Rangachari. Goatee, no less, from the party! Turned up like a bad coin. With morsels of my memory.

At breakfast on the morning of his thirty-fifth birthday, they planned a grand evening out.

'I'll be back early,' Gopi said, still in the first grip of the unfolding birthday.

'Tell Panikkar your wife is seriously ill.'

'Shhu! Why invent anything? I'll tell him the truth.'

Lekha shook her head. 'If I know that man, he'll give you overtime as a birthday present.'

'He's not a villain! Everything depends on his mood.'

'How do you know his mood today?'

'We'll hope for the best.'

'We'll go to Marina,' Shobha shouted. She'd carved out nine careful idli pieces with her spoon, surrounding her plate with them. Lekha directed a helpless glance at Gopi.

'Have you forgotten, today is Sridevi chechi's dance.'

'We'll go to Marina,' she said stubbornly.

'Why go so far? There's a beautiful beach right here,' he teased.

'Marina, Marina, Marina!'

Birthdays were meticulously routine. He'd get back early from the press and they'd first go to the Kapaleeswarar temple at Mylapore for the customary birthday blessings. From there to the Marina beach—world's second longest beach, so went the lore. Shobha bought balloons and paper kites and roasted peanuts and rode the garishly painted wooden horses on the portable roundabout, which she loved with an almost maniac attachment. She had a talent for getting herself plastered from head to toe in sand as she constructed creatures of the night, pigtail waving, tongue slipping out like a piece of pink soap. On meeting days, the Seeranai Arangam stage was lit up and the mike whistled experimentally. When the crowd was sufficient, the meeting began. Shobha went silent listening to political parties dishing out promises or evangelists singing out their words of healing. Gopi and Lekha then moved closer to each other as if they were secret lovers, seeking the age-old protection of Marina beach, immortalized in hundreds of movies, novels and legends. After the beach, it was the customary dinner at Aunt Sarada's.

This time things were different. It wasn't even two months after RV uncle's death and there was to be no celebration; 2 March would have passed like any other day but for the fact that his cousin Sridevi's dance and the Doctors Colony Association's Annual Day function were resolutely in the way and couldn't be wished away. Lekha was clearing the table. 'Wear your uniform and be ready,' Gopi told Shobha. 'I'm going down to the temple.'

'I'll come too!'

'No, you can't. You'll be late for school.'

'I want to pray.'

'Not now.'

'Then there won't be school. Ganapathy will make it rain.'

'Go and dress, Shobha,' Lekha said, menacingly.

'It's not fair—school on Saturday!' she growled and ran in.

Gopi said, 'She's right, it's not fair.'

'It's the founder's birthday, that's why she has to go.'

'Today?' He grinned. 'Must be a great man.' He looked at Lekha. 'So what else?'

'You aren't going down?' She wet a sponge and touched it to a lid containing blue powder. Gopi kept standing there. She had the pallu of her sari tightly drawn around her waist and tucked in. Strands of hair hung loose about her face. He thought she looked pale. He remembered Shankar's warning. 'What's the matter?'

'Nothing,' he said.

'Tell me.' She looked up, her eyes so distant from her smile it startled him.

'You must take care,' he fumbled. He went down quickly, leaving her staring after him.

The banyan spread its wrinkled presence. Roots climbed up and down like the shabby braids of ancient sadhus. It was a bower, private and shaded and sacred, offering relief from the elements. It also provided psychological solace, drawing residents to its bosom for fellowship and gossip. Ganapathy had been found fully formed—head, trunk, belly and all—sculpted by the elements from the flesh of the tree. The temple had been built around him, like a picture frame around a real live face.

Iyer sat on one of the three steps, rolling cotton wicks for the oil lamps. The old man gave the work all his attention, bent over and frowning in concentration. His flesh drooped over his body as if it had aged overtime. A large wart balanced on the slope of his shining bald head, a stout antenna ready to receive cosmic signals. A switch of hair dangled behind. The blood-red 'U' on his forehead announced his caste. He didn't hear Gopi approach as he was hard of hearing.

Gopi cleared his throat loudly. 'Aha, Gopi!' He always began as if he were continuing a previous conversation. 'Always so crowded in the morning. Difficult to get Him alone! Not that evenings are better.' He breathed out a whistle like a steam engine ready to leave and smiled benevolently at Gopi.

The plump elephant-headed god was swaddled in crisp white gilt-edged cloth, stretched and secured on either side to nodules on the tree. Ver Ganapathy sported a shrewd look today. Gopi stood with folded hands. 'Let it be a good birthday,' he prayed. He closed his eyes and was confronted by Lekha's face, a drawn damning expression. Oh my God, he thought, I've control over nothing at all!

'He's made me a witness to the changing times. They keep coming with so many reasons—a birthday, examination, some family quarrel, money. He has become a trader, you see, gives blessings with one hand and accepts offerings with the other.' Again the engine made preparations for departure.

'It's my birthday.'

'Don't I know or what. Wait, I'll do the arati for you.' He eased himself up with a loud concentrated wheeze. The large white cloth that he was tearing into strips fell down on the ground. Gopi picked it up, shook it clean and placed it back on the plate. The old man lit camphor on the tray and circled it before the deity. He chanted the several names of the god, and added Gopi's name and birth star as if introducing them to each other. Gopi warmed his palms over the flame and touched them to his face. 'Let Him bless you and your family for generations to come.' Iyer took a pinch of ash from the tray and applied a trickling spot of it on Gopi's forehead. He handed him a tulsi leaf which he deposited behind his ear.

Iyer resumed his seat. The exertion had brought sweat to his forehead and the wart looked redder. 'I keep remembering those days. I was in government service. Briteesh, not what you see nowadays. Our old home in Purasuwakkam—we had a large hall with a swing in the centre where I sat and chewed betel. She shouted from the kitchen and I replied from the hall. The boys were in school.' He sighed. 'Who knows what will happen?'

Gopi looked discreetly at his watch. Shobha was waiting. But he couldn't leave. A low-slung breeze paddled its way through the growing heat. The traffic from the road gathered noisy momentum and Gopi, chained and uncertain, shut his eyes tightly. Time seemed to shrivel. They were startled by a voice almost shouting into their ears.

'Vinayaka! Maha Ganapathy! Ganesha! Why fear when you are here!'

Gopi's eyes flew open. Iyer gasped loudly. Less than six feet away stood a dark bearded old man wrapped in ragged ochre. Every available surface of his pencil-thin body was smeared with ash. Gopi noticed with a deep-down shiver the long fingernails that had curled like pencil shavings. He stood there, a trembling image, revealed like some low miracle of God.

Iyer craned his neck to speak in a loud confidential whisper. 'Look, a wonderful man!' Gopi turned to him in surprise. 'He will tell you the future and all that's happened. He's come after such a long time. He travels up and down the country like this, in his bare feet. You won't believe but he's met all the important people. He has personally known Gandhiji and Nehru and Bharathiyar.' Iyer's whisper turned hoarse with excitement. 'Nobody knows his age. Hundred? Hundred and fifty? Sometimes he goes to the Himalayas and doesn't come down for years, you won't believe . . .'

'No,' said Gopi obligingly. The heat pasted the shirt to his back. He squirmed uneasily. Buses thundered past. Many of the residents on their way to the gate paused before Ganapathy for a hasty obeisance. But they were left untouched, an island of three men and a god.

The old sadhu was lost in his own world. He kept pouring out his declarations in a shrill sing-song, gradually descending a scale to silence. He wore nothing but the briefest loincloth tightened between wrinkled tiny buttocks and a weather-beaten handspun draped over his shoulders. An orange cloth bag was slung around his neck, carrying his worldly possessions. Gopi stared at the precise map of bones and ribs that left little to the imagination. Finally, feeling enough was enough, he nodded at Iyer and turned to go.

The sadhu's song came to a shivery conclusion. He turned squarely on his heels and faced Gopi. Eyes pierced into his, unreachable eyes hooded by straggling eyebrows. Gopi stood where he was, half-turned, like a frog mesmerized by a snake. Iyer hovered awkwardly somewhere in the background. Without bothering to ask his permission, the sadhu reached out, grabbed his hand and laid it out on a rough sandpapery palm. He brought it close to his eyes and peered fiercely. Gopi stood trembling. A loud exclamation. Gopi flinched. Was it a cry of horror or happiness? The face betrayed nothing beneath all that hair. The eyes withdrew even further. Iyer seemed impressed. 'Ayya, what do you see?' he called out, bent forward like a devotee seeking salvation. The sadhu remained silent, engrossed in Gopi's hand. Iyer's enthusiasm mounted. 'He hails from a great and noble family of Kerala.'

The dark old man stood indifferent to Iyer and Gopi. In that moment rendered endlessly static, only the hand seemed to matter. He gave it a final authoritative press and looked deep into Gopi's eyes. At last he spoke. 'Pray to Ganapathy. He is the Beginning.' He coughed and gave an impatient jerk of his head, cleared his throat and said, 'From here you will begin your journey.'

'What journey?' Gopi wondered if he saw travel prospects. From the corner of his eye, he noticed Iyer standing and scratching his vast belly, deaf and satisfied.

The old man ignored the question. 'You have come from beyond Time, you may have to return one day. Nothing will stop you, not even your family, not even your employer, not even the government. You will become a big man. You will break all the rules. You will repent. Because you have to come back to the Beginning.' The man stood lost in thought. He dropped Gopi's hand casually like a used tissue, and uttered a shrill sound from deep within his throat. It sounded like a brief cackle. 'In the end,' he said, 'you will come back to the Beginning.'

Gopi darted a glance at Iyer who was smiling, pleased with whatever prediction those Himalayan lips had uttered. He didn't know what to do, to retreat abruptly or to acknowledge the sadhu's message in some manner.

It seemed churlish to let him think he cared nothing for his comments. He felt in his shirt pocket. Three one-rupee coins emerged. As he held out the coins, he had a moment of apprehension. Would the old man turn indignant, 'What's this! What do you think of me? Do you know how much Gandhi and Nehru used to give me?' Or 'I'm a man of God, never touch money.' But the sadhu accepted the coins without emotion. He scratched his wrinkled buttocks diligently with pencil-shaving nails and turned back to the temple. No one else existed any more. Gopi glanced swiftly at Iyer and walked away.

PAST-ANTS

━━━━━━━━━━━━━━━━━━■━━━━━━━━━━━━━━━━━━

7 March 1998

A tourist taxi speeds me again through the besotted streets of Chennai to Rangachari's house.

Nagarajan had wanted to accompany me. 'Perhaps I can come along. Some local help you might need.' He's fascinated by the constantly changing Rangachari, weepy and soft one day, tough and businesslike the next. A sinister servant and a tantalizing twin on the horizon are intriguing.

'No problem, I can manage,' I tell him resolutely. EPA's not the point now, it's Kilikkara. I don't want some publishing minion to discover the truth behind my visit. I put him off, citing the author's bad temper. 'I can handle him,' I tell him. 'But you . . .' I pause ominously.

After a long moment's silence, he says: 'Appadiya?'

When I had woke up this morning in my room in Maharani International, I realized it was already becoming familiar, part of my life. Lekha's call had woken me. I hadn't called her since coming in. It's already been four days and that's unusual. But this city is an old wound that's not yet stopped suppurating. She asked about the journey, Rangachari, what sort of fellow he is, is the hotel comfortable, are things going according to schedule, when will I be back. She doesn't know what I know. She's long stopped ghost-reading manuscripts for me, especially since EPA's earlier diet of non-fiction never cut much ice with her. So she doesn't know the gory details of Rangachari's latest saga, just that it's still historical and I'm impressed. I told her I'll be here at least a couple of days more. I asked about Shobha. There's been a letter from her, there are two holidays next month, she'll stretch that to the weekend and come over. That's great news, I told her, we haven't seen her for more than a month now.

When I hung up, there was an emptiness she'd left me with. As strong within as it was outside, a turbulanguid vortex. To counter it, I fiddled around with those bedside knobs for music-while-you-worry. I settled for an old Tamil film song, T.M. Soundararajan's *'Ponaal Pogattum Poda'*—if they go, let them go. It's a song about death, a ballad of consoling rationalization by the super-poet Kannadasan. If it goes, let it go.

How easy that sounds. Good enough for philosophers and poets. And historians. Gloss the past. Monumentalize it, preserve it, rub it with its own ashes till it shines. Talk it out of shape. But keep going! They're all talking death. What about life? What about the live past, the still-smouldering string stretching between Then and Now, refusing to burn out?

Last night's been a bit of a this-that. First the pre-prandial revelation that Chari, grown bigger, is Rangachari. I hardly utter a word once I realize who he is. I'm going to confront him, I will, I keep telling myself. Let Kilikkara alone, for the sake of your old friend RV. It was he who kept talking. The minutes slipped through an hourglass of futility—yes I will, right now, after he's finished his next sentence, right now, right after this one—and he keeps talking, and finally the meal is over, we make some more small talk, and I'm out of the house. What else can I expect of myself? Wait, wait till a sign of fate. I haven't managed to give Them the slip, not after thirty years, my friendly gallery of judges—is this right, is this enough, is this decent? Is this acceptable? I'll wait till kingdom come.

They have this joke about the Lucknow coachmen famed for their excessive politeness. They tell each other *'pehle aap, pehle aap'*—you first, you first—each gallantly permitting the other to take out his carriage first. Till finally the prospective passenger is bored to tears and decides to take a walk instead. An extension of this is the pregnantly exhausted Lucknavi woman pushing for all she's worth, well past her due date, till the midwife realizes there are twins in there, telling each other, you first.

That's me and Fate—you-firsting each other till, of course, it's I who win each time and poor Fate has to make the first move. Yesterday, I watched dumbly as Rangachari went through his historical theories, his formulas, then went into a tempestuous fit of self-glorification, and when I emerged from it in a wringery daze, I was already out of his ambit.

The car whizzes over the flyover, a rainbow of remembrance. Below me are the shopping complexes sprouted from the dead dreams of the famous Gemini film studios. The grey American Embassy with its sordid queues of hopeful emigrants and students—flanked by relatives, friends and vendors—all waiting patiently in the sun as air-conditioned officials sift through their destinies. And, of course, the giant hoardings of giant movie stars caught in giant moments.

The next stretch is six-laned with a semblance of order. During my days, it needed a miracle to survive the traffic, and every bus driver was like the magician John Calvert who'd driven through these roads blindfolded. My taxi doesn't recognize the sanctity of lanes. It is a bus one moment, an auto-rickshaw the next, before recovering its identity. A bus now pretends it's a scooter and weaves between lanes, leaving everyone in a daze. Including my driver who looks pale after a miraculous escape and accepts defeat for the moment.

My heart returns from my mouth. I sit back and try to relax. I'm scared to begin a conversation with the driver lest his already casual driving skills become even more unfocussed.

We pass the grave of New Elphinstone, which had charged only its human clientele, offering large-hearted hospitality to movie-going birds, squirrels and rats in equal measure. It assured us of our weekly diet of Malayalam movies, but is now dead and gone. The Madras Gymkhana Club, still remembering the Raj behind a host of welcoming labour union placards. My driver now surges ahead in a burst of acceleration down the relatively uncluttered road past Dorai-on-his-Kudirai—Munroe sitting stonily on his horse. (Madras being a city of statues, even when it's prospering it's going bust!)

He takes a sharp left, squealing past red before the cop can even blink. I keep looking pointedly out of the window. The violation gives him more reason to speed, and he takes the next lights with ease, colour-blind and nervous. We zoom past Burma Bazaar, rows of shops selling smuggled and non-smuggled, spurious and non-spurious goodies where faintly guilty-looking men saunter past lazy shopkeepers with gimlet eyes.

My destination. I leave the car at a safe distance and walk. Everything is in place: shops, trucks, gutter, carts, dogs, cows, urchins. The friendly vendor is still arranging Coke bottles. I hurry past his box-shop and climb the steps to Rangachari's house. Mari frowns. More puzzled than irritated, though. He shakes his head. 'Saar is not here.' He is friendlier now that I've eaten in the house.

'How long will he be?'

'Don't know. Some meeting I think he's gone to.'

'Seshan's there?' He doesn't seem to understand. 'Mr Seshan, his brother?'

Mari frowns, more irritated than puzzled. He sidesteps the question. 'You'll be waiting?'

'No. Just tell him I was here.'

It is dusk and lights are coming on. I stop at the box-shop and buy a cigarette. The vendor gives me a friendly smile, but surprisingly holds his tongue. I don't linger. As I turn the corner from one side of a large bank building to another, stepping down where the pavement is broken, I feel a hand on my shoulder.

It is Rangachari. He looks tattered and tired. (Or is it?) He gives me a slow uncertain smile and jerks back his hand. No, it's not!

I smile. 'I was in your house. I wanted to meet you.' We stand amidst brooding shadows and stealthy voices. I take a deep breath of smoke, watching the pale streaks in the air. He stares at the smoke as though this too is a marvel from me, like the visiting card. Then he reaches out and plucks out my cigarette and flicks it away right across the road. The protest rises sharply. 'What—!'

He doesn't even notice. 'There are things I have to tell you.'

'About your books?' I ask, playing out my irritation.

'You read the book?'

'Which one?' I parry, standing in the middle of so much street activity with this tremulous twin, wanting to leave him and get into the car and get back to the hotel. He waves an impatient hand. I take a deep breath and ask politely, 'Yes, Mr Seshan?'

He looks at me strangely. 'This book. Don't play with history! It's not a game.'

'I know that.'

'I don't know who you are, but you're interested in the book. It will destroy . . .'

'What are you talking about?'

'Have you read the book?'

'No.'

'Save yourself while you can.' The yellow streetlight adds a sting to his expression. My heart starts to beat with an unknown fear. One hand descends to mine and clutches my wrist. I can see the snaky veins running up and down. 'Your history is being written.'

'I know that,' I tell him dryly.

'Stop it while you can.' A dog saunters up and sniffs investigatively at his feet. He kicks out and it retreats with a howl. I stare at him in disgust. His eyes have a ferocious expression. 'Don't accept everything—don't think you're being generous.'

'What do you want me to do?'

'Remember what I told you?' His eyes bore into me. 'Don't end up as a martyr!'

My patience snaps. 'It'll be easier if I know what the hell that means!'

He sags, upset by the tone of my voice. 'I've told you. That's all. Here.' He deposits something heavy in my hand. 'That's all.' He turns and walks away.

It is a cellophane-wrapped parcel inside a plastic cover, a hardbound book as big as a register or an album. The plastic cover shows a woman wearing nothing but a brassiere and a smile—a colourful legend says she wears only Kumar's Best Bras.

There are ten more chapters here. I return to my hotel room, order some food and begin to read.

It's like that time in Greenacres, more than thirty years ago. I was reading a comic. We didn't get comics in Kilikkara, so I devoured them during vacations. This one was about giant ants that colonized the earth, creeping in from some unprotected hole in the universe, taking over our kitchens and our offices and our schools and our lives, antagonizing us.

I was pale as I read. My head was chockful of large exploratory ants. My cousin Uma happened to pass that way and playfully crawled her fingers up my shoulder. I screamed. How I screamed! She was more frightened than me. She just stood there, frozen, watching me address the heavens.

As I read the ten chapters, the past creeps up my shoulder like some giant alien ant. Every now and then I gaze back fearfully towards a ghost-rising horizon. I admit I'm foxed. Even Goatee couldn't have casually gathered up all this in the course of a good day's work. Even if he has access to all the diaries, notebooks, textbooks and reminiscences of Kilikkara, there are still things which could be accessed only from intimate family disclosures. Even I haven't heard half the things.

I can de-chaff the grist, much of it is true history—bits I've heard, bits he's taken pains to trace and enlarge upon. Other things are atrocious. Each touch of pinched history is to be touched with a pinch of salt. I read with burning eyes what he has to say about the birth of my grandmother. The cheek!

The absolutely self-assured blasphemous cheek of it has me shaking my head in terrible merriment. I grimace, stung by past-ants.

Blasphemy isn't the word—this master of memorabbleia is placing a respectable family on the line to appease a blue-bloodthirsty world, hawking false memoirs to a trusting world.

To think he'll have the world believe that an entire family—aunts, uncles, even my own great-grandmother—laboured in unholy lust to grab possession of a diamond necklace! He mentions a curse on our family and three relationships with a neighbouring Brahmin house. He's talking about Kunnupuram, of course. But *three*?

Equally heavy on my mind is the memory of Seshan's face as he handed over this lot. Is there some sort of intrigue between the brothers? Does Rangachari know I've got these pages? He's crazy and he'll drive me crazy. He—they. Whoever!

I shake off these thoughts and continue to read.

TRACING THE TREE

∎

Kilikkara Appan founded the family.

No one else dared to take credit. The Kilikkara family members are devoted subjects of their lord and founder, the Eternal Patriarch who has His abode in the temple by the river. The eldest woman becomes the Matriarch, but the eldest male can only be Second Patriarch. So Kilikkara Appan rightfully gets one full share of the family's common properties. He is Krishna, incarnation of Vishnu—small boy ruling the universe.

Kerala comprised of the states of Travancore, Cochin and Malabar. Ravi Varma II ruled Travancore between 1478 and 1503 A.D. (653-678 Malabar Era). Towards the end of his reign, he travelled north to strengthen his kingdom.

There were several small chieftains who raised temporary armies and held on to their lands, sometimes extending them arbitrarily, leading to local skirmishes. This had become an interesting hobby. More than two hundred years before the British began their formal transition from trade to domination in Kerala, these small rulers had only a consciousness of an overlord. They were free to go about their daily business of agriculture, trade and petty quarrels without undue interference. All these chieftains owed ultimate allegiance to Travancore.

The king felt it necessary to make appropriate gestures of suzerainty once in a while. Hence Ravi Varma's tour of the kingdom. On his journey back home, he stopped and set up camp near a river in central Kerala. Soldiers and horses rested. During the night, the sky quickly changed from warm umbrella to biting deluge. Man and beast ran helter-skelter, unable to withstand the monstrous onslaught. Tents and belongings, including newly acquired gifts from small rulers, sailed away like orphaned boats. Mud churned, river rose. Soon there were bodies floating all around. Nature proved more ruthless than any army the men had ever encountered.

Ravi Varma was fortunate to grab hold of a log of wood stuck in the mud. But the river was in spate; he knew he didn't have much time. He shut his eyes and prayed. He had a vision then: Lord Vishnu appeared before him in all His glory, protector of the universe, a calm resplendence amidst the shrieking storm. The king, He said, would be saved along with his finest men and enough horses. In return, Ravi Varma should establish a temple for Him in the form of the youthful Krishna near the river bank. He should also send the most trusted and bravest member of his family to guard and maintain the temple on His behalf. Even before Ravi Varma could digest the message, the rescue began. Some chieftains, realizing the plight of their king, came with men to help them. The sky cleared miraculously. The river took a deep breath and settled down.

In the morning, another surprise. The king, walking with his men and some locals to assess the damage caused by the storm, came upon two idols. They were almost completely buried in the wet river sand. One was a large bird, probably Garuda, the vehicle of Lord Vishnu. Protected by the mighty wings of the bird was a small idol of a young and adorable Krishna.

Ravi Varma was delighted. He had an oracle brought in immediately. The oracle said a temple should be built on that very site. Since the Lord was found protected by a bird, the place should be called Kilikkara, coast of the bird. The statue of the bird should be placed in front of the entrance to the temple. Ravi Varma didn't lose time. He not only made arrangements for the temple to be constructed and the idol consecrated, he also ordered his most loyal counsellor to stay back and look after the temple. This was a handsome young cousin named Aditya Varma, who was celebrated for his skill in weaponry, his wit and intellect. The king negotiated with local chieftains and presented Aditya Varma with the surrounding land. To be held in trust for the actual ruler, Kilikkara Appan, the First Patriarch.

Aditya Varma, like his namesake the sun, shone on the virgin land. Along with his immediate family and the cream of the nearby village of Iramapuram—who went on to become the inhabitants of Kilikkara village and the personal attendants of the family—Aditya Varma settled down there and began his rule.

But all was not well. The sun grew pale, the land drooped. Agriculture failed. Trade did not pick up. When it was time for taxes to be paid, Kilikkara had no money.

Land tax is an important revenue for kingdoms that survive on agriculture. Each family head plots out his own bit of land which becomes his taravad or family home. He tills the land, lives and begets children and dies on that plot. His ashes are inextricably mixed with the soil. Unlike other kingdoms, Travancore had very early fixed an unassailable method of collecting taxes. The usual practice had been to farm out land revenue to the highest bidders; the government entrusted the job of collecting tax to them, not wanting to squint at every drop that came in. But this middlemanship spawned a great deal of injustice and corruption. The Travancore system, ushered in through a royal writ, was more effective. Government dues were fixed exactly and unalterably every year, every harvest. During droughts and floods, this was allowed to drop to one-fifth of the normal rate; more fortunate villages then paid more, to compensate.

But with no drought, flood or any other excuse, Kilikkara was still in the red. It escaped censure, being a fledgeling economy; and also because the king had a soft corner for the province. But this couldn't continue, especially after Ravi Varma's time. Sri Marthanda Varma and Sri Vira Ravi Varma followed him in quick succession. Kilikkara's fate remained unchanged.

In addition to this, it appeared that the family had run itself out. Aditya Varma's younger sister was a childless widow who showed no interest in remarriage. She turned to religion instead, caressing prayer beads and singing lullabies to her god. The other sisters were far too old. His nieces, who sportingly supported the cause, turned out to be barren. There was talk in the capital that the king might order an adoption, forcing an heir of his own choice upon Kilikkara. Vexed at this deterioration, Aditya Varma had an oracle brought to the temple. The oracle drew his chart and threw his cowrie shells and studied the signs. He then looked up and smiled. 'You have not kept your promise,' he said.

Aditya Varma, like his namesake, was capable of smiling or burning. He felt an off-with-his head rage coming on. He controlled himself and said, 'That's impossible.' Throughout the kingdom, his word was considered sacred. How dare this man . . . But an oracle's words are the words of God.

The oracle continued, 'His highness, ponnu thampuran, the most exalted ruler of our kingdom, when he was suffering in some manner, promised the Lord he would instal His idol in a temple and establish a royal family member as His representative to rule this province.'

'True. And I am that representative. And his highness himself saw the idol consecrated.'

'Yes, my lord, but there is the spirit of the word . . .'

'What's that?' Aditya Varma snapped.

'The Lord Himself—Kilikkara Appan—is the head of the family. You are merely His representative!'

Of course. Aditya Varma understood at once. He abdicated in favour of the Lord. The story goes that his younger niece was the first to conceive. Her son, Rama Varma, succeeded Aditya Varma, who lived to a ripe old age solely to egg on the family line.

By the next season, harvest was plentiful. It is written that trade links were soon established with Madurai and also some provinces in northern India, taking Kilikkara on the road to further prosperity. This happened more than five centuries ago. Kilikkara is among the oldest fiefdoms of Travancore.

And three hundred years after the line began, the title 'Raja' was conferred upon the Kilikkara chiefs. Titles, unlike today, were earned and shone like jewels. A long list of titles reflected the worth of a nobleman. But the title 'Raja' was even more important, it was hereditary—hard-earned, but forever. (In extreme cases, the displeasure of the king could lead to forfeiture of the title; there were also rare instances of the title going to some worthy thampuran besides the chief, as in the case of the poet MVR.) The king during that time was Rama Varma II (1758-98), also known as Dharma Raja. He was pleased with the support and prowess of the Kilikkara noblemen, and Valiya Marthanda Varma (1770-92) became the first Raja of Kilikkara.

The history of Travancore has been written by several people. Later records of the British read like diaries—they are mostly events built up through revenue-related, social and political reportage.

In Kilikkara, there isn't much available by way of written records. Some dusty palm-leaf manuscripts discovered during the scramblings of the first family partition contain nothing more than extracts of scriptures, copied from ancient texts; together with medical prescriptions and jottings. Everything printed refers to later periods, glossing over the origins. There is a rich tradition of folklore though, tales passed on from mother to child. The most popular story is the one about the founding.

There are thus large gaps in the history of Kilikkara, for instance, after Rama Varma who succeeded Aditya Varma, no one is sure about the Patriarchs who followed. It's as if Time paused, took a deep breath and resumed only centuries later. Some people, historians and hangers-on as well as members themselves, have attempted to draw up family trees. But the trees are stunted, varying according to these gardeners' arsenal of seeds. They reach an agreement only from the late eighteenth century onwards.

In 1859, when the poet Marthanda Varma Raja was

born. The lifespans of Kilikkara members in those days were much shorter. MVR died before he turned fifty, admittedly a bizzare and drawn-out death. His sister, Uma Amba, was only forty-three when she died. And Pooram, who received a diamond necklace from the Matriarch for magically producing a female heir amidst Kilikkara's malestorm, had the shortest lifespan. She lived a rich eventful life of only thirty-five years. Her daughter Thriketta Tirunal probably lived the longest among her generation; she died at the ripe old age of sixty. Without polluted air, adulterated food, stress or casual violence—living, in fact, in extremely protected conditions—these people tired of life much earlier than today.

Or because they'd nothing extra to look forward to? One needs a reason to live. Life leads one on with a carrot. Enticing, goading, provoking. If one had already eaten up one's carrot, one stopped. Maybe that's what happened in Kilikkara. They'd seen as much of life as they hoped to, they knew life had no more waiting surprises. So they just stopped.

But then some people also believe it's the Curse that was responsible for the early deaths and frequent family quarrels. At the end of the eighteenth century, shortly after the reign of Valiya Marthanda Varma Raja, there occured an event that shouldn't have occured.

Not far from Kilikkara is the illam of Kunnupuram namboodiris, a prosperous and accomplished priestly family. The family heads were renowned all over Kerala for their wisdom and vast learning. They were not only proficient in the scriptures, but also in science, mathematics, architecture, medicine and the arts, having stirred and drunk of knowledge in long draughts.

There was a theory that their prosperity derived from a Chakram they had in their possession. The Chakram had been crafted and sanctified by a powerful Kunnupuram namboodiri famed to have seen God. Kilikkara and Kunnupuram had traditionally enjoyed a long friendship. The Kunnupuram head was sent for with palanquins, gifts and twenty attendants each time a ceremony was held in the Palace. And Kunnupuram was one of the two illams that provided ritualists for their religious ceremonies.

In spite of this friendship, the head of Kilikkara summoned the Kunnupuram patriarch and demanded that he hand over the Chakram to him. Obviously he was high on power and low on understanding, since it is common knowledge that it's dangerous to toy with sanctified materials like that and that the powers of a Chakram cannot be transferred. The Kunnupuram patriarch refused. It isn't nice to speculate about events that occured so many years ago. Especially when there are sensitive issues involved. However, legend agrees on the following points:

That very week, the Chakram disappeared from Kunnupuram. The house was broken into and there was damage done to property. The patriarch's brother lost his life in an apparent attack. The patriarch was a powerful ritualist. He believed—going by the sequence of events and possibly an oracular consultation—that the Palace was behind the whole thing. He cursed the house and family and said they would suffer for generations. Shortly after this the Kilikkara head announced that he was having a special Chakram made to ensure the prosperity of his family. Some unheard-of namboodiri from the far north was said to be its creator. The 'new' Chakram was buried near the Devi sanctum of the Kilikkara Appan temple.

It's not nice to speculate, but the relationship between the two families did deteriorate after that.

THE STORM

∎

Excerpts from the diary of MVR:

Monday, 3 March 1884—22 Kumbham 1059 (Malabar Era)

Wrote to the India Office, London, for Prof. Monier Williams'
English-Sanskrit dictionary. Received books and memo from
Messrs. Higginbothams. Even the books, including pamphlets
of the Education Commission and a novel, could not raise my
spirits. C.H. Subramanyayyar's telegram arrived. He has been
delayed and can be expected back only in the third week.
Work on *Mohini* is thus being made to stretch on. Received
a kind letter from H.H. the Prince who has now returned to
Trivandrum after his tour. He has enquired about the progress
of *Mohini*. He suggests calling it *Mohini Vilapam*, which can
be translated as *Lament of Mohini*. I will ask Subramanyayyar's
opinion.

Played on the veena for a while. The noon was so hot that
I sat in the Palace Library reading. Dozed off for a while and

Thampan was worried about my health. Played a little tenniquoit with nephews to keep up their spirits. The heat is worse than the previous years. Got myself shaved today mainly for the reason that there is little else to do now.

Went to Kilikkara Appan and Manjoor Devi temples with Wife. Her niece Kochootti, who has arrived from Aripattu, accompanied us. Met Vasudevan Namboodiri at Manjoor Devi. He has asked me to go to Kunnupuram Illam for a Katha next week. The format is to be that of a dance drama which the players are experimenting with. They are anxious to know my opinion of this new format. Since I have time on my hands till C.H.'s arrival, I agreed.

Was with Wife in the evening before returning to the Red Room for work on *Mohini*. She was irritable and complained of my lagging attention. I explained how badly the work was going. And now C.H's delay, so the Sanskrit translations will take time. Her only comment was, 'Pick up from Life.' My Wife thinks I am unnatural in my work, she finds a lot of artificiality. Since I value her advice, I held my tongue.

Tuesday, 4 March 1884—23 Kumbham 1059 (Malabar Era)

It has been a good day. Bathed in the river and prayed at Kilikkara Appan temple. Played veena along with my Darling. She seems contrite for whatever she said yesterday. Went to the temples together for the evening prayers. A goldsmith came from Madura today and she inspected some jewellery along with her niece Kochootti. Purchased a necklace in gold with emeralds for her to her delight, and also gave Kochootti a pair of earstuds. Also a pair of smaller plain diamond earstuds for self. Instructed Thampan to write the accounts and show it to Great-Aunt before sending it to the Palace office.

She was happy and showed her happiness in a number of delightful ways. Later in the afternoon, found Uncle Ravi Varma in the Palace Library. Spoke to him about my work. He feels my Darling is right. He said I should aim for passion from Life. He said all great Literature mirrored Life. I joked that I would be straying from the Right path were I to look for passion now. Was in a good mood the whole of today, probably because of my Darling. Uncle Ravi Varma said I should be grateful to her for staying in Kilikkara against the established custom. Under normal circumstances I would have had to reside in Aripattu and come here occasionally to worship at the temple! Stayed on in the Library after he left and tried to pen some verse to keep my mind off *Mohini*. Was not entirely happy with the outcome.

The Drama at Kunnupuram Illam next week will probably be a useful diversion.

One evening, 6 March 1884, when his wife has her period and is confined to the dark room on the ground floor, MVR goes to watch the celebrations that will commence the festival season from one of the Eastern Palace buildings.

The house has upstairs rooms where, in the earlier days, women of the family used to spend the night with their menfolk. During the day, the women and men stayed in separate buildings. Some of the rooms, now empty, have been cleaned up for today. He climbs the stairs, and reaches the second floor window from where he will have a grand view of the elephants and the procession and the villagers flocking in. His wife's niece Kochootti has accompanied him. She is young and full of wonder at everything here.

'This is just like our tower room at home,' she tells him. 'You have to climb about thirty steps, all winding and narrow, and there are pigeons on the way. On top is a small room. When I was little, I used to go and sit there. No one knew where I was, but I could see everything!'

He smiles at her. 'That's what we're going to do now. Watch everyone enjoying themselves without being seen.'

The others are in another room down the narrow corridor. Kochootti runs straight to them, talking nineteen to the dozen as usual. MVR stands alone in a room, hands on his hips, like a king watching a display. Kochootti runs back to him. 'On chittappa, I think I'll watch from here. With you.'

He smiles at her enthusiasm. The gold jewel he bought her shines on her ear. 'Your aunt is missing everything,' he tells her.

She nods. 'I'll give her a long description. She told me to!'

An enormous old tree sways its branches just outside the window, blocking some of the view. Sunlight filters in through its leaves, so that the room's darkness is covered with a thin gauze of light. When the tree sways, it is as if they're in a ship, gently undulating. They watch silently for a while. His attention is gradually distracted from the elephants being brought in. Moving along the breadth of the window to keep sight of the first rows of the procession, Kochootti is suddenly pressed close to him. He breathes in the fragrance of her hair. He closes his eyes, thralled in that pool of scent. He opens his eyes and stares in surprise at her young body, her laughing gaze, as if he's seeing her for the first time. She turns to point out something. Her buttocks press against his thigh. Desire rises even as he hears the warning of his heart.

She says something, he isn't listening. Her voice is magnified as though she is whispering warmly into his ear. He catches her roughly by her bare shoulders. Her eyes look up in large wonder, mistaking his fire for anger. His hand moves up to the cool flesh of her breast. It is small, and reacts immediately. 'Kochootti!' he says.

Her eyes cloud. 'Chittappa,' she breathes, moving back.

He pulls her back to him and kisses her on the lips. 'Cheriyamma will be . . .' she reminds.

'There's no one but us,' he breathes.

He runs his hand over her awakening body.

The rain came like horses thundering across a plain.

Beating down trees and rooftops and mud. Leaves and eaves dripped in joy. From every one of the palaces, near-naked boys and girls ran out, shrieking with laughter and excitement, splattering golden mud, battering back the water with their little fists, ignoring dire warnings. Lightning snarled open the sky followed by a roll of thunder. Old buildings creaked in alarm. Servants ran about closing windows, gathering washing, retrieving naughty wet little thampurans. A wild wind rose from the river and whistled through the massive gabled houses. Large leafy trees staggered under the weight of the sky. Frogs sang, sinking into shocked silence as the onslaught roughened.

Like a line of ants, workmen moved between granary and house, bent under sacks of grain, damming columns of water that shattered to shards on their dark backs. An impatient manager under a spreading straw umbrella supervised them. As a young maid rushed out to bring in a forgotten yellow rug, some of the workmen stopped in their tracks and stared, mesmerized by her breathless laughter, straggling hair and bare wet breasts. 'Come on, come on!' shouted their manager, irritably rupturing their reverie. One of the workmen muttered things he'd like to do to her, and they all laughed. The manager frowned and waved them on.

In the evening when the rain thinned a bit, some of the ladies walked to the temple, clutching their mundus high. The temple conch blared out in long grave tones and the bell rang clear, the edakka sounded its mournful tattoo, undisturbed by the storm.

In the river, large waves rose. The boats were grounded. A deputation of villagers came and stood before the Second Patriarch, respectfully covering their mouths with their fingers. A couple of houses had been swept away by the wind, water had entered others. Could the school buildings be used till the storm subsided? Madras uncle hesitated and thought deeply. He was thus named because he was the only known person in Kilikkara history who'd been to Madras and back. Finally, watching the stray streaks of water dripping down their faces, he said, 'Yes, I suppose we'll have to do that.' He added generously, 'I'll come there when I can. Just to see them and give them some courage.'

'That's very gracious.'

'And perhaps we can give something. Some grains, some provisions. I'll talk to the temple officer.'

'Thampuran is too kind.' They bowed low, with folded hands.

The Palace always took up the villagers' cause during natural calamities or accidents. Both Kilikkara and Iramapuram villages survived under the immediate guardianship of the Palace. But Madras uncle had his ways. Every decision was weighed, every move contemplated. And whenever he was gracious or kind, it was seen as a personal gesture, a favour bestowed. He had the knack of turning duty into bounty.

During the next few days the rain showed no sign of letting up. When it seemed they were headed for a flood, an oracle was summoned to Big Palace. He had sandal paste streaks on his forehead, chest and arms, and a large red kumkum spot on his forehead. Gold chains and pendants hung around his neck, his ears spread under emerald studs. He carried his importance about him like one more pendant. He walked with a slightly swaying motion, front-to-back, and his head kept shaking, left-to-right. His gait suggested that the goddess was intermittently within him; and his eyes glowed as though she gazed out of them. A select group of ten thampurans were invited to witness the event.

The oracle said he didn't like the portents. It seemed there was to be a repetition of the First Storm—the fateful fury that had led to the founding of Kilikkara four hundred years ago. The gods were replaying their game to keep that memory alive. There seemed to be a message in it. Somewhere. He closed his eyes, held his cowrie shells reverentially to his chest and threw them. He studied their position as they fell on the small astrological chart he'd drawn on the floor. He picked them up and repeated the actions. He shook his head. 'Not reaching anywhere,' he said grimly.

'Who's not?' Madras uncle asked.

'I'm not.' His eyeballs disappeared behind their lids. 'There's a lot of years in four hundred years.'

'That's true.'

'There's more depth,' continued the oracle strongly, 'in a clear stream.' Madras uncle nodded. But his eyes returned to the ground, and the others saw a puzzled frown gather. Finally, someone asked if they should do some pariharam— atonement in whatever manner for whatever sin or sins had been committed by whoever was responsible for whatever the gods were thinking up to punish the family. 'Yes, we should certainly look into that. If we can find out why this is happening.'

'Why this is happening!' cried a young thampuran in a tone that reflected his impatience. 'It must be raining from Trivandrum to Kochi. Should everyone in the land be asked to atone?'

The oracle turned to the young man and smiled his sympathy. Madras uncle glanced coldly at the heretic, silencing him. The oracle then said firmly, 'There is a curse.'

'Curse?' Madras uncle's jaw fell.

'Curse,' the heretic said, his lip curling.

'Curse!' all the other thampurans whispered, shocked.

'Yesss!' hissed the oracle. He looked whitely at each face in turn, like a doctor revealing they all had terminal diseases. The rain had started again, spraying them icily. Thunder roared.

'Who has cursed us?'

'What did we do?'

'It's impossible.'

'Curse!' repeated the heretic, derisively.

'I'm afraid we can say nothing at this moment,' the oracle said. 'Here, I'm afraid,' he smiled sympathetically, 'in this family, the stream is not so clear!'

'What do you mean?' Madras uncle said spiritedly.

The oracle was meaningfully silent. Another thampuran, a fat young gentleman named Kochu Kelu from Northern Palace, said, 'What can we do if this is such a mystery? At least give us a hint.'

'I would if I knew,' the oracle replied. He fingered one of his pendants, lost in thought. 'It is something to do with the temple. That's what I see. The gods are not happy.'

'Why would the gods not be happy? Which temple?'

'Your family temple.' The oracle shut his eyes and swayed gently to the rhythm of the rain. 'I see it has something to with *Brahma hathya* . . .'

There was a shocked murmur in the assemblage. Murder of a Brahmin! Here, in Kilikkara? By whom? No one had heard of such a thing! Kilikkara was a fiefdom that had gathered a history of dignity, valour and enlightenment. There was no question of such a horrible thing happening.

'I have seen the signs.' The oracle spoke slowly, deliberately, so that every word was understood. 'Something is wrong somewhere. It has to do with the past. It has to do with the temple. I see signs of *Brahma hathya*. It's unmistakable. I'm only sorry that I'm unable to elaborate further.'

After the oracle had left, there was agitated discussion. Madras uncle sat back in his easy chair, fingers pressed thoughtfully together, eyes closed. He was listening intently to the conversation. The ten thampurans—uncles, nephews, brothers and in-laws—sat in chairs, on the parapet, and on a mat on the floor. They helped themselves occasionally to handfuls of puffed rice from a couple of vessels on the centre table. They all seemed put out by the accusation of Brahmin-killing. They all agreed the information should remain a secret until they were sure. The cheerless deafening atmosphere only heightened their disquiet.

As they spoke—dissecting and wondering, pondering awhile on the known consequences of killing a Brahmin, of how much suffering they could expect, why hadn't anyone told them this before—a subtle yet distinct breach could be observed. Though no one actually shifted, though the arguments and dissensions ran dispassionately through all of them, the in-laws moved away in spirit, distancing themselves from the members, like drops of oil asserting their identity in troubled waters. 'At least we're not involved, we're safe!' was their unspoken sentiment, disregarding the fact that their wives and children were indeed involved. (Because in a matrilineal family, the male is more responsible for his nephews and nieces; his own children belong to a different family.)

Some of them feigned disinterest or nonchalance. They chewed violently on their paan and spat noisily into a spittoon. One of them cracked a loud namboodiri joke, so improper they would have laughed at any other time. Another rose an inch from the ground and broke wind, bubbling sonorously and paling away against the gush of nature's mightier effort. Madras uncle went to sleep—and snored gently through his family's camouflaged agitation.

It was at this point that the door opened and MVR walked in. The rain had got him despite his umbrella. He had been poring over references, letters and sheets of notes in the library in a frustrated attempt at keeping himself busy. Mohini isn't ever going to see the light of day, he told himself as he walked out finally into the rain. She's deserted me, he said loudly, his words scattering in silvery memorials to his helplessness.

He was dripping, his long hair spotted with large diamonds of damp. He removed his wet muslin upper cloth and hung it up to dry. Kochu Kelu, a fanatic devotee of his writings, waddled up with a thorth, a thin porous towel. As he dried his tall muscular frame, the others filled him in with the news of the moment. (Madras uncle slept through it all, like a contented baby.) '*Brahma hathya!*' he exclaimed, like they all had.

'Surprises you, MVR, doesn't it?' KK said.

'It came right out of the oracle's mouth,' another cut in. 'We can't dispute it.'

'Some mistake somewhere.' MVR smiled. 'Even the word of God comes through flesh and blood. The man isn't infallible.' There was silence as they digested that. One or two of them frowned.

'You don't think it's true, do you?' the heretic asked.

'No—anyway, it doesn't matter what I think. If the oracle cannot be more precise, why sit and worry about a vague message? Let's forget it till we have something clear. Then perhaps we can take action.'

'Very true,' said Madras uncle gravely, opening his eyes, surprised to see MVR there.

MOHINI

∎

Excerpts from the diary of MVR:

Thursday, 20 March 1884—9 Minam 1059 (Malabar Era)

Have not written for three days. It is unusual. The storm has finally abated but I am going through a turbulent period. My Wife prepared some nice curries and insisted that I bring cheer to her and self by playing on the veena. I doubt whether it had any effect on either of us, cheerful or otherwise. I had to praise the curry even though I seem to have lost all taste for anything.

Received a note from the India Office, London, advising that Prof. Williams' book has been dispatched. Somehow the news has not brought the usual cheer. Subramanyayyar may be further delayed. I received the news with less trepidation than I did his last communication. I have set aside the work. But I am thinking about it all the time, I even dream about it.

Drove with my Wife and her niece to Kilikkara village

and bazaar. Though the people are still respectful towards the family, I hear some of the younger men have their own ideas. On the way back, one of the carriage horses tumbled down and a crowd gathered, but Coachman Krsna Rao managed to make it rise and drove on. Wife insisted on having an oil bath in the river, which she accomplished at the ghat along with her niece after some swift arrangements.

Went to Kunnupuram Illam on Monday the 17th. The Katha was felt to be good. Some indiscretion caused havoc during the performance and afterwards. I spent the evening and the night. I had lunch the next day with Vasudevan Namboodiri. His father Brahmadattan Namboodiri is known as Aana Thirumeni—Elephant Priest—perhaps because of his dark majesty, and is a very powerful tantric priest.

I have had no comfort since that day. Vasu thought I was not well. The Katha was *Nala Damayanthi*. I began to get an idea of the beauty of Damayanthi!

I do not think of *Mohini* as work any more. I have been debating within myself whether I should go ahead without C.H. Mohini is not grammar and reference, Mohini is a beautiful enchanting woman.

Like a sudden welcome clearing in the wilderness, clouds hushed for a while.

The Kilikkara contingent—comprising MVR, Elephant-head uncle and two young cousins Unni and Chandran—proceeded to Kunnupuram in two carriages. A slight drizzle thinned to a stop as they left the Palace arch. The namboodiri from the illam, who was escorting them, offered reassurance. 'We've made all arrangements. A strong pandal in case the rains are as heavy as yesterday. The performance will be held in the natakshala near our family temple which is, of course, well covered.'

'If we run into a storm, we may not be able to come back,' Chandran said. He was a stocky youth with long hair and small wild eyes. Both his frown and smile made people uneasy.

'The eastern bungalow has been prepared specially for the Palace guests. There is absolutely no need to worry.'

'What is it—an outhouse?' Chandran persisted.

The younger men were ahead, along with the namboodiri. The others followed in a bigger carriage. Unni said, 'No, it's their guest house. I've seen the place, it's much bigger than the usual guest rooms in front. In the early days, Kunnupuram was known for their hospitality.'

The namboodiri said defensively, 'Our patriarch is now able to assert himself.'

'I know that.' Chandran grinned. 'Aana Thirumeni—Elephant Priest!'

'Because of his scholarship and spiritual power. He's an elephant among namboo'ris.' He added stoutly, 'Today's performance and feast will show the world that Kunnupuram is still a force to reckon with.'

'I wish you the best of luck!' Chandran said.

When they reached the illam, they were welcomed by Elephant Priest. Brahmadattan Namboodiri was an old dark man with thick ominous-looking eyebrows. He thanked them for accepting his invitation and coming all the way to the illam to see the story being played out. Visitors from Kilikkara were a pleasure he had only dreamed about. He thanked MVR for persuading the others to come as well—gracious words that came from a cavern of inscrutability and seemed separate from the speaker. His eyes burned, his lips looked icy blue.

He asked his son Vasu, MVR's old friend, to escort them to the special guest house, where they could freshen up before dinner. They stretched and sighed and spread their belongings as if they'd arrived after a long journey and would be staying for days.

After Vasu had left, Chandran produced a bottle of liquor which he offered to everyone—they naturally refused—and he set about exhausting it. He was beyond the pale of castigation. None of the others could fathom the reason for his increasing jumpiness today, and his sudden bursts of merriment; they now attributed it to alcohol.

Nor did anyone notice the bulging cloth package he clutched under his arm—like poor wretched Kuchela of mythology who visited his old classmate, Lord Krishna himself, at the instigation of his much-delivered, much-suffering wife, clutching beneath his arm a small packet of puffed rice which was the only gift he had to give to the Lord. Krishna found and ate the puffed rice—and with each mouthful, there's Kuchela attaining prosperity, getting richer and richer unknown to himself, so that when he returns home it's not to his wretched little hut but to a palace crammed with wealth.

What does Kuchela's story have to do with Chandran—prodigal unpredictable Chandran? And the mysterious package under his arm. Would he seek justice from some unsuspecting Krishna at Kunnupuram? He's all set to leave a shining mark like his namesake on the brow of this night. And we'll see—in a game where he and Fate make their separate moves—what a single night can do to a series of lifetimes.

The feast is fabulous.

Undampened by the weather, in fact cheered and applauded by the skies, forty top-notch namboodiris—all there in deference to the illam's past rather than its present—congregate in order of status on low wooden seats on the floor before large lush-green plantain leaves. The Kilikkara noblemen have their food served in the guest house, since they cannot eat alongside the namboodiris who're technically superior to them. There is great joviality and easy chatter among the namboodiris.

The servers come up, carrying large baskets of pappadam, banana chips, fried brown chillies, golden boli, five varieties of pickle, ginger curd, pachhadi, avial. The rice is served, tumbling white and steaming on the green leaf. They pour ghee and dal. Some of the namboodiris make loud sounds of enjoyment. Someone shouts, 'It has been worth it, waiting for Kunnupuram to wake up at last.' Someone rejoinders, 'When are you going to wake up?' Another chips in, 'Feast for the tongue, then a feast for the eyes.'

Gold-tasting mangoes. The mango season has barely begun. 'Haaah!' 'Remember how your father cried for his mango once?' 'I don't know that. Tell us!' 'He's up to his usual stunts—' 'Anyway, tell us.'

'His father—elder Thanasherry namboo'ri, you know—was at a feast like this. The mangoes came, and the mangoes came, and no one was leaving them alone. His father was crushing out the juice of one enormous fellow. The mango slipped from his hand, jumped over five leaves and landed on the sixth person's leaf!' The discoursing diner pauses. They all wait, most of them beginning to smile, knowing what is coming. 'And then Thanasherry starts crying, howling into his leaf. They try to comfort him, it's okay, they tell him, this sort of thing happens, we'll give that namboo'ri another leaf, and let him have his lunch all over again, don't you worry, an accident it is, not a crime. And our man—your father!—cries all the more. He says, it's not that—two years ago my father was here and he had a bigger mango and it jumped over nine leaves and landed on the tenth. I can't even reach my father's record at my age! And he continues to weep inconsolably.' They all laugh, and the famous father's son looks on proudly. 'Hope you're not about to surpass your grandfather,' comes a shout. 'I'm the eleventh man from you!'

Thick white curds, shimmering like a dancer's hands. They ask for more rice.

'So, Chepally, it seems you were seen going into the Thiruvadira house the other day! What, another sammandham or what? I don't know anyone who's had so many relationships as you have.'

Chepally Namboodiri, thin and shy, looks up from his rice and smiles uncertainly. 'It's n-n-not a relationship at all. They simply called me to ask about a puja they wanted done.' They all laugh, and Chepally looks more uncertain than ever.

Four different payasams. They slurp and burp. Milk, jaggery, banana, dal.

'Not only that, his maidservant's breasts have been growing. It only shows how busy Chepally has been.' 'Be quiet! Don't bring the bedroom into the dining room.' 'For Chepally that's nothing new. Any room is good enough.' 'Poor namboo'ri. He will leave his leaf and run.' 'Don't worry about that, Chepally never leaves anything half-done.'

Poor Chepally blushes and continues to eat. He's scared enough of his own (one and only) wife, let alone go into other relationships. As for maidservants, he doesn't even have the courage to look a woman in the eye, let alone anywhere else. After his mother's death three years ago, he has—he can swear!—never felt safe with any woman. All this is, of course, well-known. But teasing Chepally has become a habit during feasts. As if it's another course, along with the rasam and the curds and the payasam!

The second feast begins—feast for the senses—in a hall surrounded by rain.

And appropriately—as they sit back rubbing their bellies and burping into the satisfied air—it's the story of a king who's also a master cook.

Nala Charitham. Nala, handsomest of men, unfortunate king, who loses his kingdom with the fall of a dice, who abandons his beauteous wife Damayanthi in the forest.

Poor abandoned Damayanthi, poor Nala. The state of kings sometimes, the state of women always! She had married him after spotting him ingenuously at her swayamvaram, the groom-selection, among mischievous gods who have turned up to confuse her, looking indistinguishably like him. But she's shrewd, doing some fine detective work aided by the goddess Saraswathi herself. She notices their feet don't touch the ground while Nala's do.

The dignitaries from Kilikkara Palace are given pride of place in satin-covered sofas in front. The aaddhyan namboodiris, cream of the Brahminical summit, sit behind them.

Everyone is alert today, dramatic history is about to be made. This presentation is a new form that's neither kathakali nor pure attam nor a straightforward play—and yet all of these. They lean forward, their critical faculties sharply honed, waiting for a stroke of genius or, more likely, a technical embarrassment. Once in a while, when there is a delectable morsel of mind-wrenching imagery, when there is the description of a woman's thighs or her bashful smile, there's still a return to Chepally, stoking his fires, spreading an air of erotic awareness all round, a brewing storm within the blowing storm . . .

Vasu comes around now and then, enquiring after his guests' comfort. The illam's servants follow him, fetching this and that—a tumbler of water, a blanket, even a pillow. They are prepared for a long night, the performance will go on into the early hours. The ladies are behind a thin curtain in a dark alcove of the natakshala, enjoying the katha as well as the amusement provided by their garrulous menfolk. Performances like this are a rare opportunity, a brief window to the world.

Chandran gets up. He's out of the hall for barely five minutes. No one notices his departure or his return. If they do, they think nothing of it.

MVR feels the onset of a headache. He has a herbal preparation back in his room in the guest house. If he doesn't take it in time, the headache, he knows, will blow up and torture him. He gets up. He whispers a word to Elephant-head uncle. No one notices him leave. He rejects the offer of an escort, but accepts a choot, a straw torch that has to be constantly waved in the air to keep the embers burning.

There is a large cauldron outside the auditorium. Young namboodiri boys are ladling bonji from it into tumblers. It is for the audience when they begin to get their second wind after the sumptuous dinner. Bonji is lime juice mixed with crushed ginger, a fresh idea from a palace down south. Unknown to the youngsters, there's one more ingredient in the drink. Now, after Chandran's unnoticed little outing, when he returns minus his bulging cloth packet.

Innocent of what they are about to unleash, these boys fill tumblers and take them out to the audience. Namboodiris and thampurans, the young and the old, men and women, they all help themselves to the bonji. Minutes pass. The play goes on. The bonji is delicious. Most of them ask for second—and third—helpings. They haven't tasted such a delicious tumbler of bonji in their lives. They can feel the warmth rising, the ice hissing down their spine. Chandran cannot stop smiling at what he has accomplished. The boys are working overtime to keep everyone happy. Perhaps even the players get an inkling of what is happening. The glorious descriptions of classical lore, the atmosphere of lashing sensuous rain, and the bonji. Most of all, the bonji! It gets to the audience. The audience is now in a world of its own. Storm and story merge. They turn to their neighbours and grin weakly, knowing they are under some strange spell.

It's a trick of fate that practically no one has refused the bonji. The very few who have remain unaffected, wide-eyed and indignant. Some of them walk out into the rain when they realize what is happening. They call out for their personal servants to get their carriage or bring umbrellas. Others watch interestedly.

The confusion begins.

One frail old gentleman climbs on the lap of a fat namboodiri and intimately fingers his hairy chest, spouting endearments.

Another gentleman, a thampuran, slyly stokes the fleshy passions of his neighbour, seeing the face of his mistress under the man's fierce moustaches.

One adventurous youth peers behind the ladies' curtain and makes seductive hissing noises. The ladies shout at him. An elderly lady reciprocates with a similar hiss.

Most of the women of the illam, sensitized to a fine degree, scamper away at the first hint of disruption.

An old servant dares to wander in. Grizzled with long years of service and respect, he sits across a pillow, paying erotic poetic tribute to the aristocratic wife of a namboodiri staying the night. She listens, magnetized by his voice and style. 'Show me your breasts,' he sings, 'sigh me a sigh.' Her sigh rises tremulously into the night. 'The world lies in stupor by the plantain stalks of your thighs.' She delicately pulls up her mundu to verify his truth. Words fail him. He stares at what his poetry has achieved. 'Come here,' she cries, also in poetic tones.

The players go on for a while. Then they stop their pretence. Roles have changed. The audience have taken over the play. So they seek the cauldron between scenes. They return to the stage and begin the performance all over again, right from the first scene, louder and more enthusiastic. When the curtain goes up on the second scene, it lifts Damayanthi's sari along with it. The man who plays Damayanthi screams in delight, displaying hefty thighs.

He bounds over to the first young man he sees. The man stares at Damayanthi with his brocade sari and painted face. Damayanthi bends and pulls up his mundu. The man cries out in alarm. 'Are your feet touching the ground?' Damayanthi yells.

This makes sense. Youngsters run around the room, pulling up mundus, yelling, 'Are your feet touching the ground?'

A thampuran—a retired Government official— charges into the ladies' section. There is screaming excitement. He grabs the hand of a woman he mistakes to be his wife and gallops with her into the rain. The storm gathers over them.

There is no precise record of who did what. In that most sacred of Kerala's sanctums, the namboodiri illam, where even the sun is denied access, all hell broke loose. Characteristic of Kali Yuga—the dark age of the dark horseman Kali—everything stood on its head! There were elders who demanded an inquiry. Others wanted to socially boycott Kunnupuram. They made a few initiatory noises before they realized that someone they knew—friend, relative, well-wisher—and couldn't afford to embarrass had been part of those prurient proceedings, who'd rather let the whole thing die a natural and silent death.

The night's epitaph can be found in the caustic comment of the Srimangalam patriarch who listened quietly to a dramatic narration of the events and shook his head gravely. 'Shiva, Shiva! The story has only one Damayanthi and several Nalas. In Kunnupuram, we find so many Damayanthis and so many Nalas and a groom-selection without rules!'

It is known that the head of Kunnupuram, Elephant Priest, took three glasses of the bonji before he dropped off to sleep. Endowed with great self-discipline and spiritual powers, he was barely affected by the drink. He did make efforts to discover the culprit who had, yes, ingenuously mixed ganja in the bonji—hemp, large quantities of 'strong good stuff'—thus bleeding art into life, redesigning the orthodox illam with purple passages. He conducted discreet investigations, but next morning, like their kitchen hearths, not a wisp of smoke could be seen.

Only the black stains remained.

MVR runs in the rain, his straw umbrella unable to keep him dry.

Once in the room, he raises the wicks of the lanterns and sits down on his bed. His head is throbbing. He dries his hair with a thorth. He grinds the herbal powder with the small mortar and pestle he always carries with him, adds water and makes a smooth green paste. He consumes the concoction in a gulp, screwing up his eyes at the taste of it.

The rain drums on the tiles. The room is warm. He decides to lie down for a while. He can hear faintly the drums from the natakshala through the rain. Drumming, drumming, he thinks, trying to keep his mind off the headache, drumming all round right into his head, the throbbing settles into a rhythm so that very soon he can't tell whether the drumming is now outside or only within his head. His full stomach, the low headache and the warmth converge upon him. His eyeballs descend far inside his head.

When he finally wakes up, it is late. Very late, he can see, or the wicks are burning too fast. The room is colder now. He gets up from the bed and stands there. The headache has disappeared. He strains his ears to hear the sound of the drums, but the pitter-patter on the roof drowns everything else.

He picks up the umbrella and walks out of the house. It is raining harder, with a flowing wind, and he tries to keep his choot beneath his umbrella so that it won't hiss itself out. It makes his face ubearably hot and his eyes water. The path is slushy and it takes all his concentration to keep himself from slipping. He trains the torch on the ground directly below him, inching sight and feet forward on the slow heavy path.

And so it's quite some time before he realizes he's lost his way.

He curses loudly into the rain. The torch begins to hiss vengefully. Through the curtain of water he can see a faint light. He halts, not sure whether it is indeed a light or some trick of his eyes. He struggles forward, slipping, cursing, sinking pitifully past his ankles in the mud. A faint yellow vertical bar of light behind the rain. A doorway, surely. He rushes forward, not bothered about the choot that singes the air, hushes and dies. It is indeed a doorway. There is a dim light somewhere inside. He throws down the umbrella and straightens up. He is soaking wet. The rain is roaring and battering. He washes off the mud and stands watching the silver curtain, then turns around.

He realizes where he is. This is a bathhouse! He knows Kunnupuram has two ponds, separate ones for men and women. He now hears the rush of rain on the water. Steps lead darkly down to the tank. He feels as if he is in a reverberating cavern surrounded by endless water. He takes off his sodden upper cloth. He shivers. He removes his mundu and his loincloth and stands naked, wringing his clothes. His shadow stands tall and proud against the wall. There is a small lantern on the ledge, and he wonders why they need a light here in the night, that too in the rain!

He hears a sound, a splashing step, and freezes. Instinctively he moves back into the shadows. A figure moves up the darkness, climbing the steps. He watches in fascination as, breaking out of the darkness, she comes up. A woman now bathed in the damp yellow glow—rising, framed by his staring eyes. He forgets the fact that he is naked.

So is she. Her body is chiselled gold, dripping on to the floor. She now stands before him like a goddess in the flesh. His heart is thump-thump-thumping within his chest, as though it would tear itself out. She is the most beautiful vision he has ever seen. Her breasts are firm and large with dark spreading nipples. As she walks up, they shiver and settle. Her belly is a flat wet plain embedded with the dark poem of her navel. And below that, melting into deep shadow, a liquid trail that disappears within the join of her thighs.

He has an eternity in which to watch her. Her hair hangs wetly down her shoulders, long and thick, blacker than the night. Her face—he has rarely seen such beauty, she is the heroine of epics, worshipped in temple sculptures. Surely she has never been seen by human eyes. Untouched by the sun, carved from pure white butter! His breath catches in his throat. Leaning forward to get her clothes, content in her solitude, she hears his exultation and looks up like a startled deer. And sees him. Naked, with the world in his eyes. For that split second, a doorway opens out of time and they stand looking at each other.

She utters a cry and grabs her clothes. She covers herself as best as she can, a cloth around her waist, another around her shoulders that still leaves the curve of a breast and a sharp nipple exposed to his gaze. They cannot completely turn away from each other. He discovers the reason for her continuing blushes and slaps his own wet clothes against himself. Their silence is composed of wonder and shame.

Finally he says, 'Forgive me, I didn't know there was anyone here. It's raining so heavily.' She stands, hanging her head. 'I'll go.' As he turns and prepares to walk away into the rain, she puts up a hand. 'Venda.' No! Her voice is like flowering crystal, shattering through rain and night. He stops and turns fully to face her. 'I am Marthanda Varma of Kilikkara. I've lost my way.' He explains himself, having no other words to touch her with.

Her smile is like the first flush of dawn stirring the sky. 'I saw you there.'

'You were there?'

She nods. Her voice is so soft that he has to strain his ears. 'I had some of that drink.' He doesn't understand. 'Something in that drink,' she says, puzzled. 'It began to burn. I ran . . .'

'I am a friend of Vasu Namboo'ri.'

She lowers her eyes. 'I've read your poems.' He catches something like pain in her voice. 'I never thought I could meet you . . .'

Something snaps. The bathhouse trembles.

They are both in the grip of a terrible fever. She stands motionless like a marble statue. His feet move without his command, splashing on the stone floor, drawn by her. He has no idea who she is, where he's headed. Lightning illumines her and the world of water behind her. As the thunder sweeps deafeningly across the skies, he raises his arms. 'Mohini!' he breathes.

She stands with her eyes closed. He reaches forward and removes the upper cloth from her, worshipping at the altar of her sacred breasts. He is unable to control himself. 'Mohini.' He gathers her to him, without knowing, without caring, heaven in his eyes.

BLOUSES AND SPOUSES

▬

Narayani was a strapping young girl of seventeen who worked in Big Palace. Her beauty, it must be said, lay in the eyes of the beholder; a mere portrait couldn't have depicted her charms. Her face lacked the perfection of line and curve that generally passes for beauty. In the case of Narayani—or Nani, as she was called—her beauty lay in what her lips suggested, in what her eyes revealed. When she walked, her heavy hips graced the air with an irresistible rhythm. When she spoke, her voice sang with a melody all its own. Her laughter rang out like a beacon drawing drowning souls.

And there were very few men who, having beheld her, did not seek out the opportunity to keep on beholding. She was clean and neat. She was happy to sweep and swab the inner rooms and do whatever else was asked of her. She would offer her life to MVR's younger sister Uma Amba, whose personal maid she was.

Her grandmother and mother had worked for the Palace. But her mother died at a young age. Nani was left in the care of her father who fuelled his life with liquor and a precarious sense of power. He treated all his three daughters alike—with a heavy hand. As darkness came and he found it difficult to keep the ache from consuming his work-weary limbs, he lit a torch, cursed a curse, and slipped out to the liquor den five minutes away.

With friendly chatter and quick quaffs, he forgot the woes of his day. When he returned home, the girls faced the woes of their day. When the marks of his hand on their flesh became too obvious to be ignored, it pained their neighbours. Word reached Uma Amba, who was shocked. 'We must see this beast is tamed,' she said. 'We owe it to their grandmother and mother who served us well.'

So she summoned one of the men who worked under their manager and sent him on a mission of retribution, armed with a carte blanche. The man confronted the girls' father along with a couple of thugs who decided to apply a little more pressure than their vocabulary permitted. The father, who was supervising work on the field, began to weep. He wiped his eyes with dirt-crusted hands and said that he loved his daughters more than anything else in the world. The girls constantly reminded him of his long-lost wife. He couldn't, he confessed, see or treat them any differently.

The thugs listened till he had finished and then did what they had come there to do. The father got a taste of his own medicine and lapsed into bitter submission.

Uma Amba did not let the matter rest there. She took Nani, the youngest, for herself. The eldest sister was married off. The middle one was sent to Eastern Palace as a maid. Ensconced in the lap of a matriarchal society, Nani blossomed. She found herself surrounded by men of all ages. They eyed her with delicious greed—and reached out to pluck her blossoms for themselves. It was a society where the myth of female superiority was propagated by men, men who were generally its decision-makers. Nani would very soon become a victim of that myth.

Employment in Big Palace was a happy experience for her. Nani had a mind and hand of her own which firmly dictated and limited the choice of her favourites. Abetting her new freedom was the benevolent protection of her mentor

Uma Amba. Nani's new life was rich. Though it was marked
by promiscuity, she preferred it to the cold and painful
guardianship of her father. Here there was laughter and good
cheer and genuine companionship. Her naturally bright
disposition found no room for complaint.

As time went on, Nani divided her time between work,
limited liaisons and unlimited visits to the temple where,
besides the comfort of worship, there was ample scope for
gossip. Kilikkara Palace was rich pickings. Besides the
eccentricities and fabulous recreations of a royal family, the
presence of so many servants ensured a steady flow of
interesting tales from the hearths of the hoi polloi. They sat
around and discussed families, big and small, of the village.

Her liaisons included hearty and casual flings with members
of the Big Palace staff as well as secret intense couplings with
certain thampurans. In those days, before the partitions, each
palace had a large number of males. Finding someone as
abundantly endowed—physically as well as temperamentally—
as Nani alone in one of the empty upper rooms was provocation
enough. Pushing her back on a bare mattress and unburdening
their stormy libidos, they felt they had achieved some kind of
spiritual release. That was the effect Nani had on most men.

Thus afloat on the predictably placid sea of her life, Nani
suddenly hit the reefs. The Blouse blew up from nowhere and
wrecked her life.

This is how it happened. In keeping with his penchant for
innovation, like that legendary trip to Madras, the Second
Patriarch had made several innovations to life in the Palace.
It was he who brought home wheat. For the rice-eaters of the
Palace, it was a strange day when he had the common kitchen
serve chapaties. Some fell in love with the new food, others
hated it and wondered how northerners could exist on an
exclusive diet of this thick and leathery thing.

Decades later, in the evening of his life, it was once again
he who brought home the very first motor car. Returning
from Kollam with his manservant, he got down at the boat
jetty and looked around for a horse carriage to take him to
Kilikkara. He had taken more time than he'd expected at
Kollam and had made no arrangements to be picked up. He

was hailed by an old man, who offered to transport him in a newly acquired Humber for a small fee. Throughout the drive, Madras uncle showed interest in the vehicle and asked various pertinent and fantastic questions. Finally the driver asked, 'Do you want it?' That silenced Madras uncle. 'I can talk to my master if you like.' So instead of driving straight to the Palace, they went to the owner of the car who, truth to tell, had been looking for an opportunity to get back to his trouble-free motorless days. That same afternoon, Madras uncle purchased the car and its driver for five hundred rupees.

When he drove home late that evening, he created a sensation. A servant ran in, shouting that a monster was roaring up the road. An old maid fainted and refused to be brought to. Children trailed behind it, screaming excitedly. A madman chased after it and threw a stone which fortunately missed the rear glass.

The car adorned a specially-constructed shed for several years. At first it admirably served as the Second Patriarch's official vehicle. (Or rather, it alternated between serving and being serviced; trained mechanics were imported from Bombay which gave the hoary Humber many days of well-earned rest.) Later, when it retired from active service, it provided hours of bliss to children who drove, fought, picnicked, daydreamed and started a sponge collection within its vast and musty interior.

Madras uncle was, of course, the first and only thampuran of his generation to go to Madras. For years afterwards, it was obligatory for visitors to sit and listen to all the interesting details of that historic trip. To assure him no one had forgotten this outing, he was named Madras uncle. And very few people remembered his actual name. Though in the glorious tradition of Kilikkara, he could very well have been named Humber uncle or Chapati uncle. Or, perhaps, Blouse uncle.

Because, in the beginning, there was the Blouse.

Serving women of the Palace were used to walking around with their breasts bare. When they went out, they might throw a casual cloth across their chest. Older women and members of the royal family tied their waist cloth high up so that it

covered their breasts as well. And very old women relapsed to
bare breasts. Madras uncle felt bared breasts were barbaric.
Having recently read a few ponderous English novels, he
turned into a votary of Victorian virginity. He began to
believe seriously in the civilizing role of the Raj. And so he
introduced the Blouse to Kilikkara. And Kilikkara to the
Blouse.

Many women saw this revolution as a symbol of repression
against their maternal instincts. To others like Nani, it came
as a shock, an embarrassment. And finally, nemesis.

Madras uncle ordered yards and yards of cloth all the way
from Madras. He took great care to see they were of the finest
colours and patterns. 'This is the first time,' he said. 'It must
be good.'

Each palace was allotted its quota of cloth, taking the
number of eligible female servants into account. Tailors were
brought in from the capital. The women were asked to send
in their measurements. The tailors sat on mats in a long hall
with their scissors, needles and threads, and they worked the
whole day long and pretty much into the night, peering at
their work in the light of several lanterns.

The stitching was a sight to behold. The tailors were
treated like actors in a play. Giggling girls and curious
children stood around watching. A group of young thampurans
came in during the afternoon and tried to guess which blouse
would fit which maid. They discussed curves and contours and
accommodations with such passion that the master tailor said
they could no longer continue their work. 'My men are getting
distracted,' he admitted. Finally, everyone had to leave and the
tailors continued their work in peace.

The blouses were ready within the week. There was a
great deal of excitement as older maidservants supervised the
blouse-fitting ceremony. There was much laughter and ribbing
because of mismatches and snapped buttons. The young girls
found this exercise of containing their bodies within garments
they'd never worn before exceedingly strange. When the
blouses were apportioned, the tailors had left and peace
returned to the inner rooms of the Palace, the real fallout
began. The consummation of Madras uncle's scheme, the

wages of innovation. And what a price it was!

It had long been the custom for the girls who covered their breasts to uncover them before the men of the family. This was a sign of respect. Now, however, they covered themselves all the time. Wearing a blouse is decent, it means no disrespect, said Madras uncle. But old habits die hard. Nani found it extremely embarrassing, this 'new fashion brought in by that old thampuran.' Generously endowed as she was, she found it difficult to wear the blouse, and irritating to keep it on. She told her colleagues, 'This is all right for white people. They wear hats on their heads. In the same way they wear these things on their breasts. How can he expect us to do that!'

She was extremely self-conscious as she went about her work, wearing a crimson flower-patterned blouse. She pulled and she tugged, she scratched and she rubbed. And all the time, she kept murmuring. When MVR came in from the library, Nani was sweeping his room. Normally, he would either leave and return once she'd completed her work, or she would lower her head and run away. This time he laughed, amused by her new attire. Nani blushed hotly and uttered a cry. She tore at the buttons and pulled open her blouse. She stood before him with her head bent, her breasts bare, as if ready for punishment. 'Nani, what is the matter with you?' he said. 'Why did you take it off?' She didn't reply. 'You mustn't remove your blouse in future,' he admonished her gently. 'That is the Patriarch's order. You must never ever remove it, not in front of people. The old times are over!' His words rang in her ear.

Things were never the same after that. Like a straitjacket, the blouse constricted all natural feeling and behaviour. Her eyes dimmed and her walk slowed. It felt as if a large rough band had been tied around her torso, squashing her breasts and pressing against her back. Her breasts felt dried-up and wasted, and she felt her womanhood itself was ebbing away. When she was in the same room as MVR, who had taken her passionately one balmy night, she felt shy and awkward. The old times were over.

But Nani's predicament was unique. The other maids

soon got used to the new attire. They enjoyed and looked forward to wearing it. Vanity entered the picture, and with it, envy and a spirit of competition. The set of two blouses per woman was hardly enough, they felt. Those who had relations living in or near the capital requested them to locate the tailors and have more blouses made, each elaborate and more colourful. There was no doubt about it, the Blouse was here to stay, years before it had reached the rest of Kerala. And the credit, of course, goes to the mulish, eccentric, forward-looking Second Patriarch, Madras uncle. The man who motorized mobility and made it to Madras, who covered breasts and discovered wheat.

Despite Uma Amba's best efforts, it was becoming difficult to calm down the new Nani. She stood staring at herself in the mirror, eyes full and faraway. She burst into abrupt tears. She stayed away from people if she could help it. Uma Amba sent her to the village doctor, who found nothing wrong with her. Uma Amba then suggested she be exempted from wearing the blouse. But Madras uncle was firm. 'No exemptions!' he ruled. 'All the good work will be lost.' He said a couple of mangoes shouldn't be allowed to spoil the entire bunch (which simile, Uma Amba felt, was in rather bad taste).

No one could bring her back. And things grew worse.

She began to open her mouth. A popular paramour who opens her mouth is dangerous. Erstwhile friends became increasingly alarmed. They even thought of taking a delegation to Madras uncle to get him to reverse his decision. Imprisoning her breasts had freed her tongue. Freeing her tongue may imprison some of us, they said, half-joking, but only half. Nani took to the streets. She would disappear from Big Palace at crucial times. Leaving floors half-swabbed and children waiting for their meals and old aunts stripped for their baths. Uma Amba listened to numerous complaints about the girl's truancy. When Nani returned, she looked absent as if she had been in the realm of birds and clouds.

Nani took to the streets and became a herald of doom. She stood in the middle of the street and announced, 'The old times are over!' Afterwards, the revelations began. The villagers reacted in embarrassment, shame and alarm. 'Those days we were free,' she said, raising her voice just outside the Kilikkara market. 'Now times have changed. These thampurans have made use of us till we are fit for nothing, squeezed out like a lime! And they are leaving us to our fate. Mark my words! See what they've made me wear. Is this what an orthodox Malayali girl like me should be wearing? See! See!' And she tugged and tore at the edge of her blouse.

One evening, as she was inviting people to see how dressed in distress she was, MVR's carriage passed by. MVR peered out, clearly showing his surprise. Nani bowed low with folded hands. 'Forgive me, thampuran,' she pleaded, 'don't take me to task. Punish me if you must, but don't discard me!' The carriage carried on without stopping. 'My thampuran was happy with me.' Nani stood staring after the carriage, wrapped in its dust, tears flowing from her eyes. 'I won't tell you how close we were. Now he's left me in the lurch. He has even abandoned his own lady. Who am I, only a servant. And you know who has him under her control?'

When she raised her voice and asked such a provocative question, how could anyone ignore her?

'How can she bear it? Leaving her in the lurch and going after . . . No, who am I to go around telling? And before that he couldn't write a word. I'm telling you, everything had dried up. He was sitting in the library and tearing his hair out. And only the hair came out, not a single word!' People stopped, listening open-mouthed; others pretended not to listen. 'And he went then to this place. I don't know where, why should I know? He went to this place and after that, the words began to flow!'

There was no doubt about it, the people of Kilikkara were caught in a sticky situation. They had tremendous respect for MVR. He was a hero of Kilikkara, the only local who had made his mark in the state. He was popular in the village, being friendly and accessible. Except for a few youngsters who refused to make much of him because they refused to make much of royalty anyway, most of Kilikkara enjoyed putting him on a pedestal. But gossip is a need that transcends good sense.

Juicy details were poised to trip off Nani's tongue! They

did not stop her. Reluctant to participate in this de-herofication, they stood mesmerized by their own eagerness to know. 'Why?' shouted Nani. 'Because he was inspired. What I couldn't give him, what his lady couldn't give him, what others couldn't give him—he got it from an illam!'

There was shocked silence. 'Illam?' The voices now began, rough, curious, demanding. 'Which one, who?'

Nani lowered her head stubbornly. 'Don't ask me!'

And that was that. Like guests invited for a feast and sent away without the payasam, they chewed their lips in frustration. MVR's latest work was inspired by a loved one from an illam? How could a thampuran find a beloved in an illam—where even the sun couldn't get in? There was only one illam in the neighbourhood. Who?

When word reached Kilikkara Palace, there was panic. Relatives started seeking clarifications from MVR in a roundabout manner. He maintained a cold silence. His sister Uma Amba heard the whispers and she knew what had to be done. She'd saved the girl once and would save her again. Overnight, said the rumours, some men came and picked up Nani from the Palace. She was never seen in Kilikkara again. People said she'd been admitted in an ayurvedic mental asylum run by namboodiris. Others came up with more chilling possibilities.

The only thing known for a fact was that she left the palace in a horse carriage, and she wasn't wearing her blouse.

MVR's wife heard of the famous street-corner revelation from two of her maids. One couldn't believe that Nani had lost her reason. The other swore Nani was seen being dragged away in chains. As they argued, MVR's wife got the bits and pieces. She'd always known he had an appreciative eye for beauty. She also knew that was all it was. But MVR had been distracted these last two years. His poem had undergone a change. She had indeed nursed her suspicions. But the illam!

Beads of memory began to gather on her worried brow. She locked herself in her darkened room and would answer no one as she sat and listed all those moments she'd let pass without question. Perhaps it was her fault. A cat let loose inside the temple couldn't be blamed if he drank up all the payasam! It was the duty of the priest to protect the cat from that sin. She wondered whether her trust in him had finally reached a crossroads. She trusted nothing but her own feelings. Now, for the first time, she began to feel the rumblings. She did what she always did; she confronted her feelings. And then her husband. She asked him if what the people said was true. Did he have someone in the illam? 'I cannot tell you that,' he said.

'I am your wife.'

'Yes, that's why.'

'Why not?' she asked sharply.

'Because I don't want to hurt you.'

'Then it's true! You do have a woman in the illam. Who is it?'

'You are my wife and I've always loved you,' he told her in a serious tone. 'But sometimes Time steps in with bigger surprises. And then there's nothing one can do.'

'I'm not one of your admirers, I'm your wife, don't give me these poetic phrases! Tell me what you've done and what you're going to do.'

MVR looked pained. He caught her gently by her shoulders and looked into her eyes. 'You've been very understanding,' he said. 'More a friend to me. I will never hurt you.'

She moved away. 'Yes, I've been understanding. It's because I knew you would never hurt me.' She held on to a post of the large carved bed. 'You didn't spare even my little niece! Don't think I'm blind. I had to send her away on a stupid pretext.' She gazed out of the window at the bright daylight. 'Now I'm not so sure any more. I see something much bigger this time. Bigger than you or me.' She turned abruptly and he saw the pain in her eyes for the first time. 'You will not only hurt me,' she cried, 'you will hurt yourself—and everybody else!'

'No, I won't,' he said. 'I give you my word.'

She said angrily, 'What can that achieve? That is an illam. And whoever it is must be married already, there's no one else.' She waited for some sort of confirmation. He stared back at her, his eyes shining brightly. 'It will only lead to tragedy.'

He said, 'You're wasting your words. You're worrying unnecessarily.' He took her hands in his and kissed them. 'I promise you this. Whatever happens, I will never leave you.' She felt the strength in his eyes. 'Whatever happens, I'll never go back to what you accuse me of. It's . . . not easy to give you this promise, but I do. You can be sure!' He turned and walked away before his eyes could reveal anything more.

In Kunnupuram, a similar scene was going on. Damodaran Namboodiri was interrogating his wife. He knew he couldn't control himself much longer, and was using all the patience he had. Damodaran was a far-removed cousin of the patriarch's wife and had been taken in at Kunnupuram at an early age. His wife was the orphaned daughter of Elephant Priest's sister. The patriarch had undertaken her guardianship and she had grown up in Kunnupuram like a cocooned pearl.

Damodaran was far-removed in more than one sense. He was from a less cultured part of the family. He worked at too many things to earn money. He kept to himself and couldn't hold his own in any forum. He was a priest at the Manjoor Devi temple and also a schoolmaster, which kept him away for most part of the day and made him a shadowy figure in the illam. In spite of the fact that he supplemented the illam's income, he didn't command enough importance.

A year ago his wife had given birth to a handsome baby boy. People felt the boy's features and fair complexion constituted a minor miracle, given Damodaran's dark and dour looks. Now after Nani's disclosures, people began to talk. They didn't talk about MVR, but of a scandal in the illam. They didn't talk about the other young women in the illam, but only of Tatri, the well-read and spirited wife of the dour Damodaran. The rumours reached Damodaran more than two weeks after Nani's departure. For another week he tortured himself with doubts and fears. Finally he confronted Tatri. Tatri remained silent. One would think she was dumb, that she'd lost all the old spirit. She clutched her year-old son to her breast and not one word crossed her lips.

'They are saying all kinds of things,' he said. 'I only want to hear what you have to say.' She said nothing. 'It seems to be common knowledge. Someone said a thampuran from

Kilikkara Palace found himself here. How? Who?' He gave her time to reply. 'So you won't tell me. I have ways of finding out. I know who it is. You'll regret it when I meet that man!' In a last uncontrollable outburst, his trembling voice kept low to keep it from reaching the rest of the family, he hissed, 'Is he really ours?' Seated on a mat on the floor with her son on her lap, Tatri gave him a calm unfathomable look that tore a tortured cry from his throat and drove him from the room.

Damodaran was content to walk the dark fringes of life. He kept so aloof that life passed him by. Now, he heard villagers talk. He caught worshippers at Manjoor Devi eyeing him strangely. The boatman who rowed him to the temple wasn't so remote any more. At the illam, his uncle and cousins avoided him more deliberately than they normally did. Everyone had pity in their eyes. He didn't like that, pity was a password people used to enter other people's lives. He flinched further into himself.

Till he realized why. At first, it was only a wicked glimmer of the sun as he walked home, or a chortle scattered in the breeze. He turned to abrupt shadows on the periphery of his vision, disappearing motes before his eyes.

One day, he was standing on the veranda, holding his baby son. Damodaran didn't coo or shush or sing. He just held his son in his arms. From the shed to his right, he could hear the vedic chants repeated by his eldest cousin's students. Their voices rose and fell in a regular rhythm. He pressed his son close and felt the softness against his own skin, flesh to carry his own flesh into the future. He saw the long Brahminical line that would bequeath, besides a family name, a heritage of pristine blood and wisdom. His love went beyond the immediacy of carrying this soft, warm, gurgling bundle.

Two men from a neighbouring village who'd been visiting Elephant Priest turned back as they left the illam. They looked at each other and something came into their eyes. They looked at his son and then at him, rapidly, not offensively or with any change of expression.

Damodaran froze. The baby must have realized something was up, he started howling. He held him in his arms, staring after them. The sun rose high, a cow pleaded loud and long, and the smell of fresh warm earth rolled up from the green fields. The baby laid his head quietly against Damodaran. His bare shoulder was wet with sweat and the baby's drool. It made a striking picture for anyone watching—the dark thin man holding the fair plump baby. The sun crept behind clouds. The cow was silent. The earth trembled, a shiver ran through its heart. No one was watching.

Damodaran stood there till little things in the past few days made sense. The boatman. Worshippers. Passing villagers. The sly sunlight and the moving shadows.

His wife was content to remain in the company of cousins or maids. She loved to read. She demanded only a continuous supply of books of poetry. She was reputed, he knew, to be well-versed in the scriptures. Her uncle, Elephant Priest, indulged her whims. In the past year, however, he'd noticed a restlessness. A sadness that went beyond the gloomy walls and loneliness, which even the little one's birth couldn't quell.

In a house he visited for a puja, a woman had become mad after childbirth. At times she was unmanagable. Before the rituals began, she ran up to present a clutch of jasmine at his feet. Since he was bathed and pure, the elders dragged her away. The flowers remained crushed in her hands. He kept hearing the woman's banshee-like screams. Her uncle later apologized and said some women couldn't bear the trauma of having to give up a life.

He'd stumbled upon his wife one afternoon in a darkened room. Their baby lay on her outstretched legs. She was singing him to sleep. It sounded like a long rhythmic sob. He couldn't bear to stand there. The baby turned this way and that. How could a mother sing this way? No wonder the baby couldn't sleep!

He remembered the Kilikkara boy Unni at the temple these past few weeks—a young thampuran who hardly crossed the river six or seven times a year. He approached Damodaran in a strange fashion—as if he wanted to tell him something but his tongue wouldn't move. He stood with folded hands and prayed, hung around for a while and left. Damodaran hoped the goddess was taking note of his complaints, whatever they were. One evening, he heard snatches of the boy's prayer.

The words escaped in pale whispers. Damodaran was right beside him and the boy didn't even notice. 'Save me!' The words came slow, barely distinguishable. 'Oh Devi, let me—let her! What have I done! Will I be forgiven? Devi! She's with child, how could I have done this to her! Alone in the dark, no one for company . . . Monster!' And more in the same vein. Damodaran had smiled—a youngster facing an unplanned pregnancy.

Today he didn't smile. Looking back, he saw moments falling into place! How had it happened? How did the boy enter the inner rooms of the illam? It was an impossible task. He stood on the veranda, holding the baby. He didn't feel any less towards him. Nor towards his wife. The Kilikkara boy, however, had it coming.

RAINBODY

——————————————— ■ ———————————————

The Manjoor Devi temple took shape within the first century of Kilikkara's founding. The small shrine of the goddess Durga was discovered tucked away in the dense forest across the river. The origin of its name is unknown, perhaps there was some inscription on its original stone bulwark. Today the temple is big, with an annual festival. There are members of the family who visit the temple every day, some go morning and evening. You have to cross the river and walk for a kilometre.

As you leave the boat, there are shops and tea stalls to greet you. The road turns sharply to the right and continues along the river to the Iramapuram village, which is nothing more than a scattering of mud houses, huts and a primary school surprised with fifty-odd children. However, if you follow the mud path that goes straight up, you reach the temple, located within a clearing in the forest. It is said there are wild animals and spirits roaming the forest. Those who return after the last puja hear jackals and small beasts, sometimes even the enquiring trumpet of an elephant. Anything more than that is yet to be substantiated.

There is a long skirting path used by woodcutters that leads out of the forest on the eastern side. It hits a road that twists and turns for some three or four miles and ends right in front of a large paddy field swaying like a green ocean in the breeze. Beyond this field is Kunnupuram illam. By the main road and over the bridge, however, the illam is all of twelve miles from Kilikkara.

One morning, two years after the infamous katha of Kunnupuram, the priest walked up to the temple and found a body sprawled outside the main entrance. There had been some rain the previous night, so it wasn't a pleasant sight at all. It was as if it had grown out of the mud and moss, crudely fabricated by Nature herself. The priest turned the body over and found himself looking at the face of a Kilikkara thampuran. The man was still alive, but barely. The priest panted back to the jetty and called the boatman who was halfway across the river.

The 'body' was entrusted to the royal doctor. The news soon trickled in that Unni of Eastern Palace had been found unconscious in front of the temple. And that he had tried to take his own life. The police weren't informed since this was a Palace affair. The uncles deliberated long and hard. The Matriarch washed her hands off the whole thing saying, 'God knows what devilry was brewing in his mind. The things our family gets into!' She entrusted the matter to Madras uncle.

Unni lay in a near-comatose doze, eyes rolled up and mouth slung down. There was a steady stream of visitors to Eastern Palace as though he was lying in state. His great-uncle—that same Elephant-head uncle whose head had reacted palely to the Sankaran episode—was quite happy to receive them and fill them in on the details. However, until Unni recovered consciousness, it was quite a game of suspense. Everyone had a theory. Someone said he had a failed love affair in the village. Someone else said he'd borrowed money and was murdered—though not completely—because he couldn't repay.

Madras uncle conducted the interrogation of the doctor

and the priest. 'Are you sure it was poison?' he shot out at the young doctor from the prescribed distance.

Dr Noble was an 'outsider', a white Christian. People in the Palace regarded his foreignness with awe and amusement as well as a conservative queasiness (because of his colour and accent and his funny gestures on the one hand and his outcaste status on the other). After he examined a patient, the patient took a bath. (Conversely, as everyone knew, the doctor never had a bath because white men remained bathless in order to retain their colour.) Dr Noble had no social access beyond the outer veranda. Medically, he was much sought after. Ladies appreciated the fact that he had to touch them (however, whenever and wherever). But without the sanctity of diognostic inevitability, his touch was severely restricted. He was known in the Palace as the Royal Cut-throat because of his expertise in tonsilitis.

He became confused in the wake of the relentless questioning. He wasn't used to being challenged. Most people took him at his word because of his learning and experience, and because he was English. Madras uncle was different from most people. He read a lot and questioned a lot, and had to be convinced with logic and evidence. The evidence had to fit in with his own reading of the world. Medicine wasn't his only domain. When a chief mason was called for a repair or construction, he first had to pass through the portals of Madras uncle's curiosity. If a new cook was interviewed, he'd better be well-versed in the whys and wherefors of preparation, protocol and serving. If the Second Patriarch wasn't satisfied, the candidate had no place in Kilikkara Palace. Gardening, weaponry, classical music and dance, grammar, pronunciation, chanting of mantras and temple behaviour, animal husbandry and ideal wifery—nothing escaped the zealous attention of Madras uncle.

The famous story about him was his interview for hiring a chief cook. A Tamil Brahmin was finally selected after heavy cross-examination. He turned out to be a handsome fellow with surprising accomplishments—he sang well, was proficient in the martial arts, had drunk deeply of Sanskrit poetry and debated deftly. The entire Palace was happy with Madras uncle's choice and hovered around the cook like butterflies. It was only when the auspicious day dawned when he was called upon to begin his career in Kilikkara's common kitchen that it was discovered that the only thing he didn't know was cooking.

'Absolutely sure?'

'Yes, of course,' said Dr Noble.

'Why do you say that?' The other uncles sat in a semicircle behind Madras uncle and smiled commiseratingly at the doctor with the strange golden hair.

'His condition and colour,' said Dr Noble expansively, even a little irritably, since no self-respecting medical practitioner explained himself to laymen. 'And, of course, the spittle that stained his mouth.'

'That's all?' said Madras uncle in the grim tone of One Who Knows.

Dr Noble became agitated. Within the bounds of respect due to the Palace, he squirmed and frowned in silent rebellion. 'As far as a doctor can know. You could always summon an expert from Trivandrum.' Silently he warned the older man: a little knowledge is a dangerous thing.

Madras uncle smiled, turning to draw the other uncles into his fold. He realized he'd, perhaps, gone a bit too far. 'You ruled out snakebite?'

'First thing,' the doctor said crisply.

'We'll leave that at that.' He shot out, 'Why did you say suicide? Couldn't it have been attempted murder?'

'Yes,' agreed Dr Noble, leaving Madras uncle foxed. Once again he smiled knowingly at the other uncles. But they remained silent, letting him fry in his own fat.

'Murder?'

'If you say so.'

'I? I don't say so!'

'Neither do I. And since the tham-poo-rran is still alive, we can be happy that it's neither.' He was beginning to enjoy himself.

'We'll have it your way then. This boy consumed poison and threw himself before our Devi temple.' He shook his head.

'I still don't . . . Anyway, what do you think made him do that?'

'Medically, I couldn't make a guess,' said Dr Noble.

'He was a patient of yours, wasn't he?'

'In the same way the other lords and ladies of the palace are my patients.'

'Still. What was his condition?'

'I would say he was a healthy young man. Except for a touch of T.B.'

'T.B. Mmm-mm.'

'I'm sure most of you would have a spot of T.B. if you tested for it,' said the doctor easily, leaving them looking at each other in alarm. That concluded the interview and they exchanged a few purposeless pleasantries to record the visit as a casual one.

After that came the priest who officiated at the Manjoor Devi temple, Damodaran Namboodiri. In spite of his more-than-equal status, he was somehow—through a stuffy behavioral Morse code—made to realize he was, after all, only a priest at their temple. In the social heirarchy of namboodiri families, the day belonged to those who had the maximum wealth without visibly doing anything to earn it. Kunnupuram illam wasn't very high on any list, they hadn't been for a century. They had a rather modest income from agriculture and rubber and one or two members of the family regularly performed outside pujas. And who was this Damodaran Namboodiri, relegated relation of the Kunnupuram chief's wife?

'You were going in for the puja, weren't you?' Madras uncle began gently enough.

'A little later than usual because of the rain.'

'Quite understandable,' the patriarch said patronizingly. Like a snake patronizing a frog. 'Coming from Kunnupuram you have to take the back road, the forest path and reach the temple through the other side. But you took the boat, didn't you?' There was a pause. Damodaran swallowed tensely. The other uncles watched in surprise.

'It's not safe, that forest path. After the rain you get

snakes coming up the path to sun themselves. You find
jackals. It's safer to take a cart and come round. And then
take the boat.'

'That must have delayed you even more.'

'No, I was in Iramapuram, I sleep in the school sometimes—
better not take a risk. It's difficult to be on time coming all the
way from the illam.'

Madras uncle frowned. 'Why,' he asked carefully, 'did
you cross the river when the school is on the same side as the
temple?' The other uncles stared in awe. Having heard of
constables grilling villagers at the police post, they realized
that here was a natural-born griller!

'I did go to the school,' said Damodaran, 'but I couldn't
sleep, some great pressure. When I closed my eyes I felt myself
being dragged up.' He looked at the assemblage for their
appreciation. 'So I got up and walked all the way to the jetty
for some milk. But they had shut their shops and were
leaving—so I got into the boat and came to Kilikkara.'

'To the Palace?'

'To Achuthan, your priest here. I had some herbal tea and
spent the night in his house. Early morning I bathed in the
river and took the boat to the temple.'

Madras uncle shut his eyes in confusion. 'You saw the boy
yesterday, didn't you?' he said, changing track.

'He prayed and he left.'

'You're sure?' The priest nodded. 'Nothing unusual about
him?' The priest shook his head. 'When you found the body,
you were surprised, of course.'

'Yes, I would have returned immediately for the boat, but
I stopped. It wouldn't have been human to leave him there.'

'So you bent down and touched the body.'

'To find out if he was still alive.'

'Knowing you had to go and have a second bath.' Madras
uncle frowned. 'It could have been an untouchable.'

'He wasn't. I saw his sacred thread.'

'All right. And then?'

'I called the boatman. We dragged him to the boat and
took him across.'

'You saw spittle on his face. You didn't think of wiping it?'

'No,' said the namboodiri in some disgust.

The Second Patriarch gave an artificial laugh. 'Wouldn't it have been the human thing to do?'

'The doctor saw him exactly as I found him.'

Madras uncle nodded grimly. The interview was over. The others chattered excitedly. Madras uncle was silent, leaning back in his easy chair, deliberating over the mysterious incident. After twenty minutes he came to a conclusion: if anyone knew what had happened, it must be Unni.

When Unni came to, he was surprised to find himself the centre of attention. In the general vagueness of his life, here was a sharper uncertainty.

'What happened?' he asked, coming to for the third time that morning.

Elephant-head uncle and the others waited. Would he dive back again? But Unni gulped in air and turned abjectly to each face in the crowd. He felt hundreds of people were stuffed into the room, staring steadfastly at him.

'He's coming, he's coming!' ran a whisper. The crowd parted like a neat miracle and the Second Patriarch walked through.

'He's awake,' Elephant-head uncle beamed.

Madras uncle sighed. 'After all this time,' he said accusingly.

He looked intently at Unni, touched his forehead with two fingers and nodded gravely. Unni lay still and unblinking like the subject of an important experiment.

'I want a chair,' Madras uncle said. A chair was brought and Madras uncle sat. The crowd waited. 'I want you all to leave,' he said. That was easier said than done. They all lingered, muttered, pushed and each one acted as if he alone was exempt from the order. Finally, when only Elephant-head uncle was left, he pronounced, 'Now we will begin.' Unni waited nervously. The uncle stared at him, trying to frame his question. Then he asked, 'What happened?'

'He wants to know how you came to be in the temple,' Elephant-head uncle translated helpfully. 'And why you took that extreme step.'

'Temple? Oh yes.' He looked bewildered. 'Step? What step?'

'Why you tried to kill yourself,' said Elephant-head uncle, looking at Madras uncle for approval. The Patriarch nodded grimly.

'Kill myself?' Unni laughed. 'I didn't.'

'We know that,' said Madras uncle patiently. 'But you tried. Why?'

'I didn't! I don't know why you say that.'

'Let's put it simply. You were found half-dead at the temple entrance in the rain and slush. What happened?'

Unni struggled to sit up. A pained expression crossed his face as he tried to recollect. 'What we're asking is . . .' began Elephant-head uncle. The Patriarch silenced him with a hand.

'I–I had gone to the temple,' Unni blinked rapidly, trying to focus on Madras uncle's face. 'I've been going there every evening. For more than a week now. So I went last night . . .'

'Not last night. It's been two days.'

'I went—that night—I was there a long time, after everyone else left. It began to drizzle then. So I . . . remained inside. I thought I'd walk with the priest—Damodaran Namboodiri—till the river. He was going to stay in the school because of the rain.' He shut his eyes. 'I felt funny, head was spinning. My heartbeat . . . I couldn't even stand . . .'

'The poison!' breathed Elephant-head uncle.

'I was burning inside. I had to get out of there. I came . . . out of the temple. It was raining—Damodaran called me back. He said, come back! He wanted to know why I was going. And then . . .'

'And then?'

'And then?' Elephant-head uncle held his breath. He looked as if he would burst.

Unni looked puzzled. 'I turned and . . .' He swallowed painfully. 'I was attacked . . .'

Elephant-head uncle let out his breath in a windy explosion. The sudden sound startled Madras uncle, who jumped. 'Who?

Who attacked you?'

'It was he. He called me back. And when I turned, he
. . . slapped me right across the face.'

'Why?' Madras uncle's voice cracked with tension. 'Why
did he slap you? Why should anyone slap you without
reason?'

'His expression—as though he hated me.'

'Damodaran?'

'Right across the face—as if he was punishing me . . .'

Sitting in a space neither here nor there, Damodaran
stopped his world. And refused to move. He didn't go to
Manjoor Devi. Or to the school. He sent word that he
couldn't perform any of his scheduled pujas. He simply sat at
home amidst the debris of his delusions.

Giving Unni the spiked holy water, slapping him in
sudden rage and then leaving him to die were unpardonable
crimes. He had 'found' the body next morning. He'd been
tempted to leave it in the mud for a few more hours. But some
worshipper arriving early to find a not-yet-dead body would
have been embarrassing. Now, of course, he knew it was all
Her will. She'd saved Unni from decomposition. And
Damodaran from a fate worse. If not, he'd have had to live
with the poor boy's death.

It was common knowledge in the village that Unni's
remorse had nothing to do with Kunnupuram. It had to do
with Nani and her pre-blouse dalliances. Now Nani was with
child and Unni firmly believed that he was the father.

But so did a lot of other deserving men in the Palace and
village. Nani's sincerity was such that it evoked paternal
feelings in each of her partners. She had whispered, 'Even a
dead seed will flower if the earth is fertile!' The words sent a
thrill through their hearts. Even an old thampuran, who
solicited her coyly from a third-floor balcony and achieved
relief even as she was climbing the stairs, now felt responsible
for her pregnancy. They thought they owed her something
more than sympathy. The mere thought gave them comfort.
Unni, however, was temperamentally more fine-tuned. He not
only sympathized and felt he ought to do more than sympathize,

he actually did more. He went straight to Uma Amba of Big Palace and confessed to his crime. 'Yes, it's mine,' he told her.

'What is yours?' she asked, wondering if he was claiming things from her palace.

He looked about him, lowered his voice and said: 'The baby! It's mine!'

'I'm afraid there's no baby here,' she told him gently.

'But there is!' he whispered.

'If you're referring to my daughter . . .'

'No, no, no!' He waved his hand impatiently. 'Her baby, Nani's.'

'Nani's?' she repeated stupidly.

'Yes, it's mine!'

'Nani's baby is yours?'

'Yes, it is. I accept it wholeheartedly.'

Uma Amba stood uncertainly. She didn't know what her role was. Everyone knew Nani had spread her affections far and wide. Everyone knew she was with child. For a man, that too a thampuran from the Palace, to come and confess in this manner was rather strange. She wondered what advice or comfort she could offer him.

'Very well.' She nodded gravely.

'You don't believe me!'

'Yes, I do.'

'Really?'

'I don't see any reason why I shouldn't.'

They had reached an impasse. He paused like a spirited athlete who overshoots the tape, lands in a different track, and skids to a halt before a crowd of bewildered spectators. He wanted to back away, but the drama of his arrival required an effective exit. It wasn't every day one confessed to an illegitimate paternity. He had expected anger, threats and much, much more. Uma Amba's calm, slightly bemused reception unnerved him. 'It's my duty,' he said. 'But please don't tell anyone.' He added, 'Unless you have to.' He left her standing and shaking her head.

But finally, when all is said and done, it was Unni who was responsible for Nani's incarceration. It was to him that

Uma Amba came with her strange request. When Nani stood in the village street and shouted out her mind. When she started giving out names, becoming an embarrassment to the Palace. It was more in Nani's interest that Uma Amba acted. Kilikkara would not tolerate Nani for much longer, and there was no saying what form their reprisal might take. So she turned to the only person she could think of: Unni who had already proclaimed his responsibility. He was bound by this feeling.

Uma Amba called him to Big Palace and told him what she wanted. At first, Unni was hesitant. He hadn't expected a solution which excluded the presence of Nani. He'd even been prepared for the ultimate recourse of marrying the girl. It took a week of introspection and soulful solitude to make up his mind. After that he travelled to Trivandrum. On his return he visited Big Palace for the last time—to report to Uma Amba and to fill his heart with a last vision of Nani. He walked into the courtyard and asked bravely for Nani to be brought before him. It was a strange request in the background of Kilikkara's rigid heirarchical structure. Nani was brought amidst raised eyebrows. Unni saw her crimson blouse and the new depth in her eyes. He saw the gentle swell of her belly. He smiled sadly across the courtyard.

Within the week Nani was taken away to a distant illam where she was entrusted to the care of an old and respected ayurvedic practitioner and his assistants.

Damodaran woke up from another of his dreary catnaps. He came out into the courtyard of the outhouse where he stayed. The sun was warm, throwing zigzag shadows of the iron bars above. He washed his feet and upper body, pouring water from the brass spouted vessel. He washed and scrubbed his face till it began to hurt and his eyes glowed red. He retied his long hair. He crossed the courtyard, entering the main building through the side entrance. As he was about to enter the veranda he was stopped by voices. The Elephant Priest, and another voice he couldn't place.

In the cover of shadows he peered out. The Elephant Priest reclined in his easy chair, fanning himself with a straw fan, holding it high up with three fingers as he usually did. In another chair, hands folded across his chest and looking grim, sat MVR from the Palace. Very close to him, burdening another chair, sat that fat thampuran Kochu Kelu. The Elephant Priest's son Vasu sat on the parapet. He seemed distracted, raising himself in a series of nervous push-ups.

The patriarch spoke in a low voice. 'We have taken more than we can bear.' They didn't look at one other. The patriarch gazed out where the birds still flew, the trees still reached for the warm blue sky. 'We've tried our best to be at peace with the Palace. We have a name and a tradition . . . You remember the story about the Chakram.'

'I don't think there's any reason to go into that,' MVR said moodily.

'Is it possible,' the Elephant asked, 'to close our eyes and carry on as if we haven't suffered? A namboo'ri from Kunnupuram stood by the founder of your family. Our family is old, we were directly in touch with the gods. That Chakram protected us and brought us prosperity and guided our family through good and bad times.'

'We know all that,' Kochu Kelu said. MVR was silent, looking weary. Damodaran began to pity him.

'Yes, we all know!' The old man's voice crackled briefly with his famous anger. 'Things were never the same since the Chakram left us. Both our families have suffered.' He turned to MVR. 'You know what I mean.' MVR nodded, their eyes meeting for one burdened moment. The Elephant Priest looked sternly at Kochu Kelu, who leaned forward, looking more than ever like a soft giant-faced ball. 'Don't think this namboo'ri is raking up conflicts a hundred years old.' Kochu Kelu continued to stare with unblinking eyes. 'And now.' The words dropped like heavy metal pieces, splashing the silence around them. Damodaran saw MVR clutch his hands together in his lap. 'During the night of the play, nearly two years ago, there was a theft in our illam.' Damodaran saw them arranged in a dark tableau against the bright sun. What was the patriarch talking about?

The Elephant Priest continued, 'Damodaran is my wife's

relative. He's a great help to the illam, though he may not realize it.' Damodaran listened in surprise. 'If he finds out about his boy . . . Already he acts strangely. I suspect he knows something.' Damodaran held on to the door jamb. The veranda and the three men and the slice of bright blue sky rolled. He blinked to keep them in focus. The Elephant Priest pronounced, 'Enough damage has been done.' MVR sat still, like an ancient figure cursed to remain frozen. Kochu Kelu looked anxiously at him. 'I will give you a way out.' Damodaran heard the bass voice roll from the end of a long tunnel. 'You will forget her, of course, that is understood. In addition, you will ensure that the Chakram comes back. Don't think this is a barter. You must understand—whatever is happening is due to the influence of the Chakram.' He looked squarely at MVR. 'Do you understand, thampuran?' he asked politely, even respectfully. 'Or I will order a vicharana—an enquiry—against Tatri. And she will have to come out with the truth in front of the whole world.'

'You will do that to your own niece?' MVR's face looked drawn and pale.

'Let's discuss this,' Kochu Kelu said, cutting in.

'That is what we're doing. Emotions must be set aside.' His voice turned thin with a strange harshness. 'I will not hesitate to do this for the sake of my illam.'

'What will it achieve?'

Damodaran felt a cold fear come between them. 'If that Chakram doesn't come here . . .' the old man began. 'Do you remember the old curse upon your family?' He looked at MVR and hissed, 'There will never be peace!'

Later, MVR sat in the carriage hunched over like an ailing old man. Kochu Kelu kept his eyes on him. As the carriage clattered noisily over the bridge, he said, 'Don't worry any more. I will take care of things for you.'

The oracle Raghava Panikkar was Damodaran's old classmate. He belonged to a family up north that had produced several celebrated temple oracles.

The oracle would arrive at temple festivals in a trance-like run, wearing a tail of youngsters, armed with the deity's blessings and his curved sword. People came out to greet him with offerings. Little children would scream in delicious terror, hiding behind doors and elders. He drew colourful ritualistic patterns on the ground and accompanied the deity in procession. When the goddess was upon him, he shivered and moaned, caught up in an exalted trance. His forehead broke out in crimson trickles as he struck it repeatedly with his sword. He finally danced with fervour upon the powdered patterns, wiping them off.

He didn't come to the Kilikkara temples, but Damodaran had kept in touch over the years. The oracle listened quietly to his friend. He had studied astrology under his father, and was blessed with the touch of truth on his tongue. While he made a meagre livelihood from oracling, his astrological services were for free. His father had given him the advice passed on by a long line of gurus—never charge unless you want to lose your skill.

Raghava Panikkar threw his cowrie shells and studied the signs. He closed his eyes and meditated for a while and peered at the shells he'd thrown. He threw the shells again. 'This is not the end,' he said.

Damodaran looked agitated. 'What do you mean?'

'Things will not end here. Both families will see more in the decades to come.' He looked up. 'There will be more tragic relationships. It isn't as easy as you think.'

'We'll . . . suffer?'

'I can only tell you the signs.' He saw the pain in Damodaran's eyes. 'Thirumeni, you ask me too much.'

Damodaran folded his hands. 'Tell me as a friend. I can take anything now!'

'What can I say? The Chakram is causing all this trouble. It has to be retrieved and consecrated and buried in a safe place near your family deity under proper conditions. Unless that is done, both families will suffer.'

'We will have it done,' Damodaran said.

'It's easy to say. Sometimes people see and yet they cannot

act.' The oracle put the shells back into their little pouch. 'What is Fate if not that? It's your karmam.'

'I'll see it is brought back. Uncle has warned the Kilikkara people.'

'What is written will have to happen.'

Damodaran's dark face seemed carved from stone. 'I don't want my Tatri to suffer,' he said.

TEN MONKEYS AND AN ELEPHANT

———————————————— ■ ————————————————

Oars sliced black waves with a cottony whisper.

The moon in panic had wedged itself into the sky, disappearing if you peered. They sat in the large wooden boat, hushed and unreal, sharing this journey out of life. Clouds spread outward like fading tattered pieces of a grey curtain. They heard the screech of an owl from a distance. They looked at each other for comfort. An icy breeze sailed over the water and ruffled their clothes. The boatman was a dark creaking creature of polished stone with shining muscular arms. His eyes were white fluorescent marbles. They watched him uneasily as he rowed. His hands went up and down, circling, grasping the oars with easy strength. When he leaned forward to splash them into the liquid bosom, the entire boat seemed to sway with the motion.

In a corner of the middle seat facing the boatman sat Thambi, a small balding gentleman, a cousin from Northern Palace—busybody, poor-cousin and assistant to the temple manager. His hobby was playing good Samaritan, and he didn't mind accepting spontaneous gifts in return. Thambi was a nickname that told an old amusing story no one remembered.

Black glowing waters streaked with silver. On either side stood enormous hooded trees like blind sentinels. The boat was headed towards a forest, a dense forest where yakshis sat on treetops thirsting for the blood of passers-by. They accosted them in the guise of beautiful girls, smiling and seducing before baring sharp teeth.

He trembled, with cold and the wonder of this morning. He'd been feeling feverish since rising from bed. Lekha leaned forward. 'Let's say goodbye now,' she murmured in his ear. 'He's surely going to have us for breakfast!' He stared at her. She spoke in English, with no change of expression. He shot a glance at the boatman who rowed impassively like clockwork. Laughter exploded through his pursed lips and nostrils, coming out in a snort. The boatman looked at him with some interest. Thambi half turned his head, then decided it wasn't any of his business.

He wiped his mouth and looked away. It was amazing. She was still keeping a straight face. His hand crawled forward and found hers lying on the seat. He squeezed it. She looked up and grinned. She looked fresh and happy, like a bright sprite of the night. Her hair lay loose and gleaming black around her shoulders. She wore a green blouse and a white mundu-sari, both bordered with gold. They had risen at half-past four, had a bath and set out for the river. The boatman had been informed the previous day. It was customary for family members arriving in the Palace to attend the early-morning puja at the Manjoor Devi temple the following day.

The boat gently bumped into the shore. The boatman jumped out and pushed. He then stood aside, shining a large torch as they got out. Thambi first, he followed, then she. When she jumped down, he was there to help her. He staggered back against her weight and she laughed and he stood holding her. Thambi, a small black bag clutched within his armpit and looking importantly deferential, waited for them to finish their little amusements and come on. He too carried a torch, and played patterns in the dark while he waited.

Further up they could see a row of thatched huts standing squarely in their way. They were shops, barricaded for the night. The path ran in front of the shops and along the river towards Iramapuram and the village school. Another less conspicuous pathway tumbled away from the shops and into the forest. Thambi nodded curtly at the boatman and walked up in front. The sparse torchlight showed them virtually nothing and they had to keep close behind him. It was a path only because people walked that way every day. Bushes brushed, branches reached out and touched them as they walked awkwardly in single file, pulled by the straggly yellow light.

The dark cold air girdled them. It was like walking into the womb of the night. The reedy, sudden, full-throated and startling sounds of the forest, some far, some disturbingly near, made them walk faster, single-mindedly. The shrill silence kept the blood nervously alive and pounding within their head. He felt a pressure growing inside his head.

'This forest is supposed to be inhabited by yakshis,' Thambi said conversationally. 'They come upon you, as beautiful as Mohini. They entice you and that is the end of you.'

'They're sitting up there on all these trees?'

'Perhaps.'

'You really believe that?'

'What is there to believe?' Thambi said. 'If our hand burns, we know what is heat!' The silence that followed was denser.

They came across a lighted clearing and the tiled gables of the temple rose like a sudden impulse of the night. Thambi stood aside. 'Come on.' At the entrance, the men removed their shirts. They left their slippers outside and walked in, lifting their legs over the high stile. The sanctum was still shut, the puja was in progress. They stood with folded hands, listening to the mournful beat of the edakka, the small flat drum played in monotonous rhythm by a small boy. There was dew in the air. A cold breeze wreathed his bare body, touching his bones. But even with that, he was sweating. She drew in her shoulders. Thambi's little black bag peered out

from his armpit and he played idly with its zip. The boy with
the edakka leaned on the stone wall, sleepy and torpid,
playing dreamily, bringing a new quality of langour to the
rhythm.

The priest threw open the doors. She appeared in a blaze
of light. She wore a scarlet sari and carried a trident. The
edakka surged. The priest showed the many-tiered arathi
gleaming with flame, dripping and dancing and rocking the
idol with its effulgence. They shut their eyes, merging into this
sharper reality. The priest came with the prasadam. He threw
the leaf containing kumkum and sandal paste into their palms,
careful not to touch them. He trickled holy water into their
palms which they drank. They brought their palms together
and prayed. This is the Earth Mother, Mother of the Universe,
essence of all life that ever was, is, will be. She encloses all life
in the palm of her hand. A special puja, arranged for him by
his mother, was then performed in their presence. They all
prostrated themselves. They circumambulated the temple. By
the time they were ready to leave, tiny tendrils of light were
curling around the branches of dense foliage.

They walked back in single file. Suddenly Gopi stopped.
'Oh-ho!'

'What is it?'

'My wallet! It must have fallen.'

'Where?'

'I think when I was prostrating. Or I must have left it on
that ledge.'

'We'll go back and get it.'

'No, no, you stay, I'll go. Two seconds!'

She stood watching his back. They could hear the twigs
beneath his feet long after he was out of sight. Thambi tried
to make conversation but she wasn't in the mood to listen.
Blue-silhouetted forms were rising into view. Birds sprang up
and cried and rustled leaves. They could hear the sound of
water from a distance. A fractured column of pale golden light
swirled down through a brown gap between two tall trees.
After a while, she said, 'What's happening?'

'Mmm . . . he said he'd be back in seconds . . .'

'It's already ten minutes.'

'Don't worry, he must be talking with the priest or something.'

'Leaving us waiting here?'

So they walked back, she in front. They walked into the clearing and had almost reached the entrance when she stopped with a gasp. Gopi lay sprawled on the mud. His arms were splayed, one hand clutching his wallet. 'Oh my God!' She ran forward. But she couldn't bend down and touch him, she stood frozen. Thambi hesitated. He glanced apologetically up at her and placed his fingers beneath his nostrils. 'It's all right,' he smiled. Her face was pale. 'We must get help, we'll get the boatman.'

Gopi remembered nothing.

'How did it happen?'

'What?'

'You fell?'

'I don't know. I was just tired.'

'Was someone there? Did someone attack you?'

'No, of course not!'

'We heard Thambi was talking of yakshis. Couldn't have been that, I'm sure!' He didn't reply. He felt he'd become part of someone else's ridiculous dream. He looked at Thambi who stood with a half-shy twist of a smile. 'But you have a wound, don't you?' He felt gingerly behind his head. He could see Thambi's fingers mirroring his own, slipping from glassy plain to thick forest fringes. He winced and nodded. 'That happened when you fell? You left them and went to pick up your purse. You remember that much?' He nodded, yes. 'And then they waited and waited.'

It became the talk of the entire Palace. Eager questions were directed at Gopi and Lekha and Thambi. There was one word on everyone's lips: 'Omen!' 'Why is it an omen?' he asked. And they answered reasonably, 'Because it is.' Finally, as it was bound to happen, after circling over and over, the trail pointed once again to Kunnupuram. 'You were chosen,' they told him. 'That's ridiculous!' he said. He remembered Kolappan sitting in the drawing room, saying solemnly, 'Brother took it upon himself.'

His mother said, 'You don't lose anything, just go there

and talk to them.'

Gopi laughed. 'I can't believe you believe all this! Some Chakram—'

'Don't forget, that's why you're here in the first place. Please, Sarada will be very disappointed if you don't go to Kunnupuram.'

'Don't worry,' Shankar said. 'I'll take him there, it was chettan's last wish.' Leaving Gopi with no choice in the matter, having come all the way on an errand for a dead man.

Kunnupuram illam was a dusty set of buildings around a large inner courtyard. It was plainly very old, carefully constructed and very badly maintained. There were fields all around, both cultivated and fallow stretches, and two tanks inside the property with bathhouses for men and women. Most of the land, however, was overgrown with shrubs and weeds and unexpected snakepits—ragged mud shapes rising like forgotten earth-frozen hermits.

No one used the tanks or bathhouses any more. The waters, choked with weed and moss and perverse lifeforms, still managed a ripple or a bubble or two. Perhaps sighing out their memories of bygone conversations, forgotten laughter, doomed rendezvous. Decades ago, the family had begun thinking of covering up the tanks. They were still thinking.

After Narayanan Namboodiri's death, some of the younger men wanted to sell off a part of the land to two tile factories. Their elders intervened with the standard line: 'Go ahead and do what you want, but after our time. We won't see our home being chopped up.' The tile factories came up elsewhere, nearer the river, belching black smoke and red slogans. A little after that, a half-acre of illam property was gobbled up by the state government, acquired for a paltry delayed remuneration. The land was fenced in and cleared for a state guest house. The government fell soon after, and the new ruling coalition had no M.L.A. in the area to pursue the matter. So the guest house remained on the drawing board. The younger namboodiris came out with bitter I-told-you-so's. As always, Kunnupuram existed in a crossfire of doomed and delayed decisions.

Accompanied by Shankar and Thambi, armed with the

blessings of everyone in the Palace, Gopi alighted from a taxi outside the illam. An awkwardly moving young man ran up to welcome them. 'Come,' he said. 'Uncle is waiting for you.' They climbed the steps to the inner veranda. The head of the family was Raman Namboodiri, a dark old man with hooded eyebrows, discreetly known as the Elephant, since he was reputed to resemble his legendary ancestor.

'I'm happy. It's been a long while.' He shaded his eyes and gazed like an anxious fisherman peering across the waters. 'Narayanan's son. You were only a boy when I came to the Palace for his death ceremonies.' Gopi was silent. The ceremonies in Kilikkara had been against convention impelled by his mother's iron grief. Both Palace and illam had frowned upon her decision. 'You should come more often,' the old man said. 'After all, we're family. I used to go over to see your mother. Nowadays I don't leave the illam.' He pointed at Shankar. 'He has been coming over recently. It's good to keep in touch.' Gopi turned, raising his eyebrows, but Shankar didn't meet his eyes.

They sat in the warping warmth, talking idly about this and that. Thambi asked about the piece of land that had gone. 'Yes, you have to remain quiet and accept what they say.'

'You can fight to increase the compensation.'

Raman Namboodiri shook his head with a dry smile. 'Those are long-drawn processes. Who'll keep running in and out of courts?'

'Only aristocrats and namboodiris are like that,' Thambi said spiritedly. 'Anyone else will fight for their rights. What about those tile factories, you could have made some money there.'

'Money is not everything.' Leaning back impassively in his easy chair, the old man looked like some dark idol against a haze of sunlight. 'We'd be sitting here with smoke and noise and dust in the air.' He waved a hand. All about them were curtains of brown and green, shimmering silently in the sun. 'At least now though the land isn't ours, it isn't anybody else's either.'

'The government can use it whenever they want,' said Thambi.

'For now, it is peaceful.'

A rusty fan with a lot of complaints tried to give them comfort from the heat. Shankar picked up a magazine and fanned himself. Gopi wiped his forehead with a corner of his dhoti. Pulling his chair towards the trajectory of the fan, Thambi made a weary noise: 'Shhh-hhhuuu!' A small naked child came to the doorway and smiled at them, waving a dripping lollipop. As they considered his offer, a dour-looking middle-aged woman came up and snatched him away. A stray breeze shook the branches, came in and touched them with its heated edge.

Shankar turned to the Elephant. 'We came primarily to discuss the Chakram.' A frantic bicycle bell sounded from the road. The old man didn't reply. He was so still they wondered if he'd dropped off to sleep.

'That Chakram,' the old man intoned. And went back to his silence.

'We're not happy about the past,' Shankar said. 'We came to make amends and to ask you to join us for a puja in the Palace.'

The namboodiri looked up. They weren't sure of his expression. 'It's been centuries. Now, all of a sudden . . .'

'Everyone had a different opinion. This time even our Patriarch is keen that we get closer to Kunnupuram.'

'There's been some trouble?'

Shankar looked at Gopi and Thambi. 'Let's say we want to avoid trouble.'

'After all these years.'

'An oracle could tell us what to do.'

The Elephant made an imperceptible movement of his head. 'What,' he asked unexpectedly, 'is a curse?' Even Thambi turned from the fan to stare at him. 'Words uttered in anger and bitterness, isn't it?' He leaned forward and fixed Shankar with his eyes. 'Words have tremendous strength. That is why mantras, repeated with conviction, can achieve so much. Words travel across time.'

They sat buried in the heat.

Gopi felt stifled. He rose abruptly. 'Can I go out and take a look?'

They looked at him in surprise. Shankar said, 'Wait, we haven't finished.'

Raman Namboodiri said, 'You have to be careful, there may be snakes.' Gopi nodded. 'I'll send someone with you.'

'No, I prefer to walk alone. I've come here with my father once.'

'I remember that. You started to cry, wanting to return home.'

He told Shankar, 'I'll be back,' and stepped out into the heat. He walked past their line of vision towards the shrouded greenery. He stood uncertainly, wondering what he was doing there. Once their voices resumed, he moved forward. Even the undergrowth behind Big Palace was neat compared to this! There were hundreds of coconut trees, several mango and jackfruit trees as far down the land as he could see. Other trees, tall and dusty, leaned in leafy clusters, accepting limited measures of sunlight.

The whole place had an ancient untouched air. He walked through the heavy clutch of bush, looking in vain for a path, feeling like an explorer cutting through virgin forests. He remembered the Elephant's warning about snakes and slowed his pace, watching the ground vigilantly. He heard an abrupt sound and froze.

A large bush before him shuddered. It wasn't the breeze, there was something in there. A strangled sudden scream stunned him. It was followed by a long half-human chattering sound. He started to turn back, but his leaden calf muscles rooted him. In the rush of desperation, he wanted to call out. His mouth remained dry and pasted shut. Panic rose slowly like dark blood.

He moved cautiously back. The chattering sounded again, sharper. He moved blindly, wading past complicated branches and leaves, scratching himself badly. Suddenly a dark shape leapt out of the bush and flew up, landing on a branch. Gopi hissed out his breath and smiled, looking at the large male monkey glaring at him, squatting like some prehistoric demigod. He began to edge away. The monkey stayed where it was. Another monkey emerged noisily from behind the bush, head, body, then a slyly curling tail. It was smaller. It jumped, and

joined the first one on the branch. Gopi waited till it had
settled, then he began to move again.

A scream and a chatter. He froze. Another head peered
from the bush, then another. A fourth. It grinned at him, its
teeth gleaming devilishly in the green dimness, a furry death's
head. His heart began to wobble against his chest. His hands
were clenched to his hips, nails hurting his palms. They were
going to attack. He prayed, Kilikkara Appa, save me, help me
just this once! There was a deafening flurry of movement that
dazed him. Sent him staggering back, red-faced, fast-hearted,
blinded.

As he watched aghast, more monkeys leaped onto the
branches below and above the first one, chattering, uttering
small screams, baring their teeth and gesturing. He felt a
sinking sensation from throat to the pit of his stomach. He
counted mechanically. There were ten monkeys, big and small,
some excited, some grave, others watching malevolently.
Something snapped within his head. He moved back, crashing
through the bushes, hurting himself. The animals stopped their
noises. They sat motionless, all of them, suddenly caught up
in silence, watching him carefully like a well-behaved audience.
He kept backing away. They're not going to follow me, he
thought with heart-wrenching relief. Then the first monkey,
enormous and grim-faced, jumped down from the branch with
a clatter.

Gopi turned and ran, not looking to see if he was being
followed. He had lost all sense of direction. He knew he was
getting deeper into the thicket but he couldn't stop. The
bushes fell away, giving way to mud and grass. There was a
tile-roofed shed before him, its door standing ajar. He almost
fell in, banging the creaking sluggish door behind him with the
full weight of his body. He stood leaning against it, breathing
raggedly, for a long time, listening intently through the roar
of his breathing and his wild heart. When he could hear the
silence again, he crept back to earth.

He looked around. He was in a bathhouse, dirty and long
unused. He could see a green glow towards the ledge, a dull
reflection of the water. Someone knocked on the door, startling
him. 'Who is it?' he called out cautiously. There was silence.

He repeated the question, certain it couldn't be one of the monkeys!

From the other side came a woman's voice. 'I thought there was someone! Who is it?'

More confident now, and not wanting to spend the afternoon playing knock-knock, he pulled open the door. A girl in her late twenties wearing a white cotton sari stood before him. Her eyes looked back at him with wide seriousness. Her hair was brushed away from her broad forehead and lay in neatly oiled waves behind her face, tied at the back by braided strands. There was a bright sandal mark on her forehead and her eyes were lined thickly with kohl. In the transparent silence of the hot afternoon, they stood regarding each other.

She spoke first. 'You're from Kilikkara, aren't you?' He nodded, staring at her. 'Then we're cousins.' His heart began to gallop again.

'I'm Gopi,' he said.

'Grandfather is looking for you. Tea is ready.' She smiled suddenly. 'You weren't having a bath, I'm sure. The water's rotten. What were you doing in there?'

'There was a big bunch of monkeys, snarling and ready to attack.' The more he thought of it, the more vicious those monkeys became. 'I ran and came in here.'

She frowned. 'We do have them in the illam, but they don't attack people. I've never heard . . .'

'They didn't actually attack—they certainly looked as if they would!' He stopped. 'How cousin?'

'I'm Raman Namboodiri's elder son's daughter. He and your father were cousins, weren't they?'

Gopi said, 'That's true. So we're cousins. What is your name?'

'Sridevi.' She began to move away. 'Come, they'll be waiting.'

When they reached the veranda, the Elephant said, 'Ah, here he is, she's brought him.'

They were having tea and hot crisp vadas. Thambi made slurping sounds, articulating his enjoyment. Shankar frowned at him as he came in and then concentrated on what he was eating. Gopi told them about his strange experience with the monkeys.

'Mmm—' The old man looked thoughtful.

Sridevi stood by the door, listening to them. Gopi put down his tumbler and sat back, once again arrested by her face. Framed by the dark doorway, the girl looked like a white reflection, or a ghost. He turned away but then caught himself staring compulsively at her through the corner of his eyes.

The old man broke the silence. 'Have you read your grand-uncle's epic?' Shankar nodded, looking up briefly from his plate. 'When the king's son rushes into the forest after Mohini, he finds her gone and only the bird left behind. And then he's chased by a bunch of militant monkeys. You remember?'

'Yes. He's rescued by the king's soldiers who take him home.'

The old man peered outside, leaning forward in his chair. 'There's another thing. The day MVR died, it is said that Kilikkara Palace was overrun by monkeys.'

'I didn't know that,' Gopi said.

'I've heard that too,' Thambi said. 'My mother used to say that.'

He smiled, looking at each of them. 'If you look at the sky right now, you will see dark clouds building up. I think we can expect a storm soon.'

Shankar walked to the parapet and looked up. 'You're right,' he said. 'Big storm coming up.'

'That is if,' the old man continued, 'you believe in omens.'

THE TRY-HARD SPIRIT

Gopi returned home in a peculiar frame of mind.

The day had begun normally enough. He rose early, bathed and worshipped at the Kilikkara Appan temple. While circumambulating, he spent extra time at the Devi sanctum where the controversial Chakram had once been buried and then excavated, to be lost forever. The floor was smooth and unbroken. The Devi looked calm in the light of the three oil lamps, not too worried about excavations and thefts. The date for the placatory pujas would be fixed by weekend, everything would be well—he sat down on the cool floor and prayed that everything should go well.

He went home to breakfast and his mother's unbeatable kai-swadh, the distinctive 'hand taste' of the truly good cook. When he ate more than double his quota of soft steaming idlis, Lekha made a dramatic gesture of surprise. 'You're hungry today!'

His mother laughed. 'He won't be by the time he leaves Kilikkara.'

'Don't make him fat, ammey!'

'He's thirty-five, he's entitled to be fat.'

'In fact, now's the time to start worrying about health!' Lekha directed a meaningful look at Gopi, who began to scowl signals at her. But Lekha, being Lekha, said nothing more.

After breakfast, he settled down in a couch and they immediately touched upon his mysterious fainting. His mother tried to remain calm. 'You'll see a good neurosurgeon the moment you reach Madras.'

'They said it's only an omen.'

'Yes, but we'll also rule out the medical part!'

'I was feeling feverish that morning, that's all.'

'Then I'll call our doctor, let him check you first.'

Gopi couldn't proceed beyond his first protest. His temple tumble had already passed into public domain; he had done his part, now others were taking over. The incident had excited all of Kilikkara, most of all Thambi who had turned into a sought-after reconteur.

They talked of their visit to Kunnupuram. Shankar said, 'We'll probably go down in history as the ones who lifted the curse.'

'Sarada will be happy. She thinks RV's death has something to do with this.'

'That's our friend Kolappan's contribution!'

'There's supposed to be a victim in every generation.'

'Maybe you'll get by without one after all,' Lekha said.

Gopi burst out unexpectedly, 'Frankly, sometimes I think I'm the one!'

They stared at him, not knowing whether to laugh or sympathize.

Gopi's dark mood continued when he dragged himself from his couch. 'This eating and sitting and gossiping will bloat me up. I'm going for a walk.'

Lekha asked, 'You're all right?' He nodded shortly and walked out.

He strolled past the temple to the bathing ghat. The river lay sparkling in the sun. There were stray groups of people at various points in the distance, swimming, washing, bathing, idly fishing. The boat was midway from the opposite bank, carrying a few aimless-looking passengers. He smiled, thinking how harmless the boatman looked in broad daylight. He thought, beyond the river, across the forest, a few kilometres away, and there lies Kunnupuram. It was funny how a place could be so near and so remote at the same time. It ought to have been a much bigger part of his life. He saw Sridevi outside the bathhouse, her sudden smile as she said, 'You weren't having a bath, I'm sure!' And afterwards, standing in the doorway, lighting up the room in her white sari. He stood staring at the river and thinking of her before he was jolted back to the heat of the morning and realized how long he'd been standing there, staring at the river and thinking of her.

As he was walking back, he saw the Palace office open, and went in. He made out three men sitting and playing cards. The air was dim, choked with cigarette smoke. He didn't recognize the two younger men. The third was Vikraman, a cousin from Eastern Palace. Seeing him, Vikraman cried halt. He introduced the others as friends from the village, and waited pointedly till they'd said their pieces and left. He stretched up and threw open a window, letting in light and air. Gopi sat down and lit a cigarette.

Vikraman asked, 'Do you want some coffee?' He shook his head. 'Water?' He nodded. Vikraman filled a glass from a mud pot and gave it to him. The water was cold and tasted muddy.

'Where do you get coffee in this place?'

Vikraman shook his head, grinning. 'I simply hoped you'd say no!'

'How's your Institute getting on? Last time I remember you couldn't control admissions, people were crowding in.'

'That's true,' he said in a flat voice. He had very fair skin and combed-back oily hair. His eyes were almost green. The sleeves of his blue shirt were folded halfway up his arms and Gopi noticed a sheen of shabbiness around the folds. There was a wasted look about him, as if his personality was being suppressed and kept from reaching the world. Gopi watched him and found a new hesitation, like someone recovering from a surgery or personal loss. 'It's doing well, isn't it?' He sat rocking determinedly, his chair wildly hitting the wall. Gopi waited, two double hits and one down, vigorous but vigilant, a thought between movements—tak-tak tak-tak tak. He tried to figure out the expression on his cousin's face. 'Must be doing well. I'm sure it is.'

There was a moment of awkward silence. Their cigarette smoke found flat shafts of light from the open window.

All of Kilikkara had rejoiced in the success of Try-hard Commercial Institute with its typewriting-shorthand courses, accountancy and BCom. coaching (which involved procuring notes from a Madras college and dissecting question papers from previous exams). Proprietor Vikraman was himself a high school dropout. His teaching staff consisted of very old men whose retirement from whatever it was they'd retired from couldn't be considered in terms of dates, achievements or certificates. Nevertheless, Try-hard grew popular. Students rushed in, magnetized by the prospect of doing something when all about them loomed unemployment and pricey college seats. It was a growing phenomenon in the highly literate state of Kerala. Education led to unemployment, and money, pawned-borrowed-begged-bled, led to that four-letter world Gulf.

The unemployed in Kerala found time heavy on their hands and turned intellectual for want of anything better to do. They found philosophy in politics, books and films, and in their own sad personal relationships and even in common household objects. They philosophized their predicaments and saw themselves as romantic symbols. Sometimes they fell into a depression and committed suicide. They sailed through local institutes and parallel colleges, prolonging their scholastic bliss before stepping out on the scalding sands of adult responsibility. Regular colleges were full of strikes and political intrigue; and working days could be counted on one's fingertips. Institutes and parallel colleges were more serious places. Students were crammed into tiny rooms and often yelled at by their lecturers, most of them couldn't even obtain hall tickets for public exams—but work went on, and parallel was metamorphosing into mainstream.

Vikraman had certainly tried hard. That was why people wanted to see him succeed. They felt he was one up on history, or that fortune was finally smiling upon his family. His legacy was such . . .

His grand-uncle had been a failed lawyer. In fact, a failed law student. After failing in three sincere attempts to get through his BL, he returned home darkly determined to make something of his education anyway. 'I'm going to write books,' he announced. 'My learning will stand me in good stead.'

Kilikkara, especially Eastern Palace, had a healthy respect for those who could tear themselves from their leisurely predictable lifestyles and venture into alternate areas of experience. Whether he was an army sepoy, a clerk, a doctor or judge, the standard response to the non-resident Kilikkarite was laced with wonder and admiration. The grand-uncle was given a grand reception. They cleared one of the upstairs rooms and placed it at his disposal. The family donated paper and pencils and pens as well as books to add to the library he'd brought home from college. He sat down and wrote long and hard. No one disturbed him. It was, no doubt, the genesis of the Try-hard spirit.

He churned out book after book. Each one was privately published as a hundred-page paperback, and released with pomp and celebration. In the beginning, he wrote *Acts and Contracts, Common Law Property* and *Common Property Law*. Then came *Marital Law* followed by *Martial Law* and *Maritime Law*. (It was generally agreed that this uncle had a poet's feel for words.) The family was startled when he followed that with the next series which contained *Brother-in-Law, Father-in-Law* and *In-Laws In Law*.

The family intervened at this stage, feeling that he needed a change of scene. He was aired out of the upstairs room and pushed into a history teacher's brief vacancy in the Palace school. The position was briefer than anyone expected. The headmaster, walking past the uncle's class a week after his appointment, noticed strange and frenetic activity going on inside. He looked in and found the uncle at the head of the class, sternly instructing his students, 'Sit—stand—sit—stand—sit—stand . . .' The children were obeying him, looking exhausted and pale, having been sitting and standing continuously for close to an hour.

That was, mercifully, the end of his teaching career. He returned to his world of books and proceeded then from *In-Law* to *Illa* which, in Malayalam, means 'no' or 'not available'. Probably making veiled references to his mealtimes he entitled books in his next series *Uppil-law* (no salt), *Molakil-law* (no chilli) and *Swadhil-law* (no taste). By now he was regularly being visited by a retinue of doctors and well-wishers.

Finally, one morning when he refused to open his study door, seemingly engrossed in his current masterpiece, the Eastern Palace senior ordered they should break open the door. With a curse or two poised on her lips the old lady strode into the room and stepped back, dumbfounded. The author sat straight in a high-backed chair in the centre of the large room, wearing a flowing lawyer's gown of black silk, stiffened in rigor mortis. His eyes were wide open. On an open notebook placed on the table nearby was scrawled a single word: 'pattil-law', not possible.

The legend Legal uncle hadn't faded when the family threw up yet another pioneer. This was different from anything anyone had ever tried in Kilikkara. Vikraman's maternal uncle was a fine gentleman who'd joined the army in the twenties and risen to the rank of major. He took premature retirement with full benefits. He returned home, carrying nothing but a small bundle of personal belongings wrapped in saffron cloth and dressed in ochre robes that displayed most of his chest and legs. The family was disconcerted but rallied around, true to their spirit of trying anything once.

The uncle went and sat under a tree near the Elephant Estate. Shocked, some of his cousins tried to persuade him to do whatever he had in mind within the confines of his palace. The uncle smiled. 'I sacrificed all that long ago.' Like Emperor Ashoka who renounced the world in the battlefield, Major uncle had rapidly and successfully moved from arms to ashes.

Let's be fair to the man. In his case, the family is more to be blamed. When he embraced the tree, they fenced off the area to give him exclusivity. When he was content to sustain himself on a simple diet of vegetables and fruits from nearby plants and trees, they brought him milk and fruits from home. When he expressed a desire to be alone, they spread the word that he had suddenly become divine, unleashing a daily stream of besotted visitors. When he sang personal songs to his god, his newly acquired devotees followed him in chorus. When he touched a baby's forehead for the sheer joy of touching a baby's forehead and inexplicably its week-long fever subsided, he was touted as a miracle healer, a skilful toucher of foreheads.

The family was responsible. They turned a simple man of god into a god of men. Major R.V. Raja, retd, became Major Swami. Streams flowed. Faith chanted. Life stilled.

One day, Major Swami brought out his hand from beneath his upper cloth. He brought out an orange along with it for the simple reason that he had been holding on to it all the while. Unfortunately, there was a crowd. 'Look, miracle, miracle!' ran a cry. And he was indelibly branded. This would have gone on, their simple faith and his innocence and the incidental healing of the sick. He would sing, they'd chorus; he would ramble, they'd listen. All would have been well. Arms to ashes, army to swamy.

But then he started believing in himself. He succumbed to swamihood. He tried to replicate his miracle. He started producing oranges from upper cloths. He showered holy ash on the palms of people. He started guessing things about his devotees—their domestic problems, what horrors lay in store for them, what sort of financial future they could expect, even approximate dates of death.

But life is often cruel. It takes back its gifts with such unthinking callousness. Never blessed with sleight of hand even during the height of his gun-handling days, Major Swami began to fumble. He dropped oranges in the middle of miracles. His left hand betrayed a secret cache of holy ash even as his right hand was 'producing'. When he sang, he forgot the words. His tunes sounded suspiciously like old

Hindi film hits of Surendra and Noorjehan. He started guessing wrong.

Faith is seldom as deep as its wounds. They got together and gave him an ultimatum. They made it clear that his status as a Kilikkara thampuran (even though he had renounced all that) was the only reason for their charity. The ultimatum was: 'Get out of Kilikkara or else.' Such a thing would have been unthinkable some thirty years before. Now People Power was here, and here to stay. Major Swami wasn't in the least bothered. As he came, he left. It was said he spent his last days at the Guruvayoor temple, eating prasadam, singing his own personal songs to God and even touching a few baby foreheads with impunity. His battles were finally over and God was as close as he would ever get.

When Vikraman made good, it was expected that the family had regained the straight path.

'But I couldn't manage it,' he told Gopi finally. 'They kept telling me thampurans like us are only fit for eating, sleeping and having oil baths.' He went tak-tak tak-tak tak. 'Perhaps they're right, we aren't capable of anything else.' He squinted crossly at the bright light. 'When the family suffers, your pioneering spirit goes for a six! Soon we were spending more money than it was coming in, and they politely told me to stop. You know how it is, you've gone through this whole thing, haven't you?'

The smoke left agitatedly through the window. The two ex-entrepreneurs of Kilikkara Palace sat gravely facing each other. 'So what are you doing now?'

Did he smile? Gopi couldn't be sure. His expression was ambiguous, it showed bared teeth and inflamed eyebrows. 'Nothing,' Vikraman said. 'I debate and play cards. I eat and sleep and have oil baths like any self-respecting thampuran. I've joined the Communist Party—Marxist. That keeps me somewhat busy.'

Gopi nodded. 'Communist Party, eh?'

'They're happy to get someone from the Palace.'

'What do you do? Hold flags and shout slogans?'

Vikraman said. 'I'm in the literacy wing. Propagating

scientific rationalism. It's unusual for the people, seeing someone like me speak.'

'Because of all this?'

'I'm the first thampuran hereabouts who's actually joined the party.'

Gopi considered him. 'You believe seriously in . . .'

He smiled at Gopi. 'We've had some times together, haven't we? When we were small.' Gopi nodded, returning his smile. 'The river, the temple, the classes—Monkey! Exciting excursions downriver.' Gopi kept nodding and smiling. 'That's all over!' Vikraman delivered a smart karate chop on the table. 'Let's say this is all behind me. I find party work much more life-affirming than anything I've done before.'

'It's not a full-time thing . . .'

'Oh, yes.' Vikraman stopped himself. 'You're right. It's no substitute for a job.'

'I didn't mean . . .'

'I get a lease from the fellow who took over the Institute. That's enough for me. As long as I don't do anything foolish like getting married.'

'Isn't that going to happen some day?'

He drove the chair forward and sat hunched. 'They keep bringing up horoscopes and emotions and threats.'

'And?'

'It's not a must in my life.' He was silent, turning his face to the window. The light drew his profile. 'If there comes a stage when I must bend before life, then . . .' He clicked his tongue. 'I don't know, I may surrender totally.'

'Why are you so gloomy?' Gopi asked with a briskness he didn't feel.

'Because we're from the Palace, does it mean we live charmed lives?' His voice sounded harsh. 'Float around in the air and allow nothing to touch us?' He ran a finger up the window bar. 'That's stupid! You should know that, living away from all this.' Gopi waited, wanting to get out of this room and walk away. 'Look! Look at me!' Vikraman said roughly. Gopi moved his head back, frowning. 'Come, come!' Vikraman got up, pushing back his chair with a scraping sound. 'Come!' He almost dragged him to the door and pushed his face forward into the stark sunlight. His green eyes glinted sharply.

'What is it?' Gopi asked, irritated.

'These eyes are slowly fading away! I'm on medication, but it's going faster than the doctors can cope.'

Gopi was stunned. 'Your eyes!'

'Yes, my eyes!' A look of desperation came into his eyes and he shut them tightly, irritably. 'I told you, there'll soon come a day . . . Till then . . .'

Later he stepped out of the building and stood arrested in the sun. He saw his shadow grown small and squat. He felt dislocated, in the grip of emotion, but he also felt an unnamed relief.

When he entered Raga Sudha, he was in a stranger mood than when he'd left. He washed his feet and climbed the steps. He stopped in the cool drawing room, his eyes caught by the large oil painting in its carved frame directly before him. *Lament of Mohini*. Dark trees, a burning sky and the girl in sorrow, her upraised arm and swollen breast. For a fraction of a moment, she seemed to him to move forward from the flat clutch of the painting. Staring at him from the shadows, those eyes unbearable in their misery. He stared back, consumed by the closeness of the room, feeling they were together in some dark and ancient prison, ravaged by centuries of suffering. Vikraman's voice rang in his ears.

In the rear hall, his mother sat talking to someone.

'Gopi, come and see if you recognize her.'

He walked up. 'Of course. Sridevi.' The girl was wearing a yellow red-bordered sari. Her hair was tied up in a knot behind. He thought, for the second time, how open and warm her large kohl-lined eyes made her look as she smiled to greet him. He went and sat by the bay window.

'You've made quite an impression on her.'

'I'm sure!'

'Really.'

'What—the bravery?' he asked. Sridevi laughed.

His mother looked relaxed. She had put on weight since

his last visit. Her hair was still black except for strands of unexpected white streaking down on either side. Her face was full and pleasant, undone by the dark curves beneath her eyes—but Subhadra's eyes were stern and discouraged people from taking her at face value.

'She'll be thinking of monkeys whenever she sees me!' Sridevi laughed again. He enjoyed the clear timbre of her laughter. Lekha came in with coffee and biscuits. 'Here—' She served them and curled up in a chair with a cup.

Gopi said, 'If this was fifty years ago, would you be walking about like this?'

'Oh, why?'

'Because you're a namboodiri girl,' his mother told her.

'Well, times have changed. Even my mother was a graduate.'

'That's fantastic. Was she at home when I came?'

'She's no more,' his mother said. 'Last year she passed away.'

Lekha said, 'Isn't it strange, you're cousins and you haven't even seen her mother.'

Sridevi smiled. 'The namboodiri part of the family is usually out of bounds.'

'Don't I know that!' Subhadra said. 'At least now things have changed. Most of the girls in Kunnupuram are working.'

Lekha said, 'Sridevi's definitely come out into the world. She's a wonderful dancer, trained at Kalamandalam.'

'Sridevi's also headed for Madras,' his mother said. 'Sarada has arranged some performances for her. Poor Sarada, she's been on the job for nearly a year now. And when things finally get going, this is what happens!'

'I could have waited, this is hardly the time for a performance . . .' began Sridevi.

'No, Sarada is going ahead with it. It will be a diversion for her. And anyway, Shankar said he'll take full responsibility.'

'I'm troubling all of you!'

'Nonsense! Don't you worry.'

'Where will this be? In her Lotus Ladies' Club?' Gopi grinned.

'Lotus, sunflower, whatever. You people should give her a break. See that she conquers Madras!'

Shankar, descending the stairs, called out, 'Listen, all of you, I've taken her under my wing!'

CONFRONTATIONS

■

9 March 1998

Time's running out and I'm still here, playing games.

'You haven't been transferred to Madras branch, yaar!
Screw Rangachari. We need you here,' Mehra yells touchingly.

'We're nearly there,' I breathe into the phone,
communicating sincerity and unquenchable optimism.

'Oh, come on,' he says with grudging admiration, 'give it
up if it's so difficult.'

After that it's Lekha. 'There's a delay,' I tell her.
'Unavoidable, but I'll be back before Shobha gets there, that's
for sure . . .'

And it's time for the definitive meeting with the man
himself. Taxi. Anna Salai. Hoardings. Red-amber-green
senseless signals. Trapped in traffic. Landmarks. I sit wrapped
in thought. Horns-curses-screeches-grinding-revving. Crowds.
I get down gingerly, still preoccupied. Gently flowing filth-
streams. Roads merging into pavements merging into huts and

makeshift shops merging into human beings and their makeshift lives. Life trips on like an injured ballet dancer. Everything is the same. The bell. Mari. Changing Mari. Inside. Waiting.

Rangachari strides in, smiling. He walks up to me so that when I stand up, we're closely face to face. I move back, hit the edge of the chair and sit down.

'He's there. Inside,' he says, tilting a thumb. 'Came back.'

This is a Rangachari willing to initiate chit-chat into personal realms, Friend Rangachari this time. He smiles agreeably. I don't respond since I'm still unsure of the Seshan factor. Compulsively committed to starting with pleasantries, I startle myself by coming straight to the point. 'So, the book?'

'I read your conditions. There are a couple of things we have to clarify, but it's not really important. By and large, it's good.'

'Good.' Does he sense a change in me? Mari brings coffee and biscuits. I lean forward to pick up a biscuit and come away with two. I bite into both, scattering biscuit bits in a yellow shower. He watches through half-closed eyes.

I look straight into his eyes. 'Of course you know who I am.' The smile remains. This had to come sooner or later, that's what he's thinking too. 'I'm sorry I didn't introduce myself properly.'

He laughs. 'That's all right.' I'm apologizing to him! I tell myself, wait!

I finish eating the biscuits, dust the crumbs from my lap. I pick up the coffee and blow to cool it. I take a few tentative sips. 'We must discuss the book again.' I swallow nervously as he stares at me. 'In the—you know—changed circumstances.'

'Nothing has changed. I think we'll go ahead, Gopi. I can now call you that.'

I nod with a tight little smile. Sure, call me anything you like. 'Sir, I've read twelve chapters. There's no doubt at all.' Something of what I feel escapes into my voice. His smile carries his surprise. It's also a slightly pained, let's-be-reasonable, it's-me-DrChari-after-all! smile. 'I came because I feel strongly about this. Of course, I didn't know who you were.'

'RV was kind enough to let me see some of the diaries. He

knew I wanted to write . . .'

'A novel?'

'Not in those days,' he admits. 'Just the historical aspect.'

'But now it's much more.'

'Yes.'

'First of all, I'd like to know how you got all this information.'

'I told you, he helped me.'

'There's so much that came to light only after his death.' I wait long enough for him to try and break the silence. 'It can't be published.' For once my voice is firm, almost harsh. 'It's about our family, it can't be passed on to the public.'

'I'm a historian,' he says slowly. 'All my works have that base.'

Sitting in a padded cell, confronting this feisty old man whose stories are based on reality but whose life probably isn't. For the hundredth time I wonder why I'm bothering at all. Who will read this book? If EPA doesn't touch it, he'll go back to the Mumbai thriller-dealer. To a readership which couldn't care less. I doubt if anyone will find the links I did.

'It's a reopening of old wounds, and the reader won't even know the fictional parts are fictional!'

'I think you're, perhaps, being too sensitive. There's nothing that . . .'

'Twelve chapters are enough to see how it's going.' Waiting for his anger to break, I've grown tense myself.

He replies in a matter-of-fact tone. 'How can you stop it?'

We gaze at each other, combatants in a ring, sizing up each other. 'Who gave you all this information?'

'You don't know?'

I shake my head.

So we continue to sit, chess players without a board.

And then all at once—for the briefest moment—I catch his vulnerability as his eyes dart away, and for the first time I see myself feeling sorry for this man as he reverts for one cracked-up sad moment to his old self—Dr Chari, earnest and filled with convictions that nobody else is willing to accept.

'I've been carrying this with me for a long time,' he

begins. He focuses on me with that same earnestness, trying to establish a meeting point. 'It's been haunting me.' I cannot think of anything to say. 'But you should realize it's your burden, Gopi, as well as mine. You'll understand that when you read what I have to say. It's your duty as well as mine.'

'How? What do you mean—duty?'

'If you read the rest of it, you may have a different perspective.' He gets up abruptly and goes over to his labour ward. He picks up a plastic-covered bundle and brings it to me. 'These are fresh. Even Kittu hasn't seen them.'

He stands before me, clutching the bundle in front of him, so I don't immediately make a move to take it from him. He's smiling now, he has accepted me as a fellow-creature.

'I'm a historian first,' he says. 'But history is common ground, you can go around and watch it from different angles, and it stays where it is—it should! My interpretation that first time—what shall I say—it didn't impress people, I was left alone like a failure. That was when I brought in my own personal convictions and added them to it. I came up with a new form.' As I watch him holding his novel and talking to me, I feel like some sweet-toothed child whose father holds out a big box of sweets and lectures all the while on the dangers of eating sweets.

'I realized that the novel, if it's genuine, if it's real . . .' He pauses and makes a quick characteristic gesture of impatience. 'I realized when you put the mask of your convictions on the face of history, it can turn out into a nice little story. And there's your novel.' He appraises me. I fidget, half-rise to take the book and sit down again. 'Your anxiety is understandable. I'm not blaming you. But the history of your family needs this mask so that you can look at it afresh. You will need to understand and accept your history. That's why I call it truth-story-history. I won't make you wait any more. Here.'

I accept the parcel. It remains on my lap. The plastic cover has the picture of the same buxom lady above the legend: Kumar's Best Bras. (So someone's a secret bra-wearer in this house!) 'That's it,' he says. 'It's complete.' It sounds momentous.

'Thank you. I'll get back to you by tomorrow evening.'

'I'm sure it will be a positive decision.'

I rise. But he is still standing there, blocking my path. His face tells me there's so much more he has to communicate that he'd rather exhaust himself now than wait for later. 'I'll come back tomorrow.'

'Yes, you must. We've lost enough time, haven't we? What I'd like you to do is to read it and try and understand my mind.' I nod gravely, wondering whether he has ever sounded so pathetically persuasive in all his life. 'You realize this book is a workshop, a laboratory experiment—I'm in the process of fleshing out a theory.' I nod politely and wait for him to move aside. 'I've already told you how I view history. I have a theory.' He pauses long enough to give me the impression that I'm going to remain a prisoner in this house. 'Western history, as you know, is so much less complicated, there's a constant search for tangible conquerable things. In our case, it's not so easy, we're still and rooted and . . . We must keep looking for that balance, that centre of gravity that keeps us where we are, looking within . . . I don't know if you remember, I called it the inner story, that's what we have to look for and understand.' He shakes his head like a frustrated man. 'Anyway, read the book.'

He follows me to the front door and then taps playfully on my shoulder. 'Would you like to see him?' He gestures towards an inner room. It's almost a taunt.

I nod, then almost in panic change my mind. 'Next time,' I mumble. I'm not ready for this as yet!

As I step out, in that mid-world between inside and outside, evening and night, doubt and decision, I think of his words, it's your duty as well as mine, and I suddenly know who it is who's given Rangachari all this information. The information he's been guarding jealously all this while, allowing it to ferment and reach epic proportions so that it will form the pinnacle of his writing career.

And for the first time, I feel uncertain about what my decision will be.

One moonlit night when a deep sky sailed the waters of the Kilikkara river, disaster struck.

A dark human shadow moved rapidly towards the Kilikkara Appan temple. The moon was enjoying a well-deserved rest after its heady run through the clouds. Midnight was approaching. A dog howled somewhere. The shadow disappeared briefly within the clutch of trees. It then emerged near the wall of the temple.

It paused for a moment. Uncertain, reconsidering. Or simply taking a deep breath. Even the night paused like a tense bride. Then the shadow moved along the line of trees. It resurfaced after a long while, perched on the branch of a large leafy tree with stretching branches, a tree easy to climb. It moved carefully on the branch till it reached the broad parapet of the temple wall. It seemed to hesitate. Finally, taking a decision, it crossed over to the wall. Another moment, and it jumped down, vanishing from the sight of the night. All was still again.

Shortly afterwards, another shadow, smaller and bulkier, disengaged itself from the silhouette of a building not far away and ran swiftly across the maidan in the thin milky light. It repeated the actions of the earlier shadow, movement for movement. When it reached the parapet of the temple wall, it stayed recumbent on the branch, listening, for perhaps five minutes.

Muted thudding sounds rose from within the temple. The shadow started up, then lay waiting. After several more minutes, it inched over to the parapet and dropped down on the other side like the first shadow had done. It landed on the platform abutting the temple well, conveniently situated right below the branch.

Damodaran suspended his labours to catch his breath. He squatted back on his heels and used his upper cloth to wipe his forehead and chest. All around him lay debris of the shattered flooring. After the pounding pickaxe on the cold ancient floor, the stillness—except for the ragged current of spated breath, the thunder of his heartbeats—was frightening.

He turned completely away from the idol of the Devi, afraid to face her. Still, a small flame stayed caught in a corner of his vision, refusing to be doused. The pain, which had begun to bother him in the afternoon, resumed now like hammer strokes. He sat clutching the left side of his chest, then began to rub hard with two fingers. His face twisted in pain. He shook his head and wiped the sweat off his face with his forearm. 'This won't do, have to move fast,' he said aloud. He picked up the pickaxe and began to strike at the floor once again, ignoring the ache percolating down his left arm and coiling around his fingers. Each hit of metal resounded in his ears as if it showered within his head.

His eyes felt a red pressure building up. They blurred under an oily film of sweat. The pickaxe suddenly broke through a thin layer and fell, pulling him down heavily. Then there was a dull hollow clatter. He froze and sat absolutely still for a whole minute. He set the pickaxe aside and carefully lowered both hands into the crevice. They came up again, scratched by the uneven edges and hurting with the weight of the brass box.

He placed the box on the floor. It was plain, small and heavy, only slightly bigger than a betel nut container, tied shut with a black string. It felt lukewarm to his touch. He stared at it. Then untied it clumsily, and opened the box. His fingers shook uncontrollably. The pressure within his head intensified. 'Don't worry,' he whispered, 'you'll go right back to where you belong.' Even as his voice died into the night, there was a disturbance in the darkness before him.

He looked up with terrified eyes. The pain was now eating into him. He saw a figure rise and move forward with a long sigh and a soft rustle of cloth.

'Do you . . .' it began. It looked like a creature created by darkness.

Damodaran stumbled up, a thick cry escaped his lips. He fell forward and landed on his face on the floor. His chest hit the open box.

The Palace and the illam woke up to tragedy.

Damodaran's body was found beside the Devi's idol in the Kilikkara Appan temple, a darker outgrowth on the rubble. His dark face retained a chalky sheen as if even death couldn't complete his shock. The temple was closed for purificatory rites.

No one outside the Palace knew of the Chakram till days
afterwards. The floor had been broken open with a pickaxe.
A small box was found among the debris. The box was empty.
There were tense parleys in the Palace. Madras uncle listened
gravely to every opinion that was aired.

'How come the priest of one temple is found in another?'

'That too, dead.'

'More important, what was he doing there in the middle
of the night?'

'More important, how did he get in there?'

'That's easy, there's a convenient tree outside and a
convenient platform inside.'

'You're very observant.'

'What was he after?'

'That's like listening to the Ramayana and asking who is
Rama! He came to take the Chakram!'

'Then where is it?'

'He took it.'

A caustic laugh. 'Took it where?'

'His assailant took it.'

'There was no assailant. Doctor says he had a massive
heart attack.'

'In that case, he came with a companion. The Chakram is
with the companion.'

'Where?'

'How should I know?'

'Who was the companion?'

'Why do you expect me to know everything? As if I was
there!'

'Anyway, it's in Kunnupuram now. One namboo'ri died
to get the Chakram, the other got it.'

'How can you be so sure?'

'By using a little common sense.'

'The Elephant will have to pay for this.'

'For taking back their own Chakram?'

'How can you say that?'

'You remember what the oracle said about Brahmin-killing? That happened when we grabbed the Chakram centuries ago.'

'How can you say that!'

'You're saying we should let this go without a fight?'

'Is there a doubt? Justice wins in the end.'

'So anyone can break into our temples?'

'And now,' said Madras uncle, practical as ever, 'we'll have to look for a new priest for the Manjoor Devi temple.'

When a group of thampurans stalked to the illam, ignoring all pleas for restraint, they were confronted by another tragedy.

That very morning, Damodaran's wife Tatri had been found in her room, sprawled on the floor, strangled to death. There had obviously been a struggle which no one had heard. A maidservant had gone into the room, hearing the child's piteous cries in the morning. He was sitting on the floor, trying to wake up his mother. A handwritten copy of MVR's *Lament Of Mohini* was found nearby.

The Elephant sat gloomy and silent. He told the delegation from Kilikkara, 'We thought at first she had taken her own life. She had enough problems. But the vaidyan is sure it's murder. Our youngsters are determined they won't rest till they've found and punished the perpetrator of this crime.'

'It's very sad,' said a thampuran, anger having dried up quickly.

'It's a bad day for the illam. My niece and her husband have both fallen . . .'

He lapsed into a rigid silence.

'What do you think happened?'

'What was he doing in our temple?'

'How would an outsider have dared to enter the illam?'

'Shh—if they can come into the temple, can't they come here?'

'How? Someone would have heard.'

'There was a struggle, that's true.'

'What about the Chakram? That's the strange thing.'

'It's not in the illam?'

The Elephant gave him a look. 'We don't have the Chakram.'

'Then where is it?'

MVR heard of the death of Tatri and collapsed in a faint. Later, when he came to, there was a wild look in his eyes and he cried out, '*No, she lives!*'

JEWELS OF DISCOMFORT

■

History is written in fits and starts, but it doesn't happen that way.

After several years of childlessness, Gopi Narayan's great-great-grandmother conceived and brought forth a beautiful female child who was welcomed with great happiness—but only by her Big Palace relatives. Being a matriarchal society, there should have been no frowns when the little girl came into the world. In fact, what a welcome relief from the row of males who kept succeeding each other in Eastern Palace! But Triketta Thirunal's birth was a special event at a special time.

During the previous few years, gender apportionment had been surprisingly seasonal. One season produced all-male deliveries followed by a second season of totally female output. (This included children of males married and settled elsewhere—who were technically not Kilikkara offspring—as well as those of the Kilikkara ladies themselves.) The symmetry was broken at Eastern Palace where a group of cousins produced a series of boys in an almost conspiratorial manner. The season changed, but the sex didn't. It was like an epidemic, and what started off in Eastern Palace grew to alarming proportions and spread to other parts of Kalikkara. This was noted with surprise, and then disapproval.

It was publicly circulated in the year 1900 that the member of the family who produced the next female child would be presented with a diamond necklace by the Matriarch.

Many doubts were raised. What if there were more than a single female birth? If there were twins, would the mother get two necklaces? Someone sneered that the family would be reduced to penury if all those nocturnal labours bore the desired fruit. The Matriarch, a prim and touchy old lady, scotched all discussion 'The first girl child is eligible. No one else.'

The tension was terrible, and the spirit of competition furious. Nights blushed with frenetic activity. Determined ladies, who allowed themselves freedom and langourous leisure by permitting their menfolk to wander off to other lands and other households, sent out frantic missives, entreating them to come and join them for a day or two of trial and error. It was a time of sustained no-holds-barred activity. The diamond necklace lingered like a wicked temptation in the dreams of every daughter of Kilikkara.

There was rivalry between the various branches, between and within palaces. Men, as much as the women, viewed each other with distrust. Female servants were sent running from household to household to ferret out information about impending pregnancies. A list of husbands present during the week was compiled. Old uncles with a speculative bent made learned guesses about possible winners. Some placed secret wagers. Even the common people in Kilikkara village piled up huge bets and waited anxiously. This, of course, would have been frowned upon most severely by the Matriarch had she known.

There was a constant crowd around the rotund person of Kochu Kelu of Northern Palace, who'd been entrusted with making the necklace. They were eager to get a glimpse of the gift that would—God willing—come to them, Kochu Kelu was large and stubborn and held the Palace above everything else. 'He won't hesitate to kill for the sake of the Palace,' people said, glad that such an opportunity hadn't yet presented itself. No one knew who was making the necklace, and where and how. Not a word came out of Kochu Kelu. All they knew was that he seemed uncharacteristically gleeful during those days, despite the fact that his great idol MVR was out on a pilgrimage in the northern states and he himself was stuck here.

The air was tense with tugging umbilical cords.

'Do you know there's a chance of miscarriage in Northern Palace?'

'Really? Who?'

'I don't know who. They just say Northern Palace.'

'Who?'

'Talk.'

'Just rumour. Not worth listening. Just because there's a necklace involved, these people will stoop to anything.'

'I heard your Vimala's also in the race.'

'That's nothing to do with all this. As if we're interested! Just a coincidence. Who told you about Vimala?'

'I told you, talk. When did she know?'

'Oh, a couple of days ago.'

'That's what I thought.'

'What are you sniggering about?'

'Nothing. You're right, it must be a coincidence.'

No one could be trusted. Each one feared he'd be held responsible for leaking out secrets if he wasn't guarded enough. When the men gathered under the entrance arch for their evening gossip, they had nothing but the necklace in mind, but they talked of everything else. The subject stained the air like an unholy unction. You could reach out and touch the embarrassment. Some old uncles broached the subject with characteristic indelicacy, but were met with a studied silence.

A couple of accidents did disgorge some secrets.

For instance, one uncle, an aged gentleman who had married into Northern Palace, collapsed one smooth balmy night, going into convulsions and yelling obscenities. The servant who rushed to assist him covered his ears and muttered, 'Shiva, Shiva!' All the ladies in the room were asked to move out of hearing. It took half an hour for the doctor to make his appearance. When Dr Noble was dragged in, half asleep, the old man was describing in graphic ecstatic detail an encounter he'd enjoyed twenty-five years ago with a gifted maidservant. 'What arms, what thighs! What a grip—like a big fat bear! I could have died in that grip!'

The doctor stopped in his tracks, wide awake now. He listened with great interest till the servant reminded him that his master needed urgent attention. 'Oh, he's healthy enough, healthy enough,' the doctor said admiringly.

Whatever the facts, the story was widely circulated, providing immense amusement. The old man, it was said, desperately wanted his wife to get into competition with the rest of her family. He grabbed the lady, a seventy-six-year-old with white hair and defeated limbs, and grappled with her in their marital bed which had supported the conception of seven healthy Kilikkarites. Trying to revive memories of his libidinous youth, he conjured up all his passion with superhuman effort. It is anybody's guess, after all there was no witness! Within fifteen minutes of their retiring into the room, the old uncle had gone into convulsions. The aunt had high fever for a week after.

'Is he all right, doctor?' one of the seven children, a retired bank officer, asked anxiously. 'Nothing serious, I hope?'

The doctor scratched his head in wonder. 'No, no, just a stray incident. I've given a little something to quieten him down.'

He confined his diagnosis to that. But gossip soon revealed the startling disclosure he later made to some of his close friends in an officers' mess in the capital. There'd been semen stains on the bed. 'Oh, come on, not at that age!' 'Dash it, it's what I saw, and it's not impossible.' 'Not at that age!' 'My dear chap, I saw it!' 'Could've been some other feller walloping around before he came in!' 'And the old bat, I'll never forget the shock in her eyes!' 'I still don't believe it!'

Another player was Thangam, a widow from a small

branch of Eastern Palace. She was on the wrong side of forty, and notorious for her lascivious recreations. The entire family considered her a blot on their fair name. She lived in a small room off the main veranda of the house that she and her younger sister had inherited. The room was cut off from the rest of the house, and anyone could come and go with impunity. Nightfall fractured the staid tranquillity of that dark gloomy house. Loud laughter and gay songs could be heard from time to time.

The family was disgusted, especially her sister, who was of a quiet and pale-complexioned disposition. The sister's husband was a short dark man who was stone-deaf and didn't take enough interest in anything at all, much less in reforming his sister-in-law at this point in life. So Thangam continued with what she did best.

• During Diamond Week, ears were finer-tuned than usual, eyes were sharp as knives, hands were eager to open doors, and the need for knowledge intense. And thus it was that the tale of Chandran of Northern Palace being snared—a case of the joker becoming the joke—came to be told. He was returning from a night out with village locals in a somewhat inebriated condition when Thangam, suffering the painful pangs of deprivation, pounced on him. She began humming a romantic duet from a currently popular play. He struggled valiantly in her grasp, muttering in shock, 'Cheriammey! No, please! God will never forgive this!'

His protests were of little use. She dragged him to her lair. The youth began to see horrible visions that taunted and screamed at him through the alcoholic vapours stinging his eyes. Take them off, take them off, they cried till his ears could take no more. She undressed him with love, like a mother spider full of tenderness and admiration. 'Ha, ha! What is this, my boy! what have you been hiding here!' She climbed on him and began to play, then forced him—painfully, protesting weakly—to reverse position. Chandran screwed up his eyes and began to pray frantically to Kilikkara Appan. Maternal fingers caressed wretched parts of him that would surely disintegrate and drop away under the enormity of his sin. Finally, when he was relieved of his soggy misery and she had retrieved her equanimity, he fell away like a larval casing cast aside and she disappeared into the toilet outside to clean up.

Things would probably have stayed quiet and secret if that was all there was to the incident. A night of indulgence between an over-sexed older woman and a reluctant relative who'd probably gloat over the event in later years, despite the incestuous vapours swirling to claim his conscience. But Fate, in a playful mood, can become excessive. Elsewhere in that same house, similar passions were being aroused. Perhaps it was indeed a spell cast over all of Kilikkara, conjured up by the Matriarch and the dream she'd launched, provoked by irritable gods who resented criticism of their gender-conferring rights.

Thangam's brother-in-law was caught in a similar wave of lust. His mellow wife instantly screamed and pushed him away and staggered into the kitchen, shedding copious tears. None of the servants or their twelve-year-old-son, who scampered in inquisitively, could get her to reveal the reason for her grief. It was thirteen years since her godlike husband had descended his podgy body onto her. Neither of them had found any reason to disturb the long ocean of abstinence that followed that bland exercise. And now, when she was regarded as the ideal moral foil to her sister's wicked ways, here was her husband acting like a ruffian off the streets.

But his lust grew till he couldn't see or walk. He pushed himself out of the bedroom and out of the house, moaning in agony. He had never in his life been victim of such a cruel illness. The mild marital movements he'd performed on his wife in the early days were like pale watercolour reproductions of love compared to the monstrosity of his oily craving. He weaved along, refusing to be mollified by the cool jasmine-scented breeze; indeed, the caress of the breeze inflamed him even more.

He staggered back to the house, clutching his vitals. In the veranda he remembered his sister-in-law. He murmured to himself in delight. Who else! Reason fled as he ventured blindly into her quarters. The door was mysteriously unlocked. A little fazed by the ease of his entry, he lurched forward in the darkness. He knocked himself against the bed and cursed softly. He made out her hazy figure on the bed in the moonlight that squeezed through some tiny aperture. He untied his dhoti and hobbling forward, fell on her like a starving man. She was absolutely devoid of clothing!

'Oh my God!' he muttered, and began to make love without further ado. She seemed to accept his advances because she was also moving passionately under him. He felt her nails tear at him. She even bit him. He carried on with renewed passion, laughing exhaustedly.

And then someone struck a match and lit the kerosene lamp. In the searing light and through the rubbing and the blinking, he could see to his shock and shame and misery that his sister-in-law was standing before him, staring open-mouthed, with only a wet towel around her waist, her still-healthy breasts heaving mischievously at him. 'Then who's . . .' He reared back to look at the animal scratching and bucking under him, and even his deafness dissolved before the yelled obscenities of the hapless young Chandran from Northern Palace trapped beneath him and the screamed laughter of his wretched sister-in-law.

Who let out the secret? It's difficult to say. The man was too scared to even recollect the event in tranquility. The boy would have died with shame were he asked to describe the successive assaults on his modesty. Perhaps Thangam told one of her friends in an unguarded moment of hilarity. No one talked of it. And yet it wasn't ever a secret.

The incident was not without outcome either. Whatever the connection, the wretched victim from Northern Palace drifted into street politics and changed into a rude, easily ignitable village hood whose instrument of persuasion was a knife, whose tongue was coated with curses, whose only hope of redemption was a hangman's noose that would stop him from staining his soul any further. Chandran married a low-caste girl and produced a son who was mentally retarded.

People don't talk about Diamond Week these days; not

members of the family anyway. Even the arch gossip is silent. Those who dare bring it up are silenced effectively. It remains a lurid red package, folded up and stored away, and everyone pretends it isn't there.

The activities continued happily. Till one day the bubble burst. An uncle from Northern Palace discharged himself into the Eastern Palace courtyard, his face red as a tomato. 'Did you hear? Did you hear? The atrocity!' The old aunt there consoled him and instructed a servant to bring him a tumbler of buttermilk; she asked him what the matter was. 'Ammu went to the temple today.'

'That's good.'

'That's not it. She goes every day.'

'Yes, I know,' the old aunt smiled. 'I see her every day.'

'This morning, Cousin from Big Palace was there. They talked.' He paused with furious dramatic effect. 'Do you know what has happened?'

'In the temple or in Big Palace?'

He made a clicking sound. 'Pooram hasn't been coming to the temple for some days.' He referred to all his female relatives by the star under which they were born.

'That's true, she hasn't been well for some time.' The old aunt shook her head. 'Poor Kamalam.'

'That's not it! Don't you understand? Pooram is carrying!' He looked at her with a combination of hurt and triumph in his watery eyes. 'All the while! And not a word to anyone!'

'I didn't know that. Did she say how long?'

'At least two months now.'

'That's certainly unbelievable. No wonder she hasn't been coming to the temple. Is she having a problem of it?' The old aunt shook her head in wonder. 'To think we didn't get a word out of them.'

'That's what I'm saying. Are we her uncles and aunts or are we not?'

The old aunt tried to pacify him. 'It's all right. Perhaps they were waiting to be sure.'

'For two months?'

'It happens.'

'Not that I've heard of. Why hasn't she been coming to the temple?'

'Morning sickness, tiredness, who can say?'

Another clicking sound from the uncle. 'I hear Cousin's taking consecrated ghee to her in secret.'

'It's no crime to eat ghee.'

'This is because of the necklace! Every young girl in this place is trying her best to get that damned diamond thing—and here she calmly enters the race before time and keeps quiet till things are too obvious to hide any longer!'

'Let it go. What does it matter? She has as much right as anyone else in Kilikkara. And, anyway, how are you so sure it will be a girl?'

The news spread like forest fire. Everyone viewed Big Palace with suspicion and irritation. Two months! It meant a solid lead. She'd be sitting there feeding her baby, wearing that wreched jewel, while the other candidates waddled about uncomfortably, all pains and complaints. All that effort wasted! Unless God was kind and gave her a boy . . .

God was kind and gave her a girl. And thus was born—to Kamalam alias Pooram Thirunal, the candidate who wasn't a candidate at all—one of Kilikkara's luckiest matriarchs, Thriketta Thirunal, Gopi's grandmother, born under the star Thriketta.

All of the Kilikkara family, barring her own Big Palace, frowned on Pooram's good fortune in getting the coveted prize and cursed her openly. She at first maintained a stoic silence, but then dissolved into tears and determined fasting that left her pale and wasted, threatening to affect the health of her new baby daughter as well. Finally, one day, she flung the prized necklace from a third-floor window in sudden inspired rage, to the utter consternation of her cousins. Then Fate decided that it would, as usual, take another line.

An athletic young uncle from across the road cleared the wall of Raga Sudha in a raucous leap and swooped on the abandoned necklace. Perched on the wall, holding it triumphantly, he yelled, 'Look, look, there are ways and ways of insulting your elders, but this, I must say, is quite unique!'

And he jumped back on to the road, only this time he landed
on a startled calf that gave a last piteous bleat of panic before
bidding farewell to its young life. There followed then such a
slanging match between the uncle and the animal's bereaved
owner—it was confined wisely to slanging since the aggrieved
party soon realized on surveying the muscles and stance of the
young athlete that a safe distance was the better part of
valour—that very soon the entire Palace gathered outside
Raga Sudha where Pooram was resting after her farewell to
the necklace. There was much shouting and brandishing and
threatening. The commotion had reached a crescendo as the
athlete—real name: Ravi Varma, nickname: Muscle Raja,
called: Anandan—became the unenviable focus of all attention.
In the sudden eerie silence that followed, his dry painful croak
rose, 'Where's the necklace? I had it with me!'

Again, all hell broke loose. This time, wrath came
collectively. The entire Palace descended upon him as one.
'You! You! You!' The calf was relegated to its rightful place
in animal heaven. The jewel was far more precious. In the
meanwhile, someone had sent for Madras uncle.

'Who had the necklace?' he asked gravely. 'How did you
get it? It was Pooram's, wasn't it?'

'She threw it away. I was only retrieving it.'

'Did she throw it on the road?'

'No, of course not. It isn't possible, you know that.'

'Then how did it come to you?'

'Well, I–I was walking and I saw her throw it . . . I got
it from Raga Sudha.'

'You got it from inside Raga Sudha! You jumped the
wall?'

'Y-yes.'

'Interesting,' said Madras uncle. 'Very interesting. Do you
know what they call people who jump over the wall and come
away with diamond necklaces?'

'Please, please! I was only trying to help.'

'Is that so? Tell us how you were trying to help.'

'I was drawing attention—she threw the necklace away. A
gift from Great-grandmother herself! How can anyone throw
it away?'

'And so you decided to take it.'

'No!' He was almost screaming. 'Honestly—I was only trying to draw attention.'

'Yes, we heard. But why did you leap back outside? We'll forget the dead calf for the moment.'

'I refuse to forget! I demand immediate compensation from this young rascal or his uncles . . .'

'We'll come to that. Let's finish this part now.' He turned back to the chastened youth. 'So you vaulted over the wall, picked up the diamond necklace and vaulted back, fatally injuring a cow in the process. That's all very well. With a little bit of chastising and an apology and adequate compensation for the dead animal . . .'

'And a propitiatory puja, since this is go-hathya—killing of a cow is a terrible sin,' interrupted another uncle.

'Yes, yes, after all that, the matter can be closed. But what I'm asking here is: where's the necklace? If you had it with you barely fifteen minutes ago, where is it now?'

'That's exactly what I'm asking!'

'You're asking me?'

'No,' said the muscular lad miserably. 'I'm asking myself.'

'Let's get this straight, Anandan,' said Madras uncle, trying not to show how immensely he was enjoying the younger man's discomfiture and his own judicial role. 'Let's be very reasonable. You picked up the necklace—where is it? We can't be more reasonable than that, can we? We'll forget about everything else. After all, this is no ordinary necklace, it's a present from the Matriarch and it's a diamond necklace. Valued at several thousands of rupees. It can't vanish!' Anandan stood staring glumly at the ground. There was nothing he could offer in explanation. 'We can't stand here all day. Where is that necklace? Come on, Anandan, hand it over if you have it.'

Anandan bristled. 'I told you! If you suspect me, why don't you search me?' He raised both arms and bowed his head in the attitude of a martyr.

'Now this is very strange. A necklace cannot just disappear.'

'Maybe someone took it . . .'

'Are you accusing us?' one of them shrieked.

There was another round of shouting, accusations and counter-accusations. When some of the participants, in their enthusiasm, began to progress from verbal assaults to pushing and nudging and prodding, Madras uncle realized the gravity of the situation. 'Let's not fight among ourselves. We'll get to the bottom of this, and all of you will hear about it.'

This ended the debate, but it proved to be a miserable reprieve for Anandan. During the next couple of days, he was harassed by everyone he met. Even his own palace surveyed him from head to toe as they would a criminal. In the village, respect turned to smirks and exaggerated politeness. Amidst the grunts and thuds of studiously heaving torsos in his gymnasium, he felt himself isolated. His second uncle, his mother's younger brother, who never exercised his avuncular option to chastise his tough nephew, now harrangued him at the slightest opportunity.

'Never thought such shame would descend on our family. All because of a mere necklace! Does our family need such an ornament? They say a girl's most valuable jewel is her chastity. Our family's ornament is our honesty, the respect and good name we've earned. Till now . . .' he ended darkly. Muscle Raja, far from flexing his muscles, sat weak and helpless.

As Anandan—his happiness evaporated—wandered vacantly in the murky moors of his misery, and the Kilikkara family let the story cook mouth-wateringly and discreetly in their courtyards and inner rooms, and the villagers wondered about this new development in the family they loved to revere and imitate and gossip about, Pooram Thirunal, disgusted by the turn of events her daughter's birth had caused, proclaimed that she had no desire to own the necklace. She'd accepted it only because the Matriarch had given it to her. Now that it was missing, she felt no regret at all. 'Let others not suffer on my account. By the grace of God, I have enough. Enough of this talk of jewels!'

Strangely, this did not anger the Matriarch, who was celebrated for her bad temper. She sympathized with Pooram. She felt guilty in some way, and admired Pooram for facing the situation with fortitude. She proclaimed (and her proclamations were instantly law): 'I take responsibility for this whole pathetic affair. I'm going to make sure the child does not suffer because of this. I hereby announce that one single additional portion from the common temple funds will go to her branch. The funds will not be immediately disbursed, but will accrue and be given out at the end of the year. This is my desire and no one will question it.' She added cryptically, 'We women should stick together.'

Of course, there was a storm of protest. 'In her old age, she's totally lost her senses.' 'Senile old woman. How dare she play around with our wealth!' 'What if they get the necklace back?'

'In that case,' retorted the old lady acidly, 'she'll have both.'

Thus Triketta Thirunal proved her worth right from the beginning. She got her family an extra portion from the temple funds within a week of her birth. And lo, the infamous necklace was discovered two weeks later by a low-caste sweeper, who had discreetly excavated a mound of earth outside the Big Palace gates to bury the smelly leavings of an indiscreet stray dog. Guileless and scared, he stood there moaning. The necklace lay triumphant in the mud, all heavy gold, its large diamonds winking at him in the sun. 'Ooooooh!'

A crowd soon gathered around him, careful to keep a safe distance in deference to his caste. 'Stop that noise at once!' said an uncle roughly. 'How dare you . . .' His voice trailed into silence as his eyes followed the sweeper's feebly pointing finger. 'The necklace,' he breathed.

'The necklace!' A collective gasp rose. Some of them eyed the wretched weeping man with suspicion, but Madras uncle walked up as if on cue and had the situation easily under control. He picked up the necklace and held it up for all to see. The diamonds smirked. 'Anandan dropped it on the ground in all that confusion. We must have kept stepping on it till it was covered in mud.'

'What do we do?'

'Do?' Madras uncle said in surprise. 'We return it to the

Matriarch, of course.'

'Or to Pooram?'

'That's left to the Matriarch to decide. We found the necklace, we do our duty. That's the extent of our obligation.' He directed a withering glance at the sweeper. 'Stand aside! Let's not have any more trouble from you, understand?' The sweeper backed away with bowed head.

And the small procession, led solemnly by Madras uncle, wended its way to the Matriarch's palace. The Matriarch was beside herself with happiness. 'We go to Kamalam this evening and present the necklace to her once again with due ceremony.'

And that is what happened. That evening, with pipes and drums in attendance as if the temple deity were being transported and the breeze sprinkled with the scent of sandalwood, the old lady hobbled across at the head of a retinue of relatives and servants to the temple and first offered her gratitude to Kilikkara Appan. She would have preferred to hand over the necklace at the temple itself, but Pooram Thirunal, her dear Kamalam, had not yet been purified after her confinement and couldn't enter the temple. So they then proceeded to Raga Sudha, where everyone had been waiting for the past hour for this visitation. The Matriarch handed over the necklace to Pooram and was rewarded by a weak tearful smile.

'You've been doubly blessed by Kilikkara Appan,' the Matriarch said graciously. 'You will be remembered by the very last of our descendants. Your daughter will grow up to be a Kilikkara Matriarch beyond all compare.'

Kilikkara Appan sat on her tongue as she uttered those words. The family not only enjoyed a larger share of temple funds from that year, but was also the proud possessor of the controversial necklace, which was handed down from generation to generation, always going by common consent to the eldest daughter.

After Triketta Thirunal, came her daughter Subhadra, again born under the Pooram star like her grandmother. She married a namboodiri and had two children: Kamala, named after her great-grandmother, and Gopi Narayan whose second name was obtained by accident. In a matriarchal society, he should have inherited the maternal family name rather than his father's. But Gopi studied for two years in a Trivandrum convent school, where he was entered in the records as Gopi Narayan, son of Narayanan N. by a missionary principal still getting used to the peculiar ways of this state, and that's how it remained.

MAGIC MOMENTS

■

A little girl of ten was getting married. Her groom was seventeen years old. The state capital Trivandrum was preparing itself for the wedding. People talked of nothing else. 12 March 1906 was the auspicious day chosen to put up the very first pillar of the massive marriage pandal. The services of an elephant were required for the operation. The wedding would take place two months later.

It all actually began with the Senior Rani of Travancore celebrating her tenth birthday. Her elders decided it was time to look for a groom. Girls had to get married before they attained puberty. The groom, Rama Varma of Ananthapuram Palace, Haripad, was chosen after much discussion and letter-writing. And a delicate little pointing finger. The little Rani looked down from an upper floor window. Two brothers from Haripad stood there, sent to earn the Travancore maharaja's approval. The elder had a muscular body, and was tall and handsome. The younger one was smaller and had a sensitive face, a look of vulnerability. She pointed her finger at Rama Varma, the younger one.

When the royal invitation reached Kilikkara, Madras uncle was in bed with arthritis and exhaustion. He declared in his soft determined tone that MVR, who had also received an invitation, would represent the family. Surprisingly, another letter followed shortly after, inviting Thriketta Tirunal, who was all of six years, and her mother Pooram Tirunal. Only a year ago, when they'd gone to Trivandrum, the little Rani had declared herself to be enchanted with the 'little Thriketta'. There was some rumbling in the Palace about this strange choice, since now, in the absence of the Second Patriarch, Big Palace would exclusively send all the delegates! But who could argue with the decision of the Senior Rani, the bride herself? So a week before the wedding day, MVR, along with his niece Pooram and grand-niece Thriketta, started off in a horse carriage on the first leg of their journey.

They took a boat that same day. MVR writes in his diary that none of them slept a wink the whole night because of the escapades of a 'small but deadly species of mosquitoes'. Otherwise, the boat trip was pleasant.

Little Thriketta enjoyed herself thoroughly. Specially prepared food served in silver plates was brought in from some of the places they halted at. Sometimes they ate sitting on deck, especially when they were passing uncrowded areas. Their evening meal was always on deck. Two large lanterns were hung up and they sat in the moonlight, watching the light-spotted shadows, the sudden spurts of lustre as they passed a festival or celebration; listening to sky-borne snatches of someone's rough song, a dog at the water's edge howling at them.

Thriketta was on deck most of the daytime as well, watching the green landscape sail by. The sun was merciless. Her mother said, 'At this rate, you'll turn into a black little child by the time of the wedding, and no one will recognize you!'

Thriketta replied, 'Yes, ammey, but for now let me stay.'

MVR smiled. 'I already see the future of this girl,' he said.

They worshipped at several temples on the way. Arrangements for their stay and worship had been made in advance. For Pooram, it was a relief to get out of the claustrophobic confines of Big Palace.

MVR felt the trip was a 'feast for the senses'. For the first time in all the years since the horrific events of March 1886, he discovered afresh the breadth of the earth and the sweep of its people as he stood on deck like a dying emperor, marvelling at what had passed him by. He leaned precariously to scoop up water using large ladles, worrying the boatmen as well as his own attendants, and washed his arms and face with it, smiling strangely. Occasionally, he withdrew to a corner and wrote feverish pages, heedless of everything else. He spoke to people on the way, sometimes even calling out to labourers working in fields, who bent low in startled respect, covering their mouth.

Minor government officials met them at some of the places they visited. Many people, familiar with the works of Kilikkara Marthanda Varma Raja, came up to express their opinions and clarify doubts. A few had read his recently-published epic *Lament Of Mohini*. They visited Mavelikkara, Attingal, Kayamkulam, Quilon and Varkala. In Quilon, they accepted a spontaneous invitation to watch a tennis match at a local club. At Mavelikkara they were treated to a Kathakali performance that went on from two thirty to five a.m. The story was *Keechaka Vadham*, the killing by Pandava brother Bhima of his disguised wife's disgusting pursuer Keechaka. Thriketta was terrified but sat through the performance.

Four days before the wedding, they reached Trivandrum and sought and got an audience with the Senior Rani, Sethu Lakshmi Bayi. After waiting for about ten minutes, they saw her walk down the long hall. She was a small and dainty figure and walked rather self-consciously. MVR later commented that she seemed 'a bit too shy, and it was the sight of our Thriketta which drew her out.' Her complexion was fair. Her hair was arranged in a sort of large bean-shaped bun above the forehead. The tight red silk jacket she wore looked too elaborate on her slight frame. Below the jacket was a plain pleated skirt. She had on gold chains, one of them studded with gems, and earrings.

They bowed low with folded hands, and the Rani asked them to sit down. Pooram presented the wedding gift they had brought for her, a small gold vessel beautifully engraved with the Shankhu Mudra, Travancore's conch insignia, on one side, and the Pakshi Mudra, Kilikkara's bird insignia, on the other. The Senior Rani examined it carefully, expressing her appreciation.

The ten-year-old Rani was delighted to see 'little Thriketta' once again and remarked that she had grown so much in so short a time. MVR thanked her for taking time off so close to the wedding to see them. He suspected she must be feeling quite nervous and tired. She said it was all very exciting, and the seven days of celebrations would be a lot of fun. She then asked them where they were staying. MVR said they were staying in Kilikkara House, just outside East Fort. She enquired whether they were comfortable there. 'Don't hesitate to ask if there is anything you need,' she said gravely, sounding very grown-up. She suddenly smiled and said she would be very happy if Thriketta and her mother could stay with her till the wedding was over.

'With Your Highness?' Pooram asked in surprise.

'Not here, of course. The Palace will not give permission. But you could stay nearby with my aunts. You will take part in all the preparations.'

And so Pooram and Thriketta were, the very next day, taken to stay in one of the smaller palaces along with other important female guests. At the feast the following day, Pooram met ladies from the royal houses of Chirakkal, Kilimanoor, Haripad, Mavelikkara, Poonjar and Thiruvella. Soon she was renewing old acquaintances and making new friends. She encountered snobbishness, gossip, excitement, envy, affection and friendship. She encountered familiar emotions and came to realize that, wherever one went, things weren't too different.

MVR continued to stay in Kilikkara House. He had leisurely oil baths, consumed elaborate meals, and enjoyed long debates and games of chess with guests from other palaces. He later indicated that 'those last few days in

Trivandrum' were especially satisfying—'like the satisfaction derived by the fatted calf.'

On Sunday, 6 May (24 Mithunam), at six a.m., the bridegroom Rama Varma, dressed in a golden closed coat, salwar and cap, astride an elephant, was taken in a long procession to the Thevarathu-koikkal Palace. His bride waited there, seated in a room adjacent to the naalukettu, the closed courtyard where the ceremony would take place. The rituals began. At nine a.m., they were married in the presence of the Maharaja, government officials, relatives and many, many guests. Pooram and her daughter were given pride of place, beyond all call of protocol, at the insistence of the little bride.

At six a.m., MVR had finished his bath in the temple tank, worshipped, and was back in his rooms to get ready. He was to join the last stretch of the procession along with some friends from Poonjar Palace. He had finished tying up his hair. He was reaching out to pick up his upper cloth when he realized he couldn't move.

He strained and pushed himself forward, sweating profusely. He managed to get to the bed, half-crawling. In the process he knocked down a small stool with a pot of drinking water and a tumbler. Hearing the noise, his personal assistant Thampan ran up. He found his master on the wet floor near the bed, flailing one arm like a swimming champion. He called out in panic, 'Thampuran, thampuran!'

Since a doctor couldn't be located in all the rush in the Fort, a local vaidhyan was bundled in. MVR's cousin, Rajan, who stayed in Kilikkara House, was of tremendous help. He made haste to procure the medicines prescribed, and did everything possible to make MVR comfortable. MVR tried to speak but the words seemed reluctant to emerge and he had to thrust them out, half-broken. His niece must be informed immediately. Rajan comforted him and at once sent someone with a note to the Palace.

After more than two hours, Rajan came into MVR's room. He had an odd look on his face. 'My man spoke to someone from the Palace,' he told MVR, his voice expressionless. 'He said it's best to keep quiet till the celebrations are over. He will have a competent English doctor here, latest by tomorrow. Till the celebrations are over, he has suggested that we don't mention your illness to anyone.'

MVR stared at him. 'Not—not let them know?' The words struggled out in a spray of saliva and futility.

'Don't worry,' Rajan said blandly, 'we'll manage. Why get them worried?'

There was a long silence. They heard the sounds of the crowd outside.

'What's . . . happening to me?' MVR burst out.

At that moment the Nayar Brigade began to fire a feu de joie in the distance. The artillery followed from outside the fort with a twenty-one gun salute.

It was nine a.m. The royal couple had just been married.

My mind dances in ecstasy like the vaulting waves.

Listening, filled to bursting with your song, heady with the honeyed hymns of heaven. Mind and body tuned to the throb of your breath, and revelling in the rhythm of restless rebirths. Take me!

Take me now so that life measured out in careful cadences of seconds, minutes, hours, days, weeks, months, years, decades, centuries and yugas will converge in one mindless moment of stinging white purity. Like the haunting curve of the vaulting wave. Poised on the brink of nothingness. Dancing eternally on the hair's-breadth between creation and destruction. Take me so the world exults. Let your song be mine now.

This is the moment of truth, the proof of existence, yours and mine. This is the purpose of birth, the skein of life unrolling its magic moments like tumbling tributaries whose final destination is once again, of course, the ocean.

Do you remember? My song wove patterns of delight through the moonlight, coupling shamelessly with the sensuous rhymes of your fleeting anklets. And a hundred sparks of joy were born unto the night, guiding other lovers, travellers and seekers, others of a younger world.

Do you remember the laughter of the moon, births and rebirths?

Take me, seductress! Merge me into you. Accept me within the refulgent darkness of your womb.

Live me unto death, sweet gentle Mohini.

Lying alone in the sullen room, listening to vibrant life flowing by outside, MVR sees his own life break down into colourless visions before his eyes. He relives the passion and the pleasure, sheds colossal tears. MVR. Great ancestor, grand old man of literature, greedy lover.

Even Thampan had slipped away to catch some of the excitement. Now he was left with phantoms. As he lay there, helpless and alive, he could feel her arms about him, hear her whisper in his ears. The laughter of wonder, warm breath of her desire. All through the deafening gigantic rush of water . . .

He paused in amazement when he realized who she was, an antharjanam—the one inside—whom even the sun wasn't allowed to see. Here she was in his arms, her breasts rising proudly beneath his palms, her lips casting soft aspersions on his greedy eyes, her thighs closing in, unable to check their magnetic movement towards him.

He tried to understand her ardour even as he held her at arm's length and studied her sudden shyness. Was it the drink she said she had during the performance? Or the power of his verse that had conquered her? He was used to ladies of noble birth demanding private audience, secret aesthetes seeking special readings, needing the poem and then the poet. But she wasn't like them at all, her quiet dignity raised her above them. Her eyes gave up everything. Her body clasped him with no conditions, no keeping back.

He was all the more shocked because she was a wife. It was as if she'd been waiting for him all her life, as though she had known he'd come. What if they find out, he asked, they'll kill you and then me! She looked at him with unclouded eyes. Are you afraid, she asked.

He ran his hand through the black river of her hair, gripped her shoulders. Holding her close to him, breast to breast, breath to breath, he told her, as long as we're together, never. His wife, her husband—no one mattered. His life was only now beginning. On this cold night, lying on the naked floor, rain lashing about them, they knew they had no one but each other. He said, and there was no poetic drama in what he said, our lives may be doomed but not our love. He said, now my poetry awakens. At last, I can write. She smiled, I'm happy.

Are you afraid, he asked.

Of you?

He nodded. Of my reputation.

She shook her head. Everything about you is here, before me, mine.

Still! There's my wife, there've been other women. Aren't you afraid? She shook her head again, smiling. How can you be so sure?

I know, she said, taking him with her eyes.

Her world was so different. He came to know of the cavern of terrible tradition and ritual within which she existed, her life of hard work and prayer, of serving the men in the illam with single-minded piety, the hidden relief of literature after an exhausting day, the occasional performance glimpsed greedily from a shared darkness with the other silent women of the illam. 'There's nothing else?' he asked in astonishment.

'During festivals we get together and sing and dance,' she smiled.

'And the world doesn't know!'

'The world is kept out.' His eyes filled and he held her tight.

She told him of a carefree childhood when she played and studied with her brothers and sisters. They played hopscotch and made snakes of straw and studied the scriptures under a teacher known for his learning and benevolence. Even then, even in childhood, the boys were always right. If they fought, it was the girls who were punished. At mealtimes, the boys always ate first and they ate on silver plates, always a step ahead. And then childhood ended and life began and brothers became strangers and the sky clouded over, descending heavily over the roof of the illam.

But half of what they said had no words. That night, protected from the world by rain, they consumed each other, body and mind, like twin flames conjoined. She listened hungrily to his verse, he urged her to respond. He caressed her body and her spirit. He held her swollen breast and drank from it as a thirsty child, she laid her head against his chest like a loving daughter; they were everything to each other, and that is why a mere half-night seemed like forever.

We may never meet again, she said, but now I'm taking you away for all time, and he held her close and replied in silence. They parted; they had to. Only they could sense the smile behind the scowling sky as they ran out into the drizzle. The storm had calmed, shamed by a stronger ardour.

What else is there to say? He wrote out his dream and called it *Lament Of Mohini*. It had nothing to do with legend or grammar. It shone brighter and touched more hearts than any epic. It had blood running through its veins, words that laughed and cried.

They met just one more time, later that year, at the same place. Only a poet could have arranged such a tryst. He sat and painstakingly copied out the first part of the epic. He sent it to his friend Vasudevan Namboodiri through his personal assistant. His friend was pleasantly surprised to get the book, he hadn't realized MVR thought so highly of him! 'Let the people at home read it too and let me have your opinion at your convenience, the second part is waiting,' he wrote in an accompanying note.

In the very first verse, describing the ashram of the Brahmin priest, the poet talks of the bathing ghat and mentions a date a few days after full moon and a time just before midnight. This is when Mohini's mother comes down to earth as a spirit to enquire after her beloved daughter. She got the message of course. They met once again, this time in moonlight, a night sky churning milk in thirsty waters. They swam and gave their bodies to each other and talked like little children.

I'm even more happy this time, she told him as he prepared to leave. You have been growing within me for the past four months. His son was born to her before that year was out. By the time the child had completed his first year, she was dead.

MVR lay on the bed, fighting his shadows. Too late, he realized his mistake—it was the wrong title. She was gone, escaped into the mists of yesterday. It is my lament! I'm the one shedding hopeless tears, my body already dead, my mind always with her.

Some days later, when his niece and her daughter returned to Kilikkara House, they were shocked to find a veritable vegetable waiting for them. They took him back to Kilikkara, an extinguished poet.

THE SLAP

❖

'I'm going to make you an offer you must not refuse.'

That was Panikkar speaking. Gently arching back his body, resting elbows on either side of him and leaving his lower half like a trained animal to splash the urinal in a vicious monsoon. Gopi looked away primly, preferring to be left alone at such times.

'I'm going to make you an offer,' Panikkar swivelled abruptly, a loud zzzzeeep, and he turned to the washbasin. All through the second series of splashes and grunts as he washed his face and arms, Gopi tried desperately to figure out this booming message.

'Okay, sir.' Panikkar looked at him questioningly. 'The offer, what is it?'

Panikkar grinned. 'Yes, offer you *must* not refuse.'

'What is that?'

'Now that you're coming up in life, Gopi Narayan, so to speak. Isn't it?'

They stared at each other across four urinals. Panikkar

nodded at him, turned and walked away. 'What,' Gopi asked
three mothballs and a deodorant bar, 'is that supposed to
mean?'

The party was on the lawn, sequestered from the rest of
Panikkar's club crowd. Slipping through cocktails and snacks,
slapping off mosquitoes. Sniffing through well-heeled smiles at
the smell that emanated from the canal close by. The stench,
of rotting meat and subterraneous slime, hovered periodically
like a ministering butler.

It was a strangely assorted crowd, young and old. All of
them sat gingerly like characters in a stillborn play.

Panikkar presided over the table like a giant priest,
relishing his whisky and tenaciously showering opinions on
the guests. He tried to animate them with strenuous attempts
that got nowhere. His wife, wrapped in a yellow georgette,
flamed the night. She and a middle-aged female companion
bobbed in rhythm as they conversed in low voices, presumably
about shared social concerns. Sulu pouted red lips and fluttered
long misty fingers. She shot rapid vapid questions that vaguely
disturbed them—as if she were subjecting them all to dark
double-meanings. She pointed a finger like a compass at Gopi.
'Gopi,' she said. She studied him with dark and melting eyes.
He noticed strife-lines on her forehead and around her mouth
as a flame flickered to light someone's cigarette. Everyone
nearby stopped talking. Gopi lowered his eyes and Sulu turned
away abruptly. A serious-eyed young man turned to Gopi.
'What do you think he's called us for?' He smelt minty and
seemed anxious to understand Panikkar's intentions. Gopi
shook his head in reply, took a larger sip of his drink and
wondered where he'd seen the man before.

The invitation had surprised all of them. Gopi and Shankar
were here only because of Aunt Sarada's insistence. 'It's time
you got out a bit,' she said. 'After all, it's Panikkar. I can't get
out anyway, I'll stay and look after Kolappan. He's not been
feeling well—some sort of gout, I think.' Lekha decided to
stay back with her at Greenacres. 'You go, moley, I'll look
after the little one.'

But Lekha was firm. 'This is a good excuse, I'd honestly
hate to go!'

So Gopi and Shankar sat with Panikkar, Leela and Sulu, and eight other invitees. Someone mixed a drink and placed it before Gopi. He was surprised at how easily his hand stretched to take the glass, how willingly his tongue accepted the taste of it.

He remembered who the serious young man on his left was. He'd been at the party the night RV uncle died. Rohit Sharma, the ad film-maker—problem was he'd shaved off his moustache. How did he expect to be recognized if he kept changing his face like this?

Jacob the ex-planter, sitting next to Shankar, cut a patient piece of prawn and forked it carefully into his mouth. 'See where—all life takes us.' He placed the fork down, took a sip of whisky, a drag from his pipe, and continued, 'Last party we witnessed a death.' His eyes glistened as his pipe blew staccato bursts of scented smoke. 'And look where we're now.' Shankar didn't reply. 'I cannot forget. He was one of my oldest friends.'

'I know that,' Shankar said quietly.

'We know when an era passes,' Jacob said. 'Things familiar start dying.' He held the bowl of his pipe with both hands. 'You won't believe it, Shankar, I'm eighty.' They were silent, mulling over the fact. 'In the old days there used to be a system. Paths and turns and everything very clear. Now no one knows where we're going.' He looked around the table. 'Do you know how many of us there are?' As Shankar started to count, he said, 'Thirteen.'

Shankar smiled. 'I didn't know.'

'That's how many there were at the Last Supper—thirteen.' He laid a hand on Shankar's arm. 'And the world was never the same.'

Shankar considered the old man with interest. He had never before wondered what lay beneath the skin of his bluff, at times acerbic, exterior. 'Do you believe in omens?' he asked.

'It's what you make of them, isn't it? A blunt wind blows through the estate and we predict a listless day. Thirteen is lucky for some.' Shankar thought the hand trembled on his arm. 'Last time your brother-in-law died. My oldest friend in

Madras. What omen was there? Today we're thirteen.' He took a deep wheezy breath. 'What will happen?' As Shankar sat back to digest that, the old man's mood quickly changed. 'But you still haven't told me why you took off to Kashi.' Shankar looked taken aback before breaking into a grin.

Rohit Sharma was explaining ad films, how special effects highlighted products so they leaped out among everything else. In the middle of his exposition, a waiter walked across the lawn ringing a bell. 'That's for children to quit,' Sulu explained loudly. Rohit Sharma, interrupted, was left hanging in the air. The white digital compass once again pointed at Gopi. 'Come, do you want to see the rabbits?' He looked at her, not understanding. 'Come, come, come,' she said in her husky voice, 'our club rabbits!'

He acutely noticed nobody noticing them as they rose. The rabbits were at the other end of the lawn. They ignored everything else and indulged in one-to-one games. Sulu paused before the smelly cage as if it was one of the wonders of the club. And perhaps it was. She drew close to him, her sharp perfume mixing heavily with the smell of rabbit-droppings. 'You know what Daddy wants you to do?'

'No.'

'Become part of VAP,' she whispered, keeping the rabbits out of it.

'That I am,' Gopi smiled.

'Really, I mean. Financially, like one of us.'

Gopi put up his hand. 'Like what?'

'He wants you to put up some money. Get a percentage share. You've come into a bit of dough, haven't you?' she said seriously.

'Well, I haven't—yet.'

'Invest a token amount now. When you can you come out with the rest.'

'I don't think . . .'

'You know VAP well enough. That's why he called you tonight.'

'To ask me this.' In the toilet! Bargains in the bog, loo-liasons. He looked sullenly at her, somehow feeling like a villain's helpless helper in a Hindi movie.

'I think it's a great opportunity,' she sighed, smiling up at him. She touched him lightly with her hip, shoulder and unforgettable left breast. 'We're all with you.'

She reached up and caressed the air close to his cheek with fairy fingertips. Her breath danced on his neck. He thought of Hindi movies again. He thought of Lekha, briefly. He turned away prudishly from the rabbits shamelessly going at it.

Gopi was at his desk at Vimala Art Printers on the morning of his birthday, braced to face anything following his bus ride.

Shobha's school was beyond the Circle, a crowded ten-minute walk from Doctors Colony. He was fortunate to get his bus almost immediately afterwards. The ride, during office hours, was hardly more endurable than a participatory stagger through medieval torture chambers. Catharsis that shook up passengers and taught them the value of humility and sharp-edged luggage. It was written that Gopi Narayan should suffer each morning. Why else would anyone leave his scooter standing safely at home and allow Pallavan Transport Corporation to violate his body and spirit? His own logic was simple, and indicative of his philosophy of life: rather be a passive passenger than a responsible rider.

He picked up his pen and pulled in the proofs. He was soon caught up in a morass of words, deletions, corrections. The first document was a Rotary club roster. This involved matching forty photographs of members with names, addresses and designations. Last year, there'd been a disastrous mix-up. VAP picked up a retired Customs officer and a young management consultant and gave them what life hadn't. The old man, a childless widower of seventy, got a new wife and two small children while the consultant was retired prematurely. The club president's message read, 'Our respected Governor is responsible for the new year's suspicious beginning.' When the roster was distributed, the crusty Customs man disowned his ready-made family and created a scene, and the president threatened to sue VAP.

K.P. Panikkar thrived on such scenes. He shouted in turn at proof-reader Jackson, an ancient Anglo-Indian curled up dreamily in a box-cubicle. Years ago, Panikkar had purchased him along with the press in a package deal, but had never regularized him. Bad light, myopia and wayward fingers had conspired to let Jackson down in his most crucial moments. No manuscript was proof against him. He bovinely allowed Panikkar to use him as a whipping boy, nodding patiently at every abuse. When he felt he needed a holiday, he simply stayed away, and Gopi—VAP's most ambiguously designated staff member—was routinely dumped with the remains of his labour.

Gopi often wondered why the boss couldn't simply ask Jackson to pack up and leave. Panikkar wasn't the man to allow sympathy to interfere with business. His sole concern was to keep the wheels moving. Vimala Art Printers was a temple at which he worshipped from 9 a.m. till well past 8 p.m. The customer deserved the best, the worker should break his back.

He also shouted at customers. The prices he quoted were sacred. Anyone daring to protest risked a shredded eardrum. Panikkar pulled out price lists of paper and ink, and discoursed vehemently on the high cost of labour and establishment. He took the startled customer on a guided tour of the press. He pointed out peeling walls, broken benches, minute chips on rubber rollers, even the cockroaches moving briskly about their business. 'See? If I overcharged, you think my press will be going to the dogs?'

Panikkar was a slave-driver who strode the press like a colossus, pausing at a treadle here, a Heidelberg there, pointing out lapses and tweaking nervous ear lobes of raw machine helpers—a contact with labour that would surely spark a strike anywhere else. His voice boomed, competing with the chatter-click of machines or ruptured out in a guffaw like the heavy plop of a cannon.

Gopi had a healthy respect for him. Their relationship was ideal: Panikkar kept off Gopi, Gopi avoided Panikkar. How could he forget, when he was wasting away at home, it was Panikkar who had offered salvation—it was an undying obligation.

Though in the past few months he'd begun to feel that stepping into VAP had been like slipping into a whirlpool—

being sucked royally in, losing control and judgment. While Aunt Sarada and his mother had jointly sponsored his unemployment, there was now no one to guide him or turn to. Earning a salary made him appear self-sufficient to his former mentors—Gopi's come into his own, he's a Man now! It was a vicious circle. His income meant that he could spend, and spending drained his income. In a gruesome monthly exercise, he cut short his feet regularly to fit his shrinking slippers. Until, finding Panikkar's salary too meagre to meet this hungry endless conveyor belt of domestic disbursement, he made his first mistake. Ignoring Lekha's advice, he borrowed . . .

The office staff sat on the first floor, along a long rectangular hall. Panikkar's room and old Jackson's bedroom were at the far end. The east wall had been sliced into six large bright windows opening out on the narrow Appa (née Chetty) Street and a murky row of tall buildings beyond. The actual press was on the ground floor. Their immediate neighbour was Rasi Talkies, which specialized in reruns of old Tamil films. Sitting in the office, they heard emotional dialogues and dire songs and boisterous dishum-dishum from fight scenes from the time the matinee began until late night, resurrecting youthful images of MGR, Sivaji Ganesan and B. Saroja Devi. Compositors jerked awake, recognizing instantly the general mood and progress of the stories, saved by nostalgia from tipping noisily into their galleys.

Gopi sent in the first few proofs through the buck-toothed peon Chelladurai. Chelladurai bowed theatrically and accepted the proofs. He tossed up a mop of hair and walked away in style, humming in a medley of male and female voices. But the next time around, he shrugged meaningfully and thrust an expressive thumb in the direction of the press.

The implication was lost on Gopi. Last evening he'd been out on collection, and had gone straight home afterwards. This morning as he walked into the press, he wasn't paying much attention. As his eyes ran through lines and lines of heavily inked print, as his hand mechanically marked instructions, as his brain registered spelling mistakes and redundant lines; he was actually toying with the eerie vision of the hairy old sadhu, arriving as it had entrenched in the lap of this sacred birthday morning. 'You'll become a big man,' he'd told him. And Gopi's mind mischievously invoked his impending prosperity and Panikkar's party-night proposition, and two and two were soon adding up to mind-boggling mega-figures.

But sitting there, deciphering those photographs, wits sharpened to avoid a mix-up like last time, Gopi began to catch a little of the vibrations. Nothing much, a hushed message between tables, a tightening of the atmosphere, faintly disturbing sounds from outside the room. At one point he even wondered if someone wasn't arranging a birthday surprise for him. Slowly, the percolation began. When lunch bell rang, Gopi was tense. Something was definitely wrong. He put away his papers and opened his lunch box, which Lekha had packed with curd rice, a spicy curry, a cabbage side dish and fried savouries, a mini birthday feast. The aroma made his mouth water.

He took his first mouthful and Sushila, the frail-looking Malayali typist, fluttered her eyes. She said, in sing-song English, 'So Gopi sir! You're not keeping touch, it seems?' She pulled her pallu tightly about her. An oval breast emerged innocently below, straining at her white blue-washed blouse. Gopi kept his eyes averted. 'Didn't hear about labour trouble?' She had raised a ball of rice to her mouth. When the mouth opened, she changed her mind and put the question instead.

It didn't register immediately. 'Labour trouble? Where?'

She smiled. 'Workers will be striking.' She popped the ball in and chewed gently. When she finished chewing, the smile was still there, as if it had been a funny thought. Her free hand came up and a finger dipped into her blouse, scratching casually.

'In Vimala?' Panikkar had finally gone too far with his pinches and bellows.

'Where else?' She flashed a glance at Gopi, then down at herself and quickly covered her breast. But the last thing on his mind was the typist's breast.

He ate with slow deliberate movements of his jaw. In spite of his growing nervousness, his taste buds tingled from the delicious curry. 'There's been nothing wrong.' Gopi spoke carefully, waiting for the whole thing to turn into a mild office joke. 'Raghavan was saying we're one happy family. They've had so much overtime lately.'

Supervisor Sebastian gave a loud grunt and belched. 'Yeah? There's going to be a family feud.' He was a tall thin-framed Goan, settled in Madras for decades, raising a pot-belly and long gel-sleeked hair. A pungent fish-and-garlic smell wafted from his lunch box as he clicked his tongue. 'Overtime's least of it. See their list of demands. Poor boss—he's going to bloody die of BP.'

'What I mean is—it's sudden, isn't it?'

Another grunt. The garlic proclaimed itself in a stronger dose. 'Oh, we buggers know damn-all. Nothing we can do, see? I bloody lost my temper. Yesterday in the letterpress, man. They took so bloody long for makeready, so bloody long for locking up, so bloody long for inking simple corrections. I bloody let the buggers have it, yelled my bazooki out! And they stood there, like, listening. Not a bloody word. And all the time, you just imagine the situation. Buggers thinking. Plotting, man! All because of that bastid.'

'Which bastard? Tell him, yaar!' This was Nazeer the accountant, chortling.

They all seemed to think this was great fun.

'Karuppan, union chap,' Sebastian explained. 'Jet bloody black, like his name. Bugger's got pull, it seems, in the ruling party. Two weeks ago, he takes them to a park—park! Now what do you say, do we guys know a thing? Bugger bought them coffee and gave one speech—usual blah-blah. You guys know what fellows in other presses are getting? You guys are starving. I'm your friend, trust me and I'll personally, like, see you buggers benefit. Shit like that. I know and my bazooki knows, bastid's going to do nothing of the sort. Swallow money from them, money from old man, that's it. You know what he says, I've got party influence, we'll force a settlement. Only thing bugger'll settle is his own future! And bastid made a fancy list for them.' Sebastian waved a piece of paper.

Sushila laughed and fluttered her eyes. 'What I'm thinking, Gopi sir, if they're striking and getting some increment and all, why not we also ask?'

Sebastian punched his palm. 'That's the trouble with you Kerala guys. Run around looking for a strike. I've been in three other presses—not a bloody peep out of anyone. I, like, enter this Malayali joint and, there!'

Gopi, less interested in ethnic proclivities, reminded him: 'Their demands?'

'This is the list.' He held up the paper at a distance and peered. 'Here—

'Uniforms for workers—what do you think? We're running a bloody school or what?

'Free tea twice a day—yeah, and pizzas and cakes, go the whole hog.

'Wage increase. Nice thing to ask Panikkar! Fifteen per cent up in overtime wages, why not?

'Compulsory overtime at least once a week.

'One extra bonus.

'Contract binding staff must be made permanent. Yeah, not to forget old Uncle Jackson. He'll want to become permanent too.' He rolled the paper into a tight little wad and bounced it on the table. 'That Karuppan bastid has a real flighty imagination. But he hasn't, like, got the whole jingbang lot as yet. Some are saying, go to hell, we're not listening.' He sighed loudly, easing into a belch. 'Tomorrow's D-day, ultimatum.'

'So the strike's final?'

'What you think I been telling all this time? They and Karuppan bugger assemble in front tomorrow, shouting demands. And they'll stop anyone who wants to work.'

There was silence for a while. Sushila and Nazeer took their lunch boxes to the washroom. 'You think there'll be trouble?'

The familiar workers transformed into a gang of strangers.

Sebastian held lunch box and lid apart, clanged them together like cymbals. 'Maybe, maybe not. One wrong word, one bloody gesture—' He made a popping noise with his lips.

'What does Panikkar say?' He suddenly felt the need to know. 'This must be the first time he's facing a strike.'

'Ten-twelve years ago, there was some dispute, like. Nothing big. Two buggers were kicked out. Became violent, shouting at old man and banging his bloody car. The labour officer came and settled it to our advantage.'

'What does he say about this?'

'Old man? Furious, of course. Bloody rattled people should turn around and challenge him. Called me to his room first thing in the morning. Said you go talk. He's afraid I'm, like, encouraging them! So I go. What do I lose? They'll eat up my bazooki or what?' He leaned back in his chair and smiled. 'Buggers refuse to budge. Do or die. They're saying old man downs even one of their demands, he's had it. That's how bugger's brainwashed them.'

The bell rang signalling the end of lunch break.

Chelladurai cleaned the tables with a wet cloth, humming a martial-sounding film song. The sound of machines resumed. Sebastian went down to the press.

Gopi pulled the proofs over. He had difficulty concentrating. Words ran into each other, bizarre meanings took shape. Photographs made faces at him. His hand trembled as if the pen were directing shots of current up to his elbow. Why's everyone else so casual?

They were always there. The large windows on the wall were spyholes as he sat hunched over his work. Everything he did, every departure he made, was dictated by what They thought, what They expected. Was he being too intense, too loud? Should he be humble, mild, self-effacing? Challenges were always followed by a nagging afterthought—would he get out with self-respect, dignity, alive? Would he measure up?

For heaven's sake, this is nothing but a strike. People you've known for ages! And the easiest thing is to take leave and stay at home. And you act as if it's a firing squad. Gopi, my boy, some bazookis simply aren't up to it!

A hand closed on his shoulder and he jumped. Manager Marthandam's dark pockmarked face materialized, trying out an uncertain smile. He was Panikkar's right-hand man, forever apologetic and stranded in the wings of life.

'Gopi.' The low bass voice suggested something between a secret and a solicitation. 'Boss would like a word with you.' In the midst of his preoccupations! Not to wish him a happy birthday? Perhaps to plead with him to take over the press with immediate effect?

Gopi got up and followed the short bulky figure. Sushila, Nazeer and Chelladurai were watching. He ignored them studiously. The thinly veiled bald patch bobbed up and down inches before his nose. Marthandam opened the door to Panikkar's room. They passed inside, into another world.

The cool air, the shuddering old air conditioner, the smell of fresh paper and ink and tomato sauce. It took a while to get used to the dimness inside. Gopi blinked. There was the squeak of a swivel chair and the air dipped and rearranged itself. The door closed with a soft thud behind them. He blinked again, frowning to pierce the darkness. 'Yes, Gopi Narayan. Come in and sit down.' The voice was thick, heavy with exhaustion, the words not very clear.

Gopi waded forward. The room was falling into proportion, objects began to take shape. It was a room he'd always marvelled at, a dim-lit aquarium where the big fish brooded. It brought to mind a lush royal courtroom gone musty and frayed with disuse.

The thick green carpet had ink stains and trenches and tattoos of mud. The tasteful wallpaper was losing its touch. Two cupboards, like squatting monsters, with diamond-faced glass windows were stuffed with leather-bound books, font catalogues, income-tax manuals and print periodicals. On the far side of the room, below the air conditioner, was Panikkar's rosewood table with chairs for his audience including, incongruously, a few steel folding chairs. The table overflowed with things—paper, coffee-stained cups, pencils, rulers, files, catalogues. A lunch plate with a half-eaten cutlet drowning in tomato sauce sat balanced on a mountain of ledgers.

A cough and an agitation. Panikkar rose from his swivel chair like Varuna from the sea. His arms, surging with hair, emerged from the rolled-up sleeves of his pinstriped shirt like heavy awkward columns. Panikkar was six feet tall, slightly hunched. He removed his shell-framed glasses from his face and wiped them, coughing. He sat down and asked Gopi to sit down. Marthandam mumbled and moved back, lost in shadows. Panikkar leaned back and studied his face.

'Gopi Narayan, how are we getting on?' Gopi started.

Boss making small talk. He produced a polite sound that emerged as a giggle. 'And your wife and son?'

'Fine, sir. She's—a daughter.'

'How's your aunt getting on, she's recovering?'

'She's okay.'

'How do you find the work here? You're adjusting to our pace?'

'Yes, sir.' I've been around almost a decade, for heaven's sake!

Panikkar cleared his throat loudly. He studied everything in the room, except Gopi, with the air of a man who's suffered and is willing to plod on a little longer. 'You remember our little talk a few days ago?' Oh yes, in the toilet, and your daughter and the rabbits too. 'Our press has been in existence for one-half century,' Panikkar said conversationally. 'I took over twenty, twenty-two years ago.' He leaned his chair back as far as it would go. The chair moaned. He seemed in a mood for confidences. Gopi sat back, relaxing.

'I didn't change the name. The press didn't get too many orders those days. When Kovilpatti was running it,' he shook his head stiffly. 'If orders came, they came. If they didn't, they didn't. Kovilpatti Narayanan was a politician and social worker. He wasn't really interested in running a business, wasn't even capable of it. That's the tragedy. He only wanted a journal to fight for freedom. So he started this press and brought out a Tamil weekly called *Porattam*—the struggle. And within some three or four years, the country became free. Now where's the question of a struggle? Vimala began to lose heavily. We don't know who this Vimala was, by the way, some girlfriend or concubine, Kovilpatti being a bachelor. I took over from him and made it what it is.'

Panikkar sighed. He closed his eyes and folded his arms across his chest. The Concise History of Vimala Art Printers Private Limited! Well, he was fated to hear it one day or the other. And he'd picked up an interesting detail: Panikkar's press was probably named after a freedom fighter's concubine. 'Or mother,' Gopi thought, and said it aloud. Panikkar frowned at him but didn't respond.

'I took over this press,' he continued, 'when it was at the

bottom. It couldn't sink any lower. I touched it only because
I was sorry for an old patriot. Twenty years I've been doing
nothing else.' Another silence. 'And what do I get for it?'

Gopi jumped. The question boomed out, catching him off
guard. 'Sir?'

'I put my whole life into it. You people don't know
anything. I was here day and night. Working myself to the
bone to make something of this press.' Panikkar sat trembling
in his chair, glaring at Gopi. His eyes swam with nostalgia and
the pain of unburdening himself. His fluffy square moustache
held his face together, giving it identity. Without it, his face
would crumble, dissolve into a surly pool of flesh and bone.
'And then some bandicoot walks into my office and says my
workers have demands. My workers! Does an outsider
understand them better than I do?' He laughed. More a snort,
sick and abrupt, like the prelude to a dirge. 'They're going to
have a strike. I've never had a strike in Vimala before.'

Had Sebastian been dreaming? 'I heard there was one
twelve years ago.'

He looked surprised that Gopi could actually speak.
'What?' Gopi repeated himself resolutely. 'A minor trouble.
Outsiders were not involved. I called the authorities and the
fellows had no chance at all.' He waved the incident away
contemptuously. 'This time it's different. Almost all the workers
are in. They're a dirty set of people. Show them compassion,
give them an advance and sanction their leave, and they climb
up on your head. Let them have their strike. Who's bothered?
I'll call in the police and have every last one of them behind
bars. Kazhuverikal!' he exploded. Fellows-fit-for-gallows!

An impasse. Panikkar's red eyes nailed him. Feeling
embarrassed, Gopi lowered his head and found himself staring
at the disgusting piece of bloodied cutlet.

'They'll stand outside and stop anyone who wants to
work', he murmured.

Panikkar pushed away books and paper and leaned across
the table. 'We must see things don't go so far.' The anger and
bravado disappeared. Now he assumed a grave expression,
full of sagacity, a general plotting an ambush. 'Gopi Narayan,
you will have to talk to them.'

'Sir?' Talk to the workers—what a day this was turning out to be!

'Marthandam, come here,' Panikkar bellowed. He realized then that Marthandam was behind everything. He'd been missing all morning, feeding ideas into Panikkar's receptive ears, hatching plots to break the strike.

Marthandam appeared. He pulled back one of the folding chairs and sat down. He cleared his throat. 'We have to settle this somehow, Gopi. If this strike is permitted, our entire schedule will be upset.' He picked up a round glass paperweight from the table and considered it respectfully. 'Someone should go and talk to the workers, make them see reason.'

'Why me?' Gopi asked bluntly.

'He thinks you can,' Panikkar cut in. 'You're in direct contact with press and office—management and workers. I definitely won't go and talk to those people. Sebastian may jump to their side after a while, you can never say. Marthandam is out-and-out management, they won't budge an inch. There's nobody else. You're quite friendly with the workers. Yes, yes, I understand they all like you. I'm not trying to flatter you, just telling you what I've heard. You put our problems before them. Take each of their demands, one after the other. Tell them our stand. They know you'll be neutral. We'll—ah— brief you just before you go.'

Marthandam gazed at the glass globe as if he could see his future in it. Without raising his eyes, he said, 'We've asked Mr Janardhanan to come and assist. He's one of the best in labour relations. We'll begin at seven tonight. There'll be a meeting with Sir and you, a worker's representative and the union leader Karuppan.' He covered the paperweight with both hands as if he could hatch it. 'But before that we'll iron out as many differences as we can.'

'I want you to become a force in this press,' Panikkar said loudly.

They sat like three corners of a triangle. Gopi felt the pressure converge upon him. If he didn't make an escape right now, he never would. 'Actually I had planned to take my family out in the evening.'

'Family!' He sounded shocked as if it was an obscene word.

'Yes,' Gopi continued compulsively, 'for a dance.'

'Dance!' There was an uneasy silence.

After that Panikkar spoke so easily, taking his acceptance for granted, that he sank without resistance. A part of him dreaded the reactions of Lekha and Shobha. But still he sat, hands on his lap, looking steadily at Panikkar, not saying a word. The air conditioning sagged like thick gloom over his shoulders.

He called Lekha under Panikkar's watchful eyes. There was total silence as he waited for her. At one point Panikkar made an impatient movement with his shoulder and elbow. Gopi felt obliged to explain, 'It's the neighbour's phone. She has to come from upstairs.' Panikkar turned away, pretending disinterest. When she came on the line, he tried to explain the situation.

'But why can't you simply get out of it? Have you told him it's your birthday?'

He shot a glance at Panikkar. He was observing him keenly now. 'Lekha, listen, I don't think that will make any difference. This is a serious matter. And he's right here beside me,' he warned discreetly.

'Then give him the phone. Let me talk to him.'

'What will you say?'

'Just give some advice,' she said belligerently. 'To act more human at his age. When it's his problem, it's a serious matter; when it's yours, it's nothing!'

Gopi coughed loudly to drown out her voice. 'Yes, yes, positively by nine.'

The conversation went on in the same vein. Lekha said grimly, 'All right then. I'll go to Greenacres. From there, we'll go straight to the auditorium. You can come there if you like.' She took a deep breath. 'I'll leave coffee in the flask and some idlis just in case. Key with Sundararajan.' There was a pause. 'And one more thing—'

'Yes?' he asked in a small voice.

'Shobha will never forgive you!'

The afternoon crept by. At four, Panikkar called him once again for a briefing. Holding the list of demands marked with Panikkar's comments and suggestions, Gopi went down to the press. He had no idea what he was going to say. He felt like a student minutes before a major exam. Or a prisoner about to be hanged. Butterflies had a ball in his stomach. Downstairs, he gave himself time, turning into the dark stinking toilet.

As he washed his sweating face and arms under the tap that delivered a sigh of brown air before oozing out a reluctant string of water, wet his hair and finger-combed it back, he heard, drifting in from the high smoky window, a melancholy song from Rasi Talkies. An oppressed heroine invited him to share his afflictions with her. He was studying himself in the mirror as if for the last time when Raghavan peeped in. He was the compositor who did most of the Malayalam jobs. He was keeping away from the strike. Raghavan smiled at him and said, '*Ividey endha*? I heard you were going to mediate!'

'How do you know?'

'Word gets around. Marthandam doesn't want to get involved, that's why he selected you for this. The others also have refused.' He paused, grinning. 'You never say no.'

'They've asked others?'

'Short of Chelladurai!'

That smooth-tongued snake Marthandam! And Panikkar: 'I want you to become a force!' He'd believed it. He was only a pawn. But as he came out of the toilet, he thought, in spite of everything, right now I'm the most important person around here, they've no one else to turn to. Perhaps he was the force! The thought played in his mind and by the time they were inside the letterpress section, his nervousness had almost evaporated. The machines were running. He spotted half a dozen workers gathered by the Mercedes, conferring. Raghavan placed a hand on his shoulder. 'Be careful. One or two have come drunk after lunch.' Gopi nodded.

What I need is courage, God help me. He walked up to the conferring group, between machines clattering loudly. He could see the interest in their eyes. They all know of my mission, he thought. The group disbanded, formed into a tight semicircle. He stopped near them. The smell of stale liquor hit him. At random he counted Vijayakumar, machine man; Pandian, machine man; Krishnan, compositor; Rayappan, binder. A cluster of men in torn smeared vests or T-shirts or simply bare-bodied in the heat, wearing expressionless faces. Krishnan was more approachable than the others. Gopi looked straight at him and said in Tamil, 'Krishna, I've come to discuss your demands. I'm sure we can come to an understanding.'

'It's too late for that,' Pandian said, a young and touchy fellow. The words slurred. 'Wait till tomorrow morning.'

Gopi swallowed. These are people I know, these are friends! 'I haven't come to force anything on you,' he said, enunciating each word like a sincere schoolboy. 'I just want us to be sure of our positions. Management has arranged a meeting tonight. We have to discuss a few points before that.' He rustled his paper sheepishly from somewhere near his hip.

Krishnan smiled, it seemed a wise smile. At last here's a reasonable human being! But he said, 'You shouldn't be talking to us. Management is only using you to serve its own ends.'

'But our objective is the same, isn't it?' Gopi said, wondering where the words were coming from.

'And what is that?'

'The good of the press, of course. Isn't it?'

'I only think of the workers' interest. No one can bulldoze their way through us.'

So the battle lines were drawn. The armies were ready, waiting impatiently for the conch to blow. Machines snorted and stamped their feet. One side was here right before him, the other waited upstairs. He was the royal messenger sent to offer terms and discuss peace. His white flag was being steadily ravaged.

'We'll find a solution acceptable to all concerned. Let's take up your demands one by one. We'll see what Mr Panikkar has to say about each of them.'

'That's not your job. Why should you get hurt?'

That stopped him in his tracks. A blood-curdling scream; he retreated a step. But it was only a bus braking on the street. He laboured under a slow nervous smile. 'Why should I get hurt?' he asked, echoing the words stupidly.

'That's right. Don't get involved unnecessarily. We've

made our demands. We won't back away from a single one.'

'Fair enough,' Gopi said, growing desperate. 'But let's just go through . . .'

Rayappan held aloft the knife from his paper-cutting machine, a warrior poised to strike. His forehead glistened with sweat and righteousness. Remember that sacred rule: never, never strike a messenger! Still, he took another step back. 'It won't take any time at all.' His voice had grown weak. He waved the ridiculous piece of paper like a flag of peace. The air around him reeked of pre-war fumes of bitterness. This was the arena. Tomorrow, as he walked on the battlefield, wading through streams of blood, whose headless trunks, whose trunkless heads, whose widow crying her heart out, what symbols of senseless cruelty would he encounter to shame and torment humanity for years hence?

Krishnan's wisdom shone. He turned to smile briefly at his confidants, then beamed benignly at Gopi. He it was who knew the past and the future, the just and the wrong, his decision would be bathed in the light of righteousness. Shall I surrender everything at your feet, Krishna? Krishnan said, 'You're wasting your time. We prefer a direct confrontation with Panikkar.'

At this point Fate, in the form of Raghavan, came up from behind.

Raghavan said, 'There's no harm if we hear what he has to say.' The atmosphere bristled. Vijayakumar, a fat dark man in an ink-stained vest, wagged a threatening finger. 'You keep out of this. You're not participating in the strike. You've no business here.' He lurched forward, belly first. The conch had had no chance. The first movements of battle were already in sight. A grimy finger stopped an inch short of Raghavan's nose. Gopi forced a smile. Raghavan shouldn't get hurt. His heart was thumping. 'Let's not get over-friendly, Vijayakumar.' He placed one hand on his tummy, the other on his shoulder and gently pushed him back. He chuckled desperately to underscore their camaraderie in spite of everything.

'Don't lay hands on the workers!' There was a roar. The dust rose high and swirled. The sky bellowed and burst into flame. A hand jumped on to his chest and shoved him away.

The hand sprang back. A blur of movement and a smell of grease and ink whipped by, *crack*! Gopi's face jerked violently. He staggered back, a flashing darkness before his eyes. His left cheek was stinging, as if on fire. He clutched the nearest arm. Raghavan's, he realized with almost tearful gratitude.

Not even my father! It was his first thought. It's done. The moment's come and gone. Why me? Why *me*? The blood rushed to his face. His entire body trembled, he couldn't stop it. His head settled and the darkness eased. An excited chatter of voices broke into his consciousness. In his shame, he wished the press floor would open up, suck him in, like Mother Earth had taken Sita.

The workers crowded around. The battle was over with a single blow.

He saw Pandian's face, startled bulging eyes. He heard his voice, flaccid and shrill, 'I thought he was going to attack the workers.' He shut his eyes and everything began to whirl. When he opened them, still rooted in embarrassment-anger-frustration, he could see other faces: Panikkar, Marthandam, the entire staff. Sushila's wide-open eyes, Chelladurai cherishing the drama. The workers, reduced from blustering to anxiety. How long had it been? An earthquake or fire in the press, anything but this. He was the centre of it all, he couldn't stand being an entertainment, a tamasha! Gopi heard a giggle in the background.

Panikkar stepped forward and took control. 'That's enough now. Don't keep standing. You people get back to work. I'll talk to you later. Gopi Narayan, come, we'll go up.'

Something broke inside him. Through clenched teeth, stuttering, he managed to say, 'I knew this would happen. I want you to do something.'

Panikkar cocked his head, trying to fathom this new behaviour. 'Come, come, let's go.'

'I want you to do something about this.'

'It's all right—'

'Forget it, Gopi.'

'Or else I will!'

Marthandam drew intolerably close. 'Gopi, it's wise not to make too much of it.'

Through clenched teeth, 'I'll file a suit!' He heard another giggle.

'Calm down, Gopi.'

'Things will change! See what I'll do to this press!' Anger pulsed through him, fuelled by terrible embarrassment. Marthandam hovered about, grabbed his arm. He shook it away. 'I'm going straight to the police.'

'Now look here, Gopi.'

'I have connections . . .' He heard another giggle in the background. 'Things will change!'

It was finally Sebastian who steadied him, put an arm around him and escorted him out. He laughed. 'Don't fret, man. It's how the whole bloody thing works. They need a big ball to throw at each other, just their bloody game. Who wins, who loses, makes bugger-all difference to the ball. It just hits shit the moment game's over.' Comforting words indeed! Sebastian laughed again to cheer him up. 'Balls have a shit life, man. Don't you worry your little bazooki.'

Trembling at the knees, a part of his brain recording very faithfully the entire ridiculous drama of it, Gopi Narayan walked out into the burning street. Things will change!

They certainly will.

SONG AND DANCE

■

He staggers out of the bus and reaches home. He stands with the sweat streaming all over and looks bitterly at the large lock hanging on the door, mocking at him. Of course, he thinks, offering an imaginary bow to whoever has thoughtfully scripted this birthday scenario for him, anything else would be an anticlimax! He continues to remain blank for a long while before thinking of Sundararajan. A ventriloquacious crow eggs him on from the vacant parapet.

He isn't disappointed there either. Sundararajan's door opens and the large kindly mami in her ever-flowing green sari smiles sympathetically. 'No, he's not here. Wait for half an hour and he'll be back.' As his shoulders sag and he is turning away, she calls out, 'Wait!' He stiffens, ready for the next. 'Your mama phoned. The one who comes with the beard and jubba. He wants to talk urgently. You'll come in and call?'

The mami brings him a glass of water as he fumbles in his bag for Shankar's agency number. He drains the glass in one neat swig. Shankar's tone is impatient. 'I waited for nearly ten minutes. And then they came back and said there's no one in the flat.' Gopi explains dully that Lekha and Shobha are at Greenacres and that he has just returned from work. He doesn't dare to mention the slap. Nor does Shankar ask him what he's doing home so early in the evening. He sounds more brusque than he probably intends to be. 'It's off,' he says, 'your deal. The lawyer called this afternoon. Fellow can't pay.'

'What deal?' he asks, his heart sinking.

'I'm sorry, Gopi.'

'Why is it off?'

'Forget it, Gopi. We'll get a better one next time.'

'What about the advance he paid RV uncle?' He can barely hear his own voice.

'That you can keep, he's broken all the time clauses—see, that's one advantage!'

'Seventy-five thousand?'

'Not all, of course. Return half—you know, as a sort of goodwill gesture.'

He laughs bitterly into the phone. 'Goodwill!'

'By the way, happy birthday!' Shankar says. 'Anyway, I'll be seeing you at the dance.' Reminding Gopi to be in the auditorium by seven sharp, he rings off.

The mami hovers up. 'Everything all right?'

He wipes the sweat off his face. 'Oh yes, fine!'

In limbo with his bag, he stands outside Sundararajan's flat and wipes himself carefully and thoroughly with his handkerchief till the handkerchief can take no more; and then to kill time he goes down to Iyer and Ver Ganapathy. Not far away, a pandal has been put up with a wooden stage for the Association function tonight, and there are thirty or forty people running around, arranging chairs and intoning solemnly into a mike: 'Testing, testing, mike-testing, one-two-three!'

The banyan settles over Gopi like an obliviating dusk. Birds shriek beyond and swoop, sweeping the purpling sky. Like the gurgle from a giant stomach, the ocean endures in the background. One or two people come up to pray. Iyer shows them the arathi and gives them prasadam. They sit in silence, Gopi clutching his bag to his chest. Iyer starts humming snatches of a song. Gopi feels a chill run up his spine. The

song is in Shree Ragam, it never fails to bring tears to his eyes.
Iyer has a thick broken voice that negotiates even delicate
turns with robust ease. Every pause is a wheeze. The busy men
and their voices and all else fall away and they are alone, Iyer
and Gopi. He turns away, feeling the familiar emotion seize
him like a catch in the throat.

The first time, he recollects, was at a concert he attended
with a couple of his college friends. It was December, and the
American Jon Higgins who'd championed Carnatic music was
on stage. The hall was full; people packed the steep upper
gallery and lined the aisles. Midway, he began 'Entharo
Mahanubhavulu'. Gopi sat in his seat, shaking his head and
snapping his fingers. As Higgins ran up and down the notes,
Gopi was whipped away into a tornado of time, dizzily,
uncontrollably. He emerged shaken. The raga had taken him
through boundless grey passages past childhood and birth, he
felt he'd touched the very root of his lifeline. When Higgins
finished and thunderous applause swept the auditorium, he
was perhaps the only one who sat still, frozen and beyond
response.

Today he was sliding to a similar tumult. Iyer's rough-
hewn song churned all the snarled emotional debris within
him. Like a decrepit diner in a restaurant finally forced to
order something, he knew he had to speak. So he recounted
the day's adventures. And then, because he couldn't stop, he
spoke about Kilikkara and Kunnupuram and the mysterious
Chakram and the curse that everyone was talking about; he
told Iyer about RV uncle's death and his first drink. 'I was
forced—no, how can anyone force—point is, I drank.' He
swallowed and looked away. 'They wouldn't let me go in the
ambulance. They said someone should stay back in the house.
But I know why . . .' He told him about the Sindhi's letter and
his terrible fears, the deal that almost went through. 'And now
see where I am!' A hollow laugh strained out from somewhere
within him as he mentioned Panikkar's generous offer and
then recounted with grim monotony what had happened in
the press, acutely embarrassed all the while as he kept shouting
to oblige Iyer's deafness.

Iyer listened quietly. Whenever Gopi's voice dipped low,

he let the long blanks remain and listened as if he heard. He swept a stretch of the stone floor with the back of his hand and began to write on it with a finger. 'Do you think He creates you and then leaves you to yourself?' He smiled and shook his head.

'And on top of all that, I've been locked out!'

'What?'

'I've been locked out,' Gopi yelled.

Iyer laughed. 'No, you haven't.'

'I just found out.'

'You're not locked out, the key is always with you.'

'No, it isn't!' He shook his head in frustration. He wanted to tell him about Lekha and Sundararajan and the key which he honestly didn't have, but it was too complicated and he'd suddenly run out of words. The sea breeze rolled in, rustling dark branches everywhere. Ganapathy glowed brighter before the oil lamps. The burden within Gopi was being tossed about. 'Just keep praying,' Iyer said, 'and everything will be all right.'

'Oh my God!' Gopi shook his head peevishly and shouted, 'I don't know how you say that. Look at me, nothing's going through. I keep praying. We're up against things we can't even begin to understand!'

'That's wise,' Iyer laughed. 'Admit we don't understand.' A rough laugh rose and died in a wheeze. 'You're on the right track,' he gasped.

'So why make images and perform rituals as if we understand . . .' Iyer studied him, mouth slightly open. This was hardly one of their usual theological debates! 'You remember the old man this morning?'

Iyer nodded. 'Great soul, he doesn't even know how old he is.'

'He said I'll become a great man.' Iyer smiled in acknowledgement. As if he'd heard. 'And see what's happening!' He lowered his head, seeking to calm himself. 'Some things never change!'

The evening was now upon them. Lights perforated the skulking structures of the colony. A couple of mosquitoes danced to music above their heads. The pandal was now

almost deserted except for a couple of men playing around
with long wires.

'It's your life but you keep depending on so many people.'

He knew Iyer's faith was so deeply ingrained that he saw
the practical world more practically than anyone else. 'What
should I do?'

'Once things get settled inside, they settle outside as well.'

'Right now, everything's unsettled!'

'That's how it is, life. You're talking about some curse
and some Chakram. You think that's why you have all these
problems.' Gopi frowned and remained silent. Iyer waved a
fat finger at him. 'You close your eyes and the world disappears,
nothing exists. You open your eyes and the world is all about
you, isn't it? That is what we call maya, mirage of life. We can
conjure up a whole world with hope. Or destroy it with
anxiety!' The finger sailed close to Gopi's face. 'Curses,
Chakrams, all very nice—entertaining! You try and explain
what you can't explain with stories.'

'What am I to do?' He added in a calmer voice, 'It's part
of our history.'

Iyer reached out and patted his knee. 'Things will keep
happening. Haven't you heard the English saying: what-what
will happen will happeney-happen!'

What-what will happen . . . Laughter frothed up as if he
was a child being entertained by Iyer.

'We should learn to be bigger than our history, appa!'
Gopi waited as Iyer went through a prolonged and painful
wheeze. 'Because what-what will happen . . .'

'Will happeney-happen!' Gopi laughed out into the night.

Later, restless and full of an unknown excitement, he
stood in the balcony and took on the sea breeze.

On the maidan below, straggly groups made their way
home. Wiry men and thin-armed women. In a few minutes,
their voices rose raucously. Gopi stood staring at them. On a
sudden impulse, he left the balcony briefly and returned
carrying Kamala's velvet jewel pouch. He pulled up a steel
folding chair, took out the chunky gleaming necklace, laid it
out on his lap and sat looking at it.

What a beauty, an ornament fit for a queen. He drew it

up and coiled it back into his palm, repeating the gesture again and again, enjoying the smoothness and the nip of gleaming gold, the sparkle of the three large diamonds. He held it up carefully and tried to see if he, an amateur, could repair the damage. He tugged gently with his short nails at the chain hanging like a partially-amputated limb. The chain produced a small click and came away in his hand. He stood holding the two pieces, his heart beating rapidly. Now what was Kamala going to say about this! He sat looking gloomily at them. He raised his hand and let the necklace flow for the last time.

When it landed, he found there were now three pieces instead of two. The larger chain was actually hollow so the thinner one could be twisted inside. The new piece had dislodged itself from within the hollow and fallen out. He picked it up with two fingers, a small metal sheet rolled tightly into a thin pencil. Even before it dawned upon him, before he realized what it could be, his fingers were trembling. With great reverence, nervously, he smoothened out the thin copper sheet.

He sat there in the balcony, staring at this little piece of magic on his palm.

A scent of perfume and silk, jasmine and musty excitement filled the hall. Shankar ran around, wearing a volunteer's badge. It shone like a large satin flower grown fresh on his breast. Shobha knelt on the seat next to Lekha's in the front row, and peered at people with her programme sheet rolled into a telescope. Beside her sat Sridevi's father, a thin namboodiri in a pale shirt and dhoti, nervously fiddling with his fingers. He seemed eminently ill-at-ease in the front row. A shrill bell sounded and the lights were doused.

Shankar peered from the wings, then ran down, bending his tall body like a modest ostrich. He sat down near Sridevi's father.

It was the interval that Gopi finally walked in. He sat back and gave in to the music. An invocation began, and in its wake, Sridevi danced on to the stage. She looked so different! He thought her movements added new meaning to the words of the song. Each mudra, look and smile, the arch of her eyebrows. After a while, swimming in winged waves of sound, his mind began to wander.

No one knew when the air would turn. Lives yielded and fallowed, rose and fell, glowed and darkened. There was magic and sharpness, colour and drabness, the air sang and shrieked. It was, finally, nothing but a vaporous movement between happiness and yearning. He wondered how long all this would last. He was transported from his surroundings, even the dancer was just a bright moving figure like a mote in his eyes. He drew all the world within himself and floated in a hazy universe, and suddenly something brought him back with a jolt. The clipped voice announced the next item— churning of the milky ocean for nectar. The gods got the nectar, fooling demons. They were helped by the enchanting Mohini.

The song began: '*Kannil irundhu pozhindhadh-amudhamo, Illai nanjo?*' Is it nectar that flowed from your eyes, or venom?

Sridevi emerged like a flare of enchantment. She was Mohini. Her anklets flashed. She was in white silk. The jasmine on her hair made her appear swathed in white from head to toe. Gopi's heart missed a beat. Suddenly everything was sharp and clear. His trance fell away in droplets and he rose like a swimmer surfacing. The song was in Shree Ragam. His fingers picked up the beat. His eyes were stinging. She smiled and enticed.

It was no longer the girl from Kunnupuram with her shy laughter.

LOST WAVES

A secret that had stung the air for three hundred long years. The magic of Mohini on earth. And the Voice of Doctors Colony, Dr Poduval, in spate.

During Association Day, annual day of the Doctors Colony Residents' Welfare Association, anyone who had anything to show showed—anything from ikebana to dressed pottery, amazing things out of toothpaste tubes and soap pieces, Pomeranians in fancy dress, and clever children who recited, debated, sang and danced endlessly in competition.

There were also 'culturals', where old amateur performers pulled out rusted tanpuras and violins and mridangams and mouth organs to wheeze out their talent, entertaining proud family members in the crowd.

Ganapathy, colony guardian, was spruced up for the night and dressed in gold-laced finery. He was bathed in rose water, holy ash, milk and panchamritham, a thick sweet five-ingredient mixture that stumbled on the tongue. Iyer was constantly on his feet, dispensing prasadam, conducting arathis and conveying blessings.

Association Day was serious business. The judges were specially invited from outside. People dressed their best. Sound and lighting were entrusted to professionals. Rehearsals and soap-shaping, plant-pruning and violin-tuning became obsessive pastimes. Dr Poduval, the Voice of Doctors Colony, held a series of meetings with his star speakers right from the beginning of the month.

Lekha was a popular soldier in pre-programme strategies. Shobha looked forward to the evening because of its no-holds-barred atmosphere and unlimited access to the mike and, of course, every child received gifts and ice cream and sweets.

Sridevi's father had a headache. He asked for a glass of buttermilk and turned in. The men were sleeping in the hall, the women in the bedroom. Lekha had no time to cook, so they decided to go down to the food stall.

The banyan was ablaze with light and laughter. A young resident sang, accompanied by a home-grown band. His voice rose loud and quivering, handling uneasy emotions. Children ran wild, belonging to no one. Shobha heaved a delirious sigh and melted into the crowd. Lekha took Sridevi's hand and waded in. And Gopi, arriving later with snacks and drinks as per Shankar's instructions, parked his scooter and walked rapidly, his head lowered, avoiding the crowd. He went briefly up to the flat to get ice and glasses and plates.

He spotted Shankar sitting on the deserted beach. A bright moon, ignored by the revellers, held sway over the stretching sand. A few of the usual dogs lay beneath the shadows of fishing boats. The waves thundered in silver splendour. The fishermen's huts in the distance were lit by hurricane lamps and one or two tubelights, and they could hear a radio. The noise from the celebration had also followed them here. 'Let's get comfortable,' Gopi said, pushing himself into Shankar's restless silence.

They spread a mat and arranged bottles, glasses, ice bucket and snacks. A few crabs darted on the mat and out. A dog with a bitten tail came up and watched them with hungry eyes till Gopi shooed it away. Then Shankar did a strange thing. He put an arm around his shoulders and hugged him tightly. 'My dear Gopi!' Gopi was taken by surprise. Shankar briskly mixed their drinks. 'Don't worry, Gopi,' he said, 'everything will turn out right.' He raised his glass. 'To this night.' They drank and watched the sea for a while. The breeze was cool. Gopi felt glad they were out of the colony's sweating lights. 'You've noticed,' Shankar began, his voice thick like ladled-out porridge, 'how I worked to get Sridevi's show going.'

'Yes, of course.' He looked at the dark froth-lined churning waves. He turned to Shankar and tried out a laugh. 'I just wondered why you were running about so much organizing her show!'

He couldn't see Shankar's expression. 'You wondered, eh? Why's he making a fool of himself in his old age?'

'Of course not.'

Shankar said, 'Long ago I made a mistake—ever since then I've been alone. When we were coming down in the car . . .'

He was silent for such a long time that Gopi asked, 'What happened?'

'What?'

'No, in the car, what happened?'

'I asked her.'

He turned to him in surprise. 'Asked her what? Asked who?'

'Her.'

'Sridevi?' He stared at him. 'Really?'

'Really. You must have guessed, of course.'

'No, I didn't. Guessed what?'

'It's been like this for some time. Today, I thought—so I asked finally.'

Gopi's face broke slowly into a grin. 'In front of everyone? Lekha, her father . . .?'

'Yes, I asked her.'

'Just like that?'

'Yes.'

'And?' He felt his excitement drop as Shankar took his time, gravely holding his glass before him as if to collect some of that wayward spray in his drink. It was the last thing he wanted tonight; he didn't know how to console him.

'She accepted.'

'What?'

'She said yes.'

'Just like that?'

'Just like that.'

'Out of the blue?'

'We've been somewhat together last couple of weeks.'

'Somewhat together! We didn't even know.'

'It began much earlier for me. You must have guessed.'

'No, I didn't guess anything. All those Kilikkara trips?' Shankar turned to him and grinned. 'We didn't even know!'

'That was the general idea.'

Gopi said awkwardly, 'And the father?'

'He's not bothered—he's one of those free-thinking men. He said, why not. If she's happy, that's all he wants.'

'That's great!' He let out a guffaw that burst out of his earlier uncertainty.

'At this age—'

'So what?'

'I'm almost double her age.'

'How does it matter if you're both happy?'

'She's a namboodiri girl.'

'Forget it, the father said yes, what more do you want?'

'It's what I've been dreading.'

'That's really mad!' He refilled their glasses and held out the plate containing chilli-smeared potato chips. Shankar carefully picked out a single chip and popped it into his mouth. 'All these days,' Gopi shook his head in wonder. 'Now that it's here, you're having second thoughts!'

'No second thoughts,' Shankar said. 'Not at all! This is what I want.'

Gopi took out a cigarette and lit it after a brief battle with the breeze. He was beginning to feel like a father confessor.

'The trouble with true love—it's true to itself, not to lovers!' Shankar made a sound in his throat that could have been a laugh. 'I never really missed anything with my kind of life.' Gopi sat still, watching the moon as it peered over water's edge, drawing worry lines on the face of the sky. 'And when she came, I didn't imagine what would happen. It's like going swimming in the sea, and then realizing the waves are stronger than you.' He stared at the water, his eyes alight with a grim sparkle. 'What a beautiful night—see the moon having a drink!' Gopi grinned. 'The waves are inviting us . . .' They soaked in the night, two solitary figures on a bare patch of beach. 'Sridevi—your Sridevi . . .'

'What do you mean, mine?'

'Your cousin, isn't she? And I felt, this is it, at the wrong end of life!'

'So what's your problem now?' He felt embarrassed by all this thick vagueness. He thought, maybe the confessional works the other way around, preventing the priest's discomfiture from showing through!

'You know what happened to MVR, don't you?'

'What?'

'That's another story. Our poet and his doomed love. You'll know. You'll know everything one day.' He paused. 'Let's hope people are more sober this time around.'

'This is now! 1985!'

He turned away. 'How many lives before you finish learning!'

Gopi looked at him with concern. 'It'll turn out well,' he said.

'Of course. Just my little worries!' They drank. The waves approached closer and the sky seemed to dip. The moon was running for cover. Gopi felt his head begin to softly spin. What about the poor priest, he thought, how does he unburden himself? He wanted to tell him about the strange morning with the old man, of Panikkar's petty conspiracy, the slap— what did he think of the slap, was it just a personal hurt or would it shake up the family tree? And see what he had in his pocket, who'd believe it, it's what everyone's been agitated about for centuries! He saw the priest tearing down the partition and shouting, see, this is me, spare a thought for me! As if on cue, Shankar turned to him. 'This must be a pretty unusual birthday for you!'

'Mmm, I've had some ready-made entertainment.'

'Good. What happened at the press? Lekha said you stayed back to handle a strike or something.' A hundred words waited but he couldn't begin. 'What happened?'

'Nothing. I handled it.'

'So how was your day?' It sounded like a question in the air, comfortable by itself, so he let it float away. Shankar remained thoughtful, holding an empty glass. 'But we'll make amends,' he said suddenly. He turned to Gopi. 'I can see a procession of faces before me tonight. All come back and looking down upon us. MVR, Kochu Kelu, Damodaran, the Elephant Priest, Unni, Nani.'

'Who are these other people?'

'You'll know. And then, of course Tatri.'

'That was her name?'

'Yes, an angel behind locked doors.' He turned and smiled at Gopi. 'Even our story will be told one day.' Shankar sat as if he really could see images rising in the cold shredded sky.

Gopi felt waves rise within his head. 'Anyway, we're free now,' he said awkwardly.

'Free from what?'

'Kilikkara is free.'

'Tell me!'

'Finally—Chakram and curse and all that . . .'

'What about them?' He regarded Gopi with an amused smile.

Gopi swallowed. 'It's all over.' He felt his hand begin to tremble, and put down the glass on the mat. He felt in his shirt pocket and touched the thin paper roll, but he was so flustered that he withdrew his hand. Finally he simply said, 'We've run out of ice.'

He saw Shankar frown. 'Okay, we'll do without.'

'No,' Gopi said quickly. 'I'll go and get it.'

'Sit down. I'll survive without ice.'

'Besides, I'd like to stretch my legs.'

'If you're so determined.' His voice was expressionless. 'And go and freshen up while you're at it.' Gopi picked up the ice pail. His feet had gone to sleep. He stomped around for a moment. Staggering in the sand, he heard Shankar's voice, 'Be careful, go slow!'

He trudged along, his head and feet leaden. The waves seemed to follow him as he walked. The function was in full spate. In the midst of it, Dr Poduval was holding on to the mike, discoursing on Water. 'Corporation must realize we won't take any more of their nonsense. They think we're camels or what? We can store water in our back and carry on for weeks like that?' Someone hooted from the far edge of the crowd. Dr Poduval shouted, 'The fault will be ours and ours alone if we remain passive. Friends, tonight we will pledge to give our descendents, the future generations, a grand watery inheritance . . .'

Gopi blinked at the bright lights. He couldn't spot Lekha or Shobha. The more he stared, the more blurred everything became. He turned and walked to 'C'. It took him several minutes to climb the stairs and his calf muscles hurt. He stopped on the landing, panting. The door was ajar, a slim line of light fell on the floor like the Lakshman-rekha, transgression line.

He crept in. Sridevi's father lay in the couch, covered completely by a sheet, snoring to wake the dead. Gopi paused in the centre of the room, suppressing sudden laughter. He washed his face and arms at the kitchen sink, and felt better. He prised out an ice tray from the fridge. The cubes clattered loudly as they fell into the pail. As he tiptoed out, he looked at his watch. Eleven fifteen. Fortunately, there was no school tomorrow, no office, no problems, just a long and lazy morning.

He froze in the landing. He heard a soft cough above. There was someone in the terrace. Thief? Who? His better judgment said, forget it, go right back to the beach. Forgetting his better judgment, he placed the ice pail carefully on the floor, right on the line of light so he wouldn't miss it later, and crossed the line. He cautiously climbed the narrower stairs up to the terrace.

The terrace was misted in white. At first he couldn't see anything as he adjusted his swimming eyes to the night. It was a large expanse, growing TV antennas, flapping clothes and superannuated flowerpots.

There was a figure standing at the far end. He moved forward slowly. It was a woman, her back to him, thick long hair trembling in the breeze. She wore a white sari, drinking up the watery moonlight. A string of jasmine tumbled on her

hair. It must have been the quickening of his breath or his feet
must have scraped the ground. She turned.

He saw Sridevi. He saw her large eyes and the bindi-like
a small moon on her forehead. They stood staring at each
other. 'What are you doing here?'

She smiled, her teeth shining. 'I didn't know you had such
a nice terrace. I came to see if Father needed anything. I heard
a sound—came up and found the door open.'

Gopi took a long breath. 'I was with Uncle Shankar.
We've been sitting on the beach.' She smiled and then lowered
her eyes. He stood watching her. The breeze swept up from his
left, bringing into relief sweating grains of sand on the back
of his neck. 'I wanted to congratulate you,' he said, suddenly
lost as he looked at her. 'The dance, and now this.' Tendrils
of hair fluttered against her face. The moonlight made her
appear vulnerable and pale and so young. The fragrance from
the jasmine reached him and he breathed it in deeply. He felt
his blood rush. 'I was sitting in the front row,' he said. 'You
were like—you were Mohini. I couldn't believe it!'

Sridevi laughed, acknowledging the compliment, and for
one moment he had a wild and terrible craving to gather her
into his arms, press his hot feverish face against her cheek,
shout out a prayer into the night, and then disappear forever
from the face of this wretched earth. He staggered back
against its ferocity, then steadied himself and moved forward.
'I'm sorry!' he said, putting up his hand. He was so close to
her now. The air throbbed with jasmine. Mohini, Mohini! He
could almost feel her breath on him.

'Gopi etta, you've been drinking,' she began. He caught
his breath sharply, hearing his name on her lips.

She made a disturbed gesture with her hand. He backed
away, his heart still, the blood evaporated from his face. As
he reached the door, he saw, with a sinking heart, Lekha
climbing up. She looked up curiously at him. Something in his
eyes, some little part of his pain, must have reached her.
'Sridevi,' he gulped quickly with a little laugh. 'I was
congratulating her—' He nodded stiffly. 'He's waiting there,
on the beach.' She stood in the narrow stairway, holding the
banister, her expression changing. 'Ice will melt,' he muttered,

pushing past her. He snatched up the ice pail and stumbled down the rest of the stairs. So many wild images flashed before him as he ran, cursing himself, 'What the hell's wrong with you!'

Dr Poduval's voice stormed on as he ran. 'We will, we will, we will—'

When he reached the sand, Shankar was sitting all hunched up like an old man. 'Here, ice.' Silently he made a drink for each. He had to gulp down half his glass before he found his voice. 'I saw Sridevi. I congratulated her!' He sank back in the sand, subdued by the enormity of this night.

'The women are okay?'

'Yes, yes, upstairs and downstairs . . .'

Shankar raised his eyebrows but didn't comment. He looked as if he'd been sitting there, brooding. After a couple of minutes, he said, 'That's all right, but what were you saying about the curse and the Chakram?'

Gopi pushed himself up and said firmly, 'I'll show you.' He fished in his pocket and pulled out the rolled paper parcel. He unfurled it carefully against his thigh and removed the paper. The thin sheet of copper shone dully in the moonlight.

Shankar stared at it. 'What is it?' he asked, barely whispering.

He moved it up and down with both hands. 'You tell me. What is it?'

'Show, give it to me.' Shankar reached out. For a brief ridiculous moment, Gopi held it back as if from a child, smiling awkwardly, trying to be playful. But Shankar's expression showed he was hardly in the mood to play; he quickly handed it over to him.

'What is it?' Shankar asked, peering like a bewildered jeweller.

'What do you think?'

He looked up and studied Gopi's expression. He cleared his throat. 'Where did you find it?'

'It was in the necklace Kamala brought from Bangalore, rolled tightly inside. It's obviously hundreds of years old.'

'Two hundred, that's all we need!'

'You think it really is?'

Shankar shook his head. He held the thing up before him but he was still staring at Gopi's face. 'Who knows?' A slow grin made his face look a little maniacal and a lot older. 'Everyone's looked and it's never been found. Where else could it be?' He laughed. 'Stands to reason that Kochu Kelu— no wonder! Good Lord!'

'Our Kochu Kelu?'

'Yes. I think things are beginning to fall into place.'

'Not for me!'

He spread out the copper sheet on his lap. 'We'll have to go to Kunnupuram and get this verified.' He looked up and grinned again at Gopi. 'You know what this means? If we return this and it gets back to where it belongs . . .'

'Maybe you can go ahead without too much guilt after all!'

'Good God, one night was all it took. Just this one night.'

Gopi's smile grew strained as he recollected what else the night had unleashed. 'You're happy?' he asked.

'Of course! I'm the happiest man.' He carefully rolled up the copper sheet along with the paper and slipped it into his pocket. 'I'll take care of this.' He sat and stretched out his arms and legs, cracking the joints. 'This is the happiest night of my life, Gopi.' He got shakily to his feet and stretched again. 'I'm going to wet my feet.'

'In the sea?'

'Where else?' Shankar shouted, looking like a totem pole in a kurta, taller than Gopi had ever seen him. He ran towards the waves, elbows close to his body, fists circling like a jogger. Gopi lay and watched, grinning at his exaggerated movements. After wetting his feet, he went in further. 'It's great, water is splendid!' he called out. Or something like that, the wind got most of what he said. His arms went up in a happy wave. Gopi watched till he was covered up to his waist. 'Are you going to have a bath?'

He couldn't be sure if his uncle heard him but he turned back again with a cheery look. Crazy, going in fully dressed, but then, so much happiness got you rather crazy. Gopi chuckled and lay back on his elbows. Though his body felt sluggish, he saw everything very clearly in the sharp moonlight.

Soon the water was up to Shankar's shoulders. What was he doing? A dog roused itself and began to bark. When even the head had disappeared and there was no sign of Shankar at all, it stopped barking and went back to its boat-shadow.

Gopi felt panic rise. As he struggled to his feet, he thought he saw the head bob up one more time. And then there was only a misty shivering world of waves and moonlight. Gopi trudged up to the water. Nothing at all! As if all that had been a dream. He called out two or three times. The full import of it struck him. He ran along the shore like a madman, calling his uncle's name. His face crumpled as he ran wailing like a child, trembling with fear.

He crashed painfully into a sudden shadow. He fell, and saw risen above him the dark and terrible figure of Kali, her red tongue hanging loose, her breasts and her trident and her powerful eyes. Even as he clutched his knee and pushed himself up, he saw the trident slowly move down upon him! He screamed, and his scream melted into the night.

THE END

Even as I strain to emerge sane from all this, there are two things that buoy me up, keep my head above water. Rangachari. And a realization.

The realization is enough to clear my head, take me a step forward, so my perspective is altered and I can see what I hadn't before. It's precisely what Rangachari expected when he handed me the rest of his manuscript.

I vanish into my room with the strict instruction I'm not to be disturbed. As I read, several events in my life take on new meaning. When I pull down strands of past events and try to match them with our present tapestry, they do so easily. There's no doubt about it, Rangachari's done much for us.

I sit out in the balcony with cigarettes and a thermos full of coffee. The printouts have been taken at some professional place, they're neat and professional, and bound within a file. The breeze riffles through them, trying to read faster than me. I sift through Rangachari's eccentric prose and observations. He's thorough, there's no denying that. Diaries, notes and letters have been avidly consumed. The bulk of it is from MVR and Kochu Kelu, while Uncle Shankar is a tortured link in time. Rangachari has made a 'fact-finding' trip to Kilikkara in the early '80s along with RV uncle.

In the balcony, cigarette between my fingers, watching coloured centipedes crawling and scattering on the black road below, I think of the past that's delivered me here at this point like a blind courier. I sit and see what happened that night more than a hundred years ago.

Damodaran, digging to bring up the Chakram. Cheeky Chandran, rising before him like a nasty vision. The poor man, blighted beyond belief, succumbs to the shock, leaving the Chakram behind, unable to effect the counter-snatch! And Chandran, street-smart and tough though he later became, grabs the Chakram in his confusion and faithfully retraces his steps to his Uncle Kochu Kelu feeling, no doubt, it's the cronylogical thing to do.

What happened that night was surely an accident. I can't imagine Chandran going wilfully beyond snatching Chakrams, at any rate not before his street-baptism—and this incident was five or six years before even Diamond Week when the demon-seed was presumably planted in him. Following the prowling priest to the temple was hardly part of a plan. Returning hazily home from his nocturnal diversions, Chandran spots a skulking priest-shadow disturbing his profile of the perfect night. Later comes the pounding in the sanctum and he ventures down for a little chat with the intruder. But it isn't bad Chandran who's responsible for Damodaran's doom, it's a bad heart. And Chandran's left holding a gift. He can't believe his luck. Though I bet the boy was soft enough to have panicked when he found Damodaran dying on him during the course of a wild and cata-Kelusmic night!

Our large and timeless KK. He takes one look and says, 'That's it, the Chakram—we'll have to return it. You will return it, Chandran!' It's a gift from heaven. KK recognizes that. It's the perfect denouement to a sinking scenario, and a way out for his idol MVR.

'Return it?' Chandran stammers. 'To Kunnupuram? I?'

KK smirks. He's obviously good at smirking—that's the way his picture's painted by the grandmother who sits on the floor and rubs her stretched-out legs, surrounded by a retinue of wide-eyed little listeners, paling the night with his escapades for the sake of generations who've known him only as a diehard daydreamer.

'Who else?' KK says softly. 'Who knows the ins and outs of Kunnupuram? Who's been brave enough to play practical jokes, right there on those sacred premises?'

And Chandran knows he's trapped. What an uncle he's gone and got himself! He's well and truly bound to him by that one sordid incident—maybe through Chandran's own big mouth—and knowing that he's got himself a lifelong crony.

There are possible answers in Shankar's notes, several of them.

Chandran sneaks into the illam, dazed by Damodaran's death and oppressed by his uncle. He knows the way of course! (Though, as Shankar writes, he never got beyond the specially erected pandals on the day of the feast, so the main building was still new to him.) He stumbles through the darkness of the illam and, instead of proceeding straight in to the little alcove where Ganapathy sits behind an oil lamp, guarding the illam against marauders and misfortune—instead of finding Ganapathy and entrusting the Chakram to Him, so the morning would present a real miracle for the ill-fated illam—instead of finding Ganapathy, he stumbles into Tatri's room.

Elephant Priest and his sons are sleeping in the front hall of the first floor. The other men stay in the nearby outhouse. Surprised by Tatri, Chandran panics. Tatri begins to cry out. The child probably wakes up and witnesses his mother's struggles. In his panic, attempting to silence Tatri and her child at the same time, Chandran strangles her—accidentally. Under the eyes of the child. When he reaches home, still carrying the Chakram and horrified by what he's done, KK comforts him. 'We'll keep the Chakram,' he says. 'Right here in Northern Palace. It's been decided by Fate. But not a word—no one should know.' That's story number one.

There's another version in Uncle Shankar's notes.

After MVR's traumatic trip to the illam, KK tries to reassure him. Dark clouds rise within his brain. He's like a blinkered beast foraging a way out. His logic is simple: MVR and his wife are precious to Kilikkara, the namboodiri woman isn't. Getting rid of her would remove a big thorn bleeding the reputation of the Palace. And he does what he has to do. Interestingly, even as his toughs are on the job, the woman's husband meets a similar fate in Kilikkara. So Tatri is sacrificed and life goes on.

Both these stories were recounted by KK's grand-nephew, who was close to Shankar. The second story is harsh and involves yet another—premeditated—Brahmin-killing. So do a couple of more preposterous alternatives he's listed out. Shankar prefers to believe the first one, the misadventures of a blundering well-meaning youth. It's kinder to Kilikkara.

The rest is mostly conjecture. Years later, when the Matriarch announced the necklace as reward for a female child, it was her favourite Northern Palace nephew who was ordered to have it made. I can see it—the glee on KK's face as he decided to leave it to Fate, and fashioned the diamond necklace, inserting into it that same stolen Chakram. A game of chance—let them keep the Chakram who gets the necklace! All's well that ends well. No one will know. The Chakram officially remains stolen. Kilikkara, rightful owner through acquisition, unofficially retains it.

Diamond Week. And women of the Palace sweat to possess the necklace. How KK must have smirked. Fighting each other to gain a cursed Chakram! And imagine his sense of satisfaction when Fate pronounces—and the house responsible, Big Palace, is left holding the baby. Because it's responsible for the adultery, and it's also responsible for the original Chakram-snatch in the first place, for in those early days there was only Big Palace which later branched out into all the others. In a perverse sort of way, he's wrapped up the entire problem and handed it back to MVR.

My mind is filled with visions of Tatri, the intelligent beautiful wife of the dour Damodaran, MVR's Mohini. The unexpected meeting in the bathhouse, storm outside, storm within. What a moment for an eternal love affair to blossom. Her brief flashing freedom from a repressive illam. Their shared moments of poetry. The fruit of their love, a child they cherished. And then death. The world crashing around MVR's feet. For a long while I wondered about that child, love child of Tatri and MVR.

What happened to him following the death of his parents? His natural father could hardly have staked a claim to him. It was years later, one evening in Kilikkara, when we were chatting under a star-crazed sky that I actually put the question. My mother shook her head and said it was sad that one family had to go through so much. The boy, she said, was brought up by Elephant Priest and his sons. 'They actually brought up MVR's son?' I asked in surprise.

My mother looked at me steadily. 'He was Damodaran's son.'

He'd been a quiet and brooding boy, a good student, and when he turned fourteen, he told his friends he was joining the army and ran away from home. He never turned up? I started to ask, but I didn't—why should he come back to reclaim an identity he never had in the first place?

Last night, I woke up from a strange dream.

A pushing crowd of women, led by the Northern Palace Matriarch who'd given the necklace. She looked grim and her old eyes glittered, but the others were laughing and noisily trying to get past her. She held them at bay with two frail arms, proclaiming in a cold voice, we women should stick together!

I spotted my mother, Aunt Sarada, Kamala, Lekha, MVR's wife, Nani, the sensuous Thangam, Sulu Panikkar and the toothless thoughtless grand-aunt who'd congratulated my mother on my father's death, among others. Hovering over their flurry, isolated and silent in the wake of that cry—we-women-should-stick-together—I sensed the dark lamenting presence of two outsiders, Tatri and Sridevi.

I replace the pages of the manuscript in their plastic busty-lady cover. I call downstairs for a taxi. There's much that is still unformed in my mind, but I must meet Rangachari first. There's a deal we have to make. It's time the book got moving.

The street is more chaotic than I've ever seen it, some agitation or discontent simmers in the air. The horns, shouts and screeches are deafening. I walk through three dusty squabbles, one of them involving an entire crowd.

An ambulance pulls away from the pavement. Its wheels gather momentum and a siren starts up, startling me. It takes me a good moment to realize it had been standing below Rangachari's house. By the time I move, the ambulance has jerked past me, split the crowd and is already on the other side of the fights.

My heart beats fast as I spot Mari. I run, crossing the road. He is turning to the stairs. 'Mari, stop!' He turns. 'Ambulance, what happened?'

He waits for me to calm down. He himself doesn't look too cool. I follow him up the stairs, clutching the plastic bag. The front door is wide open. As he shuts it behind us, the room becomes dark, silent. The walls converge. His hand rises and there is light.

'What happened?' He doesn't reply. 'Where is he?'

The sweat hasn't dried on his forehead. His eyes are young and worried. 'He just went.' He holds the top of a chair, gazing down at the floor. When he looks up, his eyes are bright and moist. 'Doctor came around one. He was bad. Then he said he must go to hospital.'

'How bad?'

'Shouting and throwing things.'

'Has he been like this before?'

He nods. 'But I didn't call the doctor. This time . . .'

'Who called the doctor?' I'll have to pull this out in instalments.

'Kittu anna.'

'Who? Oh, Krishnamurthy. From Coimbatore.'

'He came last evening. They had words and Saar was angry.'

'This happened because of that?'

'I don't know.'

'Did they fight over his new book?'

'I don't know.'

'Did they mention me?'

'I don't know.'

'And Kittu called the doctor?'

'Yes.' I sit down in my customary chair. 'I'll get you coffee,' he says.

'Wait, come here.' Mari stands heavily. 'How was he? Did they have to . . . use force?'

Mari rubs his eyes roughly with thumb and forefinger. 'Saar was calm in the end. I'll go, he said.'

'He said that?'

'Yes. He said, take me.'

'Do you know for how long?'

'Doctor told Kittu anna it's not very serious.' He straightens up, trying to look brave. 'He must take medicines, that's all. One week, two weeks. But he must rest.'

We're silent. I can smell the Dettol I've missed all this while. 'Mari. I want you to remember everything that happened. What exactly did the doctor say?'

'He said Saar is confused right now, the medicine will make him all right. He was all right before Amma died. Now I'm not able to do anything for him.'

'It's not your fault.' He furrows fingers through his poky hair. It's the first time his vulnerability is so open to me. 'This is just temporary,' I tell him. 'Professor's a strong man. If he takes his medicines, he'll get well. It's like a fever or cold. He's just worried, that's all.'

'About what?' he cries. 'There's nothing for Saar to be worried about.'

'That's true.' I say it, thinking of the *White City* idealist forced to come to terms with the world, the man in the Vyasa mould bundled into a crimson sea of sensationalism. 'Did he leave a message for me?'

'Yes, yes, a letter. In the afternoon he was calmer. Then near the door, he stopped and told Kittu anna to get him paper and pen. The doctor let him sit down and write.' Mari goes to the writing alcove and returns with a folded sheet of paper. It's hardly a letter, just a couple of lines in his thin tortured scrawl.

'It's yours. Do what you will.'

Nothing more. After all these days of bickering and steaming, this is it. Do what you will. As if he's exhausted, and has passed the buck. I continue to stare at the shivery letters, knowing that I must resolve this problem on my own, torn between my family and this man's mission. Mari stands waiting for possible answers from the letter. 'It's okay,' I tell him, smiling awkwardly. Has he got me committed with a single note? And yet again I bend to pick up the woman who smiles because she's wearing Kumar's Best Bra.

The moon sheds a radiance that filters through straggly vertical banyan arms. The temple and its surroundings are set apart in a denser light field as if in preparation for an impending nocturnal ritual. It is late. For a long while I sat on the beach, watching the waves roll up. So many years they've been trying to pass on messages to me. So many moments buried within them, so many lost forever. Others returning again and again, to be picked up, retreating unrecognized. I sat and tried to identify a pattern in their coming and going. When can I come back to these sands without shame or regret? Sifting sand through my fingers, wondering how close I'm to exorcizing my own ghosts.

I'd woken to find the breeze had died. I was feverish and my body felt painfully swollen. I don't know, I can't remember, how I trudged back through sand and thick air to the colony. All I know is that it hit me badly—the sudden lights and laughter and the crowd and the songs from the mike—and I screamed. That's the only thing I remember from that moment, screaming.

They froze, turning from whatever they were doing as though they'd finish with me and then resume. Lekha came, running and terrified. She came to me like a balm, touching me on the forehead and relieving me of my fear as if I could entrust myself to her this time as well. I told her in jerky painful words that Uncle Shankar had just walked into the sea, and then I collapsed.

The night passed. When they got his body the next day, bloated and white and looking like the body of a man thirty years older, I was also standing in the crowd. I tried to connect the cheery wave and the last words and the sadness with this wet recumbent figure on the sand that looked like a wax caricature of a fat man. But they were two different men, the one who went in and the one who came out. A fisherman in his dripping loincloth looked proud. 'Very difficult when the waves are rough,' he explained.

Some men and children from the previous evening stood hushed as they watched. This was a different kind of entertainment. A couple of policemen asked me questions in what they thought were gentle tones and I repeated what I'd been saying to everyone else who asked.

They had found nothing in his pockets, some soaking notes and coins, but nothing else. The Chakram had been sucked into another world along with whatever had animated this useless frame. I stood for a long time in the sun, staring hard at the waves, now calm and merry with none of that terrible hunger of the night. I stood there waiting for one of them to roll up and deposit the Chakram—or whatever it had been—at my feet.

I then went back to bed. Days passed, and nights. Once I found Sridevi near me, touching my forehead and bringing me my rice gruel. I turned away, unable to bear her eyes. Later, I clutched Lekha's hand and wept silently. She sat next to me calmly, patiently, waiting for me to finish. I didn't see Shobha for a long time. She'd taken leave from school and was staying at Greenacres. Aunt Sarada refused to have her brother brought back to Greenacres, saying she couldn't bear to see that as well, so he made his last journey from Doctors Colony. Our hall could hardly contain the people who wanted to see him. They stretched in a serpentine queue down the corridor and stairs. There was such a mixture of whisper, silence and briskness, a casual observer might not have immediately identified the nature of the gathering.

As usual, it was Chandrachudan who looked after everything. He and MMA dominated the morning. Phonograms and calls went to and from Sundararajan's flat. Kilikkara was mentioned every now and then, but I was the only one from Kilikkara around. I somehow couldn't go with them to the cremation ground. No one forced me.

Some days later, I woke up from a nightmare and sat dripping with sweat. I got up and went to the balcony. It was dusk with a strange yellow glow hanging over the sky. I heard the sound of drums and conch and bells. I looked down and saw a funeral procession crawling from the slums. The body was neatly shrouded. Men danced energetically in the forefront, drunk with life and death. In momentary confusion I thought, there he goes and I'm up here and no one's even told me.

I spent the following days fighting the phantoms of that night. Everyone knew it had been an accident, it had been the happiest night of his life and he'd gone out for a dip and lost his balance. But deep within, a voice still mocked and taunted, 'There's got to be a victim in every generation!', a voice that dared to question. Why, I cried out, why should he deliberately throw away his life and the Chakram, the possibility of a new life for our two wretched families?

Perhaps it was the magic of the night. That same perverse magic of the night that had refashioned our destinies again and again, the madness of Diamond Week, the choppy events of that crazy Kunnupuram night, the horrible destruction of Damodaran and Tatri, and of course, my own monstrous moment on that terrace. It all added up somehow.

Within two months, we went our separate ways. Aunt Sarada sold the house and went back to Kilikkara. Kolappan was finally packed off to Poonjar. I forgot about inheritances. I said good bye to Doctors Colony, Iyer and Ganapathy, to VAP and Panikkar, and bundled my family to Bangalore. Shobha is completing school at an Ooty boarding. We stay close to my sister Kamala, who occasionally airs out the diamond necklace for our benefit. When the famous inheritance finally came, I shoved most of it into a long-term bank deposit and also bought into Enterprise Publishers and Associates, mainly because my brother-in-law had a friend named Dilip Mehra. Sridevi underwent two deadened years of mourning and then resumed her dancing. My mother is still trying to get her married.

Sitting on the sand, his words came back to me clearly. Even our story will be told one day. Those words had dodged me amidst others, in the blur of words and faces and thoughts. Now, from an uncluttered horizon, they rose home to me.

Sand, sky and stars. Waves. Endless stretches wherever you turned. The fierce Kali, the broken-down wall, the fishermen's huts, hungry dogs. I picked them all up and left.

POINT ZERO

———————————————— ■ ————————————————

This is the beginning. With my memories and faded stories, and carrying a new burden. Ganapathy sits in his fortress, lit by a tiny unquenchable flame. I'm his only witness.

When I'm here, I'm newborn, like a canvas of the sky, yet to register words or moods. I can remember nothing, I feel nothing but the moment. That's the magic of this place. There, on the sands with the waves crashing ceaselessly, air salted with the wounds of the past, I can bleed or cry or smile. Here, I don't remember. Razed-hazed-erased, I stand free, a consciousness sponging in the moment.

The little shed by the temple is empty. The last time I was here, there'd been a priest, Iyer's successor down the line, snoring away into the night. Now the shed's bare, its wooden door staggered open. A holy old man, a wandering monk who'd wandered far in space and time, once said like a voice from the sky, this is the Beginning.

The story is already written. Rangachari, with Uncle Shankar's help, has painstakingly charted out the story of our family in his peculiar personal prose. And now he's given me carte blanche. My literary ambitions are finally to be realized—through another man's book. Do what you will—I've nothing to add but the story within, a tribute to the past and a confession—our atonement. By the time this story gets out, we'll be ready to face the world again, my ancestors and I.

Truth-story-history. With new names and new reasons. It is said Ganapathy held his broken tusk poised over the page to record the Mahabharatha as Vyasa began to dictate, telling of his own family and its turbulence.

Shankar said, Don't worry, our story will be told, we'll make amends.

MVR cried out, There's only one way. I must pour out my truth before it bursts within me. Words are the only balm on my wound, I have to write.

Words moist with womb fluid, born from the desire to exist. So the umbilical cord can be cut. And we'll begin, under a sky awash with fresh colours, rescuing the past from its greyness and offering it up to a new dawn. The heady smell of fresh jasmine and within my head, an outpouring in tantalizing Shree Ragam, to invoke my muse.

Mohini, let us begin. It's the dim hour before dawn. That hushed instant before curtain-rise . . .